BLOOD RELATIVES

STEVAN ALCOCK

BLOOD RELATIVES

FOURTH ESTATE • *London*

First published in Great Britain in 2015 by
Fourth Estate
An imprint of HarperCollins*Publishers*
1 London Bridge Street
London SE1 9GF
www.4thestate.co.uk

1

A catalogue record for this book is
available from the British Library

ISBN 978-0-00-758084-2

Printed and bound in Great Britain by
Clays Ltd, St Ives plc

For Peg

I

Wilma McCann

30/10/1975

The milkman found her. On Prince Philip Playing Fields. He crossed the dew-soaked grass toward what he took to be a bundle of clothes, but then he came across a discarded shoe, and then t' mutilated body.

Her name wor Wilma McCann.

An hour earlier, wi' t' daybreak a mere streak across t' Leeds skyline, Wilma McCann's two kids wor found by t' police, waiting in their nightclothes at a bus stop in t' Scott Hall Road, hoping to see their mother on t' next bus from town.

Later on t' morning the milkman made his gruesome discovery, after he'd told the police, made a statement, phoned his missus from a box on Harehills Lane, the milk float wor working almost parallel wi' our Corona Soft Drinks wagon up and down Harehills' red-brick back-to-backs. It worn't usual for him to be in this street at the same time as us. He wor running way late. Eric, my driver, parped the horn. The milk-float driver beckoned us over, his face taut and joyless.

'Stay here, Rick. Watch the van. Summat's up.'

This irked me. My mind wor already racing ahead to t' end of t' working day, to t' terraced house in t' cul-de-sac where t' Matterhorn Man lived, and now Eric wor blathering on wi' t' milkman and the day wor stretching itsen out before me.

I plonked both feet sulkily on t' dashboard and mulled on t' lines of washing slung between t' backs of t' terraces. Billowing sheets, flapping underwear and wind-socked nylon shirts. Washing slowed us down even more than some poor cow's corpse. I'd have to march before t' wagon wi' a long pole and hoist up all t' washing so our grimy vehicle could sneak beneath. The women would hear t' van and look out skittishly as we passed, watching to make sure their pristine laundry worn't soiled on t' line.

Then we'd stop. Stacking half a dozen bottles up each forearm we'd move deftly from back kitchen doorstep to back kitchen door; from Asian kitchens where t' hands of t' women wor stained wi' turmeric, to t' kitchens of black women who laughed and joked wi' us in their patois, to Ukrainian and Polish kitchens and English kitchens. Kitchens filled wi' t' smells of spices and baking, dank kitchens of stomach-churning grease, dirt and indifference.

Over t' road, the milkman and Eric wor still confabbing. The milkman wor pointing somewhere. I swore, slammed my fist hard against t' cab door, clambered out onto t' back of t' wagon and noisily dragged some crates about.

It wor a friggin' age before I heard the whine of t' milk float pulling away and saw Eric bustling over, face like a pig's arse. He sat in t' cab, clutching the steering wheel wi' both hands and staring flatly ahead.

'So?'

'So he found a body this morning.'

'What? A dead one?'

'Uh-huh. Thinks she wor done over last night.'

Eric picked at his teeth wi' his forefinger, leaned over t' round-book.

'Number 43 wants a crate of cream soda.'

* * *

Cos of all t' palaver over t' body it wor late morn before I found mesen propping up the door frame of Mrs Husk's living room, bottle of ginger beer dangling 'tween my fingers. Mrs Husk wor slower than any corpse, and only a smidgen of t' hour from becoming one. She'd grind time to a halt if she got her way. I should have been in and out of there an age back.

'Oeff!' spluttered Mrs Husk. 'My leg.'

I looked on as she doubled over in her chair, rubbing her calf, picking uselessly at the fraying edges of her bandaging. Her heavy brown wig had slipped slightly to show wisps of white hair, floating and anchored, like sheep-wool traces caught on barbed wire.

'Oeff,' she repeated, eyeing me beadily. 'It don't get no better.'

Nor would it. I prayed the old cuckoo wouldn't ask me to rewrap it. Not again. Not today of all days. I worn't a friggin' nurse, fer Chrissakes, I wor here to deliver pop. Her leg wor so ulcerated and pitted, it wor like massaging cold chicken skin. Not even industrial depot soap could rid my hands of t' stink of her ointment.

The day wor stacked against me.

The milkman had found a body.

Mrs Husk wanted her leg seeing to.

I would be too late for t' Matterhorn Man.

Mrs Husk motioned me further in, her jaw slackening and closing wordlessly, like a ruminant chewing cud.

'Best I stay over here, Mrs Husk, stood in some doggy-do earlier on.'

Which wor a lie. Course, I'd wanted to clap eyes on t' corpse. Couldn't be any worse than t' cat I'd found in a water barrel wi' a ligature round its neck. Just a quick gander at death, then I'd go and sell pop. People die, people are born and people buy pop.

Mrs Husk wor levering hersen out of her chair wi' both arms.

'Oeff!'

My nostrils flared, catching the manky whiff of her room. Such a dingy room, the floral wallpaper a discoloured shade of piss, the moth-eaten rugs scarcely hiding the bare floorboards. Two mangy armchairs wor angled toward a gas fire that hissed bleakly from t' fireplace, the stuffing oozing from one of them. She slept in here, the old bird, slept in one of them there armchairs.

She took the new bottle of ginger beer from me and shuffled off into t' kitchen. That's it, under t' sink, go on, that's where you keep it, behind that grubby gingham cloth. Mrs Husk wor faithful to her one bottle of ginger beer.

Still, I thought, scratching my knackers through t' hole in my pocket, she ain't a bad old crow. Not one of them cringeing, whingeing old crones on t' round who peer at you through t' crack of their door chains, or clack-clack their dentures at you about young folk or darkies or t' war.

The old littered the round, holed up in their stinking flats and decrepit houses, smelling of stale piss and imminent death. She might wear a hairnet and have a whiffy leg, but there wor summat brusque about Mrs Husk. She never apologised for being old. Not Mrs Husk.

She edged her way over to t' table by t' window, where she set down t' empty.

'Bugger the doggy-do, come in proper while I get you t' money.'

Her dappled old hands quivered as she reached for a buff envelope from behind t' mantel clock. The clock had an assured tock-tock and an expensive chime. An heirloom, perhaps. Even t' most addled old girl would notice if that went walkies, and Mrs Husk's mind wor lemon sharp. That clock wor probably the only thing of value she had. Then

6

again, maybe she wor secretly loaded. The elderly accumulate. They hoard, they store, they stash.

Summat brushed against my feet. Lord Snooty, her unfeasibly fat tomcat, lurking under t' table, blinking up at me like it knew what I wor thinking.

I said, 'I can't stay long, we're running late.'

'I thought maybe you worn't coming. That you'd missed me out again.'

'Would I do that, Mrs Husk?'

She tucked an errant lock of hair beneath her net, looked at me askance. I twitched to be gone as she painfully counted out t' money for t' ginger beer. She always got it wrong. Her hands hovered shakily over t' coins; she wore a gold wedding ring, and another ring on t' same finger set wi' some fat dark stone. The rings seemed welded into her bony finger; anyone wanting to remove 'em would have to hack 'em off.

'They found a body this morning,' I said.

Mrs Husk ceased moving coins around. She examined the pile of coppers, tanners and bobs as if she wor reading t' tea leaves.

'A body? My, my. It's a rum world, ain't it lad?'

One by one she placed the coins in my hand.

'Is that right, then?'

She wor four pence short. 'Aye. That's it.'

In t' evening I lay sprawled across my bed in a sour mood, watching two flies playing tag. By t' time we'd finished the round it wor too late for me to pay my usual visit to t' Matterhorn Man.

I could hear Mother in t' bathroom, swishing her hand through t' bath water. From her room across t' landing, sis's tranny wor blaring out Radio 1. Mitch wor downstairs, glued to t' footie.

To make yersen heard in our house you had to yell your lungs out.

'Rick! Get yersen down here. Now.'

I stuck out my limbs and flayed like an upended woodlouse. Through t' floorboards I could hear the rabid rat-tat-tat of t' footie commentator. I banged my ribcage mechanically wi' my fist, making a 'vuhh-vuh-vuuh-vuuuh' sound.

'Rick!'

That one wor closer. Like nearing explosions. That one came from t' foot of t' stairs. I pinched my nostrils between my fingers and held my breath 'til I began to feel light-headed.

'R-i-i-ck!'

I sat bolt upright, gulping in air, shaped my hand into a gun and fired through t' floor. I mouthed each shot soundlessly. Pow! Pow! Silencer on.

I scuttled out of my room, flattened mesen against t' landing wall and peered over t' banisters. In t' hallway below I could see Mitch in his flip-flops and trackie bottoms, the neat little pate on t' crown of his head like a bare patch where a bucket had stood on a lawn. In his hand he held a bottle of brown ale, which he wor giving a good blathering to.

'What is it, eh, my little friend? What is it wi' folk?' Then he emptied his lungs. 'Ri-i-i-ick!'

He wor out of sorts again. Likely as not, his two great passions, country music and footie, had been unable to raise him from his misery pit. Back to t' wall, I fired again: Pow! Pow! Then I heard the sloughing of his flip-flops as he went back into t' lounge.

'Now what!'

I knew what. The TV screen had slipped again, presenting a game of two halves. Players' upper bodies and players' legs, dissected by a thick black line.

'Bugger!!'

I heard a fist thump the top of t' telly.

'You do it on purpose, don't you?'

I sniggered. Mitch wor always chuntering on to objects. Probably cos they wouldn't answer back. Although sometimes they did, in their own way.

'Now, if I park mesen, you'll behave. You want chuckin' out, you do. Any day now, you're a gonner. R-i-ii-ck!'

Mother came out of t' bathroom and almost collided wi' me. She wor wrapped in her quilted dressing gown, ready for bed. 'Leave him, Mitch!' she squealed into t' hallway below. 'Whatever it is can wait 'til morning.'

She smiled tightly at me. Stripped of her make-up, her fox-like features seemed harder than I wor used to seeing, and her hair, minus grips, hung girlishly about her face. She had a magazine and a biro in her hand. One of her friggin' competitions. Mandy's tranny wor blaring out Abba's 'SOS'. Mother tidied her hair behind her ears.

'You wor late home again this evening,' she said. 'Is this a regular thing now?'

'Dunno, depends on how we're running.'

'I'll keep you some dinner back.'

'Ta, but no need.'

She pulled at a thread on her sleeve. 'You'd best go see what he wants. You know what he's like when he's riled.'

A beam of light wor still shining from under Mandy's door. Sis worn't a morning person, she needed chivvying at every turn, all sullen, her school tie knotted between her breasts, her socks around t' ankles, brushing her hair at the breakfast table, never wanting to eat owt, so that Mother had taken to slipping bags of crisps into her school bag in an effort to get summat down her. Waste of friggin' time, if you wor to ask me.

'Mandy,' Mother called out. 'Radio off, lights out, please.'

Hearing no response, she opened t' door. Mandy *wor* asleep. I could see her, face-down on t' bed, still dressed. Her skirt had rucked up around her waist, showing her knickers. One arm wor hanging floppily down t' side of t' bed and her hair wor hiding her face.

While Mother sorted out Mand, I headed downstairs. Mitch's Adam's apple wor piston-shunting as he glugged the pale-ale dregs down his throat. His small, droopy moustache glistened. He wiped the back of his hand across his mouth.

'Didn't you hear me calling?'

'Along wi' half of t' street. I wor kippin'.'

'You're missing a bloody good match here.'

I shrugged. He closed in on me. I caught the whiff of ale on his breath.

'I do believe, lad, you got paid today.'

'Might have.'

'Might have? Never mind yer might haves, let's be having you.'

I took t' buff wage packet from my jeans pocket and surgically peeled off a mangy tenner, holding it by t' corner 'til Mitch's fingers tugged it from me.

'Ta,' he said, the note vanishing behind his palm like he wor performing a card trick.

I said, 'When I started this job you said that half wor going toward my upkeep and that.'

'It is, my lad, it is. But then, who got you this job?'

'I know, I know, you did. Only, you said that ...'

'Me! Right! And just one word wi' Craner and I can take it from you again. You pay me and then I'm cheaper for your mother, then she's got more for your upkeep. That's common sense, that's logic, that's good housekeeping, geddit?'

'If you say so, it must be so.'

Behind him, the TV screen wor barrelling again. There wor a long 'Oooooh' from t' crowd. A near miss, which made him turn toward t' screen.

'Fer Chrissakes!'

10

He leant over t' back of t' set, swearing und
fiddling wi' t' horizontal adjustment.

I said to Mitch's back, 'They found a dead woman
morning. She'd been done in. A prozzie. It wor in t' news.
Makes you wonder, don't it?'

Mitch straightened up and backed gingerly away from t'
telly. 'Does it?'

'I mean, if I've ever sold her a bottle of pop or summat. If
t' next time I walk up to some door in Chapeltown or Halton
Moor or wherever someone'll say, "She won't be wanting no
limeade where she's gone." Then I'll know, won't I?'

Mitch grunted. 'Now, you stay, I tell you. Stay!' Like he
wor commanding a dog. A black line slid mockingly down t'
TV screen.

Next morn I wor up wi' t' lark. Mitch wor up before t' friggin'
lark. I watched him through t' ciggie burn in my bedroom
curtain, loading boxes into t' back of his rusting Austin
Cambridge van.

I wor threading boot laces in t' kitchen when Mother
sauntered in and plonked the kettle onto t' gas ring.

'Wor that Mitch?'

'Uh huh. Just missed him. Just gone off.'

'Gone off? Off where? He's supposed to be running me
over to your gran's. Didn't he say when he'd be back?'

'Haven't spoken to him.'

I'd sussed where he wor heading, but it worn't my place
to blather. Eric said that women worn't meant to know
everything, which wor why they wor always trying to. Eric
wor a philosopher on all things women. Mother picked at
her old nail varnish as she waited for t' water to boil.

'Will you be late again tonight?'

She wor fishing again. I leaned over my boots so I
wouldn't have to look her in t' eye.

11

'No, so long as we don't break down.'

I wanted to keep my options open. Maybe I'd go see t' Matterhorn Man.

'Those vans do seem to break down a lot,' she said. 'Someone should get them seen to.'

The Corona Soft Drinks depot wor t' last in a row of gun-metal-grey industrial units up in t' city's northern suburbs. As soon as I stepped into t' depot it lifted my morning bones; the metallic acridity of nails, rivets, corrugated panels, the headiness of t' exhaust fumes, the saccharine odour of t' pops – lemonade, limeade, cream soda – and squashes – orange barley, lemon barley, blackcurrant.

Going on twenty vans wor being readied. From Craner's office came t' chink of change being checked.

'Morn, Mr Craner!'

The gaffer didn't take kindly to me being so chirrupy first thing, which wor why I greeted him thus. Irritate the morose bugger.

Behind me came t' jangle of nudging bottles on t' end of a forklift. Coke, Tango orange, Tango lime – empties all being stacked; or full crates – orangeade, dandelion and burdock. Someone else wor dragging a crate along t' floor – Tango lemon, Tango lime, malt vinegar.

I punched the clock, took our float and sought out our van. The load had still to be sorted and signed off, the engine checked for petrol, water and oil. That wor every van boy's job.

I lifted up the bonnet and withdrew t' rapier-dipstick, wiped it, slid it back into its sheath, withdrew it slowly, assessed the oil-line level, wiped it on a rag and then reinserted it. While I wor busying wi' this I could see Craner in his office, balancing on his swivel office chair, chalking up crew names on t' wall blackboard behind his desk. Cos he could barely reach the board wi' his short arms outstretched the names sloped off at one end. I could make out my own initials alongside a capital 'E' for Eric.

I wor screwing on t' radiator cap when from behind me came t' unmistakable sound of glass splintering on concrete. One of t' new lads, balancing too many bottles up each arm. He'd learn. If he lasted. The lad's face puckered up like a butchered pig as dandelion and burdock meandered toward a sludge patch of oil. The crash brought Craner out of his office.

'You! Yes, you, fatso! Chuck some bloody sawdust over that spill,' Craner barked, his voice eaten up by its own echo. I grinned at Fatso, who wor just gawping at Craner like a friggin' idiot. It wor t' same here as in school: being podgy – especially being nearly friggin' immobile – you worn't part of t' main gang. Craner pushed his glasses further up his nose and seeing me smirking, shouted in his favoured mocking tone, 'Still here, Mr Thorpe?'

I unhinged the bonnet support strut and let the bonnet crash down. Craner flinched.

'Good as gone, Mr Craner, good as, just waiting for Eric.' I nodded toward t' toilets. 'He's just taking a dump.'

I climbed into t' cab to wait on Eric. In truth, I wor wary of Craner. Craner and Mitch went way back. I gobbed out onto some sawdust by t' van wheel. It brassed me off, being in Mitch's grip, but I also knew that Craner owed Mitch for summat. A little back-scratching, a little palm-greasing, and here I wor, my first proper job. Most times Craner wor holed up in his depot fiefdom, so it worn't as if he could come check up on me. Although wi' Craner you never knew, Craner seemed to have his spies everywhere.

'Boo!'

'Jeeeesus fuck, Eric!'

'Ready?'

'MIS–TER FAW–LEY!'

'Craner wants you, Eric.'

'The four-eyed fart. BE RIGHT WI' YOU, MR CRANER!'

Eric scuttled over to Craner, flattening his hair wi' one hand and tucking in his shirt-tail wi' t'other. Craner liked to make you feel t' wrath of God wor about to fall on your head, then deliver some quiet little aside about owt and nowt. Craner's way. Eric wor playin' out the game. He picked up the round-book and the float, and turned to grin at me, swinging t' van keys round his forefinger.

'Ready, Mr Thorpe?'

'Ready, Mr Fawley.'

We wor done by late afternoon, so I got Eric to drop me off in town. I waited for t' van to turn at the lights, then hurried on up Woodhouse Lane.

To see t' Matterhorn Man.

I'd first met the Matterhorn Man that summer, just shy of my sixteenth birthday. He lived at 5 Blandford Gardens, a short cul-de-sac Victorian terrace. Almost no one in t' Corona round-book had a proper name; most wor identified by some peculiar or particular feature: fist knocker, fishing gnome, third blue door, rabid mutt, buck teeth woman.

I'd been idly peering through t' front bay of 5 Blandford Gardens when I spotted a mural covering one entire wall, a photo of a mountain, rising snowcapped against a blue block of sky. Same as I'd seen on a calendar in our local Indian takeaway.

So I scrawled in t' round-book: '*Matterhorn Man*'.

Matterhorn Man wor a thin, gimlet-eyed Scot wi' a small, dark moustache and sideburns. One bottle of Coke and a bottle of tonic water every week.

Most weeks our van would reach Blandford Gardens in t' early afternoon. Often as not the Matterhorn Man would open t' door in his cordless dressing gown, holdin' it together wi' one hand while he fished in a small velvet drawstring pouch for change. Then one day he said, 'Come in a wee mo', won't you?'

Not wanting to appear rude or owt, I stepped into his hallway. Onto t' hallway runner wi' t' wear hole. He skedaddled into t' kitchen out back and came back wi' t' change and an empty. His dressing gown fell open. He had a lean, hirsute torso and thin, dark legs. His underpants wor a washed-out mauve.

Every week he held me up, rummaging for change, proffering up titbits about himsen. So I learnt that his name wor Jim, that he wor twenty-six year old, the sixth of eight brothers and sisters, all t' rest of 'em still up in Scotland save for t' one, who'd emigrated to Canada. That he worked the graveyard shift in a bikkie factory, 'putting the hearts in Jammie Dodgers', and that's why I always caught him half-dressed, or in his dressing gown, and that he used to have a lodger, but they'd argued over t' rent and so Jim lived alone now.

As Jim wor placing a florin into my grubby palm, he murmured quickly, 'Why don't you drop by a wee bit later on?'

'What?'

The question took me unawares, surfacing all of a sudden like a shark from t' depths. I felt t' blood whooshing to my cheeks. In Jim's face I saw t' horror of a man who'd misread a situation. The door wor beginning to close.

'No, wait. But I can't say when I finish. It might be a bit late.'

'I start work at seven.'

I nodded. 'If we make good time, I can be here before then.'

* * *

Jim scuttled about t' living room, tidying up, while I looked on nervously, wondering to mesen if I should have come at all. Then he went to t' kitchen to brew up tea. While I waited on him I let my thoughts wander. I sat on t' sofa edge at the foot of t' Matterhorn mural like I wor in a photographer's waiting room. I imagined mesen being photographed in front of it – 'Mr Thorpe, over 'ere ...' the flashbulbs blitzing, the world's press thrusting forward, all jostling for my attention: 'Richard Thorpe! Over here, Mr Thorpe!' 'Richard! Richard, just one more photo for ... for ... the World News.' Click. Flash. Flash. Click. 'Richard Thorpe, how does it feel to be the first man to conquer the Matterhorn single-handed and without a rope?'

'Hey, be careful there, you'll knock your tea over.'

'Oh, sorry, I wor just ...'

I flushed furiously. Jim beamed his easy smile and sat beside me. He took a sip from his tea and set it down on t' flecked brown-and-orange rug. We stared straight ahead like an old couple on a park bench. I caught t' strong whiff of his aftershave, which he must have splashed on for my benefit while he wor out in t' kitchen. A woman passed by t' bay window, a blur of raincoat and headscarf, a brief shadow across t' room.

'Ta for t' tea.'

'You're most welcome.'

Silence mushroomed. I wor missing *Doctor Who*. I'd be late for dinner.

I picked up my tea, took a sip, put it down, picked it up again, sipped, set it down. I feigned interest in t' row of scraggy paperbacks propped between two wooden bookends: *Valley of the Dolls, In Youth is Pleasure, Myra Breckinridge.*

'I can't stay long,' I murmured, my head still cocked toward t' book titles.

I felt a hand settle on my leg, as if it had fluttered down to rest. *Giovanni's Room, The Persian Boy, The Plays of Tennessee Williams* ... my head wor being gently yet firmly turned away from t' books by a man's palm. My face wor too close to his to focus. I knew at once that I wor about to be kissed. I leaned toward him, allowing it, wanting it.

The kiss felt strange. The neat moustache brushed against my mouth, the lips moist, the tongue wor warm wi' ... I pulled away.

'No sugar!'

'Sorry?'

'You don't have sugar in yer tea!'

'Sugar? Aye, I don't. Shall I rinse out my mouth?'

I glanced uncertainly out the window.

'Nope, it's fine.'

'Aye, well, if you're sure now?'

'Certain.'

And as if to show him that I wor, I kissed him again, a long, slow and exploratory kiss, while reaching down to place my hand on Matterhorn Man's evident stiffy.

'Shall we go upstairs a wee while?'

'Upstairs?'

And so it started. The Saturday afternoons after work. The curtains drawn against t' fading day. Lying naked on purple nylon sheets.

The name, I wor to discover, wor apt, cos the Matterhorn Man's erect cock had a kink in it, a bit like t' mountain itsen.

That wor also t' summer that Granddad Frank died. Mother's dad, not Mitch's – his folk wor gone before I wor slapped into t' world.

Not a week after he wor buried I wor idling in t' hallway when through t' gap between t' half-open door and the doorframe I saw Mother, standing in t' middle of t' living room,

17

eyes closed, arms extended. She began to rotate, slowly at first, then faster and faster, like a kid twirling in a playground, whirling and whirling round 'til she stopped suddenly and had to steady hersen against t' dining table.

Then I heard her say: 'What are little girls made of?' and reply to hersen, all breathless, 'Sugar! ... and spice! ... and all things ... nice!' and in my head I finished the rhyme off for her. 'What are little boys made of? Slugs, and snails, and puppy dogs' tails,' and I knew she wor remembering Granddad Frank, cos he used to swing us round like that when we wor small and shout out t' same rhyme, so I guessed he'd done it wi' her an' all. Only she'd had him to hersen cos they never did have another.

She slumped down onto t' carpet, sobbing gently, so I slunk into t' kitchen, opened the back door and banged it shut, like I wor just coming in.

Granddad Frank had died alone. Alone, under blistering arc lights, alone amongst a load of nurses and doctors, clamped to a defibrillator. He'd been cold twenty minute by t' time we pitched up at Leeds General Infirmary. The dour nurse on reception said that someone had brought him in by car.

'Who?' barked Grandma Betty, stabbing the air wi' her forefinger. 'Who brought him in!?' Grandma Betty had her frosty side all right, but never before had I seen her face all screwed up like a ball of paper.

'No idea,' the dour nurse stuttered. 'Whoever it wor didn't leave a name, and I wor on my break anyway.'

We plonked oursens on plastic chairs and waited. Except for Mitch, who stayed in t' Austin Cambridge, engine idlin' cos he said the ignition wor faulty. It had been just fine yesterday. Mother wor clutching her handbag like it might float away. Grandma had both hands wrapped around a plastic cup of hot tea, her lips pressed tightly together.

We waited an age, watching people drift by. Sitting opposite me wor a tramp wi' a gash on his hand. He wor mumbling and scratching his chest hairs furiously beneath his half-open shirt. He stank like a mouldy cheese. Two seats to his right sat a nervous Asian woman in a cerise sari and a brown anorak, rockin' a bawling baby.

Grandma wor muttering under her breath, 'I know who it wor, I know!'

When I asked who, she shook her head and blew her nose on a tissue that Mother passed to her.

After an age, an African doctor came up to us and ushered us all into a side room, where, he said in a cantering voice, it would be quieter.

Emily Jackson

21/01/1976

'Seducing a woman,' Eric wor saying, 'is like throwing a pot.'

It wor t' arse end of January, and after t' frenzy of pre-Christmas sales the soft-drinks trade had gone belly-up. We wor running light and ahead of schedule. So here we wor, parked up in Spencer Place, Chapeltown, heart of t' red-light area, scoffing chip butties and watching rivulets of rainwater scurry down t' windscreen. I worn't in no hurry today. The Matterhorn Man wor up in Glasgow, visiting his sick mother. Eric held his chip butty in front of his gob, undecided about how to attack it.

'To start wi',' he said, spraying breadcrumbs as he spoke, 'it's all shapeless, and you don't know if owt will come of it, she wobbles unsure in your hands. Then, if you're workin' it right, she yields and starts to take shape, until ...'

'... You've made an urn?'

'Ha, bloody ha. Listen to Eric and learn, lad. There ain't nowt I can't teach you about that mysterious being called womankind.'

Eric's other favoured analogy wor t' lightbulb and the iron. In t' world according to Eric, a man is turned on like a lightbulb, but a woman heats up more slowly, like an iron. He said it wor his dad's explanation of t' birds and the bees. Lightbulbs and irons.

'What if you've got two irons? Or two lightbulbs?'

Eric licked the salt off his lips and tossed the crumpled chip paper into t' road.

'Two lightbulbs? What kind of skewed thinking is that? You'd blow a bloody fuse, that's what. Two bloody lightbulbs indeed. Sounds a bit peculiar, a bit daft. A bit queer, if yer ask me.'

I flushed. I'd been blowing fuses on every visit to t' Matterhorn Man.

On my third, or maybe fourth visit, we'd lain in bed afterward listening to Velvet Underground on t' record player. Jim wor idly stroking my head and smokin' a ciggie when he asked me if I ever had any problem wi' what we wor doing. I just laughed.

'It wor Maxwell Confait,' I said. 'He wor t' one.'

'Eh?'

So I told him about how, late one evening, I wor slumped on t' living-room rug in my pyjamas after my bath, one eye on t' telly, t'other on t' music paper beside me. Mother wor mulling over a competition where you had to write a slogan to win a caravan at Skegness. The late-night regional news drifted into a documentary about t' murder of some male prostitute called Maxwell Confait.

'I pity people like that,' Mother said, raising her eyes toward t' small screen. Then she told me to move, cos I wor blocking all t' heat from t' gas fire.

I shuffled back a tad and reread some Black Sabbath tour dates. But really my lugs wor glued to t' smug, southern voice of t' reporter, who wor saying that Maxwell Confait wor 'a self-confessed homosexual who was murdered in South-East London', and that three teenage lads had been charged wi t' murder. One of t' lads wor only fourteen year old, same as me.

It wor like a firework had been lobbed into t' living room. I remember thinking, clear as anything, 'That's me he's talking about. That's me. I fancy boys.'

It befuddled me that anyone my age could commit murder. What wor that about? Adults murdered, kids got murdered. Like that Myra Hindley and that bloke that murdered loads of kids and buried 'em up on t' moors.

All t' while Mother wor pretending to be reading her magazine, but I knew she wor listening an' all, cos she kept clicking her ballpoint on and off. Then, when I saw his face on t' telly a strange thrill coursed through me.

Jim sat up against t' bedhead. 'It did?'

'Aye. He had these big, pleading eyes and unkempt hair and this black gash for lips. Cos we hadn't got our colour telly then. But I knew. At that moment, I just knew.'

'Well,' Jim exhaled, 'if I recall rightly, they were all acquitted in the retrial.'

I turned over in t' bed to ease the pressure on my elbow. 'Since then, I've always thought that one day I'll be a famous pop star, or be murdered. Or a famous pop star who gets murdered. Or a pop star who gets murdered and then becomes famous.'

Jim laughed and tousled my hair. 'Just don't end up like poor Janis. All washed up on heroin.'

Eric started up the engine, let it idle over. 'Come on, we've enough time. Let's call on Vanessa, if she ain't too busy. Then we can have a quick cuppa, all right?'

It worn't good to get too far ahead of schedule. Harehills and Chapeltown before lunch, then on to t' big housing estates of Belle Isle, Gipton and Halton Moor in t' afternoon, then finally the tower blocks and maisonettes up Seacroft way. Too early, or too late, and sales would be lost. And Craner wor intent on improving sales. Even a push on malt vinegar had failed to revive the flagging figures.

We pulled up outside Vanessa's, and Eric headed in while I waited in t' van.

It must have been a grand house once, but now it wor in a very sorry state. The stone wor sooty and pitted, the rotting gutters all clogged wi' wet leaves, the paintwork flaking away. A board had been nailed across one of t' etched panes of coloured glass in t' front door. In t' overgrown garden, a few spindly roses soldiered on.

Eric reappeared in t' porch. 'Bring a bottle of Coke!'

I fished one off the van and strolled up to t' house, tossing and catching it as if it wor a baton.

As I pushed the door wi' my shoulder a breeze gusted in, lifting the hallway linoleum at its edges.

Vanessa lived on t' ground floor. I paused in t' hallway at the foot of t' stairs, my eye following the sweep of t' banister rail upward into t' gloom, my nostrils twitching to t' stale traces of over-fried and boiled food, my ears hearing the steady plopping from t' laundry slung over t' banisters.

Although Vanessa's door wor open, I knocked anyway and entered without waiting.

'Here he is!'

I set the coke bottle on t' sideboard, parked mesen on one arm of her grubby sofa.

Vanessa wor a big woman wi' matted strawberry-blonde hair and a round, pocked face. I tried not to stare at t' folds of pale skin slithering from her faded pink halterneck dress. Worn't she cold? I dunked my teabag as she gabbled on in her brittle voice, talking about business mostly. All t' while she kept one eye on t' street, t'other on t' nipper in plastic pants that wor shuffling itsen toward me across t' lino floor. Vanessa crossed her plump legs and let one shoe dangle. Her feet wor deformed by years of stilettos. Chips of red varnish on her toenails.

'God, I hate this weather – didn't know you'd got hitched, Eric,' Vanessa said in one breath.

'I'm not.'

'What's wi' t' ring then?'

'Engaged.'

'Ooh, engaged? To that ... what's her name ... Julie, is it?'

'No, not her ... to Karen.'

'Last I heard you wor knockin' about wi' a Julie.'

'Aye. Aye, I wor – but it's Karen now.'

The subject of t' ring shunted off into a siding, Vanessa turned her attention to me.

'Heard a lot about you,' she oozed. 'Eric tells me all sorts, he does.'

My innards wor squirming like a bag of mealy worms. When, for pity's sake, did Eric get to blather on to Vanessa about rings and marriage? We only stopped by when we were on t' round, didn't we?

They wor both looking at me expectantly. The ring. Now that I'd clapped eyes on it, it had a permanent look. No hacking that off.

'All good, I 'ope,' I mumbled.

'Well, now, that would be telling, wouldn't it?' Vanessa teased. 'Nice-looking lad, though, ain't he, Eric?'

'If you say so.'

'Trust me. Make some girl very happy one day, mark my words.'

Friggin' 'ell. Not the done thing – glowing like hot coals in front of a prozzie.

'Oh, he's not still a virgin, is he Eric?'

'What you asking me for? He's a bit of a dark horse, this one. I reckon there's summat going on, what wi' me dropping him off in town after t' round every week, but he's keeping mum about her.'

Eric winked at me.

'A dark horse, eh?' Vanessa purred. 'I lay bets on dark horses, them quiet ones wi' t' broad smiles and not much to say for themsens. They're t' ones you have to watch.'

Luckily for me, Vanessa's attention wor distracted by her toddler, who wor balanced on fat little legs, trying to clamber onto a chair, fingers stretching toward t' Coke bottle.

'Leave it. Leave it, Jase! I said effin' leave it!'

She scooped up the toddler wi' one arm and plonked him firmly back onto a different part of t' lino. The room filled up wi' a piercing wail.

'Effin' kids! Always wantin' whatever they clap eyes on. I want this, I want that. I want, I want, I want. Well I bloody want, but it don't mean I can 'ave!'

The wailing brought in Vanessa's older kid from out in t' corridor, yelling excitedly. Spotting us, he hid himsen behind his arm, gigglin', 'til he spied the Coke bottle on t' sideboard too.

'Yer can 'ave some later, Barry. Wi' yer tea. Take Jase out in t' corridor, there's a luv.'

Barry ran out again. The toddler set off after him, toppling over, making us all erupt, then hauled himsen up again onto his crooked little legs.

Vanessa moved to t' window, from where she could keep an eye open for business. There wor fewer punters about in t' daytime, but then, she said, fewer girls wor out working. The banter turned to Emily Jackson, the murdered woman, who like Wilma, like Vanessa hersen, wor a mother an' all.

Vanessa repositioned the one-bar electric fire toward her legs.

'I didn't know her, Emily. She worn't no regular. I hear she used to hang out at the Gaiety and the Room at the Top club. But that don't mean owt.'

She patted the corners of her mouth wi' a tissue, her gaze fixed on t' gap between t' gateposts. For a moment it seemed she had a punter. She sat upright, patting her hair, projecting her breasts. Then she relaxed her posture. The punter had moved on.

'He'll be back,' she said, taking a long drag on her ciggie. 'The girls,' she said, exhaling upward, 'are mostly working team-handed. They'll keep it up for a week or two, and then they'll forget. Trust me.'

She screwed her fag end into t' ashtray and lit another. 'When you've been in business as long as I have, you can smell a bad'un.'

She smiled at us both, a smile, I saw, that wor too light for t' effort she gave it.

I lay on my bed leafing through t' local rag. They didn't waste much ink on Emily. Just a brief mention of a second prozzie murder in Chapeltown, and a fuzzy photo. Whores get what's coming is what most folk thought. If folk thought at all.

I could hear sis in t' bath. She wor always having baths. No wonder t' reservoir levels wor so low. I slipped across t' landing into her bedroom and, sliding open a drawer, took out the diary from under t' layers of knickers. I flipped it open where a blue biro wor resting in t' spine.

My fingers danced grubbily through t' pages. Her scribble wor hard to read, and she'd been scrawling biro flowers and stick figures in t' margins. It wor t' usual friggin' rubbish. Some boys had been carving band names in t' wooden bus shelter (boring), summat about copying her French home-work off Emma in return for buying Emma some fags (learn-ing fast there, sis), and some boy called Adam had smiled at her in t' corridor.

I turned the page. Sunday. She'd been listening to t' top thirty pop charts and marking down t' chart positions in a special chart book. What friggin' chart book? My eyes skimmed over t' shoes and bags strewn across t' carpet, the teddies, frogs and gonks on t' bed, the washing slithering out of t' wicker basket. My hand hovered over all t' girly clutter on t' small dressing table that Mitch had put together for her in t' garage last winter, not wanting to move owt in case she clocked it.

I realised I could hear t' bath water gurgling away down t' pipes. I flipped the diary shut and scuttled back to my room. I threw mesen on t' bed and laughed deliciously. A close call wor always more satisfying than getting away clean and easy.

'Charts!' I snorted under my breath. 'Charts!'

Marcella Claxton

09/05/1976 (survived)

Friday night, as usual, we all went for a chinky and then on to t' Marquis of Granby at the end of our road.

Even Gran came along these days, now that she wor on her tod. Mandy, being too young for pubbing, said she wor going to Emma's to listen to records. When sis wor fibbing she talked like a dalek and fiddled wi' her hair. She wor off to see Adam. Her latest diary entries wor full of him. Adam-friggin'-Adam. Mother didn't say nowt, except 'Don't be late.'

The Marquis wor a large, noisy pub wi' swirly blue-and-green carpeting, a jukebox and a dartboard.

Mavis, Mother's mouldiest friend, had pitched up, as had the neighbours, Nora Gudgeon, her diabetic mother Denise, and her daughter Janice. Mavis squeezed her ample backside onto t' bench seat between Gran and me. She wor wearing a trowel-load of slap over t' thin veneer of abuse doled out by hubby Don, and a pong so raking I thought I'd gag if I so much as flared a nostril. I spotted her abuser, across t' bar, through t' curling smoke, wi' Mitch and two other blokes I didn't know, drinkin' themsens into a slurry.

Janice wor sat opposite me, face like a pickled egg. Struck me she wor all dolled up like she'd been planning on being elsewhere. I could sympathise. It didn't suit me none, sitting wi' all t' brassy women, but Mother wor being as stubborn as a goat, using that 'family together' baloney to blackmail me into feeling guilty for wanting to stay at home and play my records.

Janice fiddled wi' t' buckle of her wide, white belt. Her nipples wor pushing pertly up against her cheesecloth smock-blouse.

'Our Janice is getting spliced soon,' chirruped Nora.

'Married? Is that right, Janice?' said Mavis, leaning forward, her glinting hoop earrings leaning wi' her, her breasts bunching together in her low-cut glitzy top. 'When wor all this decided?'

Janice dropped her chin, and all eyes followed to t' gentle bump. Looked like it wor decided about four month gone, I thought.

'So, come on,' Mavis said. 'Who's the lucky fella?'

'He's called Drew,' Janice said, lighting a ciggie and blowing smoke from t' side of her mouth. Denise flapped the smoke away wi' a flash of pink nails.

'Drew? Short for Andrew, is that? So where is he? When do we get to meet him?'

Janice crossed her arms over her stomach. 'He's on a geography field trip. Wi' t' school.'

Mavis said, 'Kids today, eh. Who'd have 'em?' Then wi' a toss of her head toward Mother, she added, 'If I remember right, Pam, you married dead young, didn't you?'

'He wor a mistake,' Mother replied waspishly. 'We wor divorced before a year wor out ... Oh, Janice, luv, not that I mean that it won't last between yersen and ... and ...'

'Drew.'

'Drew ... just that I married a wrong'un, that's all.'

'What wor his name ...?' Denise asked, pitching in her tuppence worth. Mavis snatched up her lighter, clicking it furiously against t' tip of another ciggie 'til Nora struck a match for her, then lit one for hersen.

Mother hissed, 'You know damn well, Denise. You know damn well his name.'

Mother stretched out a smile. I didn't know if she wor

shunting off the topic for her own sake or mine. What wor to know that I hadn't learnt already by earwigging and nosing about? Some friggin' carpet salesman, twice her age, who she'd married and divorced like t' church had revolving doors. It all happened a friggin' age before I came on t' scene. And owt that happened before me didn't really happen. Except in history books and on t' telly. Of course she didn't want to blab on about it.

Denise worn't done yet.

'Didn't he take you down to London on honeymoon? Started out wi' a stall in Leeds market and before you could say shag pile he had his own warehouse in an old church, heavin' wi' carpets and linos. Proper little peacock, he wor. Always wore a suit, and drove a car wi' a walnut dashboard.'

This wor a stinking, fresh cowpat of news to me.

'What kind of car?'

Mother looked like her hair wor on fire.

'A bloody posh one,' said Mavis.

'So, Janice,' said Mother, trying to park the conversation elsewhere, 'any name yet for the ... for the ...?'

'Damien,' Janice said. 'Or Rosemary, if it's a girl.'

'What unusual names, Janice,' Mother said.

'I think,' said Mavis, 'we should all drink a toast to Janice. And to Nora on becoming a grandmother.'

Nora bridled. I surmised that 'grandmother' didn't sit well wi' her just yet. She nodded at me, and said to Mother, 'Well, I'm sure this one will do you proud when t' time comes.'

'Not me. I'm never getting married,' I said.

The women guffawed.

'I'm not.'

Behind Janice's head I could see Don's barrel bulk heading our way, parting the drinkers like a shire horse fording a river. Denise, who hadn't clapped eyes on him yet, wor saying, 'Course you will, Rick. Some lovely lass will catch your eye, and then before ...'

'I told you, I'm not getting married. Ever.'

Mother's brow knitted painfully.

'All right, ladies?' Don's eyes combed across Janice's breasts. Janice averted her gaze.

'We wor,' piped up Denise, 'until we saw you waltzing over our way.'

'Gerald!' said Gran, as if she'd just hit on t' answer in a friggin' crossword puzzle. 'His name wor Gerald. Had his own carpet business and a big house up Alwoodley way wi' a garden, a big car and ...'

Mother flashed me a pleading look. I said, 'Gran, we know. Give it a rest.'

Gran cocked her head at me. 'A gin and tonic, please, young man.'

'You've got one, Gran. Look – right in front of you.'

It wor odd for Gran to call me young man. She usually only called anyone young man whose name she didn't know or couldn't recollect. She picked up the glass, downed it in one. 'Gerald,' she murmured, looking pleased wi' hersen. 'His name wor Gerald.'

The next morn, Mother wor leant against t' fridge, watching me wolf down beans on toast before heading off to work. Our fridge wor covered in friggin' fridge magnets. Sunflowers, London buses, Smurfs, Disney characters, cacti, flags, all plastered over t' ruddy thing like fridge-magnet acne.

I wor wanting to ask her about Gerald and his car wi' t' walnut dashboard and that, but I could see she worn't going to spill. Her face wor taut, her hair still unbrushed and she hadn't put her lippy on. Mother said little above t' necessary to make brekkie function.

'I might be late again,' I said.

Mother repositioned one of t' fridge magnets.

'Again? I'll keep some cold ham and beetroot for your dinner.'

She spoke slowly, like she wor really saying summat else. I scraped back my chair.

'It's all right, I'll get chips.'

Mother winced.

I rattled Mrs Husk's letterbox. 'Corona pop!'

'It's open, luv.'

Mrs Husk wor swilling out a teacup under t' kitchen tap. She shuffled into her front room wi' t' teacup dangling from one finger. After a momentary difficulty freeing her finger from t' cup handle she said, 'Did yer get my whisky?'

'Yer whisky?'

She eyed me beadily. I laughed and took the small bottle of Bell's from my coat pocket and set it on t' table, together wi' her usual ginger beer. The things we're friggin' well asked to do.

Mrs Husk patted her hairnet. 'Have you had a win on t' pools or summat, lad?'

'Being happy's not a crime is it, Mrs Husk?'

'It's a rum world, lad, when folk are happy for no reason. Sit a moment.'

I sat. Today I had time. Eric wor knobbing some house-wife at number 78, but I worn't going to tell Mrs Husk that. She sloughed into t' kitchen to fetch her empty. From my spot in t' lounge I said in a loud voice, 'My gran's just moved house.'

I didn't usually blather about t' folks, but if I kept Mrs Husk conversationalising then I knew where she wor. Gran had upped sticks, sold sticks and moved about a mile across town into a small, modern, first-floor flat. Fitted carpets, new boiler, double glazing, window locks.

She'd taken as good as nowt wi' her, but had instructed Mr Cowley – *Second Hand Furniture – House Clearances*, screamed the black letters on t' day-glo orange sign – to cart away all t' stuff that Mother had grown up about, sat at, played under, slept on. 'Sold without sentiment,' Mother had said bitterly. 'Sold for a pittance.'

Mother then blathered on about feeling 'complicit in a dirty crime', denying a man barely cold in t' ground all trace of his time on this earth. Wiping him clean of our lives, she called it, as if, she said, it wor *her* own childhood that had been parcelled up and disposed of in such an underhand manner. I wor thinking, 'It's only stuff.'

I thought Gran had done t' right thing. It meant we didn't have to have any of it. Mind you, we did end up wi' some friggin' boat-shaped lamp wi' a parchment sail shade.

While I wor waiting on Mrs Husk to come back from t' kitchen wi' her empty ginger-beer bottle I picked up a framed photo from t' side table. An old photo of a man and woman at t' coast somewhere. They wor posing stiffly and smirking at t' camera. The wind had blown the woman's hair across her face and the camera had caught her pushing it aside wi' her hand.

'Is this you and Mr Husk?'

'Is what me?'

'This photo. Is it you?'

She sidled over, handed me t' empty ginger beer bottle and peered at t' photo.

'That? Aye, it is. That wor took at Whitby. A long while back.'

She took the photo from me and set it back on t' side table. 'Now I want you to rub some ointment into t' back of my calf. I can't do it mesen, I go all funny.'

I sighed. Mrs Husk parked hersen in her chair and rolled down her knee-length stocking to expose her bare leg. Taking the ointment from her, I squeezed a little onto my palm. Her skin moved in loose ripples under my kneading fingers, as if she wor in a coat too big for her tiny frame. I distracted mesen by thinking of Eric's bare arse rising and falling over at number 78. I wor getting a stiffy, so I decided it might be better to make some more idle chat.

'So, when he died, I guess he didn't leave you much, then?'

'When who died?'

'Mr Husk. When he passed on. I wor saying that he didn't leave you no money?'

'Hah! Die? Who said owt 'bout him being dead? For all I know he might be still swanning about somewhere. No lad, he walked out on me a long while back, went off wi' another woman. There, I've said it, never thought I'd say these things to a complete stranger.'

'I'm not a stranger, Mrs Husk, I'm your Corona van boy.'

'Well, no, I suppose not, lad. It wor my fault, you see. I put him on a pedestal, which never does, does it, putting a man on a pedestal? Put a man on a pedestal and it goes to his head. He came back one time. We wor living over Beeston way then. There wor a knock on t' door, and there he stood, bold as brass in his brand-new overcoat, suitcase by his side, looking reet dapper. He didn't say nowt, just stood there, waiting for ... waiting for me to let him in, I suppose. Trouble wor, I had a friend round for tea, didn't I? So I said to him, I said, "It's not convenient, come back later."'

'And did he?'

'Did he what?'

'Come back?'

'No lad. Never saw hair nor hide.'

'Sorry to hear that, Mrs Husk.'

'Aye, well it's a rum world, it is that.'

Mrs Husk looked down at her leg.

'I think that's enough. I'll bandage it later – let the air at it a while. I'd better not keep yer dallying, now that he's finished wi' her over yonder.'

I peered through t' nets. Must have been a real quickie, cos Eric wor already on t' back of t' van, restacking crates. Mrs Husk sluiced her tea through her dentures and peered into t' bottom of t' cup.

'Oh it's a rum world, all right,' she muttered to Lord Snooty, who looked up at her and mewed, then drummed his claws furiously against a chair leg.

After t' round I got Eric to drop me in town.

'Give her one from me!' he shouted.

I legged it to Blandford Gardens, then stopped at the end of t' road, doubled up wi' a stitch. I knew at once that the Matterhorn Man worn't home. The house wor in darkness. The street wor eerily empty, wi' all t' cars parked where they wor last week, like they'd never been driven. The sun wor slowly sinking behind t' buildings opposite. I rapped on t' door. The knocker had a dead knell. I waited, then rapped again. Standing in t' gutter, I scoured up at the bedroom window. Where it happened. Where it should be happening now.

Before Jim, I'd never slept under a duvet before. Before Jim, I'd never even shared a bed wi' a man, a proper grown-up man, wi' a grown-up man's stubble, and dark breath, hands wi' hairs sprouting from t' backs of t' fingers, muscular calves and the amazing, perfect, slightly kinked cock.

At first it hurt a bit, like he wor trying to jab it in me, but that wor only cos I wor all tensed up. Jim said I had to learn to relax and imagine I wor drawing him in, and that it wor like learning to swim or riding a bicycle, wi' practice and persuasion I'd soon be flying. Jim wor patient and gently insistent, and then suddenly I wor up in t' clouds and there wor no bringing me down again 'til t' inevitable happened.

And afterward I lay on t' purple nylon sheets wi' my head on Jim's chest, listening to t' squelches and gurgles in Jim's stomach mingling wi' Pink Floyd's *Meddle* LP on t' stereo, feeling warm and safe and sated 'til Jim said it wor time for him to go put the hearts in Jammie Dodgers and for me to go home.

I peered through t' letterbox into t' hallway. All wor dull and silent.

Flummoxed, I plonked mesen on t' bay window sill, tapping my shoe-end against t' brick. I decided to take mesen round t' block a while. Maybe I'd just been unlucky and Jim had slipped out to t' shop for some ciggies.

I gave it a good half-hour, then, still finding no one at home, I trudged off toward t' city centre. At the junction wi' Woodhouse Lane I found mesen facing the Fenton, a pub, I remembered now, that Jim said he frequented. I chortled. I'd find Jim again, easy peasy.

I ducked into t' Fenton, hiked mesen onto a bar stool on t' public bar side and ordered a pint of lager and lime. There wor a couple of flat-capped men in t' lounge bar and, two stools along on my side, a rough-looking woman in a gaudy dress. Sixty dressed as thirty.

I drank heedlessly, tracing circles in t' beer slops. I wor downing the dregs of my third pint when I heard t' rough old bird say, 'You want to go easy or you won't last.'

Setting my empty down on t' slop mat, I looked stonily into her face. A face that wor t' wreckage of another age. Even her voice had been shredded by t' years. She creaked out a smile, displaying the last of her wobbly, lipstick-stained teeth, and told me her name wor Dora. I nodded at her like I wor batting away a fly. She pulled her fingers through her dyed straw hair and adjusted one strap of her dress.

'You not talking, stranger?'

I slid off my stool and headed for t' door.

'Hey, handsome, where yer going?' she called out in her rickety voice. 'Aw, don't go yet. Buy me a G & T if you like? I'm good company ...'

I trudged the quarter mile back into t' city centre, a foul fog filling my brain, cutting through t' Merrion Centre shopping mall, which wor empty and silent save for t' flickering buzz of a faulty photo booth, passed on by t' multi-storey and out through a filthy underpass. I wor burstin' and the gents toilet in t' underpass hadn't been locked, so I reeled in. It reeked of piss.

I worn't alone. There wor this old geezer by t' cubicles, toying wi' himsen, and a younger one at the trough. I pissed long and hard, sending an arc up the metal trough back. The young'un shot a glance at me and I glanced back. He worn't much older than me. He wor half-cock, and I could feel mesen getting the same.

I nodded toward t' cubicles, but he shook his head to mean that we should go elsewhere. I followed him out and up a back stairwell of t' multi-storey. Only when we reached the very top did he turn toward me.

'Safe enough here,' he said, unzipping himsen.

I looked about. Anyone coming up them stairs would be heard long before they reached us. There wor no cars on t' roof, so no one would surprise us from that direction neither.

'You live round here?' I said.

'Just up the road. Neville Street.'

Neville Street – the parallel cul-de-sac to Blandford Gardens.

'Can't we go back there?'

'I live wi' my mum and older sister.'

'You don't know a Jim, do you? Lives in Blandford Gardens. Drinks in t' Fenton.'

His eyes widened. 'Aye, I know Jim. Been round his place loads of times.'

'Have you now?'

'Aye. I slip round there at night sometimes when my folks are all tucked up.'

A cold anger uncoiled in me. Still, I unzipped mesen and he dropped to his knees and took my dick in his gob even though I worn't fully hard cos of t' lager and the blather. I closed my eyes and concentrated on getting a stiffy. Not that I needed to. He wor good, didn't get his teeth in t' way and could deep-throat. Jim had trained him well, I thought. Opening my eyes now that I wor hard, I took hold of his head wi' both hands and held him there. I wor soon going to spunk off, so I thrust deeper and made him splutter from near on gagging. He tried to pull back, but I tightened my grip on his head, thrusting into his gob 'til I basted his tonsils. I pulled out, and spunk ran across his lips and down his chin.

Then I hit him.

Unbalanced by my punch, he fell sideways. He looked up at me disbelievingly, like a trusting dog.

I hit him again, in t' face this time, and blood oozed from a nostril. He made no sound, not a whimper. The less the reaction, the more I wanted to force one – a cry of pain, a plea to stop, even an attempt to defend himsen – but he did nowt. So I thwacked him again, hard, my fist landing firmly above his left ear. Just say summat, I wor thinking, say summat and I'll stop. But he sat there, like a disused glove puppet, his gob half-open, his dick still peeping out of his fly.

I kicked him one last time in t' ribs and ran down t' stairs in threes and fours, cut back through t' Merrion Centre and over t' road. As I crossed it I caught sight of t' old geezer emerging from t' underpass, two plain-clothed coppers escorting him by t' arms.

* * *

When I wor next delivering to Blandford Gardens, I found the Matterhorn Man all chirrupy, like there wor nowt wrong. I fathomed that the Neville Street tyke had kept shtumm. He invited me in while he looked for his velvet bag of change, which he'd mislaid in t' kitchen somewhere.

There wor someone parked on t' moss-green sofa, beneath t' Matterhorn. His head jerked up toward me as I passed by t' open lounge door.

Jim said the man wor his older brother, Steve. Anyone could see right away that he wor Jim's brother. Knock Jim over t' bonce wi' a fairground mallet and that wor what he might look like: a podgier, squarer version of Jim, wi' an extra chin, shorter legs, a beer belly and splurging love handles. Jim took it upon himsen to introduce me, which must have looked a bit odd, presenting the Corona delivery boy. I stretched out a hand, being polite. Steve looked at it wi' an expression that slithered between uncertainty and hostility, then shook it briefly. He wore a signet ring. He looked underslept.

I excused mesen and went into t' kitchen. Jim smiled ruefully.

'Sorry, kid, he just turned up out of the blue. He cannae stay. It's not the first time he's done this. I'm guessing his missus has kicked him out again – that's usually what this is about.'

He kissed me on t' nose. 'It might be best you don't call by after your work for a wee while. Just until he's gone.'

'How long will that be?'

Jim had found his velvet change bag by t' toaster.

'Last time was about three weeks. Blethered on about getting a job and all that, but all he did was doss around the hoose all day. Trouble with Steve is he thinks the world owes him. In the end I gave him some dosh and put him on a coach back to Glasgow.'

'Three week!'

Jim kneaded the nape of my neck. 'He'll not be staying that long this time, don't you worry.'

'Does he know?'

'He knows, but I wouldn't want to give him the extra ammunition, if you get my drift.'

'Meaning?'

'Meaning that you being underage jailbait, it's better that he disnae know. I cannae trust Steve not to use something like that.'

Jim handed me t' money for his usual order, and an extra bottle of Coke for Steve.

I said, 'What about t'other one? Has he been warned off an' all?'

Jim fiddled wi' t' drawstring of t' velvet bag.

'What other one?'

Craner had his feet up on t' desk, flicking paperclips at the tits of Miss July on t' wall calendar. It had barely rained since t' end of May. We wor out on t' road from dawn to dusk. Sales of pop wor skyrocketing. We sold it, drank it, sweated it, pissed it up the sides of walls and into hedges. Eric had even pissed full an empty bottle of limeade, and somehow we sold that. Craner hauled his eyes off Miss July's tits and onto my face.

'I hope you had a wash, Thorpy, cos by mid-morn in this heat you're gonna stink like a wrestler's laundry basket.'

'Always wash, Mr Craner. Just wondering if t' round-book wor ready.'

He tossed the round-book toward me. It fell short by my boots. I picked it up.

'So, Thorpy, who's going to win the cricket at Headingley, eh? England or the West Indies?'

'Dunno, Mr Craner. Don't follow it none.'

40

Friggin' cricket ruled that week. Wherever we delivered, doors wor slung open, sash windows raised or lowered, radios cranked up to distortion, every last soul hanging on to t' plummy vowels of t' cricket commentators. Some folk had set up their TVs in t' back yard, wi' t' cable running through an open window. Folk who never watched cricket wor watching cricket. Pubs had brought in TVs to drum up extra trade. Even kids had got the cricket bug, overarming tennis balls toward chalked stumps on brick walls or tapping cheap bats into t' ground in front of upended box stumps.

Up at Headingley cricket ground, the Windies wor giving England a pasting.

Craner arched his eyebrows over t' rims of his glasses and flicked off another paperclip. This one pinged against Miss July's left eye.

'Don't follow cricket? Even my good friends at the Ukrainian Club are following the cricket. They don't know a bloody thing about it, but they're following it all t' same. They know what's important in this life, Mr Thorpe.'

'Didn't know you wor a Yu-ker-ranium, Mr Craner.'

'My grandfolks wor from Lvov. Came to this country before t' first war, changed their name to Craner. So now you know. Corona supplies the Ukrainian Club wi' soft drinks and mixers. A lot of 'em are ex-forces that got left in Yorkshire at t' end of t' war. Same as for t' Poles. Lvov wor part of Poland back then. Did you know that?'

'No, Mr Craner.'

I wor thinking they could come from t' moon for all it mattered.

'All t' things you don't know or show no interest in. Connections, boy. To get on in life you have to show interest and propagate connections. It's no good sitting back and waiting for life to grab you by t' goolies. Remember that and you'll make summat of yersen.'

'Like you, Mr Craner?'

'Aye, like me.'

'Use your connections?' Eric said. 'Is that what he said?'

We wor parked up by t' side of t' road, scoffing lunch. We'd peeled off our shirts and the sun wor baking our bods through t' windscreen, our reddened arms and necks contrasting wi' t' paleness of t' rest. I liked sitting there half-naked, wi' Eric half-naked alongside me.

I said, 'Well, it wor Mitch's connection to Craner that got me this job, so there must be summat in it.'

'I wouldn't trust Craner an inch. Not an inch. As for that shite about cricket and U-Cranes ... I bet Craner don't even know where U-Crane is.'

'Hey, geddit? U-Crane? Craner? Funny one, that.'

'No bloody wonder we're losing the cricket,' Eric said, 'what wi' it being so hot and the pitch so parched and play-ing like it is. Put up a few banana trees and they'll think they're back home.'

We ate slobbily, shovelling fried duck and eggy rice wi' 'special curry sauce' into our mouths, washing it down wi' swigs of pop. Sauce droplets slithered off our plastic forks and, I clocked, splattered onto Eric's crotch area.

'Bloody 'ell,' he muttered to himsen, rubbing the spots wi' his hankie. 'Bloody effin' 'ell. These keks wor clean on this morning.'

He mopped his forehead wi' t' same hankie, screwing his face up at the sun.

'Must be up in t' 90s today. Granddad's as pleased as punch. Says it'll bring on his allotment lovely, all this sunshine will. He's out there every day, tendering, watering. Won't last, mind.'

Eric rolled up the *Sun* and squished a wasp against t' windscreen.

'So, tell Eric, who is she?'

'Who is she what?'

'The girl, stupid. You know – Saturday afternoons? You all tetchy and eager to finish the round and cash up and get away at day's end. Come on, spill all. We've all been there.'

I flicked the dirt from under a fingernail. The distant tower blocks shimmered in t' heat. Somewhere nearby, an ice-cream van tinkled listlessly.

'Ain't no one.'

'Ain't no one? Is she blonde? Dark? Pretty? Don't tell me, she's already got a boyfriend and you're seeing her on t' sly? Married? If you want any advice on the best way to ...'

'I don't need no advice. There's some stuff I prefer to keep to mesen.'

Eric scented the air like a gun dog.

'Vanessa's right, you're a dark horse all right.'

He scrunched up his foil tray and tossed it into t' road. He pulled on his shirt.

'We'd best get on,' he said, turning the ignition key. The engine spluttered into life.

'Aye,' I said, buttoning up my own shirt. 'We'd best get on.'

The heat wave lasted 'til t' end of August. The grass withered away, leaving brown, naked patches, the sunbathers and park picnickers turned red and weary. Allotments, including Eric's granddad's, wilted away and fell foul to insect plagues and hosepipe bans. The government put up standpipes. Van washing, even washing the outsides of t' bottles, had been banned, and everything wor looking grimy. In t' queues for water, neighbours rediscovered each other and chattered like finches set free.

It wor August Bank Holiday before t' heavens finally opened, but not before t' Windies had crushed England in t' final Test at Lord's. Every West Indian on t' round wor celebrating to our faces. Back at t' depot, our two West Indian drivers, Phillip and Chester, wor hollering to all who could hear, 'Who said we'd grovel? Eh? Didn't the England captain say it, eh? Didn't he say he'd make dem West Indies grovel?'

I shrugged. 'I couldn't give a rat's behind about cricket.'

Chester wagged his finger at me. 'You's saying that now! You's be saying that now!'

If it wor too hot for cricket, it wor surely too hot for murder. That summer, nowt happened.

For t' next few weeks I wor riled to find Jim's good-for-nowt brother answering the door to Blandford Gardens. I longed for him to skedaddle back to where he came from. But three week became a month, and a month became three. He wor a friggin' scrounger and a layabout if ever I saw one. He'd taken to ordering an extra couple of bottles of Coke for himsen on Jim's money. Spent his Saturday afternoons watching *Grandstand*, and most likely spent his evenings in t' pub.

I asked after Jim, keeping it casual, but Steve always said he wor either out or kipping. Besides, what wi' t' hot weather an' all, sometimes we only finished the round after Jim wor on his way to t' bikkie factory. To put the hearts in Jammie Dodgers.

Then one afternoon I found a note in an envelope under t' empties. I tore it open.

Just one bottle of tonic water and one Coke. Jim. x

He'd left the exact change. I folded and pocketed the envelope and swapped over t' bottles. Steve had finally pissed off back to Glasgow or wherever. I spent the rest of t' round singing and whistling and joking wi' Eric, and at the end of t' day I told him to drop me in town. I ran full pelt the quarter mile to Blandford Gardens rather than wait for t' bus.

Again, there wor no one home. It wor that dead hour of t' day – too early for t' pubs, but t' shops wor already shut. I hung about for a while, my mood sinking wi' t' lowering early-autumn sun. I mooched off about t' neighbouring streets and then up past Leeds Uni. I found mesen idling before t' window of some feminist bookshop, fumed up about Jim being out even though Steve had gone, not wanting to go home and undecided about what to do wi' mesen.

The bookshop wor closed. The plate window wor a proper jamboree of notice cards, adverts and magazine covers wi' names like *Spare Rib*, *Marxism Today* and *Leeds Other Paper*. On t' far wall above a tatty sofa wor a pro-abortion poster and a Che Guevara poster. Studenty-politico-women's-commie-lesbo stuff. I wor thinking about breaking in, or at least bricking the window, cos smashing summat up might make me feel better about t' world, when my eye wor drawn to a word on a lavender-coloured card that wor taped to t' side window. I took a furtive gander. The card read:

Leeds Gay Liberation Front
Meeting every Tuesday
The Empress of India
Victoria Street – upstairs bar. All welcome

No mention of t' friggin' time.

As soon as I pushed through t' pub saloon doors I knew I wor way too early. Apart from a few gruff old men strung along t' bar and a teenage couple snogging in a corner, the Empress wor deserted.

I ordered a lager and lime and pitched up at a low corner table. I sat there a friggin' age, shredding beer mats. Eventually two women entered, one of them portering a cardboard box.

At once I wor as alert as a fox. I watched 'em blathering on to t' barmaid, who wor pulling two pints of bitter. Maybe, I thought, I should introduce mesen. Hello, I'm Rick. Is this the Gay Lib meeting? Like the friggin' AA. What if they worn't lesbos at all? What if tonight wor quiz night? One of 'em even had long blonde hair. What if, being lesbos, they didn't speak to men? 'Some lesbos are separatists,' Jim had said, 'who think all men should be castrated.' I crossed my legs. 'Some of them,' Jim had said, 'tried to buy an island off the coast of Scotland,' either to put all t' men on or for them-sens, he couldn't quite recall. They wanted to de-sex the Isle of Man, and Manchester and manhole cover, and chimney-breast wor to become chimney-chest. And 'women' wor now spelt 'wimmin'. What's more, Jim had said, all lesbos wor trouble, always getting into fights and being aggressive. Once, he said, a lesbo had threatened him wi' a snooker cue, though he didn't say why, leaving me to think that all lesbos threaten men wi' snooker cues.

The women made for t' stairs, one slopping the drinks, t' other portering the box. The box, I noticed, had once held Fairy Liquid bottles. I got up from my seat and crossed to t' bar. I coughed at the barmaid who wor vigorously twirling glasses on a plastic brush head. She jutted her chin in my direction.

'Do you have a snooker table upstairs?'

'We do, luv, but there's a meeting on up there tonight.'

'So, erm ... what meeting's that, then?'

She set two upturned glasses on a red slop cloth.

'Gay Lib meeting. Sue and Lorna are setting up.'

She spoke brusquely, as if it wor owt o' nowt and time wor pressing. Her hands ceased their busying about t' bar, her chin jutted out again, only over my shoulder toward someone else. Behind me I heard a voice saying, 'Hey, Rick? Rick?'

I turned, feeling the colour flooding from my face as I found mesen eyeball-to-eyeball wi' an ex-school mate.

'Warren?'

'Rick?'

My skin wor poppin' and burstin' like popcorn on t' hob. Warren had sat next to me for t' first three year of high school. I hated him, cos he wor good at maths and I worn't. He'd shot up an inch or two since I'd seen him last, and had the wispy makings of a moustache on his upper lip. I inhaled deeply, willing Warren away, but when I opened 'em he wor still there, grinning like a gargoyle.

'Rick Thorpe. Where have you been hiding?'

I grabbed an ice cube from t' bucket on t' bar, crushed it in my fist, letting the water trickle between my fingers.

'I ... I ... might ask yersen t' same question.'

'Me? I wor just passing by when I spotted you through the window. So this is where you lurk, is it? No one sees you any more.'

'Here ... and other places.'

I smiled inanely at him. I had to escape, to reach cool water, cold air, but I wor trapped. I would have to ... have to ... Out of t' corner of my eye I clocked two men arriving. A young'un wi' a haystack of hair and decked out in Northern Soul gear – the platform shoes, the highwaister keks and a tank top wi' a star motif on it – and an older bloke, thinning on top, wearing purple crushed velvet loons and a green denim jacket spewed over wi' badges and buttons. He had the friggin' set: Anti-Nazi League, pink triangles, pro-abortion, trade unions, Chairman Mao and Che Guevara, Keep Music

Live, Rock Against Racism, and down both lapels, lines of friggin' miniature railway pins. 'YES, I'M HOMOSEXUAL TOO' screamed the first badge in my sightline.

'Oh, fuck!' I murmured. Please, Warren, please – I wor thinking so loudly it felt that I wor shouting at him – please don't turn round, don't look at those men. I put a hand on Warren's shoulder so he wor jammed between me and the bar stool.

Warren looked petrified, though fuck knows why – I wor t' one in t' pig pen.

'So,' he wor saying, 'what brings you in here, then?'

'Me? I'm ... meeting ... someone.'

'Bird, is it?'

From t' edge of my eye I saw t' two men move to t' end of t' bar, where they wor served by t' barmaid. Then, drinks in hand, they headed toward t' stairs.

'No, no, truth be known ... Well, yeah, you've got me, yeah, I am. I'm meeting this bird and she'll be here any mo', so it might be a good idea if ... Warren, I'll be back in a jiffy, I'm bustin' for a leak.'

I pelted for t' gents. Fortunately, it wor empty. No friggin' mirror. Never a mirror in t' gents. Mirrors are poncy. I rammed on t' cold tap and threw water onto my neck, arms, face. I gripped t' cool porcelain sink, inhaling and exhaling, my face tight wi' agony, wi' relief.

I could scarper. Or I could slip up them stairs. I dried my face and hands on t' dirty roller towel. What did it matter if Warren knew? Let him blab, let him tell every so-called friggin' school mate who never wor my mate, let him tell t' headmaster, all t' teachers, every last one of those friggin' tossers who said I wor a useless good-for-nowt and that I wor wasting my life. I wor out of their grasp now. No more hiding in t' science-block toilets in a blind panic or bunking off school cos I wor terrified. A strange, floating calmness coated me. I stood tall, patted my hair. I strode back into t' bar. Warren had skedaddled.

I wor miffed to find my drink had been whisked away, so I ordered another one.

Folk started arriving in greater numbers now, singly and in pairs. My finger ends wor tingling. I bided my time, watching. It wor as if I'd stumbled on some secret society, and I wor about to be initiated, stretched out naked before 'em while all manner of acts wor performed on me. It occurred to me that maybe Warren hadn't left at all. Maybe he wor upstairs wi' t' rest of 'em. That would take the biscuit. I stood there, undecided what to do. Then I took a long sup from my lager and lime and headed up the stairs into t' growing hubbub.

There wor a good thirty people there. Thankfully, most of them wor men. The meeting passed in a daze. I wor crushed by t' stomach-aching ordinariness of it all. I found it hard to fathom what it wor all about, and my attention drifted off into musings on some of t'others about me. Such as the man in t' Michael Caine glasses and mustard poloneck sweater. Or t' long-haired man in black velvet loons who perched cross-legged on his chair all evening. The woman in t' white denim all-in-one, the bib decorated wi' flower patches. The thin-faced Asian bloke who listened wi' his chin tilted toward t' cornice.

My stomach wor growling so loudly I wor sure everyone could hear it. The weasly, freckle-headed man sitting next to me must have heard. And yet, somehow the demons beneath t' skin stayed quiet.

Mustard-poloneck man stood up, took off his specs and wiped them, then welcomed everyone, 'especially the new faces'. A few heads swivelled my way, so I looked down at my boots.

There wor an agenda. And friggin' points.

Point one: Should the women have separate meetings? This wor held over, cos there wor so few women present. Maybe they wor stuck on t' island Jim said they'd bought.

Point two: Back copies of *Gay News* should be collected and donated to fish-and-chip shops as politicised wrapping. This wor passed, and two people said they'd take care of it.

Point twelve: Should PIE be part of t' meetings?

I turned to t' weasly man next to me. 'Pie?' I whispered hopefully. I wor friggin' famished.

'Paedophile Information Exchange,' he replied.

This caused a long and heated debate about t' Gay Lib position on t' age of consent, wi' some saying there shouldn't be one at all, and others saying it should be lowered from twenty-one to sixteen, which one of t' PIE men said wor discriminatory against kids, and then he got into a right shouting ruckus wi' this other bloke which ended wi' t' PIE man calling us all fuckin' fascists and storming out. Finally there wor a show of hands. I didn't raise my hand. PIE would still have lost.

There wor more friggin' points, and then we wor asked if anyone had owt else to say, and of course some goon wi' a stammer did. The meeting lasted a friggin' century, and I clenched my buttocks, trying not to fart. 'Any other business?' took a whole half-hour.

Eventually we 'adjourned' downstairs. In t' bar, the men flocked about me like gulls fighting over a morsel. Someone wor asking me loads of questions, someone else plied me wi' drink, someone squeezed my arse. I knew I wor getting khalied, cos I wor drinking too fast and my teeth wor becoming numb. I fell against a table.

'I should be off,' I slurred, unable to will mesen to move. Then, somehow, I wor pushing through t' pub doors and stumbling into a street bin. I heard a voice calling out after me, calling out my name.

Irene Richardson
05/02/1977

The Saturday after Irene Richardson wor done over, we called in on Vanessa as usual. We found her in a bit of a state. The police had been doing door to door. She had hid hersen in t' kids' room, wi' t' kids, waiting for 'em to leave. Then a reporter came nosing, doing t' same.

'She wor here,' Vanessa said, rocking little Jase on her knee and chain smoking.

'Who wor?'

'Irene. Not long before she wor done over, Irene turned up here.'

'Jeez, Vanessa, you haven't told the cops?'

'Tell them owt and they'll never be off yer doorstep. So don't you go saying nowt neither, hear me?'

Eric nodded. Vanessa eyeballed me and I nodded also. She stroked Jase's hair.

'When I heard a banging at t' door I knew summat wor up. I rolled over in bed, hoping that whoever it wor would go away. But it wor t' kind of knocking that has the devil right behind it, if yer know what I mean. Then I heard my name called – or at least the name I use on t' street – and I wor surprised, cos it wor a woman's voice. I remember what time it wor cos the alarm clock said it wor after 3 a.m.'

I could picture the alarm clock. I'd spotted it one time through t' open bedroom door: a kiddies' clock wi' Mickey and Minnie Mouse seesawing through time. Vanessa took a long drag on her ciggie.

'I got up, wrapped mesen in my bathrobe' (the pink one she often wore) 'and shouted, "All right, all right, I'm effin' coming – Jesus bloody Christ!"'

I pictured Vanessa pulling her fingers through her tangled hair as she padded barefoot down t' corridor lino and unslotted the safety chain to find hersen peering through t' door crack at a small, dishevelled woman. 'Only I couldn't see her proper,' Vanessa said. 'Not in that light. But she wor somehow familiar.'

Before she'd been able to say owt Vanessa had been hit by Irene pleading in her Glaswegian accent. 'Cannae stay ... I'm sorry, please ... I need somewhere to stay ... just a wee while, just for tonight, just one night, it's so cold, and I won' be no trouble ...' on and on she'd gabbled, plainly fearing that if she stopped for a moment the door would be closed on her.

'What could I do?' Vanessa said, looking at us both. 'I unhitched the chain and told her she could have t' sofa. She stood in t' middle of t' room in her fake suede coat, this wild look in her eye. I know that look, when someone's hanging on by their last fingertips. Scared me shitless, I can tell you. Maybe, not far behind, there wor some very angry bloke, a pimp, a punter. I said to her, "Do I know you?" And that's when she told me her name. Said she'd seen me out working once or twice, and knew where I lived.'

After that Irene had fallen silent, as if suddenly struck dumb by some affliction. She'd stood there, shivering, clutching her bag to her chest. Vanessa offered her a ciggie and she took it, then Vanessa lit one for hersen. Irene's fingers wor dark and unsteady.

'I fetched her a blanket, and told her where to find a towel in t' bathroom, but she said she wor fine. Said she'd been roughing it and tidying hersen up at a public lav. Then she asked me if I'd got kids. Turns out she'd got two an' all, only hers were in care. She said it wor just for a while, 'til she got back on her feet.'

Vanessa pulled her robe tighter about her. 'Then she asked if she could see my kids. I held the door open just a little, cos I didn't want her going in there, but then she wanted to stroke their hair. So I told her I didn't want 'em woken up.'

For most of t' night Vanessa had lain awake, anxiously listening through t' bedroom wall to Irene crashing about like a restless horse in a stall. Across from Vanessa, Barry and Jase slept on, top and tailed on t' single mattress.

Gradually the noises grew less frequent, then ceased altogether.

The next morning Irene had tried to negotiate another night, but Vanessa had told her bluntly that she couldn't stay. Irene's chillingly blank stares and constantly furrowed brow sapped Vanessa's strength, and she wanted to be shot of her. Vanessa pulled a fiver from her purse – her only punter the previous afternoon.

'Here,' she said, holding it out. Irene didn't hesitate.

'Vanessa, I swear ...'

'Forget it, luv.'

Irene quickly combed her tangles of thick hair wi' a hairbrush she'd found lying under a chair, then left without another word.

The next night she booked hersen into a grotty rooming house in Cowper Street. The papers said so. She dumped her bag of meagre belongings on t' bed, spruced hersen up hurriedly and left, telling someone that she wor headed for Tiffany's disco in t' city centre.

A jogger found Irene Richardson's body on nearby

Soldiers Field, not a hammer's throw from where Wilma McCann wor topped.

When we called on Vanessa the next week she'd gone. Eric pressed his nose up against her window and peered in. I put my hands to t' sides of my face like a horse's blinkers and peered in also.

There wor nowt but a mucky sock on t' bare floor, a sun-faded print of a kitten in a basket of flowers on t' wall, and a wooden chair wi' t' seat missing.

'She's scarpered,' Eric said.

'Looks like it.'

'Moved on, like they all do. Best strike her from t' round-book.'

All in all, I wor relieved that we worn't having cuppas at Vanessa's no more. Her teasing and questioning had always made me squirm inside. Like she knew really.

Mid-morning tea break now wor wi' Lourdes, a big West Indian woman, big, springy hair, big hips, big, unruly breasts. Lourdes wore knee-length striped stockings and played scratchy ska records. I asked Eric why all our breaks were wi' prozzies. He said prozzies make better tea.

Lourdes flashed her teeth a lot while she blathered, and her tea tasted like wrung-out dishcloth. She danced around t' room to her ska music, her buttocks shimmying like maggot-filled medicine balls.

'You dancin', bwoy?' She meant me.

'I can't dance.'

Lourdes yanked me out of my seat. 'Mi teaches yuh!' She took hold of me wi' both hands. I tried a few unwilling plods on t' spot and kicked out a leg.

'Bwoy, you ain't trying to shift a fridge! Use dem hips!' She slapped her own buttock.

I shuffled like someone wriggling out of wet jeans. She tossed her head back and laughed.

'Dat is duh ting!'

Eric wor grinning at me like he wor seeing another story for t' lads back at the depot.

Lourdes said, 'You's like ska and reggae, bwoy?'

'Punk!' Eric shouted over t' pulsating lilt blooping out of Lourdes' stereo speakers. 'He's into all that punk stuff!'

Lourdes' face crumpled. 'Punk? Wat dat? Mi nah nuttin' about punk. How's I dance dat punk?'

'You pogo!' Eric yelled. 'You jump up and down on t' spot and gob a lot. Go on, Rick, show Lourdes how to pogo.'

'Shut it, Eric. I can't do it wi' no music, can I?'

'Music?' echoed Eric derisively. 'You call that Sex Pistols shite music?'

'Spit? Nah, man. Real dance ga like tis.'

Lourdes locked her arms around my waist, pushing my leg between hers. Her clothes smelt of old smoke and school cabbage and she had sweat patches under her armpits.

'Move like you's making it wit' sum girl,' she gleamed. She put her mouth to my ear. 'I teaches you, bwoy, mi's a good teacher.'

She cackled, tossing her head again. I glimpsed two gold caps. She thrust her full hips against my thigh bones, using her weight to shunt me around t' room. I shut my eyes, trying to concentrate on t' choppy backbeat. Then, almost unwillingly, I felt t' two of us flowing together in harmony, while Eric looked on, bemused, at the West Indian prozzie, as wide as a dinner plate, dancing wi' a young white boy, as thin as a spoon.

I wor dipping into sis's diary again, amusing mesen over sis and this friggin' lad having sex in t' back seat of an abandoned car, when I heard t' front door slam and sis thundering up the stairs in her platforms. I shut t' diary and froze, waiting to get nabbed in sis's room. A prickly crawl travelled like a bushfire up my arms and neck. Oh fuck, fuck and triple fuck!

Luckily she ducked into t' bathroom. I shoved the diary back under her smalls and scuttled across t' landing to my own room. Moments later I heard the bathroom door open, then her bedroom door slam and a school bag being flung aside, then a sort of strangled sob. Summat to do wi' Adam, I reckoned.

I cut into t' bathroom, opened the cold tap and splashed water over my face and neck and up and down my arms. I let the water run across my wrists as if calming a burn. I inhaled and exhaled, long and slow, waiting for t' skin demons to retreat. I looked in t' mirror. My neck wor all blotchy, like I'd fallen into a nettle patch.

Mandy's sobs had receded into snuffles. She must have heard the tap running. I flushed the chain even though I hadn't used the loo, and went back to my room. I'd got away wi' it again, although it had been a close call this time.

I played my new single – The Damned, 'Neat Neat Neat' – full blast. When it ended I could hear Mandy screaming at me to turn it off. So I played it again. Then I played every punk record in my meagre collection while I put on my gear. I started wi' The Ramones 'Blitzkrieg Bop', followed by t' Pistols 'Anarchy' and then Buzzcocks 'Spiral Scratch'. Then I played The Damned again.

Meantime, I hiked mesen into my old paint-splattered keks, yanked on a white T-shirt and then my old school jacket. I'd already rented the sleeves wi' a Stanley knife and filched some safety pins from Mother's sewing basket which I'd pinned on randomly. I'd added a few punk badges, pins and buttons to my lapels, including my latest – a small pink triangle. I figured that no one in t' house knew what that stood for.

I sized mesen up in t' wardrobe mirror. I forked some vaseline through my hair, trying to make it look punkier. Then I nabbed some of Mum's hair lacquer and sprayed that on. I stuffed my jacket into a carrier and pulled on t' slime-green cable sweater Gran had knit me for Christmas last year.

Mother caught me sneaking out.

'Where are you going looking like that?'

'Helping a mate mend his dad's car.'

'At this hour? Well, at least comb your hair.'

'No, it's fine ... no, leave it!'

'Who is this mate anyway?'

'Just a mate, from school.'

Before she could say owt further I bolted out of t' house. At the end of t' road I pulled off my sweater and stuffed it behind a dustbin. Then I put on the jacket and ran full tilt for t' bus stop.

The Babylon Club wor a reggae hangout in Chapeltown. Maybe Lourdes came here to dance sometimes, but Wednesday nights it opened its doors to punk and became t' FK Club. It had once been some sort of school. The windows had been boarded up wi' white plasterboard and there wor two entrances, marked overhead 'BOYS' and 'GIRLS'. The girls' entrance had been bricked up forever, the boys' wor now t' fire escape.

I arrived late. On t' bus this bitten-looking old couple sitting opposite kept eyeballing me and whispering 'til I gave 'em two fingers. Then t' bloke blabbed to t' bus driver who chucked me off t' bus, so I'd had to walk the final mile or so.

I joined the ragged queue that shuffled forward noisily 'til there wor just two girls in front of me. The one wor a thin waif of a girl and the other wor a bigger girl wi' long hair and big breasts. The waif girl had on shiny black leggings, a loose white shirt and a thin black leather tie. Her black hair wor cropped. T'other girl wor wearing a tight red miniskirt over fishnet stockings. Flesh gaped through t' large tears. Their dark lipstick made 'em look as if they'd been gorging on berries.

The doorman let the three us in together, and the waif girl darted a smile at me between her small, gapped teeth. Her friend nudged her and she turned away.

I tagged behind 'em along a corridor of garish striplights toward a barrage of careening guitars and battering drums. I could hear a voice barking tunelessly into a microphone. We pushed through t' swing doors and into a wall of heat and noise in a room sardined wi' sweating bodies, all leaping and pogoing furiously.

I edged my way in. Two lads in front of me had stripped to t' waist already, and their bodies glistened under t' blue and red strobes. Sweat droplets sprayed off their hair as they each propelled themsens upwards on t' shoulders of t'other. Beside them, a girl wi' her eyes shut and her fists clenched wor pummelling the floor wi' her boots as if she wor a road-stamping machine.

The two girls wor pushing their way toward t' stage, so I followed them.

The singer on t' stage – some band called New Trix – barked and screamed and threw t' mic stand about. He introduced each number wi' 'And this one's called ...' in a thick Liverpudlian accent. Some kid gobbed at him as he dropped to his knees, the mic head half in his mouth. The gob landed on him and trickled slowly down his torso.

I became aware of t' waif girl alongside me, eyeing me severely. I nodded at her, cos she wor making me uneasy. She said summat, her mouth forming mute, indecipherable words.

'WHAT!?'

She cupped her mouth to my ear and yelled. I still couldn't hear owt. She took me by t' elbow and launched hersen into a dance, flaying around like a rag doll being tossed by an invisible hand. I shuffled about for a short while, then slipped away to watch from t' margins.

The band's brief set ground to a halt wi' t' drummer kicking over his kit. Some barmpot at the front shook up a beer can and sprayed it over t' singer, who grabbed the can, took a swig, sprayed it back at the crowd and poured the rest over his own bonce.

'Fuck you all! Fuck you!'

The waif girl pushed her way through to where I wor propped against t' wall.

'Didn't you like it, then?'

'Worn't too bad.'

'I think they're ace. The singer's a bit of all right, don't you think?'

She wor screwing her hair round one finger. Her posh voice had a mocking edge to it that made me wary. But then, she looked like she belonged at the centre of summat. I glanced over her shoulder at a lad passing behind her.

'I'm Gina.'

'Yeah, right. Oh, I'm Ricky.'

'Ricky? Don't you mean Rick? Ricky's a little boy's name. I'm sure you're not little.'

I'd meant to say Rick. Fuck knows why I said Ricky. Only Gran called me that. My ears wor popping. I said, 'I'm taller than you.'

'Everyone's taller than me, Rick. Or is it Richard?'

'I don't like Richard. Even my mother don't call me Richard.'

'You're not still living at home?'

'Moving out shortly. Soon as I get my own place. What about yersen?'

She cackled. 'I don't live with my mother, if that's what you mean. God, no.' She shook her head, laughing. 'God, no,' she repeated. Her laughter raged about and then fled.

'Are you working then, Richard?' She spoke rapidly and quietly, as if she wor afraid someone might overhear.

'Nothing great. What about you?'

'Signing on. I was training to be a nurse but I got fired. Buy me a drink?'

I bought us both cider. She drank hers down in rapid gulps. We had a couple more. Being wi' her wor like trespassing. She had this way of nibbling her bottom lip and staring into you as if you'd been caught out. She said it was only her third time at the FK Club, and she didn't think much of it. Her offhandedness deflated me like a knife in a tyre. So I faked being world-weary and unimpressed. Suddenly she grabbed me by t' arm. 'Stay here, don't move, only I've just seen someone I have to talk to.'

She darted off. The DJ played 'Gloria' by Patti Smith, then some Burning Spear, then 'White Riot' by The Clash. I bought mesen another pint of cider. And another. It wor all finishing up, an t' place wor emptying rapidly. A long-haired roadie in an Allman Brothers T-shirt wor carting out band equipment. An old woman wor pushing a wide broom across t' floor, the bristles skidmarking through t' beer slops.

Then I saw her lolling by a radiator. I wondered if she'd been watching me on t' sly. I strolled over, all loose-limbed and more than a little khalied.

'I didn't think you'd wait,' she said.

I fired off a so-what smile. 'I wor just about to head off. Did you find that girl?'

'Sort of.'

'That one you arrived wi'?'

'Her? No, God, no. That was just fat Judy.'

'She ain't that fat.'

'The girl I was looking for was the one I was snogging in the toilets last week.'

'Uh-huh.'

'Only tonight she pissed off without saying a word.'

'Right.'

'Are you shocked?'

'Do you want me to be?'

She shrugged.

Outside, a few folk wor still hanging about. Someone wor touting tickets for a Banshees gig in Doncaster. We pushed through, heading on up the dully lit street 'til we came to a junction. I stopped, one hand on my belly.

'I think I'm gonna spew up.'

I bent double, and a volley of vomit splattered the pavement.

'Oh, bloody Nora! Hey, wait!'

I staggered after her, spitting out vomit bits, 'til I caught up. She wor singing some rubbish song in a high-pitched, baby-doll voice, only she couldn't remember the verses, so she just kept repeating the chorus, emphasising a different word each time. I wiped the back of my hand across my mouth. When we reached the traffic island she said, 'This is where we part.'

'You off then?'

'I have to get home,' she said, implying some urgent reason. 'Lift up your shirt.'

She fumbled about in her pockets for a biro. 'Lift up your shirt,' she repeated, poking me in t' chest. I rolled up my T-shirt. It wor damp. She wrote her number across my chest. It tickled and I tried not to squirm.

'Don't rub it off before you can remember it.'

Then, before I could say owt more, she wor gone, darting off in t' direction of t' town centre.

The next week I tried phoning her. The line wor out of order. She didn't show at the FK Club neither. So I asked Judy about her.

'Gina? You a friend of hers?'

'Sort of.'

'All her friends are sort of.'

She finally pitched up at the FK Club weeks later. Her hair wor now dyed platinum blonde, she wore a black string vest under a biker's jacket (no bra), DMs and torn black leggings. I ignored her 'til she placed hersen in front of me, fixing me wi' a triumphant stare.

'Didn't you recognise me, then?'

'Course I friggin' did.'

'Oooooh, Mister Coool!' She chuckled and turned on her heeled boots.

For t' rest of t' night she wor firing off dark glances at me. Downstairs, a small crowd wor watching Patrick Fitzgerald's acoustic friggin' punk. Songs about safety pins stuck in hearts. Upstairs, a few stony-faced rastas slunk around t' pool table and a line of stockingless white girls in tight, spangly dresses perched on bar stools, dragging on their ciggies.

It wor then I clapped eyes on him. The lad from t' Merrion Centre multi-storey. Jim's boy.

I sidled closer 'til I wor only a few feet from him. He wor facing slightly away, making out that he hadn't clocked me, but I knew he had. He wor waiting like a gazelle: nervous, alert, almost quivering.

All of a sudden he slunk away, then glanced back at me. I knew I wor meant to follow.

He led me through t' fire doors and down t' rear steps that led to t' boiler room. In t' pitch-black hollow of t' doorway we fell greedily on each other, pulling at each other's clothes. Behind t' steel door the boiler hissed like some locked-up beast. I grazed my knuckles against t' wall. I yanked down his drainpipe keks and dropped to my knees and took his hard-on in my mouth. Moments later he spunked off wi' a solitary exhalation, rucked up his keks, palmed his hair, mumbled summat and left. I kicked t' boiler door. 'Fuck!' I hadn't even unzipped, barely got started.

'Fuck!'

I headed back up the steps. The bugger had shut the fire doors after him. I clambered over a wall and dropped into t' road. The doorman wouldn't let me back in unless I paid again cos I didn't have a pass-out stamp.

I headed home, toward t' city centre. It wor raining sideways. The road gleamed in t' wet and the city neon lights blurred at the edges.

Taxi! I saw a taxi beetling along. I stepped out into t' road, waving at it as its headlights bore down on me. The taxi slowed, then picked up speed again.

'Fucker!'

The taxi stopped abruptly, slammed into reverse. Oh, fuck, I wor thinking, oh friggin' hell. The driver wound down t' window.

'I ain't supposed to stop here. Get in, then, before t' boys in blue clap eyes on us.'

I slumped into a corner of t' cab, my mouth still tasting salty-sweet from t' lad's load.

'Bin another one,' the driver wor saying as he swung sharp right down a pitch-black side street. 'How many's that now? Of course, it could all be a nasty coincidence, but I'd say it worn't, I'd say there's a maniac on t' loose, wouldn't you? Want to know what the wife thinks about it all? She thinks it's someone wi' t' clap who's out for revenge. But then, t' wife's full of ideas like that about t' world. Me, I don't know what to think. You go up the Carlisle Hotel and you'll find 'em, strung along t' bar stools wi' price tags on t' backs of their stilettos. Some of 'em you wouldn't let a dog lift its leg on, know what I mean? Still, no one deserves to get sliced up, right? Picked up a few of their punters in my time. Well, you would, wouldn't you, in this job? As long as they pay the fare I don't look none too close. Young'un like you don't go wi' slappers like that, do you?'

'No.'

'No. At your age you shouldn't need to. This one wor done in over Bradford way. Murdered in her own bed.'

At the mention of bed I wor overcome by tiredness. I yawned.

Patricia 'Tina' Atkinson

23/04/1977

Mitch's job wor driving a refrigerated lorry, delivering raw meat and canned food to works and school canteens around South Yorkshire. He had to deliver some pig carcasses to a coalmine, and asked me if I wanted to go wi' him.

While Mitch worked Monday to Friday, I always worked the weekend, and had two free days in between. It wor siling it down outside, so I wor grouching about t' house, getting under Mother's feet or playing my punk records in my room or tugging mesen off at similar speed, so when t' chance wor offered to get out I grabbed it wi' both free hands.

Mitch's lorry cab wor decked out in country-and-western/ Southern US stuff, wi' Texas Lone Stars and stick-on cacti, US dollar bills and dolly-bird pin-ups in Confederate flag bikinis, and Leeds Utd and Elvis stickers. To Mitch, Elvis wor some sort of god. Even though he had a bald patch, Mitch still combed his few strands into a greaser style and squeezed into his winklepickers on t' rare times he took Mother out for some country-and-western hoofing.

The mine wor out Castleford way. We drove along a bumpy track between moonscape mounds of slack and scree. The air wor flecked wi' coal dust like swarms of tiny black flies. We heard a bell ring, and then up ahead we saw t' pit wheel turning, taking men under or bringing 'em back up top.

Mitch backed the van up to t' loading bay of a low red-brick building that wor t' kitchens and canteen. A large woman looked on, leaning against t' doorframe, her thick arms folded over her apron. She wore a liquid-blue hygiene bag over her tight black curls.

We unbolted the doors and clambered up into t' refrigerated air. There wor four carcasses on hooks: pale, headless, limbless, wrapped in orange meshing. They wor still swaying gently.

Mitch said, 'Help us get 'em down, then.'

The carcasses wor smooth and cold to t' touch, and the orange mesh made 'em hard to grip. It took the both of us to lift each one off its hook and heave it onto a pallet. By t' time we'd unhooked the third we wor sweating heavily.

I pondered the pile of pigs on t' pallet. Hard to think that not so long back they'd been snuffling happily about, jostling wi' other contented little piglets over t' sow's teats. Fattened up 'til they all squealed their last in t' abattoir. I'd heard it said that pigs are bright buggers and know their fate, that pigs know death.

I went to pick up t' final carcass.

'Leave that one,' said Mitch, a little sharply.

'But I thought ...'

'Well, you thought wrong.'

We lowered the pallet onto a trolley. The woman smacked each carcass like a newborn's backside, then took a clipboard from under her armpit.

A group of miners passed by, freshly back up top, hard hats in their hands, white circles where their goggles had been. I watched 'em as they headed for t' outdoor showers. Some wor already stripping off. The woman wi' t' meaty arms passed Mitch a docket to sign. Over her shoulder I glimpsed the pale arse of a miner as he nipped between t' shower blocks.

Mitch jabbed me in t' ribs. 'Stop gawping. There's a pile of boxes under that tarpaulin in t' back of t' van. Bring me five of 'em.'

I lifted the blue tarpaulin. Underneath wor about fifty boxes of hair rollers. What wor we doing wi' hair rollers in a refrigerated lorry? At a coalmine?

I handed the boxes to Mitch, who passed 'em down to t' woman wi' t' docket. She handed us a pink copy wi' a number 4 signed for, and kept a white one wi' a 3 signed for. The last pig rode home wi' us.

We'd just driven by two ravens that wor pecking at a road kill, when Mitch said, 'You keep shtumm about this, you hear?'

'What arc you going to do wi' t' pig?'

'Let's just say it fell off t' back of a lorry.'

'Or didn't!'

We both burst out laughing.

'I'll sell it on tomorrow to this bloke I know over Shipley way. When we get home I want you to keep your mother occupied while I stash the rest of them there hair rollers in t' garage. You hear me?'

'I hear you.'

Mitch curled his bottom lip approvingly. I sat wi' both feet up on t' dashboard, feeling that all wor right wi' t' world, listening to Mitch singing Elvis songs tunelessly 'til he'd had enough of it. We wor stop-starting through inner-city traffic lights.

Mitch said, 'How you getting on at Corona?'

'Better than that last job you got me.'

'Aye, well that's as may be. And Craner? How's our Mr Craner?'

'Craner's all right, I suppose.'

Mitch grunted, seemingly satisfied. He turned on t' radio, which wor good cos it meant we didn't have to sing or talk and there worn't silence neither.

That last 'proper job' Mitch got me wor in a loony bin. Work experience he called it. I lasted all of three days. They didn't know what to do wi' me, so I just mooched about like one of t' inmates.

I wor hanging about t' corridor when suddenly there wor a friggin' commotion and this woman screaming her lungs blue cos she wor being dragged along by t' hair by two men in white coats. One of 'em eyeballed me and shouted, 'Who the fuck are you?'

The next day it wor suggested I could look after some men out in t' gardens. Get out in t' fresh air. I wor happy about this, cos inside it smelt of piss and bleach. So I wor sent out into t' grounds wi' five grown men to play cowboys and injuns.

'But,' I wor told, 'make sure you watch 'em, don't let any of 'em run off.'

I looked on uneasily as these middle-aged blokes ran about and hid in t' undergrowth. It wor more hide and seek than cowboys and injuns. No one went 'Bang bang' or hollered or whooped or lay on t' grass pretending to be dead 'til they got bored and got up again.

For a brief while this wor brill. I just had to keep an eye out. When I wor a nipper I'd always played cowboys and injuns wi' my best friend, Mickey. Mickey always played the cowboy and I wor t' injun. Except one time Mickey undressed me down to my undies (injuns always wore very little) and tied me to a tree (injuns always got tied up). Then he went home and forgot about me. Not long after, these two older boys came along on their bikes. They cycled round and round the tree, laughing, but they refused to untie me. Then they chucked their bikes aside, took out their willies and pissed all over me.

I looked about for my grown-up cowboys and injuns.

I formed my fingers into a pistol and sighted one of 'em.

Pow! Pow! (Silencer on.) The man's face crumpled and he started to blubber.

I counted the men. One, two, three. Four. Only four. Where wor t'other one?

I spied him nipping into a greenhouse. I followed him in, creeping around t' ragged tomato plants and whatnot. He wor ducked behind t' seed tables, sniggering. He wouldn't come out, but just kept running about t' friggin' greenhouse and giggling. For a baldy wi' a paunch he wor fair nimble.

I'd soon had enough. I strode out of t' greenhouse, turned the rusting key, locking the blighter in, and looked about for t' others.

I shouted out, 'Hey, cowboys! Injuns!' cos I worn't told their names.

Silence. No one popped up from behind a tree or stone wall or any of t' bushes.

Behind me, the bugger in t' greenhouse wor freaking out, tugging at the door and bawling. I quickened my step, heading out, telling the man on t' gate I wor just nipping out for a paper.

A month later I wor standing in Craner's office, wishing I wor still in t' loony bin.

On t' Wednesday following Tina Atkinson's murder, Gran toddled over, as she often did, for a meal. She arrived early evening and sat at the kitchen table, fingers interlocked, pride dented, like she wor in a doctor's waiting room.

Sis flounced into t' kitchen and greeted Gran breezily. She wor chewing chuddy gum. She only chewed chuddy when she'd been smoking, so God friggin' knows why she bothered trying to mask it. Mother frowned. Gran rooted out a bag of mints from her handbag. She handed Mandy the bag and said, 'Now these are to share,' like it wor a reward for being brave cos your pet hamster just pegged it.

'Oooh, thank you Gran,' sis had simpered. She spat out her chuddy into her hand and stuck it to t' underside of t' table. I puckered my face in disgust, so she stuck her tongue out at me, popped a mint onto t' end, closed her mouth and began sucking noisily.

'Don't I get one?'

She pushed the bag toward me.

'No ta. I just wanted to see if you would.'

Gran rose from t' table, supporting hersen by t' edge, sloughed over to t' sink and began rinsing a plate under t' cold tap. 'You know,' she said, 'I wor once stuck in a lift.'

Mother wor stirring some cheese sauce to pour over macaroni. I saw her neck vein bloop. 'Yes,' she sighed heavily. 'I know.'

We all knew. Barely had Gran doled out the words 'stuck in a lift' before we'd collectively arrived at the end of t' tale. Stuck in a lift. Stuck on repeat. Made me appreciate Mrs Husk the more. Mrs Husk never said owt twice, never mind fifty trillion friggin' times.

I mouthed at sis, 'Two hours.' Sis sniggered. Mother replied dutifully, taking the rinsed plate from Gran, 'When you were visiting Florrie. Quarry Hill flats.'

'I wor stuck in that lift for a good two hour. How it stank. People had peed in it. I never thought I'd get out.'

Mother said, 'Like being entombed in a metal box.' I watched her lifting bikkies from a Tupperware container and arranging them on t' rinsed plate.

'I really should go and see Florrie,' Gran wor saying, 'but what wi' t' lift breaking down and them stairs being such a climb ...' Her voice trailed off.

Mother's face turned concrete. Mandy and I stared at each other. The story had veered from its usual course and pitched into a ditch. Mother pressed down t' Tupperware box lid firmly wi' t' flat of her hand. Florrie had been dead these three year.

A few weeks later Gran failed to show for dinner. Her phone wor just ringing out. Mother wor having an anxiety attack, her face and neck turning all blotchy. She wor all set to call t' cops, fire brigade, even the friggin' army. Barely had she had set the receiver on its cradle and Mitch wor putting on his jacket to drive over there, when t' phone rang. Gran had got on t' wrong bus.

'So where are you?' we heard Mother say.

Pause.

'Pontefract?'

Gran hadn't clocked where she wor 'til t' bus pulled into Pontefract bus station and the driver announced it. Mitch had to drive over there and collect her. He found her sitting in t' station office, chatting wi' t' off-duty drivers. When he said he'd come to take her home, she asked him if he wor a taxi driver.

Over t' next few months our worries about Gran grew. She kept buying milk, even though she had it delivered. She started to forget what she wor saying before she got to t' end of her sentences. She forgot which flat wor hers, and surprised a neighbour in whose door she wor twisting her key and swearing under her breath.

One evening Mitch came into t' lounge and turned off the telly midway through *Columbo*.

'Oi! We wor watching that!'

Mand and I wor parked side by side on t' sofa. Mother came in and perched hersen on t' armchair, winding a manky tissue round her thumb. Mitch rocked on his heels before t' gas fire, puffed out his chest a little, then said, 'Your gran ain't getting any younger. And maybe you've clocked that she's been behaving a little queer of late.'

I winced when he said 'queer'.

'Could say that again,' Mandy blathered. 'Why, only ...'

Mitch held up a silencing forefinger. 'Think,' he said, taking one of t' fake plastic coals from t' gas fire and placing it on his open palm like it wor a frog or summat, 'of yer gran's brain as a fire that once burned bright, but is now just dying embers. Or,' he added, setting the plastic coal lump back on t' fire, 'like a set of Christmas-tree lights that have short-circuited and you don't know which one's blown without trying the lot.'

I imagined a set of short-circuiting Christmas lights in t' shape of a brain.

'Well, that's what happening to your gran, and so that's why ... that's why ... she's coming to live here.'

'Here? Wi' us?' Mandy squeaked. Mother shuffled her legs, her stockings making a static rustle.

'It's just 'til they find a place for her in a home.'

'What kind of a home?'

Jeez, sis wor a sack full of gormless questions.

'A cats' home,' I said.

Mitch eyeballed me to shut it.

Mother said, 'A nursing home, where she'll be cared for proper. She'll like it there. She'll make new friends, and we'll be able to go and visit whenever we want.'

Mand glared at us all, then ran from t' room. Then we heard her bedroom door slam.

What wor she so upset about? Gran wor getting my room. Not that I had any say in it. I'd be on a friggin' blow-up lilo in t' lounge.

At Blandford Gardens there wor a shaft of light in t' hallway. I stabbed the bell and waited on t' porch. Overhead, a sash creaked. Stepping back in t' road and looking up, I saw someone who worn't Jim leaning out of t' bedroom window, someone I'd never clapped eyes on before.

'Can I help you?' the man said, pushing strands of wispy hair behind one ear. He wor wearing Jim's Chinese dressing gown.

'Jim home?'

'Who wants to know?'

'Tell him it's Rick.'

'Rick? Ah, yes. I have a message for you. Fuck off, sweetie. Show your face around here again and you'll get it mashed into next week.'

The man slammed t' window down and yanked the curtains across. I stood looking up at the window, stung wi' disbelief, waiting for Jim to appear, telling me in his sweet Scottish brogue that it wor all a mistake. But the window stayed stubbornly shut. I slumped down onto t' low front wall, welled up inside wi' anger, and bashed mesen repeatedly on t' upper leg like a self-hating Mr Punch.

I headed for t' Fenton. Maybe Jim wor there, and maybe I could explain. Instead, I found Dora, parked on her usual stool like she wor glued to it.

'Hello,' she cooed. 'You're not going to run off again, are you?'

'Jim about?'

'Scots Jim? Haven't seen him, luv.'

I ordered a lager and lime and hiked mesen onto t' stool next to hers. The pub reeked of old beer and cold smoke. Dora wor harping on about some other old crone who'd been bitching about her and how this other old crone wor jealous cos she – Dora – could still get the attention of men. Like I gave a rat's behind. Dora paused only to suck on her ciggie. She left a lipstick print on t' butt end. I drank, letting Dora buzz in my ear like a faulty fridge while t' evening seeped away and the place became crowded and boisterous.

73

Then, not long before ten, this young'un came waltzing in like he owned the friggin' joint, passing right by us and making straight for t' lounge bar. A lanky, wire-haired lad wi' his chin set a smidgen too high. Dora beckoned me close. I tipped my stool toward her and caught a full blast of her market-stall scent.

'That one, who just sailed past us without so much as a how's-yer-father, he's one of Jim's. I've seen them in here together. Jake, his name is.'

She pursed her powdered lids across t' open bar toward t' lounge-side bar stool where Jake had parked himsen. I kept my gaze fixed on him, waiting on him to look across our way. When he did, his eyes widened and flickered wi' wary curiosity, like a startled deer. Then he turned away.

Dora wor saying, 'I thought you knew?'

'Knew what?'

'That Jim picks up boys from t' railway station. He picks them up, pays them. Takes them in sometimes. But then they move on, or get bored, or they steal from him.'

Her mouth fell open, showing her lipstick-stained dentures.

'Well, I've never been taken in!'

'I'm sorry, I didn't realise ... I thought ...'

I slid off my stool and pushed through t' double doors and out into t' street. I launched my boot into a waste bin. Then I picked it up and tossed it out into t' road. A car driver parped his horn as he dodged around it.

The driver stopped and wound down his window and wor effin' at me, so I gave him a V-sign and stomped off. I walked on, the city lights squinting through t' knifing rain, passing the Poly where they used to have punk gigs, on past the Empress pub and Leeds Town Hall wi' its dome imprinted against t' sickly green sky, on through t' precinct shopping zone and down Briggate toward t' Corn Exchange. I wor all fumed up, wi' no notion of where I wor going, no aim. I just walked.

It wor then that I spied her, striding along in a shiny black PVC coat, black fishnets and Doc Marts. Vaulting a pedestrian safety barrier and dodging the traffic, I called out, 'Gina, hey, Gina!' but she couldn't or wouldn't hear me. I skimmed along t' gutter 'til I wor almost level wi' her.

'Gina! It's me. Rick.'

She stopped, turned and eyed me haughtily. She'd changed her look again. Her hair wor back to black and all spiked up like a yucca plant. Her eyes wor two smudged coal-black holes in a white-powdered face, her lips and lids a bruised purple. She wor wearing a single glove, a studded dog collar and a small crucifix earring in her right ear.

'Don't you remember me? You wrote your number on my chest and ...'

'Of course I remember.'

Her gloved hand wor holding a dog lead. At the end of t' lead, cowering in a shop doorway on his haunches, wor a man.

'That's Jeremy. You're not to acknowledge him.'

'Hi, Jeremy.'

Jeremy scowled skywards and whimpered.

I said, 'Ain't seen you at the FK Club lately.'

She snorted at the mention of t' FK Club, then strode on, wi' me dancing alongside, trying to keep up, 'til she suddenly stopped and frowned. Jeremy stopped also. She pointed at him and he made a couple of small monkey hops into t' corner of a nearby bus shelter.

'Who the fuck does your hair?'

I sifted two fingers through my locks. 'My hair?'

'If you want to be with us you can't look like that. Like a nothing. Jeremy's a hairdresser, or he's trying to be. He could do something with that mop.' She cast her pitiless gaze over me. 'Something ... radical.'

'Sure, sometime ... I've been meaning to ...'

She pressed a gloved finger to my lips and then smiled, a blackberry-lipped smile that opened and shut like a poacher's trap.

'We're going to Paradise,' she said. 'Coming?'

I tossed a coin in my head. It landed on 'yes'.

Paradise Buildings wor a three-storey sooted brick warehouse on Bradford's Sunbridge Road. There wor no windows at ground level, and those on t' upper storeys wor recessed behind iron grilles. Opposite, more warehouse blocks descended steeply down t' hill. Next to it wor t' Paradise Chapel, now home, so said a sign, to Patel's Electrical Repairs.

We came to a steel side door. Gina pressed two loose wires together, sparking a bell ring. I looked about while we waited. Beyond Patel's, where t' waste ground widened out, stood a discarded fridge-freezer and an old wicker chair. On t' far edge of this rubble wasteland, where you came to t' road junction wi' t' lower end of Lumb Lane and Bradford's red-light area, stood a lone shack Indian takeaway.

'Worn't that last Ripper murder round here?'

'Poppet, the area is crawling with the filth,' said Gina. 'If I had my way, I'd castrate the bugger. Cut his balls off. Very slowly. With a very blunt razor.'

She swore and pressed the wires again, making 'em fizzle. Suddenly the door opened, swinging outwards.

'Heard you the fuckin' first time,' said a man's voice, his Manchester accent ironing every word flat. We followed him up a cold, unlit stairwell. He wore a leather jacket wi' t' words 'Hell and Back' studded onto it. His hair wor long and greasy and wi' greying strands, reminding me of an unwashed collie.

We passed by a room of shoe lasts. A cascading heap of wooden clogs heaped against t' wall like the piles of suitcases and glasses I'd seen on *World at War* docs. We climbed another floor, on past the frosted yellow panes of some disused offices, 'til we came out onto a large factory floor. The far end wor lit by a naked bulb hanging from a ceiling hook and a fire that raged in an immense fireplace.

'Welcome to Paradise, poppet.'

'Brill place!'

Our footsteps echoed across t' concrete floor.

'Used to be a shoe factory,' said the Hell's Angel, 'but, hey, nothing lasts ... Geddit ... Shoes? ... Lasts?'

'We're all tired of that old joke, Victor,' Gina snapped. She unhooked Jeremy from his lead and he monkey hopped over to t' fire. The flames wor fierce on his face, giving him edges and hollows.

'This is ace,' I said. 'Must cost a bit to rent.'

'Rent!?' squealed Gina. 'Rent? Hah! No, my little capitalist poppet, we squat it. You know – occupy ... liberate?'

I bit my lip, feeling friggin' gormless.

'We call this place Hotel California,' said Victor.

'No we don't!' Gina flashed. 'Well, you do, but no one else does. Cali-fucking-fornia! Fuck Hotel fuckin' California! And fuck The Eagles! Hippy has-beens! Fuckin' Yanks!'

'I like 'em,' muttered Victor smally.

Jeremy sprawled himsen across an old armchair and opened a can of Red Stripe, tossing the ring-pull into t' fire, then passed the can to me. I took a sup and then handed it back. I sat on t' floor wi' my back against t' same armchair. Gina sat cross-legged opposite me.

'So,' said Jeremy, sounding both menacing and superior, 'where wor you heading, hmm? Or rather, where had you been?'

'Nowhere much. I wor in t' Fenton earlier on.'

'The Fenton? Hear that Gina, wonder boy here wor in the Fenton.'

'The Fenton, poppet?'

'On Woodhouse Lane. That bleedin' leftie-student-commie pub – you know the one.'

'Oh, *that* one. Maybe we should pay it a visit.'

Victor, who had vanished into t' inky vastness, returned carrying a bikkie tin. Mooching along behind him wor three other Paradise inmates: two long-haired men and a mousy little woman. They had, I saw as they neared, the dead-eyed look of junkies.

The men slumped onto an old leather sofa and the woman sprawled before t' fire on a dirty sheepskin rug. She wor humming to hersen and fiddling wi' an unlit roll-up. I grimaced and one of t' men, one wi' mutton-chops, nodded at me warily. We sat around like circus performers waiting backstage, supping beer and passing a spliff.

Then mutton-chops man opened the tin and took out a syringe. He signalled to t'other one beside him to roll up his shirt sleeve. He held the syringe at eye level and tapped it. I pretended not to be watching, like it all wor summat and nowt. I'd seen my share of discarded syringes on t' pop round, in t' tower-block stairwells and walkways and what have you. I'd idled in t' doorways of stinking flats wi' t' thin curtains drawn against t' daylight, wi' broken toys or shite-filled nappies strewn over t' bare floors; the gaunt faces and yellowed eyes pleading wi' me for a week's credit on their pop. But I'd never seen no one inject before.

The man wi' t' rolled-up sleeve pumped his fist a few times to raise up a vein, and t' other one kneaded his skin, searching for an entry point. As the needle slid in the man's eyelids shuttered over and he sank back into t' sofa wi' a soft sigh.

Mutton-chops man then eyeballed me levelly and said in a hoarse whisper, 'Does this disgust you?'

'Should it?'

The man cocked his head, his hair hanging in front of his eyes. Jeremy wor drumming his fingers on my shoulders to some song playing in his head.

The man held up the syringe.

'Wanna?'

Jeremy's drumming fingers lost their rhythm for a moment. A smile flickered across t' man's lips.

I hesitated, as if mulling it over. Never ever accept or reject an offer out of hand, Mitch had a habit of saying. I glanced over at his mate, who wor out of it. He wor t' lucky one. My head wor swimming wi' Jim, the Chinese-dressing-gown man, Dora, wire-haired Jake and even t' angry car driver – all wor gathered in a huddle in my head and whispering like I wor t' butt of their private joke. I tried to blot them out by focusing on t' syringe. The needle glinted in t' firelight. The room had gone very quiet.

'Not just now. Ta.'

I tried to sound light, like refusing another drink or summat. The man's face darkened over. He spat on t' floor. Jeremy's fingers lifted from my shoulders. Making a snip-snip motion in t' air he said, 'Well, are we or aren't we?'

'Oh, yes!' Gina squealed, jumping to her feet. 'We must!'

Mutton-chops junkie sniggered, got up and sloped off. T'other bloke wor still out of it, and the woman had fallen asleep on t' rug wi' a lit ciggie between her fingers. Jeremy vanished into t' shadows and returned carrying a kitchen chair.

'Well then. Let's be having you, wonder boy. Take off your shirt.'

I peeled my T-shirt over my head. He placed the chair directly beneath t' hanging lightbulb, facing away from t' fire and toward t' pitch dark. The chill brought me out in goose-bumps and made my nipples stand up. The junkie woman woke up and relit her roll-up and offered it to Gina, who waved her away.

'Not now, Julia.'

Jeremy fetched his clippers and then a bowl of warm water and a small, dirty towel.

'Sit!' he ordered.

I sat. The bowl of tepid water wor placed on another chair right in front of me.

'Bend forward!'

Jeremy shampooed my scalp, dried it vigorously wi' t' manky hand towel, then started applying the black dye. It ran in ticklish rivulets down my neck and leached into t' metal bowl at my feet. It had a raw, caustic smell. Without waiting for t' dye to set, and wi' one hand clamped on t' back of my neck, Jeremy began to snip. Clumps of hair fell into my lap, into t' bowl and around my feet. I steered my mind away from thinking about what wor being done to me and, sugared a little by desire, fantasised mesen as a criminal having my hair shorn.

Jeremy paced about me, slurping from his can of Red Stripe and snipping. Gina just gleamed at me.

'Relax, will you,' Jeremy snapped. 'I'm not going to cut your head off.'

I dropped my shoulders and stared straight ahead. Jeremy thumped me in t' lower back.

'I said relax. Not slump!'

I stared straight ahead, focusing on a far point of t' room. Beyond t' harsh ring of t' naked bulb above me, lying on a mattress that I could now make out by t' far wall, wor some-one else. I couldn't tell if they wor kipping or lying awake. I took it to be another junkie.

'Who's that?' I whispered to Gina.

'Just Tad, poppet, sleeping off a helluva hangover. HEY, PRICK-FACE, WAKE UP!'

The shape moved, shuffling and stretching, hacking and gobbing onto t' floor. Then it rose up, a shadow rising up the wall wi' it.

The shape stepped out of t' gloom. He wor naked. I glimpsed the dance of his cock as he pulled on some bleached-out drainpipes that lay on t' floor. The man said, 'I need a fuckin' piss.' He stumbled drowsily toward a door.

'So how many people live here?'

'Depends, poppet, depends. People come, people go.'

Jeremy wor slow in his labours. Eventually I wor allowed to view mesen in a large shard of mirror. It wor me, and not me. My hair wor jet-black, teased up and stiffened like oil-soaked beach grasses. My lugs wor visible, and the nape of my neck felt cold and exposed. Gina and Jeremy looked on while I stared at mesen in dumb amazement.

'Oh, fuck!'

Tad came back from pissing and stood before me, his arms folded across his chest, grinning wolfishly. He had a tattoo of an iron cross above his right nipple and a Union Jack tattoo on his upper right arm.

'Should have shorn him, Jez.'

'He doesn't want to be a skinhead, stupid,' Gina said, stroking my inner thigh. Her smile wor almost feline. 'Anyway, poppet, you're ours now!'

I awoke on a thin mattress in a room wi' a single, grilled window. The hair dye had left stains on t' pillow. My mouth tasted like a rat had died in it. Tad wor kipping on another mattress by t' wall opposite, curled up in t' foetal position, his backbone ridged up like a wolf's. T'others wor in other rooms.

I lay still while my eyes grew used to t' gloom, then got up and padded about. I peered out through t' window at the rose dawn sky. Tad rolled over, pushing his blanket aside in his sleep. I knelt down, drinking him in. As well as the tattoos I'd clocked earlier, he had a Yorkshire rose on his other arm and a serpent snaking toward his groin. A thin line of sandy hair ran up to his navel. He had an appendix scar and a faint birthmark on his lower abdomen.

I lifted the blanket back over him. He grunted, rolled over and buried his face in t' pillow. I dressed mesen in t' cold, greying light and made my way down t' stairs.

In t' kitchen on t' floor below I came across Julia, the junkie woman, asleep in an armchair, her head lolling forward and her hair covering her face. No sign of t'other junkies. I shuftied about for summat to eat, my insides gurgling like one of Dr Jekyll's potions. The breadbin wor empty. On t' kitchen stove stood a saucepan of cold stew. I spooned up a mouthful. A smear of cold grease coated my tongue.

'Yeuchh!'

I gobbed onto t' floor, threw t' spoon into t' pot, slammed on t' cold tap and sluiced out my mouth. Julia hadn't stirred. I dropped a knife into t' sink. She slept on. She must have been totally out of it. I picked up the pan and let it clatter onto t' flagstone floor. Stew splattered and oozed away like fresh cow shit. Julia didn't move. Friggin' junkies. Waking the dead would have been easier. I left Julia to her druggie dreams and cut down t' stairs and out through t' steel door, letting it slam shut behind me.

Outside, the breeze wor blowing an early-dawn chill and some ravens wor making a racket. I headed down t' steep hill toward t' junction. Just then, all t' street lights went out.

* * *

I'd expected to find 'em all still tucked up. I wor miffed to find Mother seated at the kitchen table in her nightgown. She'd been pasting Green Shield stamps into books. She didn't lick the stamps, cos Granddad Frank once told her that the glue wor made from boiled horse bones. Rather, she dipped them in a shallow saucer of water. Her jaw wor set, her cheeks pale, her lips colourless.

'So, the wanderer returns.'

I set my key down on t' table.

'You look a sight,' she said, to my back. I didn't reply.

I woke late, fuzzy-headed, daylight beaming through t' ciggie burn in t' curtains. I lay there a while going over yesterday in my mind, thinking about t' skinhead, Tad, or whatever he called himsen. Short for what? Tadpole? Not unless that wor a nickname from when he wor a nipper. Outside, I could hear Mitch hammering in t' garage. Sis wor in her room, hoofing it to Heatwave's 'Boogie Nights' and singing along tunelessly.

I got dressed and took in my new look in t' wardrobe mirror. My hair had flattened, and it stuck out in all t' wrong places from where I'd slept on it. I spat into my palms and teased it back into shape.

Downstairs, I found Mother daydreaming out t' kitchen window. She mustn't have slept, cos the washing wor done and already flapping on t' line. I opened the bread bin quietly, then slid two slices into t' toaster.

Mother said, 'I've got Social Services coming round later today to talk about Gran. If they see you looking like that you'll get sectioned.'

Social Services sent a hard-faced little woman wi' her hair scraped up in a tight bun. She perched bolt upright on t' settee, her box jacket still buttoned, her eyes flirting wi' t' decor. When she worn't trying to weigh the dust on t' picture rail, she wor examining her teacup as if she worn't sure if it wor clean. Mother kept patting her own hair uneasily. Mistrust hung there between 'em like a pane of glass onto which each exhaled icily.

'A place has been found for your mother,' the SS woman said.

I said, 'Does that mean that I get my old room back?'

Mother eyed me stonily. The SS woman pursed her lips together like she wor sucking on a sour boiled sweet. She said glassily, 'Yes, I suppose it will.'

Mother's expression dithered between pleased and mortified. The SS woman rummaged in her bag and muttered summat about formalities. I excused mesen and left them to it.

A week after Gran had gone into t' nursing home I went wi' Mother on a visit. The home wor a grim red-brick mansion of turrets and towers, wi' deep bay windows on t' ground floor that reflected the trees and the gardens. It reminded me of t' loony bin.

Mother popped her head into t' office door by t' entrance lobby and a perky young girl wi' a plate of Mr Kipling cakes on her desk told us where we'd find Gran that day. Parked beside t' desk wor a bearded bloke in a wheelchair. The girl said that his name wor Bobby and that he'd been abandoned there as a child.

Bobby had a book propped before him on a music stand. As he read he turned the pages wi' a long, thin metal hook that he waggled between his teeth. When he saw us, Bobby's head wobbled enthusiastically, the hook batoning about. He emitted a strangled 'Nnnnhhhh.' The girl reached across and wiped away t' dribble that ran down his chin.

'Bobby says hi,' she said, swallowing some cake.

'Hello, Bobby,' Mother said in a tone she usually reserved for owt mildly cute. I nodded my 'Hello', and Bobby made another excitable 'Nnnnnhhhh.'

'You'll find Betty in t' lounge at the end of t' corridor,' the girl said.

We clopped along t' dully-lit corridor of mushroom gloss walls and the sharp tang of bleach over stale piss. Mother blathered on about t' sour-faced staff and the girl in reception being t' only cheery one.

'Nice-looking girl. Don't you think so?'

'Uh-huh.'

Mother gave me an assessing look.

We entered a cavernous lounge area, empty save for a semi-circle of armchairs at the far end. Gran wor buried in one, her head bowed forward slightly, and smiling oddly, as if taken up by some pleasant scene on t' rug before her, such as a frolicking kitten. Except that there wor nowt.

We'd been told that Gran's mind wor steadily disintegrating, like cabbage boiling down to mush. But as we neared her, we saw that she'd stopped caring for hersen – or being cared for. Her cardie had a dried egg stain on it, her hair wor all matted, and without make-up, her face looked sallow.

Mother crouched alongside Gran's chair and spoke loudly and slowly.

'Hello, Mum. How are you today?'

Gran's head lolled. Mother took a hairbrush from her handbag and began tidying Gran up a bit. I walked over to t' window. In spite of t' drought, the lawns wor well watered, the flowerbeds wor flourishing. An exhausted wasp wor crawling along t' sill. I tried to lift the sash, but it wouldn't budge. The windows had been nailed shut. Mother came over to t' window, still holding the hairbrush. Together we took in t' blooms.

'They do a nice job on t' gardens.'

'Aye,' I said. 'On t' gardens they do.'

Mother's face twitched. 'What were we supposed to do?'

'Did I say owt?'

'Oh, spare me. We might not have seen eye to eye, and my God your gran could be a troublesome old goat, but that don't stop the guilt sitting in me like a stone.' She touched her stomach wi' t' back of t' hairbrush. 'We couldn't have cared for her at home, Rick.' She looked across at Gran wi' a regretful half-smile. 'I do wish we'd talked more. Before t' gate started closing.'

Gran raised her head slowly and her face opened into a wondrous, trusting smile that wor never part of her when she had all of her cups in t' cupboard. Her fingertips quivered anxiously. Mother went over and crouched beside her. Then Gran's expression darkened, as if she wor seized by a worrisome thought, and she grabbed Mother's wrist very tightly.

'Ow, Mum! Let go. Mum, let go, you're hurting me!'

But her grip wor so tight that Mother couldn't wrench hersen free. Gran's eyes widened, the whites like crazed china, her damp mouth agape as she screamed into Mother's face, 'He'll be t' death of us, child!'

'Who? Who will?' Mother cried, yanking her wrist free. 'Who?'

'Him! Frank! Frank, and that man!'

'What man?'

'That man! Him! HIM!'

On t' way home I said, 'What man?'

Mother flapped a hand. 'There wor a man who used to go to t' races wi' your granddad. Your gran hated him. Wouldn't have his name breathed across t' doorstep.'

'Why?'

'Search me.'

'Did you ever meet him?'

She rooted in her shit-brown handbag for a tissue, blew her nose and sorted out her eyes.

'A couple of times. They once took me to a race meet at Wetherby. I can't have been more than six or seven ...'

'Granddad always did love the horses.'

Mother chortled. 'I used to get sent to t' bookies' to fetch him home for his dinner. I wouldn't go in, cos the bookies' wor like the pub, a smoke-filled den of men where little girls shouldn't be seen. So I'd wait outside 'til someone noticed me, and then someone else would shout, "Frank! Frank, yer wanted!" and Dad would appear in t' doorway and tell me to run back home and say he'd be there in a jiffy. It wor what he always said.'

Mother laughed again. 'At first I used to think a jiffy wor a small car, or a horse-drawn carriage or summat, so I'd wait by t' window for his jiffy to appear.'

I looked out the bus window at passing suburban houses.

Mother then recollected how Frank's friend drove a grand old car – well, she remembered it as a grand old car. She recalled the wonderful patterns of t' jockeys' shirts and how t' horses seemed to steam and how far away they seemed when they wor racing and then how near suddenly as they charged into t' home straight and Granddad and this other man wor screaming crazily for their horse, only she didn't know which wor their horse, and she'd tingled excitedly as the thundering of t' hooves grew closer and louder 'til t' horses blurred past t' winning post right in front of her, but she felt safe cos Granddad wor holding her hand tightly and then he whisked her up and kissed her on t' nose and said, 'We've won, did you see, we've won!' and the two men threw their hats in t' air and their arms around each other and they all went to collect the winnings and Granddad bought her a toffee apple.

She remembered how on t' way home she wor soothed by t' measured talk of t' men, while she sank into t' rear seat, stroking the ribbed leather, catching the faint whiff of t' ashtrays in t' car doors. She wor their shiny little girl, they'd said, and they would take her to t' races for always and they would always win and throw their hats toward t' sky and she would smear toffee apple around her lips and suck boiled sweets for evermore.

I smirked. 'And did you go again?'

'No. I kicked up a right fuss 'til Gran clipped me around t' ear and said, "Frank only took you cos I had to visit a sick relative." But I knew that wor a fib, in the way all children know when their parents fib. Still, I worn't going to poke that fire again.'

She gave me a long look. I took in t' scenery outside t' window. I wor thinking that wor t' way Mother and I differed. If there wor an ember, I had to poke it into life.

II

Now that I wor not welcome at Blandford Gardens for some reason that might have summat to do wi' mashing up that little runt in t' car park, Gay Lib meetings wor t' only way to meet anyone likeminded. The measly gay pubs – the New Penny, the Wellesley Hotel side bar in Leeds, the Junction in Bradford – didn't seem to offer up owt much, and I didn't fancy sitting on my tod waiting to get chatted up by some lecherous old codger.

Thank friggin' Christ this next Gay Lib meet wor shorter. That butt-clenching politico stuff had been doing my nut. Afterward, in t' bar downstairs, some baldy, moon-faced boy-lover wor plying me wi' drinks and rubber-tongued talk. He cooed into my ear, 'Sadly, your age leaves you on the upper cusp of unsuitability. If only we'd met five years ago.'

'I wor twelve.'

'A delicious age.'

I slung mesen into an armchair and took in t' room. This lot worn't t' freshest display of farm produce neither. As for me, it seemed I wor too old for t' paedo, and jailbait for t' rest. Even here some old bloke wi' doughy cheeks and specs wor leering at me like a bladdered uncle at a wedding. Every time I looked his way he wor still eyeballing me. Suddenly he wor bee-lining my way.

'May I sit here?'

Before I could say owt he'd parked himsen on a buffet stool. He smiled, displaying his crooked, stained gnashers, and set his pint of Guinness on t' polished copper tabletop. A butt-end waggled off his meaty lower lip when he spoke.

'Gordon,' he said, sticking out a hand. The palm wor thick and callused, the finger ends nicotine-stained. I shook it briefly.

'I think I should start,' Gordon started, 'by saying that I realise perfectly well that you are young and handsome as all young men are handsome, and what is more I'm perfectly aware I'm not, that I'm certainly no beauty, indeed it is doubtful in my case that I ever was, although I have had my moments along the way, and that I fully recognise that I haven't the slightest chance of any carnal relations with you whatsoever, so I have expunged utterly any such notion from my mind. Indeed, that's not why I chose to come and introduce myself to your good self.'

'Eh?' Over Gordon's shoulder I caught the pitying glances of others.

'No indeedy, young sir. Quite simply, I haven't had the chance to make myself acquainted, so I thought I would do the decent thing, and ... well, I've done that bit, haven't I?'

'Aye.'

'So now we've dispensed with my name, why don't you enlighten me as to yours?'

'My what?'

'Your name. But that's all right, I believe I overheard. It's Rick, isn't it? Brusque and to the point. Very apt. Cigarette?'

'Don't smoke.'

'Good for you, my boy. There are prettier vices. Dr Choudhury says I should stop.'

He blathered on, all t' while sucking one ciggie down then lighting another. He coughed 'til his eyes watered.

The gist of what I got, when I tuned in, wor that Gordon had lived alone since his mother had 'crossed the great divide', that he wor now 'a man of leisure', but he used to have his own radio and TV repair business. That he'd always been gay, although in his day one didn't use the word, that he'd never married, that he'd had two long and secretive relationships wi' other men, and that he only came out – 'as they now say' – to his sister when he wor fifty-two, and she hasn't spoken one word to him since.

I watched his fingers mess wi' a match. Exhaled smoke hung about his wide mouth. I leaned back in my chair. Gordon leaned toward me.

'Well, you've certainly sent a ripple around the room.'

'Is that why no one's talking to me?'

'That, and perhaps that you give off such an air of unapproachability.'

'I do?'

'Utter aloofness, my boy. It's an alluring defence mechanism in one so young. You think that anyone who talks to you wants to get their hands on you. They don't. You're not really standoffish at all, are you? In fact, the moment I saw you I detected a certain crackle across the airwaves. I thought, now there's a young man who won't think I'm trying to seduce him just because I say hello.' Gordon smiled crookedly. 'I accept that I repulse you.'

'What makes you say that?'

'The young are repulsed by everything. It's what makes being young so unbearable.'

I wor feeling cornered. I stood up. 'I'm going for a refill.'

Gordon emptied the dregs of his glass in one gulp.

'You want another?' I said, feeling obligated.

'A Guinness would go down a treat.'

While I wor waiting at the bar to be served a voice murmured into my ear, 'One-way traffic, that one.'

93

The voice had a foreign note. It belonged to a man wi' a long, angular face, curly black hair and what Mitch always called 'an unwashed complexion'.

'Sorry?'

I felt a hand rest on t' small of my back.

'Isn't it always the way with the old ones? They pretend to be your friend, and then before you know it their hands are all over your deck. Trust me, dear, we've all suffered.'

I looked across at Gordon, who waved at me like a man on board a departing ferry.

'He means no harm.'

'Oh, please. He's always cadging free fags and drinks. Heavens, my dear, if I look like that at his age I'll shoot myself.'

The foreigner wor still kneading my lower back wi' a worrying expectancy.

'You're new to GLF, aren't you?'

'Aye.'

'You've heard no doubt about the protest this Friday in Bradford? I mean, fancy someone getting fired from British Home Stores just for being gay? Scandalous. So we're picketing BHS. It should be fun. Afterward we're going for a curry and then on to the Nash.'

'The Nash?'

'The International Club on Lumb Lane. Hard-core basement reggae club. Us pouftas are the only non-blacks allowed in. And the prostitutes, of course. As far as the world's concerned, we're on about the same social level as the whores.'

'Prozzies don't bother me none.'

'I wouldn't know any.'

He told me his name, and spelt it for me. Fazel. F.A.Z.E.L. He made me guess where he wor from, a game I knew he must play wi' everyone. The only places I could recall from t' school atlas wor Egypt, Arabia and Tunisia. He said wi' a curl of his lip that he worn't an Arab.

'Israel?'

'Iran! I don't suppose you even know where that is?'

'I've heard of it. So how come you speak such good English?'

'Daddy works for an oil company. We've moved around a lot.'

'I nearly went to Rotterdam on t' North Sea Ferries one February, but it wor cancelled cos t' sea wor too rough.'

'Is that right? Well then, you mustn't go to Iran first, because then the rest of the world will disappoint you. Iran has beautiful ancient cities, warm weather, great food, gorgeous men ...'

'So what made you leave all that for Yorkshire then?'

'I'm a student at the uni. Do you like it here? This septic isle? Ah, well, I suppose if that's all you've known – the cold, the grey, the damp. As for myself, I'm always trying to find interesting ways to keep warm. You know, like crawling under the covers with some willing young man.'

'I'd better take Gordon his pint.'

'All yours,' Fazel said, lifting his hand off my back like it wor scalding him.

I set the pint before Gordon.

'Here.'

Outside, it had started to sile it down. We listened to t' rain drumming on t' pavement.

'Gordon, what's wi' this demo business? Are you going?'

He sipped the head of his Guinness, leaving a froth moustache on his upper lip. His tongue licked it clean, shooting out like a chameleon's.

'I might. I'm having lunch with my good friend Charles, so it depends greatly. You should go, though. These things are important.'

The rain wor battering at the windows like it wor wanting to be let in.

Gordon said, 'Are you planning on going home in this?'

'No choice.'

'I could give you a lift.'

'What will it cost me?'

Gordon smiled his yellow, toothy smile. 'A lot less than you might be thinking.'

As it happened, the day of t' demo wor my day off work. I thought I'd go take a gander first and then decide whether I'd join in or not. I wanted to see how many wor going to pitch up, and what they looked like. I didn't want to be the only young'un amongst a bunch of oldies, uglies and lesbos.

I staked my place at a street corner across t' square. At first, it didn't look like owt wor happening. The man wi' t' badge-vomit jacket wor there, as wor t'other one in t' platforms and bell-bottoms. He had a long patchwork scarf snaking round his neck that looked like summat knitted by t' blind, and a pale orange cotton bag hanging from his shoulder. They all just stood around, blathering on at each other, judging by t' positions of their heads.

In t' end there wor about ten folk. There wor two women portering a furled-up banner between them. Not the women I'd first seen at the GLF meeting. A sandy-haired bloke pitched up, pushing a chunky bicycle. No sign of Fazel.

No Gordon neither, but then he'd said as much. When he dropped me off after t' GLF meet he'd asked me for my phone number, but that wor a no-no. He tore out a page from his pocket diary and scribbled his own number on it.

'Otherwise,' he'd said, 'most Thursday evenings I am usually in the Dog in the Pound on the Leeds Road. Do you know it?'

I said I'd been past it. Which I had. On t' way to Paradise Buildings.

Across t' square, the women unfurled the banner, which had holes cut in it to let the wind through, and 'BRADFORD G.L.F.' sewed onto it. They started shouting summat about Gay Lib and jobs and discrimination. At first they seemed a little unsure, like schoolgirls carrying out a dare, but then they egged each other on and the shouting became more forceful. Only it wor carried up on t' breeze and grew small – like a lost balloon.

I wor gobsmacked that anyone would do that. Stand out there in t' wind and rain for someone else, risking all that abuse. I pondered what the bloke who'd got fired thought of it all. Wor he one of t' ones who wor wi' them?

While t' women shouted, the men wor trying to leaflet folk who wor entering or leaving the department store. Some went over to see what it wor all about, taking the leaflets, maybe thinking it wor a freebie promo of a chance to win a car. If it had been, Mother would have been in there like a shot. Others read the leaflets briefly then tossed them away. Some just dropped them, but a fair few screwed them up and made a disgusted show of tossing them aside. One or two handed them back. Most folk just pushed on by, heads bowed, not looking.

Then a woman in a bobble hat came over, dragging a toddler by t' hand, and started yelling about God and the Bible and all that baloney. This set the toddler bawling.

Nowt much else happened for a while apart from t' shouting and the leaflets being blown about t' square, 'til someone from t' department store came out to talk to them. The lone cowboy sent out to face the enemy. He seemed all riled up. He wor flapping his arms about and pointing at the leaflets on t' ground and seemed to be vexed about summat, although I wor too far away to hear. Then he strode back into t' store.

I wor expecting that any moment a couple of bobbies would put in an appearance, or even a panda car, but nowt of t' sort happened. After an hour or so they gradually dispersed, looking undecided what to do next. Eventually three of them headed Lumb Lane direction, presumably for t' curry. I wor peckish mesen, but it might have looked a bit odd to suddenly pitch up for t' curry, so I headed into Bradford market in search of a sausage roll or a samosa, but it wor just stalls of brightly coloured sari cloth or cheap toiletries, plastic buckets, curtain net and whatnot.

I left the market at the far end where it came out near a small roundabout. I toyed wi' t' notion of taking a wander up Paradise Buildings way. It had been yonks since I last saw Tad or Gina or Jeremy at the FK Club. So much for that 'You're ours now' guff. I stood there for an age, leaning on t' safety barrier, watching t' traffic whizzing about. Then I went home.

As summer approached, folk wor getting worked up about t' Queen's Silver Jubilee. There wor to be a chain of bonfires across t' country. There wor to be street parties, wi' Jubilee streamers, Union Jacks flapping from bedroom windows, flags and windmills to wave, wi' trestle tables lined wi' Jubilee teas the lengths of entire streets, great mounds of sandwiches and cake and Jubilee iced buns, and endless cups of Jubilee tea poured from giant Jubilee tea urns, and Jubilee Coca-Cola for t' kids, and Jubilee music and dancing and much toasting and cheering for Her Majesty and all that lot. And all anyone seemed to want to know wor: would it rain? Would it rain? Of course it wouldn't rain – it never rained on Her Majesty. The sky would be a cloudless blue block wi' t' smiling, happy sun beaming down from on high.

Mother baked two whole Jubilee parkins for t' big day, wi' Union Jacks forked across t' top. Mand and I looked on in awe and befuddlement as she measured out the ounces of butter and flour, counted out teaspoons of ginger and table-spoons of syrup. Neither of us had ever seen her bake before. She said it wor cos she had no love of baking, but parkin she said she could do cos as a child she loved to sit at the kitchen table, watching Gran stir t' mixture.

'I used to beg to lick the spoon, even though eating the raw mixture gave me stomach ache. When it wor finally ready and your gran opened t' oven door, the heat and the baking smells would fill up the kitchen.'

She waved a table spoon at us. 'Then Gran would put the parkin on a wire tray by t' window, and we'd have to wait 'til it wor cool. I'd always imagine them smells escaping on t' breeze through t' kitchen curtains.'

She shook her head, shaking the memory loose, and lift-ing a dollop from t' mixture bowl, she sucked on her finger like a new-born lamb. She offered some to Mand, who screwed up her face.

'No, ta. I don't want no stomach ache, do I?'

I stuck my finger into t' bowl and tasted the raw mixture. Uncooked, the ginger kicked through sharply.

'Why have I never seen Gran bake owt?' I said.

'She just stopped one day. Stopped and never baked another. S'pose she couldn't see t' point. She still made her trifle every Christmas.'

'Way too much sherry in it,' said Mand.

Mother laughed heartily. It wor good to see her in such a happy mood. 'Well, yes,' she said, 'always too much sherry.'

An hour or so later she lifted the parkins from t' oven. Her face clouded. The parkins had burnt at the edges, and in t' centre, where they should have risen to a gentle mound, a fissure had opened up through t' Union Jack.

'Smells great,' Mand said encouragingly.

Mother hunched over t' parkins, running a knife round t' edges of t' tins, then upended them onto a metal grid. She set the grid on t' draining board and we all looked on, waiting for some sort of transformation.

'Don't we get to try a bit, then?' I said, reaching out for a corner. Mother slapped my hand.

'Hands off! They're not for you.'

'They're for t' Queen,' Mand said.

Freshly baked smells teased the air. I suggested opening the window.

'No,' Mother said, 'it will only bring in t' wasps.'

On t' big day itsen streets wor closed off all over t' city, the trestle tables wor decked and Union Jack bunting wor hung from every available pole. All morning Mother, Denise, Mavis and a gaggle of t' older folk from t' surrounding streets had been assembled in a former Methodist chapel-cum-function room, threading Union Jack bunting. I wor collared to help collect chairs from t' chapel storeroom. Outside, two young Asians wi' a bucket of disinfectant and scrubbing brushes were listlessly trying to wash away t' graffiti that had appeared overnight:

GOD SAVE THE FASHIST REGIME

While I fetched yet more chairs, Nora, portly Mrs Fibak and some other women I'd never clapped eyes on before wor laying out white tablecloths, cutlery, plates, cups and saucers and whatnot. They wor joined by Mother, Mavis and Denise. The women nattered and clattered, telling tales about hubbies, offspring, fancy men, work colleagues – drenching themsens in their own laughter as if all wor right wi' t' world.

A few excitable kiddies wor hiding beneath t' tables or tearing up the pavements on BMX bikes. Some blond-haired nipper in Union Jack shorts wor jumping up and down on a space hopper 'til he lost control and sideways hopped into a table. His mother clipped him fiercely on t' side of his head.

'I told you to leave that indoor!'

The kid just scowled, dragged the space hopper away from her and continued bouncing around.

As I came back wi' t' chairs, Mother wor blathering giddily, 'Oh, I know. Our Mandy acts like a scalded cat whenever I say owt to her.'

'It's their age, Pam luv. She's growing up, that's all,' said Mrs Fibak, wi' a skewed smile. Mrs Fibak had married a Pole who had been stranded here at t' war end.

Mother tied another knot in t' endless stream of bunting, broke it wi' her teeth, then turned to Mrs Fibak and said, 'Of course, you know all about raising kids, don't you?' It sounded crueller than she'd perhaps meant. Busy hands stilled, voices hushed. Everyone knew how Mrs Fibak fussed mightily over other people's kids, that the Fibaks had no kids to call their own. Mrs Fibak wor everyone's babysitter and folk loved her for it.

Into t' thickening silence I plonked down t' chairs and said, 'We'll need more than this.'

I headed back to t' chapel storeroom. All that remained of t' graffiti wor a white smear. The Asian cleaners wor packing up. One of 'em nudged t'other and pointed at my hair. Maybe they had me down as the culprit. If only. I grinned and they grinned shyly back, and one of 'em tousled his own mop.

'Punk? You punk, eh?'

'Yeah, punk.'

He put up a thumb. 'Punk! Me like!'

He laughed, displaying a neat set of impossibly white tombstones. I laughed also. He looked relieved. 'God save the Queen, eh?'

'God save the Queen,' I echoed. I picked up four more chairs and made my way back.

'I hear,' Nora wor saying, her voice like iron filings in syrup, 'the police wor round at the Graysons' last week, taking a statement.'

'Nora, luv, the police have been all over t' place like flies on rotting meat,' said the woman to her right, sucking on her teeth. 'Scares me half to death, all this murdering. The only good thing about it ... and I'm sorry to say this ... but thank God it's only prostitutes. Not that I'd wish ... you know ... Even so, my Derek won't let me out at night, not even to walk to t' post box at the end of our road. Drives me all over t' shop.'

'Well I wouldn't mind being chauffeured about. Save my feet,' said Mrs Fibak. Mrs Fibak's ankles swelled over her shoes, and her feet looked beyond saving.

Mavis clattered some plates down. 'Can't any of you let this Ripper business drop? It's all some of you ever talk about ... Ripper bloody this ... Ripper that ... I don't want to hear it, I ... I just want to enjoy this day. That's all. Just ... enjoy ... that's all.'

She lowered her trembling hands beneath t' table lip, where only I, standing right behind her, could see her one hand gripping t'other too tightly.

Craner had arranged for every pop wagon to have plastic Union Jack bunting attached to t' outside and plastic Union Jack stick-on flags in t' windows. We wor shifting pop by t' crateload. Halfway through t' day we wor sold up and had to go back to t' depot for a reload. By t' time we wor cashing up in Reginald Street, Chapeltown, the sun wor setting behind t' nearby terraces and I wor aching like I'd been stretched on a rack. But the bonus would fatten up my wage packet nicely.

The only fly in t' ointment that day had been Mrs Husk. That morn, she'd been all riled up about summat. She wor rubbing the stone on her ring finger, which she did when she wor agitated.

I parked the ginger beer on t' table beside her Brown Betty teapot. The spout wor chipped. She swirled the dregs of her teacup and tipped the leaves back into t' bottom of her cup.

'What's the world coming to, lad?'

'Dunno, Mrs Husk. But it's rum all right.'

She flicked me a look.

'He's going to do it again, you know.'

'Who, Mrs Husk?'

She didn't seem right in t' head today, blathering on so darkly. I just let folk talk. Always best that way, just let them blather on and don't disagree wi' owt they say. Still, I worried for Mrs Husk. Maybe she wor going a bit doolally. Like Gran. I didn't want Mrs Husk to go t' way of Gran.

'I've seen it!' she hissed, gripping the table edge wi' her bony hand.

'Seen what, Mrs Husk? Seen what?'

She wor giving me t' willies. Summat had rattled Mrs Husk's cage all right.

'Ohhhh ... ohhhh ...'

'Mrs Husk, I think maybe you should sit down ...?'

'What can I do?' she cried, looking at me pleadingly. 'What can I do? That poor girl. That poor, poor girl.'

I touched her on t' arm, but she shook me away. Breathing hard through her nostrils, she sank slowly onto a dining chair, one elbow on t' tabletop, muttering under her breath, her lips opening and closing like a guppy. Through t' hallway door, partly ajar, I could just see t' bottom two stairs. Upstairs ... upstairs ... in other rooms, the elderly hoard, they store, they stash ...

'Ain't this place a bit big for you now, Mrs Husk?'

She tilted her head toward me. Her wig shifted, and she righted it. I'd brought her out of a trance. She smiled at me kindly.

'It's where I'll end my years, lad,' she said, her voice lightening a little.

'But you just live downstairs now?'

She harrumphed. 'He's over yonder again, is he? Your driver? And her wi' legs like a corner shop.'

'Eh?'

'Never closed, lad. If she charged she'd be bloody rich.'

Mitch had hung a Union friggin' Jack from t' washing-line pole in t' back garden. He wor getting irked cos the flag kept wrapping itsen around t' pole, so he shouted at it through t' window to loosen itsen, which it wor never going to do, wor it?

Then he came up wi' t' idea that Mother should sew on a bit of line at the bottom corner, and then he'd bang a tent peg into t' ground to hold it. Only t' ground wor too dry, so he piled some stones on t' peg to hold it down.

I left him to it and went to my room where I played the Pistols' 'God Save the Queen' single over and over. Ace record. Even better since t' tossin' BBC banned it.

Mitch came thundering up the stairs and opened my door without knocking and started barneying on at me about t' Pistols disrespecting the nation cos they played 'God Save the Queen' on a boat down t' Thames in London and when t' boat got to t' Houses of Parliament they wor all arrested. I said it wor brill. This made Mitch explode.

He stormed downstairs and played Rod Stewart's friggin' 'Sailing' on t' lounge record player, cranking the volume up so loud it distorted the sound, while singing along wi' it at the top of his lungs like a drunken Jack Tar.

A few days after, The Clash got fined for spray-painting their band name on a London wall. I nicked an old tin of white paint and a brush from Mitch's garage and went out and painted THE CLASH ROOL on t' first bit of wall I could find. Which happened to be t' neighbours' garage.

The next morn I wor in Craner's office as usual, waiting for t' round float, when he said, 'Seen this, Thorpy?' He wor waving the paper about. The headline read: PUNISH THE PUNKS.

'World is full of nutters, Mr Craner.'

Craner tried to mash a fly that wor exploring his desk top wi' t' palm of his hand. The fly dodged him easily. But not for long. It landed again on a notebook, and Craner thwacked it dead wi' t' rolled-up newspaper.

The punks wor punished. The following week two of t' Sex Pistols got mashed up by Teds in London. It wor in t' papers. Made it sound like they wor to blame. Then some Teds attacked Gaye Advert, bass player wi' The Adverts, and their singer, TV Smith.

Mitch said, 'What do they expect if they go round dressed like that?'

This riled me up, so I went and got Mitch's brothel creepers, threw them into a bucket and put a match to them. Then I tried to set light to t' flag in t' garden. Mitch bolted out of t' house like a ferret after a rabbit and tried to smack me on t' jaw, but I wor too quick for him. I pushed him hard and he toppled backwards, tripping over t' stones that wor holding down t' tent peg. Then I scarpered.

When I came back later Mitch had snapped all my punk singles into tiny bits and dumped them in t' dustbin, so I refused to talk to him for t' rest of t' week.

* * *

After t' Gay Lib meeting a few of us trooped up the road to a snooker club. It had a late bar and full-size tables that you had to lean across. Also, mid-weeks it wor almost empty.

I wor improving rapidly. I had the dead eye, the steady hand. The shaft of t' cue wor like looking down an airgun sight. I had the art of leaning coolly on my cue, waiting my turn, just like in them old gangster films or on *Pot Black* on t' telly.

I did a lot of what I thought wor looking cool. Still, I could never get the better of t' likes of Lucy or Sadie, who could sink breaks in double figures then set up snookers that needed at least a three-cushion hit. These women must play snooker most nights of t' week.

Daytimes, Sadie drove a bus. We passed her one time in t' Corona van as we wor trundling up the Roundhay Road and she waved at me from her cab. I waved back and yelled and she stuck up a thumb. Eric asked me who I wor yelling at, and I told him it wor a friend of my mother's.

'And she drives a bus?'

After losing the next game I left the lesbos to rule t' table. Gordon wor leant against t' bar, letting his ciggie ash drop on t' carpet while gabbing wi' some frizzy-haired bloke called Jeff about Jesus and some friggin' poet called James Kirkup.

As I wor ordering another pint of lager and lime, Fazel sidled over and slid an invite into my hand like he wor slipping me a pound note. It wor printed on pink card.

You are cordially invited to a midsummer poufs' party
25th June 1977
Radclyffe Hall, 137 Brudenell Road, Leeds SE6
8p.m. until late
Bring a lot of bottle

On t' reverse wor a printed drawing of a woman in a twenties dress and hat (which, Gordon said when I showed him the invite, wor called a cloche), in a poncy pose wi' a glass of champagne and a long ciggie holder.

'Bring friends,' oozed Fazel. 'As you English say, the more the merrier.'

I didn't say if I had any friends I could bring.

A week later I bumped into Gina and Tad at the FK Club. Gina blathered on, but I wor barely listening. Behind her wor Tad. I smiled furtively. His hair had been dyed blond and cut back to a tuft. He wor wearing black leather drainpipes, DMs and a white German army vest. Gina wor pawing my chest while she blathered. I wor getting a semi just being in sniffing distance of Tad. I told them about t' party.

'Oooh, sounds ... fun.'

'They said I could bring folk.'

The corners of Tad's mouth twitched.

'But just you two, eh?'

'Just us?' Gina purred. 'OK, poppet, just us. Where's this place?'

'It's called Radclyffe Hall.'

Radclyffe Hall wor a large, rundown Victorian house across t'other side of Hyde Park from t' uni. Not a stone's throw from Blandford Gardens.

There wor a few things I wor to learn about Radclyffe Hall.

Radclyffe Hall wor named after a real person – some friggin' ancient lesbian writer.

Radclyffe Hall had been a gay commune since t' early seventies.

At some point Radclyffe Hall had been exorcised of t' ghost of a murdered serving maid.

The last owner kept a mad Alsatian dog and its teeth marks wor still visible on t' bottom of t' cellar door.

I didn't know there wor gay communes.

I didn't know there wor lesbian writers.

But I knew that the world wor full of mad dogs.

I pitched up on my tod shortly after 8 p.m. wi' a bottle of Bull's Blood Hungarian wine and three cans of Red Stripe. The fourth I'd drunk on t' way. I dropped the empty can over a low garden wall and rang the bell. After waiting a while I rang it again. Then I heard a shout of 'Dooor!!' and someone clattering down t' stairs.

The door wor opened by a man wearing a low-cut purple dress that showed a full mane of chest hair. He had blue powdered eyelids behind round little specs, and matching blue fingernails. I could smell fresh nail varnish.

'Well, you're an early bird. Who are you?'

'I'm Rick. Friend of Fazel's.'

'I'm Camp David. Well, don't stand on ceremony. Fazel's popped out with some friends for a curry. They'll be back later. At least you've brought some booze.'

I followed Camp David into a long kitchen out the back of t' house. All t' chairs had been pushed to t' sides of t' room and on t' table wor several large bowls of brown rice and lentil salads.

'Come on,' he said, pulling the dress together at the waist. 'You can give me a hand.'

I trailed behind Camp David as he portered napkins, forks, paper plates and plastic cups from t' kitchen to t' front room and set them down on a worn red velveteen tablecloth that covered a hefty old dining table. The carpet had been rolled up against t' wall. Above me, the ceiling wor painted black wi' sprayed-on silver stars and planets.

'That was done by the previous lot,' Camp David said. 'Occultists, apparently. We haven't got round to painting it over. Terry – he's another Radclyffe Hall inmate by the way, but he won't be at the party – well, Terry says it's inaccurate. Terry says the Pole Star is in the wrong place completely.'

'Wouldn't know. Not great on my stars and planets.'

'Terry watches anything educational ad nauseam. All the Open University programmes. Lord knows why – what use is all that knowledge if you just sit around all day drinking endless mugs of tea?'

'He knows the planets are in t' wrong place on your ceiling.'

'Darling, he does it just to feel superior. As long as you know where Uranus is, then everyone's happy.'

'Don't he work, then?'

'Trained as an architect. But then the quacks gave him aversion therapy and he hasn't worked since.'

'Version therapy?'

Camp David flapped a hand. 'Hmm, nails still a bit sticky. A–version. It's electric-shock treatment. They think they can cure us of our so-called perversions, but they can't – it just fucks you up. Fucked Terry up good and proper. His other obsession is the weather. He measures it. Keeps a rain gauge and a thermometer in the back yard. He records the maximum and minimum temperature each day, cuts out the weather report from the paper and writes down the names of cloud formations. Don't ask me why.'

'Maybe measuring the weather helps to keep him sane?'

Camp David snorted. 'Well, darling, if you ever need to know your cumulus from your cirrus, you know who to ask.' He looked at me over t' top of his specs like a transvestite owl. 'You know, I like the punk hair, and your clothes are, well, interesting, but what you need is a few finishing touches. Come upstairs. You can keep me amused while I finish getting ready.'

In his bedroom, Camp David parked himsen on a long stool at his dressing-table mirror.

'Put some music on, sweetie. You choose.'

I walked across t' shaggy, dirty-white carpet, lifted the smoked plastic lid of t' stereo and switched it on. Where t' carpet didn't reach the edges of t' room, the boards wor painted lilac. Spider plants in macramé pouches cascaded down from t' mantelpiece toward a fireplace filled wi' dried flowers and incense sticks, and in t' corner a Swiss cheese plant stretched its dust-laden leaves toward t' window.

I rifled through t' LPs, unable to decide.

'What do you want to hear?'

'Lou Reed. *Transformer*. That always gets me in the mood.'

I lowered the needle onto t' record and the opening chords of 'Vicious' chugged in, Camp David mouthing the lyrics at his own image. I sat on t' edge of t' bed. Above me wor a poster of a drawing of a man wi' a stiffy twice the size of his body.

'Aubrey Beardsley,' Camp David explained, clocking me ogling t' skyscraper stiffy via t' mirror. He patted the padded seat beside him on t' long dressing-table stool. 'Come, sit. Sit by me.'

I perched on t' seat beside him. In t' mirror's side wings countless images of mesen cascaded away. Camp David's hands hovered over t' mess in front of him, his eyes lit like a child's in search of a favourite crayon.

'It isn't an attempt,' he said, leaning into t' mirror to crimp his lashes, 'to appear female. It's about breaking down the constraints of your attire, of breeder society dictating who you are, how you should look. It's radical drag, it's gender-fuck. I mean, a man isn't a man until he's worn a dress.'

He batted his lids at the mirror, testing the lashes.

'But let's not run before we can walk, shall we? Especially in heels. What you need,' he murmured, turning his face toward mine, 'is some work around the eyes. A little kohl, a little black eyeliner perhaps?'

'Like Sid Vicious?'

'More Cyd Charisse, dearie. Those cheekbones are just begging for rouge.'

I worn't one for make-up, or drag. And glam wor so out now that Bolan wor churning out shite and Bowie had moved on. Camp David wor holding the eyeliner pencil aloft.

'All right, then,' I said. 'But just a little around t' eyes.'

I found it hard to keep my face still. Camp David wouldn't let me look in t' mirror 'til he wor done.

'You've got lovely skin,' he purred. 'Really fine.'

He leant forward wi' eyeliner pencil, t'other hand resting on my knee. I could feel his warm breath on my skin. I caught the faint odour of sandalwood soap. It wor odd that someone so hirsute should smell so maidenly.

'Like I said, fabulous cheekbones. Hold still, try not to blink.'

'It tickles.'

'Don't be daft. Now. There. No, don't look yet! You need a little more on the other side. Black on black. Give you that punk-glam look you so desire.'

He leant back a little, looked me directly in t' eye. 'Lashes,' he said firmly. 'Look up at the ceiling to my right.'

'No, no, not ...' and then t' doorbell tringed. We both stopped. 'I'll get it,' I said, springing up from t' stool.

'Ah,' Camp David sighed. 'Saved by the doorbell.'

The bell tringed again. Then we heard laughter from downstairs, and at least three, possibly more, voices talking over each other. I recognised Fazel's throaty laugh.

'Oh,' said Camp David. 'They're back. And more besides, by the sound of it.'

The partygoers soon splurged from t' kitchen into t' hall-way, t' front room and up the stairs where they queued for t' bog, and eventually into t' first-floor bedrooms. The place wor jammed now, save for t' attic bedrooms, which wor marked out of bounds. Still yet more kept arriving.

Camp David wor showing me off as 'the young chicken I found on the doorstep', and when he tired of that I wor left to my own devices. Fazel wor gliding from person to person, laughing and waving his long fingers. Another housemate, Fizzy – nicknamed cos of his Bowie haircut, I assumed – had commandeered the record deck. The Bowie obsession extended to about every third friggin' record.

I hung against t' wall, supping Red Stripe and looking on. A large woman wi' long, beaded necklaces that flew about wor dancing wi' a tall, bearded guy in a tie-dye T-shirt and purple loons whose shoulders convulsed when he laughed. Nearby, two guys wi' Afro hair wor in a crotch-locked sway, holding each other's gaze.

Who wor all these people? Where did they hide themsens? Where did they come from? I hardly knew anyone 'cept for Fazel and a few folk from Gay Lib. I wor just getting into t' groove of Wild Cherry's 'Play That Funky Music' when I heard a commotion in t' hallway. Gina. Wi' Tad in tow. So he'd come!

I shuffled along t' wall slightly so that I wor partially hidden by others, and glimpsed them as they shoved their way along t' corridor. Tad wor dangling a half-drunk bottle of gin between his fingers.

'Try the kitchen!' I heard Gina screech. I edged into t' hallway and could see them up ahead, about half a dozen heads between us. I cut up the stairs and ran into Fazel, leaning over t' banisters, peering into t' hallway below.

'Who invited her?' he snapped.

'Who?' I replied.

'Her! Gina! That fascist little cow.'

I wor wondering how the heck Fazel knew Gina. Fazel straightened up.

'It wasn't you, was it?'

'Me?'

'Just thought your paths might have crossed at your little punk thingies or whatever. I hear the FK Club lets anyone in. Even fascists. That's the trouble with democracy. It's like an open sewer.'

'Sorry, Fazel. Do you mean that punk girl who just arrived wi' that bloke?'

Fazel's wide nostrils flared. 'Yes, her. She used to come to Gay Lib meetings claiming she was lesbian. She was very disruptive. She was thrown out for threatening someone with a broken chair leg. Lesbian? Her? Ha! Her husband used to drop her off and collect her.'

'Husband?'

'Some Hell's Angel on a motorbike. Anyway, then she showed her true colours and joined the National Front. What is wrong with this country? In Iran the likes of her would be dealt with properly. I don't want her in my house.'

I looked down and saw t' spiked-up crown of Gina's head as she and Tad wove their way back from t' kitchen toward t' foot of t' stairs.

'And what about the likes of us?' I said. 'In your country?'

Fazel snorted. 'What do you know about my country?'

Gina and Tad wor now clambering over two women who wor sat on t' bottom steps. Behind me the toilet flushed and the door opened, so I ducked in, pleading urgency.

I sat on t' bog, listening, weighing the options. I wor breaking into a cold sweat. I rubbed my palms over my face, trying to stay calm, trying to marshal my thoughts. The toilet walls wor a collage of arty posters. Pasted on t' back of t' door wor some friggin' poem about Jesus called 'The Love that Dares to Speak its Name' by that poet bloke called James Kirkup, across which wor scrawled in red biro, 'Defend Gay News!!' This wor t' very poem Gordon and Jeff had been

113

blathering on about in t' snooker club. Why did folk get so worked up about poetry?

I could feel the bass thud of Bowie's 'Jean Genie' coming from below. I tried reading the first couple of lines of t' poem. But then someone wor banging on t' bog door.

'Oi! You died in there?'

'Won't be a mo!'

'Well, fucking well hurry up or I'll crucify you! I'm dying for a crap!'

I took the key out of t' door and peered through t' keyhole. All I could see wor a flower patch on t' backside of someone's jeans. I unspooled the last of t' bog roll and dropped it into t' bog, flushed the chain and opened the door.

'Sorry mate.'

I scuttled past him and up the second, narrower flight of stairs to t' attic rooms. On one door wor a sign on a card that read 'The Rochester Suite', beneath which wor scrawled in biro, 'Fazel's Room. OUT OF BOUNDS'. So I went in.

At first I took it to be a storeroom of household junk. There wor a mattress under t' steep roof slope, an overstuffed chest of drawers, thickly painted purple, and a wooden chair. Boxes, suitcases, clothes and books lay about in untidy piles.

I moseyed about. I tugged open t' top right drawer of t' chest. It wor chocful of papers: airmail letters and bills and study notes and the like. Under them I found Fazel's passport. I flipped to t' photo page. Fazel then worn't very Fazel now. His hair wor combed and shiny and he wor wearing a striped sweater that an aunt might have notched up. In t' passport wor a small buff envelope of loose photographs. Inside, two bevel-edged black-and-white photos of a boyish Fazel, studio head shots wi' glued-on smiles.

I put them back, and had barely closed the drawer when t' bedroom door wor flung open, making me spasm wi' fright. It wor Tad.

'Saw you disappearing up here,' he said. 'Gina's having a helluva bloody barney wi' someone or other. I guess we both need to keep a low profile.'

'Only if Gina grasses me up.'

'She won't.'

Tad stepped further into t' room, filling the meagre space, his head catching the round paper ceiling shade, making it sway. He still had the half-bottle of gin.

'Why not?'

'She don't do that. She's loyal. She expects loyalty in return. And she's got this thing about you, I don't know what.'

'What about you? And Gina?'

'There's nowt going on between Gina and me, if that's what you mean. She's a law unto hersen, is Gina.'

'I heard she's married. To that Hell's Angel bloke.'

'Did you now? News travels fast, don't it? She married Victor about two year back. But now she won't have anything to do wi' him. Poor sod still follows her about like a dog.'

'How sweet. Anyone see you coming up here?'

'Don't think so. And no one else here knows me. Not even your Arab mate.'

'Trust me, he's not my mate. And he's Iranian. They ain't Arabs.'

Tad took a sup from t' gin bottle and passed it to me. A fiery slug of gin coated my tonsils, making me cough.

'Sorry,' I said, handing back the bottle. We sat down on t' mattress. Tad took another sup and wiped the back of his hand across his mouth. Music vibrated through t' floor. 'Nutbush City Limits'. The bottle passed back and forth between us like a silent conversation. Tad kept his eyes fixed on t' wall opposite, as if waiting for summat to happen. My hand edged toward his leg. I didn't know if he'd kiss me or punch me. Tad took another slug of gin and turning his head toward mine, snogged me, letting the gin sluice from his mouth into mine and then down our chins. The gin made him splutter. He pulled back. I wor breathing hard, like I'd swum across a swollen river. I weaved my fingers behind his neck, tilting his head toward me, his lips giving way as they brushed across mine.

But then mid-kiss a commotion from elsewhere made us stop. We listened like lovers hidden in a broom cupboard. It wor coming from t' street, three floors below. We heard Gina's voice first, then Fazel's and another woman's, all screaming and berating each other, then a banshee wail from Gina, and then t'other woman wor yelling, 'Fuck off, you little fascist bitch!' which made Tad fall back onto t' bed, hiccupping wi' laughter. Then Fazel, shouting, 'Fuck off home! Fascist cow! We don't want you here!' And then Gina, 'You go home! We don't want you here neither! Don't push me! Don't you ever push me!'

I thought Tad would race to her aid, but he just lay there, helplessly hiccupping and laughing. I got up, went to t' window and forced up the sash. In t' street below I could see Gina, walking backward and putting up two-finger salutes at Fazel and one of t' Afro-haired guys I'd seen dancing earlier. Camp David wor at the edge of t' group, his purple dress billowing in t' summer-night breeze. The Afro-hair guy had his arm around Fazel and wor trying to lead him back into t' house.

I watched the scene 'til I felt Tad's arms wrap around me and his fingertips kneading my body under my T-shirt. 'Forget them,' he said softly into my ear.

Jayne MacDonald
26/06/1977

I woke up alone, starkers, wi' a head that felt full of wet sand.

I'd had a fitful Technicolor dream of sitting behind the immense steering wheel of an articulated truck. The wheel wor so wide that I could barely grasp it wi' both arms outstretched. I wor trying to steer t' truck in one friggin' direction while all t' time some mysterious hand wor trying to wrest the wheel from me. The truck wor veering out of control. I'd woken suddenly just as it drove over a cliff into an abyss.

I propped mesen on one elbow. Fazel's duvet had a musty, unlaundered smell to it. I didn't know if Tad had stayed the night or had left me kipping. I could only remember t' sex as a drunken, fumbling urgency and awkwardness. Neither of us could make it to t' end, as if summat other than t' gin wor preventing us, so we'd lain there, listening to t' party winding down. Had he stayed, or had he scarpered as soon as I'd fallen into a sozzled slumber? Maybe he hadn't wanted to be found here. And where wor Fazel? Had he come across us? If so, where had he slept?

I stretched my limbs like a cat and listened out for signs of life. Right now, I wor thinking, I could murder a full English brekkie. Two rashers, sausage, fried egg, baked beans and buttered toast. A nice thick slice of Mother's Pride to mop up the egg.

I kicked back the duvet, crossed to t' window and pressed my face against t' windowpane. The sky wor a milky gauze. In t' window of t' house opposite hung a solitary Leeds Utd rosette. The brickwork of t' next house along wor painted lime green, wi' purple window frames and doors. An Asian family must live there. I saw houses like that on t' rounds, the brickwork garish colours, as if trying to evoke the spirit of another place far away amidst all t' dull red brick.

A frail old woman in a floral apron and outsized slippers wor putting summat in a dustbin. I watched her as she clattered the lid, looked about, took out whatever it wor again, clattered the lid again, looked about some more, then rattled it again. She scanned the neighbouring houses, waiting. When no one appeared she rattled the lid one final time, as if saying 'To hell wi' you all then,' before shuffling back indoors.

I dressed and headed down to t' kitchen. Camp David wor in his dressing gown, upending a bottle of nail-varnish remover onto cotton-wool balls. The astringent smell of t' nail-varnish remover, cold fag ash, flat beer and old wine assailed my nostrils. Someone had made a half-arsed attempt at tidying up. A carton of empty wine bottles had been put by t' back door, and paper cups, corks, cans, ring pulls and ciggie butts had been swept into a loose pile. I scoured about for matches wi' which to relight the pilot of t' gas boiler.

'Want some tea?' I said, filling the greasy old kettle.

'Oooh, please. Better make that three mugs. There's someone waiting for you in the lounge.'

'For me? Who? Not Tad?'

'If by that you mean the man with whom you were climbing the walls last night, he left at first light. Who was that, anyway?'

'Do you think Fazel minded?'

'That you sullied his bed? Hardly. Fazel got off with John and Arnie, and went back to their place. Anyway, I don't believe he's washed those sheets in six months. That room must smell like a fox's den.'

I carried two mugs of tea into t' lounge. There, parked in an armchair, wreathed in smoke, surrounded by old beer cans and empty wine bottles and leafing through a back copy of *Gay News*, sat Gordon.

'Good morning,' he chirrupped. 'Ah, tea!'

'This is most unexpected, Gordon.'

Gordon smiled soppily, his eyes sparkling at me.

'Well, I had intended to call on my dear friend Charles. You haven't met Charles yet, but you should. Marvellous old soul. Charles and I used to go on weekend cottaging forays together, until Charles developed emphysema. Difficult to perform orally when you're constantly out of breath. But I digress. Charles wasn't at home, so I suppose he must be over at his sister's. He goes there for Sunday dinner sometimes. So then I thought, Gordon, why don't you pop in on Radclyffe Hall? And so, here I am. I have to say, you do look a picture in eyeliner.'

I wiped my sleeve across my face. 'David wor messing wi' my face last night. I should go wash it off. Folks'll think I've gone all Larry Grayson.' From t' kitchen we could hear t' radio, and Camp David trilling along to Donna Summer's 'I Feel Love'. A police panda car whizzed by t' window, siren la-la-ing furiously.

'Heavens, that's about the fourth in twenty minutes,' Gordon said, flicking ciggie ash off his trouser knee. 'I thought it might be fire engines. But fire engines have an altogether distinct sound. No ambulances either. Just the police. Something is keeping the old Bill busy this morning. I was hoping,' he continued, touching the knot of his old paisley tie, 'to invite you out on a little foray in the Humber.

But if I'm disturbing you, do say. I don't mind being on my own. I've grown quite used to it in fact.'

He pulled a large handkerchief from his pocket and parped into it loudly. My throat tightened a notch. I didn't want to be caught up wi' Gordon for t' day. My head wor fuzzy and my body wor limp. I needed some time on my tod. Most likely I smelt like a tomcat.

We heard yet more screaming police sirens. Gordon rose from his chair and filched three ciggies from a packet lying on t' dining table. 'I hope you don't mind,' he said, 'but I need a good cuppa to unfreeze the blood, and a cigarette or two to clear the cobwebs from the mind.' He lit one ciggie and put the other two in his top pocket. He inhaled deeply. 'If you won't accompany me on a drive into the country, will you at least, young man, let me give you a lift home?'

I nodded gratefully.

On t' way Gordon prattled on about his car.

'This is my fourth Humber,' he said proudly. 'My first was a Humber Snipe from the late 1930s, then I changed that for a Humber Super Snipe Mark IV, then I had a Series III saloon for a while – the one with the double headlights – and now I drive this one – the Series IV saloon. Sadly, they don't make them any more. There's no craftsmanship, no elegance in cars nowadays. We're being flooded by Japanese tin boxes on wheels. Of course, my boy, this car is a mite conspicuous when out cottaging, so I usually park a few streets away so as not to be noticed.'

The friggin' talk wor always reverting to cottaging. Any moment now, I thought gloomily, Gordon's going to suggest just that: stop off at some red-brick public lav, wi' Gordon dallying about while I'm sent inside to whip up some action. Or worse, get me and some other bloke in t' back seat of t' Humber, wi' Gordon ogling in t' rear-view mirror while he fumbles wi' himsen. Not that Gordon had suggested owt of that ilk. Mind you, if it wor Tad ... I sniffed. I could smell him on my skin.

'I'll drop you at the end of your street, shall I?'

'Might be best.'

Watching the Humber pull away, it occurred to me that I hadn't told Gordon where I lived.

I walked in on Mother and Mand having a barney. Summat about some evening job that sis had lined up. Mother's face and neck wor practically piebald red and white. Sis wor saying, 'I've already said I'd do it.'

'Well, you can unsay it. Does Mitch know about this?'

Mand pouted and looked sideways at the floor.

'He won't let me. I know he won't. I know what he'll say.'

'You don't know anything of t' sort.'

Mother looked at me like I wor summat alien.

Sis worn't done yet. 'But it's only in the evenings and I wouldn't miss school or owt and anyway I'm leaving in a couple of week and it would be brill and I know there's this nutter going about but we still have to live our lives and I'm dead careful and anyway he's only topping whores.'

'Not no more, he ain't. Didn't you hear t' news this morning?'

'Has there been another one?' I asked quietly. 'I heard t' police sirens.'

Mother's neck vein glooped like a snake swallowing a rat. 'An innocent sixteen-year-old girl! Murdered only yards from her home!'

I opened the acne fridge-magnet door. So that's what all t' hoo-hah wor about. At least, I thought, they're giving this one some attention. There wor nowt much in t' fridge save an open pack of cheddar cheese slices. I wor ravenous, and needed a shower. I opened the breadbin and pulled out two slices of Mother's Pride.

'But Mum,' persisted Mand, 'it's only a couple evenings a week in a caf.'

'Mandy, darling, this latest one, she worn't no prostitute, she wor a young girl almost t' same age as you, and ...'

'I'm careful, Mum!'

'So is HE! Careful at hunting down his victims!'

'But we don't live anywhere near where it happened ... This ain't no prozzie area! It's not fair!'

Mandy's voice wor hard, full of need. I wor wondering what kind of caf it wor. Probably some steamed-up hole wi' dirty cream walls, red Formica tables and cappuccino machines that make that friggin' awful sucking sound. Fry-ups and liver and peas and steak-and-kidney pies under cellophane. The pop rounds wor chocful of 'em.

I dropped the two slices in t' toaster.

'I'll put it to Mitch,' Mother wor saying.

Mandy rolled her eyes. 'He'll say no! I know he will. I hate him, he says no to everything. In any case, he's never here, so he can't stop me. I don't care what any of you say, I'm doing it!'

She kicked her new shoulder bag, that wor parked on t' floor, sending it skating across t' kitchen. The toaster popped.

'That's enough! You're still too young. Maybe next year.'

'Next year, next year!' Mandy yelled. 'It's always next year! Rick has a job, so why can't I?'

Grinning, I held up my hands in protest. 'Don't look at me,' I said. 'Mitch got me that job, and he takes most of t' dosh off me every week for so-called upkeep. Sis, any chance of a bacon sarnie? Bit of pre-job training?'

She scowled. 'I hate you!' she spat. 'And you smell!'

I kipped dreamlessly for a couple of hour. I wor pulled from my slumber by a rapping sound coming from t' back of t' house. I lay awake for a while, idly massaging my balls, thinking of Tad and listening to this sound, trying to work out what it wor. My bedside alarm clock said two-thirty in t' afternoon. I rose and crossed the landing into t' bathroom, opened the window a smidgen and peered down.

On our dried-up patch of back lawn wor a large tomcat wi' a bird in its mouth. Downstairs below me, Mother wor drumming her fists on t' kitchen windowpane. Then she opened the window and screamed shrilly at the cat to go away. Which it did, just a few feet, wi' t' bird whole in its gob. It dropped the bird and looked about. The bird wor flapping a wing on t' ground. The cat toyed wi' it, releasing it then pouncing on it again, rolling it across the grass wi' its paws then taking it in its mouth again.

It's just a cat, I told mesen, acting out a cat's instincts. It don't know no better. I heard the window downstairs close, and moments after Mother appeared round the side of t' house. The cat, momentarily startled, froze and looked at her indignantly. She shouted again, waving her arms.

'Shoo! Go away!'

The cat stiffened onto its paws, its back arching. Then it dropped the bird and fled. The bird lay on t' grass, quivering in shock. Mother came back inside to get summat to pick it up with. No helping the poor bugger now, I thought. What wor she going to do wi' it? Bring it indoors and nurse it back to health? Better to knock it on t' head wi' a mallet or summat.

The coast clear, the cat returned, stalking rapidly across t' grass. It pounced, dragging the bird away. At a safe distance, it bit off its head. Mother screamed. The cat scarpered, leaving a headless carcass lying on t' lawn.

I'd awoken to a tilted world. The Murder of the Innocent One! So that's what all t' sirens had been about. By t' evening we wor on t' TV, radio, even t' friggin' foreign news. Leeds wor finally on t' map for summat other than friggin' footie.

In no time the city wor heaving wi' Southern friggin' journalists, shoving their fat-headed mics in t' faces of folk just going about their business, trampling through flowerbeds, knocking on doors. An innocent! Thousands of statements wor being taken, everyone wor being questioned about their whereabouts on t' night in question.

It wor dead weird, seeing streets on t' TV that I knew brick by brick. 2 Limeade, 3 Cokes, 1 tonic water, 1 orange squash. Geranium pots, blue door, dachshund, rasta man at number 23, gnomes in t' garden. I'd walked that street, pissed in that toilet block, sat on them swings in Reginald Street adventure playground that he'd dragged her across, her heels scoring into t' ground, and where a police line wor now crawling on their hands and knees, as if one of 'em had dropped a contact lens.

A black line slid down t' TV screen.

There wor even a twenty-four-hour free phone number where HIS wife, HIS girlfriend or HIS mother could ring and leave a recorded message. For surely, the police wor saying, some woman must be protecting HIM. In a week, seven days that would normally pass in a blink of routine, we wor being made to feel bewildered, angry, ashamed. Sucked in like fish into a vast trawler's net. Folk on t' round slaked their thirst on pop like every sup might be their last. On t' doorsteps, no one spoke about HIM. Or about t' murdered Innocent One. Not to us, the Corona pop men, busy on our rounds. Not to t' milk-float driver, nor his brother, as we all worked our way round t' back-to-backs in Harehills, Woodhouse, Chapeltown. Back kitchen door to back kitchen doorstep.

When t' time came, if it did, I would need an alibi.

Gordon.

For t' rest of t' week Tad clogged up my thoughts. I wor restless and distracted, unable to settle on one thing. I'd tried to get him to go to a punk gig wi' me, mentioning that The Vibrators would be playing Leeds Poly at the end of t' week. Tad snorted his derision. The Vibrators had originally signed to t' RAK record label, home of crap chart bands like Mud and Suzi Quatro and friggin' local heroes Smokie. Mother liked Smokie. Tad hated The Vibrators.

Sis wor still carping on about t' caf job. And all cos her schoolfriend Emily had been offered a job in one. Neither of them would stick it a week. As it had turned out, Emily's folks worn't letting her work at t' caf neither, so that settled the matter. I sneaked a peek at sis's diary and she wor whingeing on about hating us all, including me, and that she wor going to run away wi' Adam. What had I done, sis? I turned over t' page.

> Thursday: The biology teacher, Mrs Burton, kept all the fifth year girls back after class. She looked at us all like she was going to burst a blood vessel and shouted 'Who has been scrawling their name on the brand new desks? Alice Cooper, stand up now!'

Priceless, sis. Just priceless.

My next day off work I schlepped mesen over to Paradise Buildings on t' off-chance of catching Tad. I had my plan. I'd say I needed another haircut from Jeremy, which wor a truth of sorts. I wor done wi' my old high-street barber's, wi' its black-and-white photos of neatly shorn necks and perfect partings, squeaky chairs wi' gashes in t' red plastic, the smell of talc and rancid barber's breath as he breathed into your ear, 'How does sir want it?' then turned everyone out the friggin' same.

I buzzed the bell wires together and waited. I wor about to give up when t' door wor swung open by one of t' junkies. He scowled and said, 'Oh, it's you,' wi' a disappointed sneer. I followed him up the stairs.

'Are they at home?' I said as we reached the kitchen level.

'Who?'

'Gina, Jeremy, Tad.'

'Haven't seen 'em.'

The junkie wandered off into another room.

Left on my tod, I moseyed about. In t' sunlight filtering through t' old industrial windows dust motes danced on t' air. At one end I noticed for t' first time a wooden trapdoor in t' floor, and hanging above it a rusting industrial winch.

I took the stairs up another level and pushed through some grey fire doors that led onto a corridor of cell-like rooms. I had slept here that first night. Each room had a small, square window of reinforced wire-glass and a cast-iron radiator beneath. The first room had no door, and there was nowt in it 'cept for a pile of wood and a bicycle wheel. The next wor empty save some tins of paint. The door to t' next one along wor slightly ajar. Cautiously, I pushed it open. Inside wor a mattress on wooden pallets, an ashtray on a sisal mat, a dead plant on an old wooden chair and, blu-tacked to t' wall over t' bed, a few mag pics of big skies and some lush countryside.

'Looking for someone?'

I jerked round. Tad, shirtless, sockless, in trackie keks, had emerged from one of t' cell rooms further along. He wor eyeing me warily, curling his lower lip, as if he'd come upon a trespasser.

'Hey, Tad,' I said, taking a step toward him. He flinched as if a fly had skirted his face. 'Jeremy about? I wor hoping he could give me a haircut.'

'Is that right? Well, you've missed him. He's out, wi' Gina.'

'Pity.'

My eyes flitted over him: the tattoos, the appendix scar, the soft hairs on his forearms, like pale, single sheaves of wheat in t' glinting sun. He sensed me eyeing him, and crossed his arms over his chest. We wor standing a little apart, like there wor a chalk line between us that neither could cross. I looked down at his feet. His big toe wor precisely that – big – and it veered slightly away from t'other toes. Each wide foot wor muscular, meaty.

'I mean, I wor hoping, if Jeremy ...'

'I'm just on my way out.'

'Right. Well, maybe I'll come back some other time.'

Tad didn't answer. He returned to his cell room, reappearing moments later in a plain white T-shirt, washed-out drainpipes held up wi' red braces and blood-coloured DMs. Safely in his armour.

'Whose room's that?' I asked, trying to smother t' awkwardness wi' incidentals. Tad blinked then turned his head slowly toward t' room.

'That wor Julia's.'

'She's left?'

'No, mate. She overdosed. Jeremy found her dead in t' kitchen. Right fucking mess. Stew all over t' floor.'

An icy little creature scurried along my spine. Wi' his eyes still fixed on Julia's room, Tad said, 'Thank your stars you'd buggered off wi'out seeing it.' His voice cracked. 'I mean, we couldn't just leave her there, could we? Dead junkie on our hands? We'd have all been banged up in no time.'

I leant queasily against t' door jamb. An echo of t' cold stew pinged against t' back of my throat. I swallowed. 'So what happened? Didn't no one report it?'

'Oh yeah, it got reported. But first we moved her body to this empty council flat a mile away and dumped her there, poor cow. Scattered a few bits about t' place, left a needle between her fingers.' He shook his head in disbelief. 'I hate junkies. Complete losers. Tossers, every one. They put themsens there, didn't they? I mean, Julia could be all right at times, total posh bird, but all right when she worn't high.

127

When she wor off her face she could get utterly fucking paranoid. Funny, ain't it?'

'Funny?'

'Her dad's a magistrate.'

'Poor Julia,' I said, stupidly.

'Don't you go blabbing about this, or I'll knock you into next week. If t' cops find out, I'll say you wor part of it. Geddit?'

'As if I'd say owt.'

Tad slapped me roughly on t' back of my neck. 'Good. We understand each other then.' He squatted down to lace up the DMs. I thought of Julia, slumped lifelessly in t' kitchen armchair.

Tad said, 'If I had the time I'd shave your head.'

'I'd prefer someone like Jeremy. Someone qualified.'

Tad snorted. 'Qualified? Jeremy? He just says he is. Anyway, I've shorn a few sheep in my time.'

Unsettling images of Tad waving sheep shears reared up. 'Sheep?'

'I wor brought up on a farm. Up on t' moors over Huddersfield way.' He grinned, his wide, boyish smile softening up his face. 'Did you think I grew up on some scuzzy council estate? Is that what you thought? Bit of skinhead rough, eh? Your skin is a fucking sheep farmer's boy.'

All laced up, he bolted down t' stairs ahead of me, two, three steps at a time. I wanted to shout out that I didn't care what my skin wor, as long as he wor mine. We wor bound now by t' truth about Julia's death, bound in blood, gin, spunk, stew. So why did I feel like a man clinging to a fraying rope? I pursued Tad down t' stairs. He palmed the door onto t' road open. We tumbled out into t' bright of day. Tad started to run.

'Tad, stop!'

Down t' road, he stopped. But didn't turn round.

'Tell me, Tad!' I demanded, my frustrations flooding me. 'What's changed between last week and this? Are you going to say you wor too tanked to remember owt? Oh, come on, I worn't first, wor I? You knew what you wor doing all right. So why are you shutting me out?'

He didn't reply. Still he didn't turn to face me. I wor shouting at the back of his head from ten paces.

'Why do you live here? In this shithole wi' these scum junkies and fascists and – you said it – these washed-up losers? Eh? Why are you denying ...?'

'Go fuck yersen!' he yelled, still not turning round. Then he started walking fast, down t' centre white line of t' road, as if he wor trying to shake himsen from me. Two doddery Asians, turban heads wi' white, woven beards, dithered nervously on t' pavement between Tad and me.

'Didn't it mean owt?'

He stopped again, turning now on his boot heels and walking backwards.

'You wor just a fuck! A one-time nothing fuck! Forget it!'

I could hear t' sob in his voice. The old turban heads had stopped to stare. Tad turned and tore off down t' street like his life depended on it.

Wi' both hands I picked up a nearby dustbin and launched it into t' road, sending tins, rotting vegetable peelings and paper spilling out. The dustbin crunched onto t' tarmac then rolled briefly 'til t' handles stopped it. A sudden gust whisked up some food wrappers and newspaper pages. The bin lid rolled along on its end, like a loose wheel hub, 'til it too came to a stop. I stood there, breathing heavily, my chest tightening, watching Tad disappearing down t' road, becoming smaller and smaller 'til he vanished altogether.

Maureen Long
31/07/1977 (survived)

In t' Corona depot all t' talk wor of Maureen Long, the latest Ripper victim. There'd been a breakthrough! The police wor in a buoyant mood. She'd lived to tell t' tale. Except that there worn't much of t' tale she could recall, having been battered repeatedly over t' bonce and left for dead. A white car wi' a black roof. Friggin' police panda cars wor white wi' black roofs. But she'd survived. HE had slipped up. HE would soon be caught.

We drove t' Corona van past graffiti that read 'Hang the Ripper'.

Up in Chapeltown, Lourdes, along wi' a truckload of other prozzies, got arrested. 'What dey tink? Now mi got to work double to pay dem fines! And dey scare all duh punters away!'

Lourdes cackled as if it wor all too stupid not to laugh over. 'Some girls, dey goes to Sheffield,' she said. 'Poleece don't interfere so much, and it safer dere.'

She cackled again like it wor all t' funniest thing ever.

'They just want to look like they're doing summat,' Eric said once we wor back in t' van. 'Clear the streets. Like Lourdes said, they'll all just switch patch for a while ... head for Bradford or Sheffield ...'

'... or further than Sheffield.'

'Or further than Sheffield,' Eric echoed, sounding befuddled.

It seemed to me that the folk wi' least to laugh about laughed the most. The distance between t' prozzies and us gays didn't seem to be much greater than between two gate posts; if it worn't prozzies that some maniac wor killing it could just as easily be gay men, and the public reaction would be t' same – they got what wor coming to them. Thankfully, no one wor going about slicing up gay men.

On t' Friday following the attack on Maureen Long, as he wor tossing out the paypackets, Craner barked, 'Henceforth, no Corona crew will be allowed out on the road in just vests. T-shirts or shirts must be worn. You are to always wear your blue Corona coats. Head office diktat.'

The men murmured, shuffled their feet. Garthy piped up that it wor cos of all t' TV crews around. The company had to be seen to be keeping up an image. Craner told him that if he wanted his tuppence worth, he'd ask for it.

I looked about for Eric. Eric wor late, very late – must have overslept again. Craner kept catching my eye, I kept avoiding his. Neither my name nor Eric's wor chalked up on t' blackboard. Wi' t' office almost empty, Craner said, 'Richard, a word.'

Craner never called me Richard.

'Mr Craner?'

He scratched the nape of his neck, reset his glasses and looked like he wor readying himsen to fire me. Craner never needed much of a reason to get shot of anyone.

'I've had a call,' he said, then paused to make sure he had my attention.

Mitch, I wor thinking, Mitch has been sticking his oar in where he shouldn't, and now I'm getting my marching orders. I opened my gob to say summat, but Craner held up his palm.

'There's been a sudden bereavement. Eric Fawley's grand-dad. He wor watering his garden wi' washing-up slop, carrying full buckets of it in this heat. He wor found dead amongst his withering roses.'

Craner lit a ciggie while t' news bedded in. 'Dead amongst his withering roses'? Had he been at the poetry? He worn't done.

'He will be interred on Thursday.'

Interred? My stomach drained and my legs tingled blood-lessly. Eric would be off work for t' whole week, maybe longer.

'So, this morning,' Craner continued, 'I'll cover your usual round, and you'll be on Leek Street.'

'Not Leek Street?'

I didn't want Leek Street. Leek Street wor a friggin' massive city in t' sky over Hunslet way, a monolithic housing estate of rain-grey breezeblocks criss-crossed by aerial walk-ways. Worse, my driver would be morose Kev, who'd lost his right little finger in a die press so his tattoos spelt LOVE and HAT.

Not that you saw much of your driver on t' Leek Street Estate. At Leek Street you pulled a trolley along t' web of open walkways, while three, four, five storeys below, your driver moved the van around t' block entrances. Crates wor sent up and down t' stinking steel lifts by a process of shouts and signals and bangs on t' lift doors. And you kept losing sight of t' van and that four-fingered git of a driver. You spent half your time leaning over t' waist-high parapets, the ground below hurtling up to kiss your eyeballs, waiting for t' van's canary-yellow roof to reappear.

'Do I have to do Leek Street?'

Craner tossed the Leek Street round-book onto t' table.

Mitch finally got shot of t' old Cambridge van, and bought a Ford Corsair off some bearded bloke over in Heaton. Bit of a bargain, wor how he described it.

'Bloke wor desperate to get rid of it.'

Mitch's bargains usually worn't, and this one wor no different. But Mother wor happy, cos it wor a proper car and not a friggin' van wi' a dodgy exhaust. Mitch said he'd take me for an evening run in t' new car, show off what it could do.

We set out. The engine coughed and spluttered on t' steeper inclines as Mitch talked to it and coaxed it through t' gears. The interior had a sickly-sweet odour that wor masking summat more unpleasant. We drove around a few city roads, and then Mitch declared that it wor sounding so smooth we should take it on t' motorway for a bit.

We hit the motorway south. After thirty mile the Corsair rolled to a gentle halt on t' hard shoulder. We'd run out of petrol.

'Didn't you fill it up?'

'Gauge is buggered. I could've sworn it wor half-full.'

'Or half empty, more like. So what do we do now?'

'There's a petrol can in t' boot. I'll walk to t' petrol station.'

'But that could be miles.'

'Two mile. I saw t' sign a bit back.'

He got out of t' car, slammed the door. I watched him in t' rear-view mirror, petrol can in hand, head bowed slightly, trudging away.

I played around wi' t' radio dial. Radio 1 wor playing Elvis's 'Always on My Mind'. I turned the dial to Radio Luxembourg, but the reception wor fuzzy. They wor playing Elvis too, 'Way Down'. Back to Radio 1, and now it wor 'Heartbreak Hotel'. I scythed the dial through t' regional stations. Another Elvis song – 'Burning Love' – then another – 'The Wonder of You'. This wor friggin' ridiculous. I hated Elvis. I left it playing anyway.

For nearly two hours I waited in t' car for Mitch to return as the traffic juddered past, waiting and enduring one friggin' Elvis song after another. By t' time I finally spotted Mitch making his way back along t' hard shoulder, thin wisps of cloud wor turning a deepening mauve against a pinking upper sky. A star, or maybe a planet, I didn't know which, hung low over t' motorway embankment, twinkling fiercely. Mitch emptied the can of petrol into t' tank and got in t' car. He dangled the keys in his hand and looked at me.

'What?'

'Elvis is dead.'

The next morn Craner had us all assemble in his office.

'I thought that this morning we should have a few minutes' silence before you head out on your rounds. I know that Elvis meant a lot to many of you here, as he did to me, and that his passing is a great, great loss.'

He slid a cassette into a portable machine that wor parked on his desk. We shuffled our feet and kept our heads bowed while listening to a mangled 'In the Ghetto'. The man to my left wor snuffling. A single tear snaked down his rough cheek. He let it run.

Granted, the death of Elvis wor a bit sad for older folk, but then, old Elvis *had* been ballooning like someone locked in a pie factory, so maybe fate had played a kindly hand. But the third death, one month after Elvis's, fair tore me up. I'd never known what it wor like to lose someone who really meant summat to me 'til then. I wor fair sliced up about it. Marc Bolan, glittery lead singer of my childhood heroes, T. Rex (up 'til 1973's naff *Tanx* album), had been driven into a tree by his girlfriend. Why did she have to survive and not him? She wor just his friggin' backing singer.

I went down on my knees before t' record player, made a small shrine out of a T. Rex photo, some badges, an old concert ticket stub I'd bought in Leeds market and some half-wilted flowers I'd filched from t' neighbours' front garden.

Then I played the whole of *Electric Warrior* and *The Slider*, and genuflected. I didn't know if I should cross left to right or right to left, and if doing it wrong I wor cursing him to Satan, so I did it both ways to cover all t' bases.

'One day it will be my turn,' I murmured to t' makeshift shrine, 'to become famous and die, or to die and become famous. Fate will decide ...'

Even though Eric had been back at work a while, he wor still down in t' mouth cos his granddad wor kipping wi' t' worms. He sure milked it on t' round – all that sympathy from his doorstep women. He'd leave me in t' van while he wor shedding the odd tear or two wi' some housewife who'd answered the door in a see-through blouse or a loosely bunched bathrobe.

When I started to tell him how it felt losing Marc he cut me short sharpish, and told me to rebuild the load, cos all t' Tango lemon wor at the bottom under t' empties. Not that we shifted much Tango lemon.

We did some four-storey maisonettes and a couple of tower blocks before lunch. Eric said we didn't need to deliver to anyone above t' sixth floor, unless they wor regular orders of three or more bottles. 'Takes up too much time,' he said.

Over t' usual lunch of chip butties and curry sauce he told me that the worst of it worn't his granddad dying, but that his mum didn't even know.

'When she walks back into our lives,' he said, 'I'm the one who'll have to tell her, won't I?'

That's the trouble wi' families, I wor thinking. Either you're trying to find someone, or trying to lose someone. Pity you can't just build your family out of Lego bricks, and then if you don't like it, tear it down and build another one.

Jean Royle (also known as Jean Jordan)

01/10/1977

In t' months since I last saw Tad tearing down t' Sunbridge Road, Paradise Buildings had been cleared by bailiffs, and corrugated metal sheets had been nailed over t' doorways. Tad still popped up in my head like Mr Punch whenever I wor tugging mesen off.

I kept a lookout for him at the FK Club and in t' Mannville Arms, but he never showed. When I worn't in t' FK or t' Mannville, I hung around various gay watering holes, drinking away t' hours, feeling like all life wor happening at t'other end of a telescope from me.

Sometimes I headed over to Radclyffe Hall. Sometimes Camp David wor there, sometimes Fazel, or even Fizzy, but most times it wor just Terry. Whenever he answered the door he would inform me drily, 'There's no one home,' as if he himsen wor of interest to no one.

'Make yourself some tea,' he'd say, before leaving me alone in t' kitchen, waiting. I'd sit there, leafing through yesterday's papers and downing their tea and toast. If no one showed up, I'd leave.

Then one time I wor contemplating attacking the Radclyffe Hall washing up out of fart-furnishing boredom, when t' doorbell rang. I waited for Terry to get it, but when it rang again, and more persistently, I answered it mesen, expecting the leccy man or t' postman or some such person. Instead, I found Gordon.

'Rick! What a delightfully agreeable surprise.'

We whiled away an hour in Radclyffe Hall's scuzzy kitchen, drinking more friggin' tea, Gordon smoking his way through half a packet of ciggies, 'til it wor as plain as a pig's backside that no one else wor going to show their face that day. Gordon exhaled and looked at me soppily.

'You know, Rick, I don't own very much – the car of course, a sizeable collection of 78s, and an old gramophone that I've had since new. I'm not entirely sure what to do about the car, but I want you to know I intend to leave my entire collection of 78s and the gramophone to you.'

'Me? What for? Not about to peg it are you?'

'I certainly hope not. Mind you,' he continued, pausing to hack up a cough, 'I don't imagine these things help.'

'Don't talk daft, Gordon. Anyway, what have I done to be so deserving?'

I had absolutely no interest in his 78 collection. Mind you, they might be worth a bob or two. Mitch might know where to get a good price. Gordon leant back in his chair and puffed merrily.

'Addicted to the spin, my mother used to say. She was right. I can look at the grooves in a 78 and tell you which part is the orchestra, where the horns come in. All that, just by holding it to the light.'

'I'm impressed, Gordon.'

'Something about the patina, the ageing, the decay even, of a 78 that makes it so alluring. The beauty of shellac.' He leant toward me confidingly. 'You know what shellac is?'

'No idea.'

'It comes from the lac beetle. Hence shell and lac.'

'I didn't know that, Gordon, truly I didn't. So the death of t' 78 saved the lac beetle then?'

Gordon rocked back and laughed 'til he had a coughing fit, which he settled wi' a large slurp of lukewarm tea.

'Possibly so!'

He ground his ciggie into his saucer. 'I want the collection to go to a good home. I certainly don't want my sister to have it – she'd just sell the lot.'

'Gordon, please don't be soppy. I hate it when you're soppy.'

'My mind is made up. The collection is to be yours.'

I figured Gordon had a good ten year on t' mileage clock, so I cast off t' guff about t' 78 collection. It wor just Gordon being gooey.

It wor t' Saturday evening before bonfire night and we wor glued to t' telly, watching *The Generation Game*, when t' doorbell chimed. Mitch had recently fitted up a doorbell that played different tunes, so it plink-plonked gamely through 'Greensleeves'. A cartload more wor stashed in t' garage. Mitch said to me quietly that I wor to say nowt about t' boxes of door chimes, and that he wor going to sell them on to some bloke over Shipley way.

Mother rose from her armchair, chuntering on about some bloody woman wi' her charity envelopes wanting to bleed us dry. She reappeared moments later. 'Mitch, it's the police.'

Mitch uprighted himsen sharpish from his slovenly position and flattened his hair across his bald patch. The constables apologised for disturbing us during *The Generation Game*. They took off their helmets. Mother turned off t' telly, plunging the room into a funereal silence that wor punctured by some kids letting off fireworks up the street. Mitch coughed and invited the constables to sit.

One of them sat himsen on t' edge of t' sofa, t'other remained standing. Mother offered them tea, which they declined. Apparently they'd just had a cuppa across t' way, wi' t' Gudgeons at number 44.

'I hope she didn't use her cracked mugs,' Mother said wi' a queer little cackle. She fetched a plate of bikkies – 'Just in case you boys might be peckish.'

The seated constable, whose hair wor very black and curly and who had a small, neatly kept moustache, kneaded his forehead wi' his thumb, as if wearily mustering his energies. He cleared his throat and apologised again. 'We're making door-to-door inquiries concerning a murder.'

'Jean Royle?' Mother replied, as if she knew her personally.

He nodded.

'It wor all over t' papers. Changed his patch to Manchester, I see. Getting too hot for him, is it, on this side of t' Pennines?'

'We certainly hope so.'

Mitch stopped picking at his fingernails, and wor trying on his attentive face. Mother's shoulders relaxed. 'She worn't an innocent though, this one?'

The standing constable spoke. 'We have cause to believe that she may have been a working girl.'

The standing constable took a bikkie, which Mother clearly saw as a small victory of sorts.

The seated constable ploughed drily through some questions, like his tongue wor sticking to his mouth. He directed most of them at Mitch. He asked him about his job, where he worked, what he did, if he knew his friggin' blood group, what car he drove, how long he'd owned it. He then asked for his shoe size, and whether his job took him over Manchester way or up to Tyneside. Mitch answered all these questions plainly.

The constable then wanted to know exactly when Mitch had changed his car, then why and where. Mitch half-rose from his chair, offering to get the address in Heaton, but the constable told him that worn't necessary, as they had a lot to get through.

Then he looked at me, and asked me my age.

'Nearly eighteen,' I replied, grabbing a bikkie from off t' plate and ignoring Mother's frown.

I watched him scribbling. He had hairs sprouting from t' backs of his fingers. And two wayward single ones springing from his pronounced Adam's apple. I imagined him starkers.

'Anyone else reside at this address?'

Mitch coughed, clearing his throat. 'My daughter, Mandy. She's gone to t' cinema wi' her boyfriend to see ...' He looked at me for t' answer.

'*Exorcist II: The Heretic.*'

'Aye. That one.'

While t' seated constable questioned and scribbled, t'other one – the younger one wi' t' baby-faced cheeks – wor nosing about t' room. Naked, he would be less hairy than his mate, if slightly flabbier. He took a long gander at the collection of framed photos on t' windowsill. He picked up the one of me taken at the end of year four, looked at me now, smirked, then set it down again. I smirked back. Mother watched him, kneading her wedding ring. The seated constable turned to Mitch. I imagined both constables starkers. Wi' me in t' middle.

'Make sure your daughter gets home safely, Mr Thorpe. Where were you on the 1st of October? A Saturday.'

'Dunno,' said Mitch. 'That wor weeks ago.'

'Saturday the 1st,' Mother said slowly, as if ruminating. 'Wor Leeds playing at home or away, officer?'

'Away,' rosy-nosey constable replied cheerily. 'Against Chelsea. I got that weekend off.'

'2–1 to Leeds,' Mitch said, groping his way toward some common ground. 'Lorimer scored the second.' He found none.

'So, you remember that, but you don't remember what you were doing or where you wor on the 1st of October? In particular, that evening. I mean, did you stay in? Go out?'

Mitch scratched his nose a tad too much.

'We have to follow everything up, you understand.' The constable clicked his ballpoint on and off repeatedly. 'You know,' he sighed, 'you should see the piles of paperwork back at Millgarth station. So much paper, great stacks of reports and notes and jottings. Confessions from hysterical women who think their husband's a serial killer, or sad gits who want to confess that they're the murderer. This business has brought them all out of the woodwork. We've got hundreds of confessions, maybe thousands. They can't tell you one bloody thing about the murders. The women swear blind that their husbands or boyfriends were at or near the scene of the crime, or that they know for certain that the Ripper is the chap next door, or the name of the murderer came to them in a dream ...' He paused, wiped his eyes wi' his fore fingers. 'But it all has to be gone into. All has to be logged.' He clicked the ballpoint head. 'And on the 9th, the following Sunday?'

Mother replied wi' an arid little laugh that she could barely recall what she'd been doing yesterday, let alone on a date plucked from t' calendar. Then she added, 'I visit my mother twice a week. She's in a nursing home, you understand.'

The constable scribbled. He wanted to know if this wor on t' same days or evenings every week. Mother's neck vein made a single gloop.

'Not always, no.'

The constable scribbled again, then paused, his pen hovering over his notebook.

Mother said, 'Mitch, worn't that the day you went over to ...?'

'No,' said Mitch quickly. 'You're wrong there, Pam. That wor t' week before.'

He caught her eye. I saw it. A fleeting exchange at once understood. Mother offered up the plate of bikkies, which the seated constable declined, and a version of t' truth, which he accepted.

'We wor right here, at home as usual. My husband wor watching the telly ... and I ... I wor ... you know ... well, being a housewife.'

Finally done, the constables thanked us, excused themsens and left.

No sooner had the door closed than Mother's expression shifted like we'd switched TV channel. The neck vein wor glooping furiously now.

'So where wor you then?'

'When?'

'Don't give me that, Mitch. You know perfectly well when. The 1st of October. You certainly worn't at 'ome.'

'Went to Shipley. Like I said. Had summat to sort out.'

Mother's jaw tightened. She collected up the mugs and the plate of bikkies and went into t' kitchen.

Mitch harrumphed and switched on t' telly again, just as the *Generation Game* prizes – an electric blanket! – a slow cooker! – a giant cuddly toy! – a set of kitchen knives! – wor whizzing by on t' conveyor belt.

A brand-new five-pound note had been found in Jean Royle's handbag. The papers wor saying that this wor t' note that HE had most likely used to pay her wi'. It had been traced to t' Bingley/Cottingley areas of Yorkshire. It had most likely been part of a wage payout to a business in t' Bingley or Shipley area. Then came t' appeals on t' telly, t' radio and in t' papers. Wives, it wor suggested, should look in their husbands' wallets, or their paypackets. 'If it's from the same bundle of notes, then we'll know which firm the money was issued to.'

When I came home late that evening from t' FK Club I found the kitchen crockery all smashed up and Mother curled up in t' corner next to t' fridge, sobbing.

'Mum?' She turned her head slightly. 'What the heck ...?'

Glass and porcelain pieces scrunched beneath my boots as I crossed the floor and crouched beside her. 'Did he hurt you?'

She had her arm crooked about her head. Her shoulders convulsed. I wrapped my arms around her and stroked the crown of her head, waiting 'til she wor ready to talk about it. She swallowed hard, as if coming up for air.

'My fault,' she wor muttering. 'All my stupid fault.'

'How can this be your fault?'

She turned her face toward mine. Between hiccupping and gulping, speaking in a hoarse whisper, she unfolded the whole caboodle. How she'd been barneying wi' Mitch about that night in October, the 1st of t' month. How he'd stormed out and left his old jacket, wi' t' torn lining, draped across t' back of a kitchen chair. How she'd taken his wage packet from t' right pocket, a square, buff envelope containing several folded banknotes. How she'd scanned the serial numbers for a match wi' t' one she'd torn from t' *Evening Post* – AW51121565 – the number of t' note found in Jean Royle's handbag. The note HE had paid her wi' for sex.

'I didn't hear him coming back,' she sobbed. 'He'd forgotten his mitts.'

I moved aside a few of t' bigger broken pieces close to me. The red plastic draining board lying on its side, the upended kitchen chair, the hanging cupboard doors told their own story. So did the tell-tale puffiness that wor already rising beneath one eye. A sea of jagged shards glinted beneath t' kitchen tube light, where flies collected to die.

'Where's Mand?'

Mother shook her head. 'She wor here, but ... I dunno. I heard her leave, I think.'

'And Mitch?'

'Took the car.'

I bounded upstairs and flung open t' door to Mandy's room. Discarded clothes covered the bed. Shoes on t' floor. The dressing table had make-up powder skidmarks as if it had all been swept into a bag. I yanked open t' dressing-table top drawer. Empty. No smalls, and no diary.

When I came back downstairs Mother had got to her feet and wor leant against t' fridge door, staring down at the debris. Some of t' fridge magnets had been dislodged.

I found a dustpan and brush in t' cupboard and passed them to her.

'No,' she said wearily. 'Let him see it. Let him walk over it.'

I set the dustpan down. Mother lit a ciggie and sucked on it.

'At least he apologised.'

'Apologised?'

'To all this. To all t' things he smashed. He apologised to each and every one. Like he wor killing it.'

Mother went to bed, red-eyed and exhausted. When I looked in on her she wor fast asleep, her hair hanging across her cheek. Her clothes lay in a mess on t' floor beside t' bed. I went back downstairs and swept up all t' broken crockery and emptied the pieces into t' dustbin. I stood for a while wi' my back against t' sink, my fingers steepled against my nose.

Mitch didn't show 'til early morning. I heard him crash against t' hallway telephone table, swearing loudly, drunkenly climbing the stairs. I lay very still. I heard him in t' bathroom, the tap running for a long time. I heard t' toilet flush. I heard nowt more after that.

144

The next day Mitch wor hiding himsen away in t' garage. The side door to t' garage wor warped, and it scraped the floor as I shoved it open. Mitch didn't look up, but he knew I wor there. He wor nailing a piece of wood. He took a second nail that he wor holding between his lips and hammered it into t' plank too hard and for too long.

I spied his old bottle opener, dangling from t' workbench on a string. When I wor eight–nine–ten Mitch would make me sit wi' him in this garage, even though I wor itching to be elsewhere. We'd play a game of trying to flick beer-bottle tops into t' wastebin. I wor encouraged to try drinking beer. I pretended to like it, even though I didn't. I pretended to like it all – the beer, the footie banter, the darts we played hour after hour. He'd always beat me, cos I wor bored. At that age I wanted to please him. Tried my friggin' hardest.

'I want you to stop punishing her,' I said.

His fingers tightened around t' hammer handle. He wor building what looked like an oversized dolls' house.

'Excuse me, hammer, one moment,' Mitch said, then laid it down, aligning it alongside a spirit level.

'What are you making?'

He didn't answer. He picked out another nail from a tobacco tin. 'Craner tells me you're his best boy. That he's given you a pay rise.'

This rankled me. I worn't here to make idle talk about Craner. I said, 'I'm not giving you my keep no more. From now on I'm giving it straight to Mother.'

Mitch dropped the nail back into t' tin and fished out a better one.

'Tell me why, oh little nail? Why I work my socks off for her – for this family? Working all hours, putting food on t' table, paying bills. And what thanks do I get? A snooping missus who thinks I'm topping prozzies, and a selfish, good-for-nothing ...'

'She knows she did a wrong thing. Isn't that enough? Why,' I said, 'do you talk to things, when you won't talk to Mother?'

Mitch kissed the nail, then dropped it back into t' tin from an exaggerated height.

'I want you to apologise.' Mitch ignored me, so I put it another way. 'I want you to say sorry. To Mother.'

'You don't tell me what to do or when!' Mitch roared, his face distorting, his eyes bulging.

Summat snapped in me. I wor whipped up wi' anger. In two sharpish steps I wor upon him. I punched him hard on t' jawbone. Surprised, he lurched sideways, then stretched out an arm to try and balance himsen, sending an old jam jar of paintbrushes onto t' floor.

'What the fu ...'

I hit him again, harder. He raised his elbow to protect himsen, and my next blow caught his forearm. Before he could proper right himsen I kicked him hard in t' ribs and he keeled over. In his eye I saw t' look of a wounded animal being turned on by its own kind. A cold hate came over me, and I kicked him pitilessly in t' legs and the back. He curled up into a ball as I laid into his arms and shoulders. Wi' each punch or kick he exhaled sharply, like a reeling boxer. I caught sight of t' hammer within reach on t' workbench. I could have sworn that it wor calling out to me, 'Do it, do it, please, do it for me, do it for all of us,' and in an icy second my fingers wor gripped about that hammer handle as it fell again and again onto his skull, the hammer cackling like a mad clown as skull-bone crunched and splintered, as blood spurted and splattered, as dirty grey matter oozed along t' garage floor.

Only some deep throb at the back of my brain wouldn't let me. Mitch had raised his arms to protect his head as I pummelled at him wi' my bare fists 'til all t' fury that wor flooding me had ebbed away.

Breathing hard, I dropped my arms by my side. Mitch lay very still, as if waiting.

I left him lying there. In my head I could hear t' hammer sniggering.

It wor two days before Mandy returned home. She wor holed up in her room, playing records, pushing us all away 'til she wor ready to face t' world again.

She'd left her diary out on t' kitchen table, so I sneaked a peek, leafing through t' pages for summat juicy. Ah. Seems that sis and that Emma snuck off to Wigan for t' Northern Soul all-nighter. Christ, her friggin' biro scrawl wor difficult to read in places. Summat about taking uppers and downers and ... and ... cider ... cadging a ride home wi' three student blokes ... back of a VW Kombi ... Emma snogging ... older bloke ... blah, blah ... yeuchh! Sis being sick on t' motorway grass verge.

The little minx!

The next paypacket I gave half directly to Mother. Without a word she folded the one-pound notes into her purse. She said that now my hair wor shorter I needed to wash my neck better, as I wor leaving a black line on my shirt collars.

Marilyn Moore

14/12/1977 (survived)

Gina pitched up at the FK Club wi' Jeremy on his chain.

I spotted them before they clocked me. Lines of tables ran left and right up to t' stage edge. The National Front mob wor in one corner, outnumbered by t' Anti-Nazi League/Rock Against Racism crowd across t' room, all badged up wi' their allegiances, ignoring each other. For now.

DJ Clare knew t' score all right, coolly mixing Patti Smith and dub reggae wi' Clash, New York Dolls and X-Ray Spex. 'White Punks on Clare', someone had scrawled on t' toilet wall.

Back in t' main room, I watched Gina drifting between t' Nazi boys and no man's land, flashing her shark smile, giving off her provocative pout. When she did finally clock me, she lowered her chin and eyeballed me like a snake hypnotising its prey. Her shark smile gleamed.

Behind her wor Tad (so he wor here!), decked out in army-surplus keks and a white German army vest, staring off into t' middle distance. For t' merest moment it rankled wi' me, a nanosecond in which I saw mesen forcing Tad's head down t' FK Club toilets and then shafting him hard up the arse 'til he begged and thanked me over and over. But maybe that would show him I cared too much.

'Look who it isn't,' Gina sneered, tapping a badge on my lapel wi' her nail.

'Hello, Gina. What have you been up to?'

She pawed at me, stroking my Buzzcocks badge, then lingering thoughtfully over t' small pink triangle nestling alongside it, before letting her forefinger slide down my chest to my belt buckle.

'Well, let's see,' she said, holding up two fingers. The ends glistened wi' dried wallpaper paste. I fathomed that they hadn't been pasting up rolls of Laura Ashley.

'Posters. For the repatriation campaign. It's for the good of them and the country. The rest of us are still out there, but Tad said he wasn't going to miss Wayne County & the Electric Chairs for anything.'

I shook my head. 'Live and let live, I say.'

'Oh, we'd let them live, poppet, they just have to live somewhere else.'

'God, you people repulse me.'

'Ooooh, hear that, Tad? We repulse him. And I thought you wanted a threesome. A ménage à twa. Tad's up for it, aren't you?'

The corners of Tad's lips curled like burning paper.

Wayne County & the Electric Chairs ambled on. They had one good number – 'Fuck Off' – which they played twice. American drudge rock dressed up as punk. The crowd wor restless and the atmosphere wor tense. The gig ended shambolically. I pushed my way down t' corridor toward t' exit, shuffling along next to a guy wi' a shedload of Rock Against Racism badges covering his striped jersey.

I started the long trudge home. It didn't take long before I spotted their handiwork. Three in a row on t' end wall of a terraced house. The posters still rippled wi' darker patches of wet glue. The lazy buggers must have put them up all around t' Chapeltown streets near t' FK Club.

Taking hold of t' top corners of t' first poster I yanked hard, sliding my fingers down t' edges. At first the pain wor indefinable, as if I'd grazed my knuckles against t' brick. But when I saw t' dark blood, waves of pain flooded my fingers. I cried out and shoved my hands under my armpits and doubled over. I heard running footsteps behind me, heard my name being shouted. Tad.

'You idiot! Oh fuck, oh Christ! You fucking idiot! Are you hurt? Jeez, you're bleeding.'

Dark rivulets scurried from shredded fingers.

'Didn't no one ever tell you they put razors behind t' poster edges? Didn't you know that? I thought you knew. I'm sorry. Jeez, I'm fucking sorry. Here, show me your hands. We need to get you to a hospital. You'll need to get that stitched. Oh, Christ, this is my fault, all my fault. I should have said summat. But I didn't think you wor that gormless.'

Tad walked wi' me t' mile or so to t' A & E at Leeds General Infirmary. He said sorry so often I told him to shut the fuck up. He wor nigh-on blubbing.

In t' waiting room blood droplets spilled onto t' floor through t' snot rag he'd given me to wrap around my fingers.

'Show me,' he said.

I unfolded one hand. Blood oozed. He bent forward to kiss my fingertips. I snatched my hand away.

'Did you put them razors there?'

He shook his head in denial.

'Look at me, you ball of shite! Did you?'

'No, not me. Scout's honour. Not me.'

Tad's face puckered like a kid who'd just kicked a ball through a window. He fidgeted and paced around while t' waiting time stretched. A copy of yesterday's evening paper lay on t' side table wi' a load of shite magazines. Tad picked up the paper. HE had struck again. Another prozzie had been attacked the previous night in Chapeltown. Tad stared at the headline then laid the paper back face-down.

From behind a cubicle curtain I could hear someone groaning and vomiting. The raw stench of vomit drifted like a toxic chemical through t' waiting room.

After an age, I wor called into a cubicle. A nurse pitched up and asked me some questions about 'all that punk stuff', and banged on about a tetanus injection. The fore-fingers of both my hands wor ripped, so wor t' second finger of my left and the thumb of my right. She stitched up the worst gashes, and cracked a joke about cross stitching that she'd probably told a billion times before. She said that I wor lucky, there didn't seem to be any grit in t' wounds. The stitches done, I wor cleaned and bandaged up and given some antiseptic ointment. My fingers and right thumb wor taped together to prevent the cuts reopening. When I emerged from t' cubicle I found that Tad had buggered off.

I walked home, cos I couldn't pull t' change for t' night bus out of my pocket. Rain spat in my face. My hands throbbed like they wor beacons. I couldn't fish out my house keys neither, so I leant against t' bell – 'Greensleeves', 'English Country Garden', 'Frère Jacques' – before t' hallway light came on and Mitch's form appeared behind t' frosted glass, like a man underwater.

'Sorry. Forgot my key,' I said, keeping my hands hidden. In his half-awake, morose state Mitch swore at me, but didn't say owt more.

In my room I managed to wriggle out of my jacket and lever off each boot using t' other foot. I needed a piss, but undoing my fly buttons wor difficult and painful. It wor like pissing wi' oven gloves on, so I pissed free-handed. My piss sprinkled over Mother's new salmon-pink toilet mat, the salmon-pink toilet-brush cosy, the salmon-pink toilet-seat cover and the floor. I crawled into bed, curled up into t' foetal position wi' my hands between my knees, and lay there, the ebb and flow of pain rocking me into an exhausting, half-wakeful slumber.

The rest of t' week I wor off work. I couldn't carry any bottles or count change. The nurse had said the stitches would just fall out, and that I shouldn't pick at them. Mother fussed about. Mitch told me I wor a right fucking idiot.

Even holding a fork or turning a doorknob or tap wor tricky. Washing mesen, cleaning my teeth or tugging mesen off were impossible tasks, so I gave up on all three, although I did slip out of t' house and find some oldish bloke in a park cottage who wor willing to give me a blowjob. It wor a brilliant blowjob, though I had to close my eyes to shut him out. Afterward the bloke kept saying, 'Thank you, thank you,' in a pathetic whisper. I told him to fuck off. Then he took his teeth out of his side jacket pocket and slid them back in his gob.

On seeing my bound-up fingers the Gay Lib crowd huddled around me, showing syrupy concern. Had I fallen on broken glass, cut mesen washing up, cut mesen at work? I put these misapprehensions right and told them about t' National Front posters wi' t' razor blades behind. I kept working over t' story, milking every detail 'til it turned into summat gleaming that I no longer recognised. I wor t' hero of t' hour.

Another friggin' downer wor not being able to hold a snooker cue. In any case, the women had stopped coming to Gay Lib meetings. Lorna had joined some breakaway group called the Revolutionary Feminists. Maybe they had better snooker players. Or had bought an island. As it happened, I wor becoming less of an onlooker from t' margins; sometimes my voice got heard. What's more, I worn't even t' runt any more. This seventeen-year-old had pitched up – cocky lad wi' long blond curls and a voice like marshmallow.

Gordon looked out of sorts. He wor standing a little apart, almost ghostly through his own wreathing smoke, waiting, I assumed, 'til t' interest in me had thinned and he had me to himsen.

'Looks like you've been through the wars, my boy.'

'I'm not your boy.'

The ciggie end wobbled.

'It's just a turn of phrase.'

He rooted around in his pockets, as if summat wor trapped there. 'No, Rick, you are right,' he went on, 'you are right. You are not my boy. I shouldn't call you that.'

I couldn't fathom why he wor so upset. He played wi' his tie end.

I said, 'Don't get me wrong. I do appreciate you doing stuff for me and playing the chauffeur and us having a pint ... It's just that, well ... Why, Gordon? Why me? You haven't made one pass at me.'

Gordon exhaled. 'I simply enjoy your company. What else should a man like me expect? Isn't that reason enough?'

It didn't seem like reason enough to me.

The nursing home called to say that Gran had had a stroke. It had left her wi' slurred speech, as one side of her face wor paralysed. It also left her incontinent.

Mother dealt wi' this news by vacuuming. She vacuumed the landing and then t' bathroom carpet, whipping the flex along behind her. Seemed she vacuumed everything three times. When she'd done t' hall she changed the attachment and sucked up every last microbe of dust on t' stairs, bashing the attachment end into t' corners. Finally she stamped on t' switch and the vacuum cleaner died wi' a decapitated howl.

Now that Gran wor rattling St Peter's gates I wor feeling a bit remorseful, cos I'd only been to see her the once. So I said to Mother that I'd go wi' her on her next visit. Mother said there'd be no point, since Gran hardly recognised anyone. She just slumped in her chair or slept, drugged up on t' pills they ground into her food or whatever they did so she didn't keep wandering off. When she wor awake she chuntered on about strangers from way back or folk long dead.

Mother unplugged the vacuum cleaner and wound up the flex. 'Whatever world your gran's living in, we're not part of it. She just blathers on about Frank and someone else. The nurses say nice things, but then they're paid to, aren't they?'

'This might sound daft, but wor Granddad having an affair?'

Mother swished a duster over some picture frames on t' hallway windowledge.

'Well, I can't say it didn't cross my mind. Him always being out of t' house. But I think that wor just his way. And I think she made him an unwelcome guest in his own home, always badgering him for treading dirt in, smoking and being so untidy, so it worn't as if he needed much excuse to be elsewhere. But as for another woman – I don't think he could be bothered. And if there wor another woman, he would have been out on his ear if your gran had got wind of it.'

She flapped the duster, releasing trillions of dust motes.

'He wor a long-suffering, easy-going soul, wor your grand-dad. Had to be to deal wi' all her bitterness.'

'What did Gran have to be so bitter about?'

Mother clicked her tongue. 'Do you know what your gran used to say to me? "Nowt good will come of you," that's what she kept saying, and if you hear summat like that often enough you end up believing it. What I don't believe – and I can say this now you're as good as grown – is that she got the life she wanted. Not from Frank. He hardly ever took her out. All right, sometimes he took her for a run-out in t' car, or dropped her off in town, but most times she wor stuck in that dreary little house while he wor off gallivanting wi' his mates. It wor a bad marriage, but they just got on wi' it. Lived their separate lives. You did in those days. I always got the idea that they never gelled in t' bedroom department, if you get my drift. Of course she never said owt, but as I got older I could sense it.'

I reddened at the image that popped up in my head of my grandfolk having sex. Fazel had said that wor t' reason straights find homosexuals disgusting. The very word homosexual triggers imaginings of us having sex.

Mother said, 'Don't you ever go repeating that.'

I promised I wouldn't. Who would I repeat it to anyway?

I wor flabbered to see how much Gran had gone downhill. Her head wor lolling on her chest, like her neck bones wouldn't hold it up. She wor drooling. Mother wiped away t' drool from her chin and dabbed her cardie, then gently cupped her hands beneath her chin and cocked her head up.

'Hello, Mum. Look who I've brought along today. Rick. You know Rick. Your grandson.'

Mother tilted Gran's head toward me. She gave out an anguished cry, as if I frightened her somehow.

'She don't know who I am.'

'Perhaps if you wore some normal clothes she would. That scarecrow hair! Makes me ashamed to be seen out wi' you.'

We offered Gran some tea in a plastic mug wi' a child's spout. Her lips parted slightly, crookedly as one side of her face wor frozen, then closed again.

'Doesn't Richard look a sight, eh? Dyed his hair all black and stuck it up wi' my lacquer, and he's got these little cross earrings ... see?'

'Mother! She ain't registering.'

'You don't know that, Rick. Sometimes I'm sure she can hear me. Mum, don't you want your tea?'

Gran drooled some more, mumbled summat. Mother ploughed on.

'Mandy's got a job. Just for Christmas. She's working in Schofield's. We're hoping they'll like her and take her on permanently. She's in women's clothing. Tops mostly. You like Schofield's, don't you? You always did enjoy a cuppa and a desecrated coconut slice in their café – do you remember?'

'Desiccated.'

Mother shot me a don't-you-get-smart-wi'-me look. We wor wasting our time here. We could be Morecambe and Wise for all it mattered.

Mother said, 'This is the worst I've seen her. Not three week gone she wor better than this. Makes you wonder what they give her.'

'Aye. Well, she sure ain't no trouble.'

As we left, I let Mother go on ahead through t' double swing doors and out into t' grounds. I saw her umbrella go up as plops of rain began to darken the gravel drive. The girl in t' foyer office wor there, wi' Bobby. I walked in without knocking.

'What do you give her?'

The girl smiled sweetly, nervously, and tucked her hair behind her ear. 'What's with your hands?'

'It's nowt. What do you give her?'

'I don't give anyone anything, but if you mean the nurses and doctors, they do give the patients a few sedatives. To calm them down. When people like her, I mean your gran, well, sometimes they get confused, over-anxious or aggressive. We don't have the staff to ...' She trailed off and grimaced tightly.

'Mmm. Nnnmmm. Hnnnn,' Bobby wor going. She reached forward and adjusted his mouth-stick, then flipped over t' page of his book for him and wiped his mouth. She wor done wi' me, and I wi' her. Bobby wor looking directly at me wi' wide, sad eyes and rocking his chair like he wor trying to tip it over. 'Hnnnn. Hnnnn. Mmmmmm.'

Just before Christmas I went back to work. Sales went ape. Worse, folk kept inviting us in for Christmas toasts – vodka and some chewy bikkie wi' t' Ukrainians or t' Poles, rum and Coke wi' t' West Indians, tots of whiskey wi' t' Irish. It wor nearly 10 p.m. before we finished up and the van wor dry. Eric and I wor both on t' wrong side of sober. When we tried cashing up our fingertips wor too cold and we kept losing count. So we took a tenner each for tips, and Eric upended the rest into a carrier bag and staggered off into t' night, saying he'd come back for t' van in t' morning.

Wi' my Christmas bonus I bought:

The Only Ones – 'Lovers of Today'
Dead Boys – 'Sonic Reducer'
The Rezillos – '(My Baby Does) Good Sculptures'
Buzzcocks – 'Orgasm Addict'
Penetration – 'Don't Dictate'

I played them all over and over at full volume 'til Mitch wor yelling from t' foot of t' stairs to 'Turn down that fuckin' caterwauling!'

I formed my fingers into a pistol and fired through t' floor. Pow! Pow! Silencer off.

Yvonne Pearson

21/01/1978

Mitch went to see a man about a dog. The dog wor a three-year-old Alsatian called Max. Mitch said that some mate of his and his family had been moved into a new council flat, which meant they had to give t' dog up cos pets worn't allowed. Likely story. Whenever Mitch said 'some mate' and had a long story attached to it, you knew he wor fibbing. The dog barked the whole friggin' time and crashed into t' furniture. Mother wor bloody livid about it.

After t' Christmas spree, January Corona sales had been a stone-cold morning after. We could take our time, take a proper hour for lunch in a warm caf serving chips wi' curry sauce, then a half-hour unthawing on Lourdes' horse-piss tea, and still be done by 6 p.m. It wor quiet for Lourdes too: the weather wor bitter, the punters broke, and the few that wor desperate enough had been scared off by t' police presence.

'Means mi has to take risk,' Lourdes said. 'Mis no like takin' risk, stayin' out late, not bein' choosy. Gotta eat, gotta pay dem solicitin' fines, but yous sees it – duh place is crawlin' wi' poleece.'

Her mirthless cackle died like a siren winding down. Eric said, 'My girlfriend, Karen, she's expecting.'

Lourdes' eyelids flickered. 'You's gonna do duh right ting, ain't you, Eric?'

'Spring wedding.'

Eric, married at twenty-three wi' a sprog on t' way. He didn't sound too sold on it. I guessed it wouldn't be long after t' wedding before Eric wor slipping that ring into his nylon Corona coat pocket and getting up to his usual antics.

Eric said, 'Well, we wor going to wait ... but I guess it's been decided for us.' He scratched his right sideburn like he had eczema. 'Can you believe she wor going to have an abortion? Go through wi' it, the whole shebang, and not a word to me. Me! The dad! Told her mother, told her sister, told her best friend, but did she think to tell me? Did she ask me what I want?'

'And what's dat, hmm?' said Lourdes, her tone softening, like summat wor melting on her tongue.

'Well, I want to keep it.'

'Men always want to keep it, honey. Dey just don't want to raise it.'

'I'll make sure she comes round to t' idea. I'm already on t' council house waiting list, and maybe I'll have to find a better-paid job, and Karen might have to do some hairdressing from home, but we'll cope. I told her we'd cope. But we talk and talk and it all gets tangled in knots. She says it's for her to decide, cos she's carrying it. But it's all I've got now.' He stopped pacing. 'We'll cope. I told her we'll cope.'

We needed to get on. I set down my mug of horse piss and I threw a pleading glance at Lourdes. Lourdes read me and stood up. 'You's got customers waiting. Maybe I's gat dem too.'

Eric slung the money satchel over his shoulder.

'Come to t' wedding, Lourdes. Bring people. The more the merrier.'

Lourdes laughed like an unhappy child.

'Me? Lourdes? Come to your wedding? What'd yer new wife think o' dat?'

* * *

Mother wor watching *The Good Old Days* on t' telly. *The Good Old Days* wor broadcast from Leeds City Varieties theatre on t' Headrow. It wor a recreation for TV of an old music hall, wi' singalongs, circus acts and saucy comedians. The audience wor all decked up in hired costumes from t' period and a frothy compere introduced each act as 'The fantabulosa, the phantasmagorical ...', the audience oooohing and aaahing 'til t' compere smashed down his gavel and the applause thundered out. Mother loved it.

A Houdini circus act came on. A man in a white suit wi' a leggy blonde assistant in a shimmery get-up. The man lifted chains and padlocks from a box and showily bound and chained his toothily smiling accomplice. She stepped daintily into t' open suitcase and the man put his hand on t' top of her head and pushed her down. He locked and chained the case, and made a show of rattling the outsized padlocks and pretending to swallow a giant key. The audience oooohed. Drums rolled. '10–9–8–7 ...!' the audience shouted down t' seconds in raucous, shambolic unison. Mother wor chewing on t' end of a biro. We knew it wor an act, the young assistant would escape without question, but how, Mother said aloud, did the poor soul cope in t' meantime wi' being cooped up in such a confined space? Did she not feel like it wor waking up in your coffin? Wor she ever afraid that she wouldn't escape? Would he let her out if she banged on t' underside of t' lid?'

'It's just an act,' I said. 'She's faking it.'

Sure enough, as the dying seconds wor counted down t' case locks began to rattle, then on t' count of one the top burst open, and there wor t' magician's assistant, dressed in a different shimmery number, arms spread wide, smile glued on, as if she'd just emerged from a fitting room. The audience whooped and cheered and applauded riotously. Mother pulled her handkerchief from her sleeve and blew on it hard.

The main report on t' 9 o' clock news that followed wor about HIM. Then t' scene switched to a reporter, clutching his tulip-headed mic. We recognised the street behind him. He wor standing next to a newspaper billboard in red letters that reminded me of Hammer horror film posters:

HAVE YOU ANY INFORMATION
ON THE RIPPER MURDERS?
RING LEEDS
36168 OR 36149

Mother said she'd make us both tea, and went into t' kitchen to fill t' kettle.

Blandford Gardens wor up for sale. And empty. The net curtains and velvet drapes had been taken down. I pressed my face to t' window, staring in, reconstructing the room in my mind – the settee beneath t' mountain, the rug before it, the Turkish table wi' t' orange telephone on it, the books on t' bare shelves. On t' far wall, across t' empty room, I could make out the shadow of t' Matterhorn.

Further along t' street some curtains flurried and a neighbour appeared, eyeing me as if I wor looking to brick the window. I walked away. When I glanced back from t' end of t' street, she still had me fixed in her sights.

I ducked into t' Fenton and found Dora parked on her bar stool, wearing a short, gaudy green dress and no stockings, so that she showed off her varicose veins. She told me Jim had gone in a hurry.

'Trouble wi' some young'un,' she said. 'Some ungrateful, spiteful little tyke ...'

'Did he leave you an address?'

She laughed emptily. 'No, luv, he did not. Why would he?'

I made to place my hand over hers, but she pulled it quickly away.

'Everybody leaves,' she sniffed. 'Either they die or they leave. My son left. Can you believe that? Left his mother one day nigh on twenty year ago, and I haven't heard owt from him since. Not a peep.'

'I didn't know you had a son, Dora.'

'Hmphhh. For all it matters, luv, I might as well not have.'

The dolls' house Mitch had been building in t' garage wor a kennel. A cartoon Scooby-Doo kennel wi' red planks and a sloping green roof. So he'd planned the dog all along.

The dog didn't take none to his new home. We looked on while Mitch ordered, coaxed, threatened, shouted, even went down on his knees and pleaded, which just befuddled it into licking Mitch's nose. When Mitch tried to drag it into t' kennel it lay down, dug its paws into t' ground and stubbornly refused to go near it.

Dog 1, Household 0.

So Mitch tied the dog to t' washing-line post by t' kennel's entrance. The first two nights the dog whimpered and barked all friggin' night to be let back in. It wouldn't go in t' kennel, not even for a trail of bikkies. No one got a wink of sleep. On t' second night Mother got up, effing on about t' ruddy dog. She let it in, laid a blanket down on t' kitchen floor. It whimpered for a while, its nose pressed against t' bottom of t' kitchen door, but eventually the whimpers stopped. Next day Mother bought a basket, a dog blanket and a rubber bone.

Dog 2, Household 0.

Mitch went into a lovey-dovey, baby-talk phase. 'Here Maxy, luvverly Max, who's a good boy then? Yes, you are, yes you are,' slobbering into t' dog's chops, smothering the poor mutt one moment then ordering it about like some sergeant major.

'Sit, Max! Stay! Good boy! Who's a good boy then? Who is? Maxie, Maxie Maxie is a good boy, aren't you? Aren't you? No! Sit! Max! Sit!'

Max sat. Alert, twitching to be off again. No sooner had Mitch taken his eye off him than he jumped up, barking wildly.

Dog 3, Household 0.

'Sit! Sit, Max! Good boy. Who's a good boy then?'

Noses rubbed again. Wet dog nose against runny human one. More barking, then jumping up for a dog bikkie. The whole spectacle wor making me squirm.

'Next time I want summat from you,' I said, 'I'll bark for it.'

After a week the dog began to settle, and Mitch took to taking it wi' him in his lorry.

'Looks like I'm a dog widow,' Mother said.

I lay on my bed, hands behind my head, listening to my records. Life could be summed up as:

1 Matterhorn Man skedaddled.
2 No Tad.
3 Foul, dark winter.
4 The Sex Pistols split. All Nancy Spungen's fault for leading fuckable Sid by t' nose.
5 Stupid dog.

Helen Rytka

31/01/1978

The Leeds gay scene wor nowt to write home about: the New Penny of course, a couple of back bars in straight pubs, Charley's – a skuzzy nightclub wi' fake wood-panel walls and thin red carpeting that stuck to t' soles of your shoes – and a monthly Gay Lib disco at the Guildford Hotel. The Bradford scene wor even more pitiful.

All t' buzz wor about some new club over Huddersfield way called the Gemini which wor being touted as the Studio 54 of t' North. Wherever t' Studio 54 of t' South wor I had no notion. In London, I supposed.

I took a weekday evening train to Huddersfield. Beyond my own mooning reflection in t' train window I could see t' yellow lights of a snaking road, the squishy red of tail lights moving along it, the blistering white lights of t' industrial estates or nearby towns. The train rattled on bleakly, causing me to nod off 'til I wor jolted awake by t' screeching of t' brakes. Friggin' Huddersfield.

Once I wor off t' train, the wet winter night air slapped me to my senses. I scurried along, head down against t' driving rain, passing a gaggle of goths huddled about a burger van, on past the shuttered shops, the blaring pubs and dark side ginnels, 'til I came out on a main road.

I'd come full circle. The railway station wor directly behind me. To my right, a roundabout and a straggle of terraced houses dipped away toward t' dual carriageway.

Somewhere here, under my very nose, wor t' Gemini club. But where, for Christ's sake? I spotted a couple of baldy men in leather jackets heading for an unlit warehouse building across t' street. They approached an unmarked door. One of them pressed a small bell. Then t' door opened and they stepped into a warm block of light.

I hurried across. This had to be it, although there wor no sign saying so. I pressed the bell, and moments later the spyhole winked. I wor left waiting much longer than t'other men. I glanced nervously about. It crossed my mind that maybe the door wouldn't open, that for me it would stay shut. But then it opened. The doorman gave me t' once-over, scanning up and down t' road as he did so.

I'd found it. The Studio 54 of t' North.

The ground-floor reception wor all red and gold. A wine-coloured carpet and damask walls decorated wi' gold-sprayed plaster-cast cherubs. More red and gold in t' cloakroom. I made my way up a very narrow, straight stairway that opened up onto t' club proper on t' first floor.

I wor way too early. Emerging at the top of t' stairs wor like walking in on a cancelled reception. It wor t' biggest and poshest club I'd ever clapped eyes on. I couldn't imagine how they wor going to fill it on a midweek night. To t' left there wor a sleek long bar, to t' right an L-shaped dancefloor that led through to a restaurant area. A glitterball rotated over t' dancefloor, refracting the strobelight beams onto t' floor-to-ceiling mirrors. The disco music porp-porped as one solitary soul in white-bummed flares (Y-front panty-line visible) pranced and twirled, dancing wi' his mirrored sen, while t' raised dancefloor flashed light squares of red, blue and yellow.

I bought mesen a lager and lime and supped it slowly, watching from my bar stool as the place slowly filled up.

Boney M's 'Daddy Cool' came on, causing a minor rush for t' dancefloor, and the twirling dancer was swallowed up in a sea of flaying arms and bobbing heads. I remained on my bar stool, supping my pint, watching the dancefloor dramas being played out.

I emptied the dregs and circled the dancefloor twice, cut into t' bogs for a leak, where a lean man in jeans, vest and leather US police cap flashed his semi stiffy at me. Like I wor that easy. I passed up his firm offer, returned to t' bar stool and ordered mesen another pint. I caught my image in t' smoked-glass bar mirrors slumping like a hunched chimp so I straightened up. Then I felt two hands placed over my eyes.

'Guess!'

No guessing wor needed. The voice, the hands. 'Tad!' I shook mesen loose and turned round on t' stool. 'What the heck?'

He wor smirking at me wi' skew-jawed wonder. His hair had grown to a sandy stubble. Gone wor t' drainpipes wi' t' thin red braces; he wor in flared black jeans and a plain white T-shirt. No rings, no chains, just the one stud in his left ear. He had a small white plaster on his cheekbone where he'd nicked himsen shaving.

'You are kidding me.'

'It's my local. What's your excuse?'

'Boredom or desperation. Take your pick.'

He laughed. If he wor embarrassed at finding me here, he didn't show it. I kept looking down at t' floor, then looking up at him and grinning like a mad'un.

'What?'

'What? You know friggin' what, you shit. While I wor having my fingers sewn up you scarpered.'

'Aye. Well. It wor just bad timing.'

I worn't going to argue. Tad wor t' last person on earth I thought I'd bump into in this place. He bought me a pint, and a vodka and tonic for himsen. It didn't take long for t' talk to turn to Paradise Buildings, to Gina, Jeremy and Julia and the rest of t' junkies. Tad said that after Julia had overdosed and the bailiffs had cleared out the place he'd thought it best to lie low awhile, so he'd scuttled back to his parents' farm up on t' moors above Huddersfield. He spoke wi' a strained urgency, as if it wor important that I understood. All t' time he wor blathering his fingers stroked my forearm or my knee.

Tad said, 'You know about t' Fenton?'

'The Fenton? What about it?'

'Believe me, I didn't agree wi' it. Smashing it up like that.'

I jerked my head. 'When wor this?'

'About a week back. I thought you would have heard. It wor in t' paper – on t' local news. A load of NF went in and starting chucking chairs about and glassing folk. I didn't want no part of it. I had a big falling-out wi' Gina over it.'

'Gina?'

'She started the whole thing. Got about twenty of them together. This poor old girl ended up needing ten stitches in her face and neck.'

'Dora!' I could feel my cheeks pounding, as if someone had slapped me.

'You know her?'

'If it's who I think it is, yes, I know her. Jeez, Tad, couldn't you have warned anyone? Not the cops, but you could have let the pub know or summat.'

'The NF would have known it wor me. They would have gone for me. They still might. I'm a marked man now. A traitor for refusing to take part. It's not that I disagree wi' what they're all about. But smashing people's faces in ain't going to win 'em any friends. And wi' all t' Pakis in Huddersfield and Dewsbury, my dad says ...'

'What about gay Asians, then? I mean, there are a few in here tonight.'

'Dunno. I dunno what I feel about that. Don't bother me none. The ones that are here can stay. I just don't want any more coming in, destroying our culture ...'

'Wi' their curry houses? Which you like.'

'You can think what you want. I don't feel like a hypocrite. Christ, if it comes to hypocrites, the NF's full of 'em. Rumour has it some of t' NF top dogs are as gay as they come.'

'You're kidding me.'

'Wish I wor. If owt, they're t' worst, cos they've got more to hide.'

He burrowed his head into my neck, and I kneaded his bristly hair. It felt nice, like a soft boot brush. He straightened himsen up and pulled me off t' bar stool.

'Let's dance.'

'To this?'

This being Thelma Houston's 'Don't Leave Me This Way'.

'Yeah. To this.'

By t' time we left the club it wor sleeting outside and the wind wor whipping round corners and rattling the lampposts. Tad had use of his mum's mustard-yellow Austin Allegro. We drove out of t' town and up into t' wall of night, climbing onto t' moors, the headlights scanning verges left and right as the single track twisted through t' inky blackness. We juddered over a cattle-grid and the road dipped sharply, then suddenly we turned onto an unmade track.

A farm loomed into view, the headlights arcing across one end and the side of a shippen as we pulled into t' farmyard, setting the sheep dogs off into frantic barking. I caught a strong whiff of chicken droppings and manure. The farmhouse itsen had a long, low roof and small, deep-set windows, so it seemed to be cowering from t' elements. Apart from a solitary light from an upstairs window, all wor pitch dark. Up here you could see all t' stars.

Tad killed the engine. An outhouse door, not properly tied, could be heard banging. Tad leaned over to me and we snogged. The upstairs light went out.

'Mother,' Tad said. 'She always stays up 'til I get home, then goes to bed. Pretends she doesn't, but she does. She won't worry us.'

'How much do they know?'

In t' shippen, the dogs wor still barking brainlessly.

'They know what they need to. I do what I want, and there's nowt they can say about it. Course, I can't say they'd be too chuffed to find you here. Dad says I don't get this place 'til I marry and breed some offspring. Like I'm a prize bull. Says if I don't he'll cut me out of t' will. I'm only back here for a while 'til things blow over. I don't want to inherit this fucking dump anyway.'

The house creaked like old joints as I trailed Tad through low ceilinged, darkened rooms full of heavy furniture and up the rickety stairs. My nerves jangled. Any moment Tad's old man wor going to jump out t' shadows wi' a friggin' axe. My innards would be pig feed. My bones would be ground-meal for t' chickens. We crept along a narrow passageway and into Tad's room.

Tad clicked on a bedside lamp and drew t' curtains. The shade had a pattern of pink roses and carmine tassels. The polished dark wood of a heavy wardrobe glinted in its soft beam. The old bed wor very high and a little short, wi' a roughly carved headboard. Generations had slept in this bed, likely as not been conceived in it, born in it, died in it, and now two men wor going to fuck in it.

Tad wor already down to his underpants. His firm, smooth body wor contoured by t' lamplight, the tattoos like ink splodges applied in anger. The room wor icy cold, so we quickly dived under t' covers. Tad squirmed.

'Christ! Your feet are freezing!'

'Sorry.'

He laughed and bit into my neck wi' a playful growl. 'I'll soon warm you up!'

Sometime in t' night I awoke. My arm, which lay beneath Tad, had gone numb. I pulled mesen clear, shaking my fingers 'til t' feeling returned.

I lay awake, watching a small shadow dance on t' ceiling. Tad wor having some dreaming argument. I spooned mesen against his back and curled my hand around his. His fingers gripped mine like a newborn's and his dreaming grew still. I lay there, listening to t' wind rattling in t' trees, to t' one dog still barking at the moon, to t' restless complaining of t' weary old house, 'til at some point I must have fallen back into sleep.

I awoke early to t' smell of burnt toast, hen shit from t' yard below, and the keen edge of winter. I wor alone. Tad's side of t' bed wor still muskily warm. From somewhere outside came t' high-pitched whine of a chainsaw.

I wor ravenously hungry. I threw back the covers and quickly got dressed.

Wiping a hole in t' frost on t' windowpane, I looked out over a sloping field, sparsely dotted by raggedy sheep. Below my window, in t' yard, stood the rusting hulk of an old car. Overnight, the moor tops had been dusted wi' snow that gleamed where it wor caught in t' pale morning sun.

Tad came back from t' bathroom, towelling down his hair and neck. I wanted to explore t' farm, but Tad made it clear that worn't an option. His folks, he explained as we headed for t' kitchen, had been up and working for two hour already. And they weren't well-disposed to him bringing strange men home at all hours. Which made me wonder if he'd done this before.

Seated at the old farmhouse kitchen table wor a young woman having breakfast. On seeing me she scowled at Tad.

'This is Rachel, my ever-loving sister,' Tad said. 'I'd offer you coffee, but I don't think Rachel will make us any. No, I thought not. You see, Rick, my folks really would prefer it if you wor a sheep.'

'Baa,' I went, unable to help mesen. Tad sniggered. Rachel's face hardened as she rose from t' table and stomped out into t' yard, slamming the back door so hard it rebounded ajar.

Tad drove me back into town. We drove in thick silence. In my head I wor going over t' right way to say it: 'Are we going to see each other?' 'Will you call me?' 'So, is this it then?' – but none of it felt right. Whatever wor t' right thing lay buried beneath all t' wrong'uns.

As we approached Huddersfield town centre Tad said, 'I'll drop you near t' station.'

'I want to walk a bit. You can drop me here if you like.'

He pulled the Allegro into a bus layby. We sat there, Tad waiting for me to get out, me waiting for Tad to kiss me, only just then two burly blokes wor passing by on t' pavement, so nowt happened.

As I got out Tad stretched out an arm as if to hold me back, but it wor too late. I walked a little up the road, then looked back over my shoulder. Tad wor drumming both his fists on t' steering wheel. I took a couple of steps back toward t' car. Then he gunned the engine, did a u-turn and drove off wi' a squeal of tyres.

Gordon set his battered old camera and light meter on t' table and ordered tea and two rum truffles, one for himsen and one for me. The absurdity of it: Gordon in his thread-bare three-piece, and me wi' my spiked-up hair and proto-punk attire, pale as a pall-bearer, sitting in Betty's posh caf in snooty old Harrogate.

We'd spent a goodly portion of t' previous hour photo-graphing the cottage opposite t' park gates. I told Gordon that if we carried on like this, snapping pics of men's lavs, we'd get oursens arrested for being pervs.

'I'm on a mission,' he explained, 'to save as many as I can from closure and dereliction. You would hardly credit how many marvellous public facilities have been closed down in the last few years. Take the cottage in the park at Burley in Wharfedale, for example. It has the most superb original Victorian faucet, and some excellent architectural features. And now it's threatened with closure. It's an absolute scandal. I've written to the local council about it.'

'What for?'

'To try and get it listed. If I can get the cottages listed, they can't knock them down. Seeing no one is interested in my book, *Urinals of Yorkshire*, that's my next plan of action.'

'Your book?'

'The Burley cottage,' Gordon enthused, 'has wrought-iron finials.'

'Has what?'

'Finials! Finials!'

He drew me a finial on a piece of notebook paper. I toyed wi' t' fringes of t' tablecloth, trying to pay heed. Post-punk growlers Magazine had been playing the FK Club the night before, and even now, sitting amongst all these posh grannies, the guitar riff of 'Shot by Both Sides' wor assaulting my head. I'd stood down by t' stage, motionless and still fired up about t' whole Tad episode. Howard Devoto wor spitting out his words for me and me alone. By t' end of t' night I wor proper khalied. Jugs the bouncer chucked me down t' club steps, and I'd lain there on t' pavement, curled up in a ball, calling Jugs a cunt.

'Rick?'

'Oh, sorry Gordon. So that's what a finial looks like.' I looked about us and chuckled. 'Look at me, Gordon. Look at you and then look at me. And look at them.'

'The bustling blue-rinse ladies of Harrogate! They'll think we're uncle and nephew. Of course, in my time that was what one always said – uncle and nephew. Especially if an older man was living with a younger one.'

Gordon often referred to 'his time', as if he'd been dumped in t' present by aliens.

'Have you ever lived wi' anyone, Gordon? Anyone special?'

He clasped his hands together, as if in prayer. 'There was someone once. Brendan. I had a thriving radio repair business. Brendan helped out. Everyone brought their radios to us. I could take a radio apart, have it all laid out on the table – filleted, I used to say, because everything was laid out flat, the valves, the wires, the whole caboodle – and put it back together again in no time at all. And it would work.'

'But were you in love?'

'Of course we were.'

'So what happened?'

'It was a bad time, back then. All these high-profile cases in the papers of men being arrested for loving other men – like the chap from Bletchley Park who worked on cracking the Ultra code.'

'The what code?'

'The Ult ... Oh, never mind. There was a Nazi machine that transmitted in code, and the man who first cracked it, whose name eludes me just now, bloody hero of course, turned the whole course of the war. Well anyway, he was homosexual, and after the war he was arrested and charged with "gross indecency". He committed suicide.'

Hearing the word 'homosexual', one of t' old dears at the next table stiffened and peered at us sternly. If Gordon noticed, he didn't show it. I didn't give a rat's backside what the posh old biddies thought or heard.

'Turing! Alan Turing. I knew it would come to me.'

'Can't say I've heard of him, Gordon.'

'Hmm. Well, he made the mistake of falling in love.' He paused, tapping out another ciggie from t' packet, then added wistfully, 'There was someone else, much later, but ...'

'Thing is,' I interrupted, 'I'm in love.'

'Ah. At your age I would have called it an infatuation.'

'Eh?'

'That would certainly account for your somewhat distracted demeanour. One moment all sunshine and light, and the next snapping like a crocodile on heat.'

'Oh.'

'Don't worry! Embrace it!'

Embrace what, I wor thinking. Playing listlessly wi' t' cake fork, I said, 'So did it end badly wi' Brendan?'

'In a manner of speaking,' Gordon murmured. 'Ah, the tea.'

A teapot wor planted between us, then t' rum truffles, nestling in their pleated cases like chocolate golf balls. I leant my chair onto its back legs. The biddies at the next table had gone quiet.

'I'll be Mother,' Gordon said, and poured the tea through t' strainer into t' china cups. He should have let it stew a little longer.

'Do you think you'll ever fall in love again?' I asked.

Gordon stubbed out his ciggie and stabbed the truffle wi' his cake fork.

'Oh, one never loses the capacity for love,' he said, pausing to raise the fork to his mouth, 'only the opportunity.'

He coughed, took a large slurp of tea.

'So? Spill the beans. About t'other one. After Brendan.'

Gordon's face darkened. 'Not many beans to spill, my boy. He was married, we saw each other off and on for about ... about ten years. We used to go to the races. York, Wetherby, the St Leger at Doncaster – we even went to Aintree. Mind you, if you want to bet, make sure you have enough to lose. These days, I don't.'

'So what happened?'

Gordon set down his fork. 'He died. Not all that long ago, as it happens.' He eyeballed me levelly.

'Sorry to hear that, Gordon. Truly I am.'

'You know, Rick, I really shouldn't smoke so much.'

On t' weekend it wor made known that HE had struck again. In Huddersfield. It wor a bit of a shock to realise that it wor t' same night, and about t' same time, that I'd been searching for t' Gemini. The latest victim, Helen Rytka, had been reported missing by her twin sister Rita. They'd both been on t' game together, working team-handed, only t' arrangement had gone awry somehow. It had taken the twin three days to pluck up the courage to open her gob. I wor thinking what she must have gone through in them three days, waiting, not knowing, fearing t' worst. Somehow, it being her twin sister made it all t' worse.

A few days later Rita appeared on Yorkshire TV in an appeal for information. She stared out at us, a round-eyed, olive-skinned, frizzy-haired teenager, and said she and her sister had 'a psyche between our minds. If she had a problem I knew. I could feel it.'

In t' Marquis of Granby a Catch the Ripper collection box wor going round. I added fifty pence. The *Yorkshire Post* announced a ten-grand reward for information leading to t' conviction and arrest. The depot wor buzzing wi' news of it. Craner said, 'If anyone here is the Ripper, would they please come and tell me privately – I could do wi' a fucking holiday.'

One of t' drivers had been reported for being seen repeatedly in Manningham. He wor questioned; turned out his girlfriend lived in t' area. No one questioned me. If they did, I'd keep shtumm or make up a lie.

The next Gay Lib meeting wor all about two things: the *Gay News* editor Denis Lemon's appeal against his conviction for blasphemy, and the safety of womenfolk in t' light of all t' Ripper murders.

Someone blathered on for a friggin' age about t' cops spending hundreds of man hours staking out public lavs to snag a couple of old fumblers when 'their resources would surely be better employed trying to catch this maniac and protecting the public'. Someone else wanted a show of hands on how many men had been stopped by t' cops and questioned in connection wi' t' Ripper. Five hands went up.

After t' meeting I made my excuses and went up the road to t' Fenton to see t' damage done. There worn't much evidence of t' fight. The broken glasses and stools had been replaced. One of t' large mirrors behind t' bar had a crack in it. The broken windows had been repaired. The stool Dora always sat on wor back in its position, an indent in t' plastic seat. The atmosphere wor muted, as if a TV had been turned down to a background murmur.

I asked the barmaid after Dora. She shook her head. I sat mesen on Dora's stool.

'Give me a gin and tonic. A double.'

Next morn at the Corona depot Eric and I wor loading the wagon when two friggin' coppers showed up in Craner's office. Craner shut the door, but we could see what wor going on through t' glass. The coppers wor stood either side of Craner, like two gateposts. I wor sweating and my skin wor starting to crawl. I wor thinking that maybe I'd been spotted in Huddersfield, or on t' train. Or Tad's licence plate had been clocked. I kept telling mesen that the chances wor about nil. I didn't want it coming out where I'd been or where I'd spent the night. I worn't sure I could even remember t' way to t' farm. And I certainly didn't want Craner knowing owt about it.

Craner wor tapping his finger on t' page of a round-book. The coppers, I could tell, wor asking him some questions, or having a few quiet words. Craner took off his specs and then put them back on again. Then he took a small book from his jacket pocket and handed it to one of t' coppers. It had gold-edged paper, like a pocket diary or a phonebook. The one copper thumbed through it while t'other one moseyed about, opening cabinet drawers. There wor more words, and Craner wor looking edgy. After a while they shook Craner's hand and left.

The newspaper billboards wor all about t' discovery of Yvonne Pearson's body under an upturned sofa on waste ground in Bradford, just behind Drummond's Mill. She'd been missing for several week, and wor certainly murdered before Helen Rytka. It wor said that cos she hadn't been discovered HE had gone back to t' scene and moved the body into view.

It wor made known in t' press that Yvonne had an address book of clients wi' 'special tastes'. The police wor working their way through it. There wor one who liked to be burned wi' lighted ciggies. Someone at Gay Lib said James Dean had liked the same done to him.

For some reason this brought Craner to mind, and the coppers I'd seen flitting through t' pages in his little black book. I couldn't help looking at Craner and wondering.

Eric said he wouldn't be surprised if t' Ripper turned out to be a Corona van driver. We wor still confabbing on this and the meaning of t' cops' visit when we reached Mrs Husk's.

'After all,' Eric said, 'it has to be someone who knows his way about. Knows the streets, knows the red-light areas. Van driver, lorry driver or taxi driver. Mark my words.'

I wor still mulling on this when I rapped on Mrs Husk's door.

'It's open, luv.'

Mrs Husk wor listening to t' radio. She had both her hands on t' back of t' chair to support hersen. The radio sat on t' table in front of her. Her lower leg wor still bandaged up, and her ankles had swollen like they wor oozing over her feet.

The radio wor a brand-new portable wi' crimson casing, a soft handle and a light-grey dial. I'd never clapped eyes on it before. Where had it come from? Who'd paid for it?

Mrs Husk hushed me wi' a raised finger before I could speak. She wor listening to *The Jimmy Young Show*. I recognised his smarmy, jokey delivery. His unfailing friggin' happiness.

I nodded approvingly at the radio. Lord Snooty arched his back and repositioned himsen in front of t' gas fire. Someone on t' radio wor being interviewed. Jimmy Young wor speaking in a slightly lowered tone, to show that this wor serious. If that wor possible wi' a man who sounded like he wor peddling balloons. That someone being interviewed wor Assistant Chief Constable George Oldfield. I'd seen him on t' telly: a white-haired, haunted-looking man. They wor talking about t' Yorkshire Ripper.

Oldfield wor urging any listener – meaning Jimmy Young's millions of women listeners – to search their consciences and report anyone (husband, brother, father or son) who'd been behaving oddly.

Mrs Husk harrumphed. 'That'll be most menfolk then,' she said as I set the bottle down on t' table.

On t' pretext of another trip out, I persuaded Gordon to drive us over to Huddersfield. Once we were there we had a swift lunchtime half in t' Greyhound, a gay pub more commonly known as the Whippet Inn. Being lunchtime, the Whippet wor almost empty, and the frumpy old barmaid set her knitting aside to serve us. I told Gordon my real intention: to search for Tad's family farm up on t' moors above t' town.

'Still infatuated, then?'

'I just want to see if I can find it. Can't do no harm, can it?'

Gordon agreed that it would do no harm, as the views up on t' tops would be marvellous on such a beautifully clear day. But first of all, he said, he wanted to drive through Holmfirth to take in t' cottage there.

We downed a couple more pints and some cheese and piccalilli sarnies before heading over to Holmfirth. Gordon wor miffed to find that the cottage wor locked up, but he took a couple of snaps of t' outside wi' his chunky old camera and and then we headed out onto t' moor tops.

As the Humber climbed, I said to Gordon that I didn't recall passing through Holmfirth that night wi' Tad, but maybe I'd just missed it somehow. Gordon said that from t' tops we'd be able to see for miles. In t' daylight it all looked different. I didn't care about t' view, since it didn't help me recollect none. The road twisted and turned. We passed by a formation of limestone rocks that looked like they might topple any moment but had most likely stood there for thousands of years.

At the top we stopped so I could take a piss into t' roadside gully. Gordon got out and leant against t' Humber, scowling at the moors. The wind blew Gordon's hair and my piss stream sideways.

I said, 'I could swear we came this way. It just feels right. We crossed a cattle-grid, and then sometime after that Tad took a right.'

Gordon huffed.

'You said that about that last turnoff, and look where that got us. Up a dead end and me having to back her ladyship out of rather a tight corner.'

I scanned the horizon. Dark patches of moorland rose then fell away to t' left, down toward t' valley. The buffeting wind filled our lugs as it scudded the clouds across t' sky and carried the bleating of late-spring lambs upwards from t' lowland fields. Gordon wor cupping his hands, trying to light his ciggie. I could sense his growing impatience.

I said, 'I know we came up that road back there, I remember t' turnoff. It must be further up.'

'Well, come on, then. We haven't got all day.'

We got back into t' Humber and headed further along t' narrow, winding road.

'There! Must be! See! That farmhouse roof in t' dip, wi' t' trees. Has to be it!'

Gordon chewed on his ciggie end. He pulled the Humber smoothly onto a single-track farm road wi' a line of grass down t' middle. On reaching the farmyard, we came to a stop. There wor a gate. I couldn't recall a gate.

'Well?'

'Dunno. Yes. Maybe ... maybe. Yes. Yes!'

Hearing us, dogs starting yapping. The shippen to t' right, the toolshed behind that, and off to t' left the old farmhouse wi' t' sagging roof and the break of sheltering trees. Maybe t' gate had been open and I hadn't noticed? But it all looked sadder and scuzzier than I remembered.

'I think this is it – yes, it is, it is! I swear!'

'So what now?' said Gordon.

That wor decided for us. A farmer appeared around t' side of t' house, flat cap, ruddy blasted face, trouser bottoms pushed into mud-caked boots, brandishing a walking stick. It wor hard to imagine this man had sired Tad.

'Who are you? What you want?' he barked, poking the air wi' t' stick.

I opened the passenger door and leant out. 'I'm looking for Tad. Does he live here?'

I realised that I didn't know Tad's proper name. The man's jaw jutted, as if he wor insulted by t' question.

'Who wants to know?'

'It's just that I'm a mate of his, and he hasn't been in touch for a while, so I wor wonderi ...'

'No one wi' that name lives here. So yer can skedaddle. Be off wi' yer.'

Just then a girl appeared, pulling on an anorak, the hem of her light skirt blowing in t' breeze. She raised an arm to her forehead, shielding her eyes against t' lowering sun.

'Rachel?' I called out. 'Rachel, do you remember me? Is Tad here? Can I talk to him?'

She squinted at me, as if trying to work out who I wor. Her father scowled. The dogs in t' shippen wor baying for blood.

'Rachel, get yersen indoors!'

'Rachel. Is Tad here?'

She glanced quickly at her father, then shook her head briefly. 'Gone,' she mouthed, before ducking back inside. Tad's father gripped his stick tightly, his thin lips whitening.

'Like I said, there's no one here wi' that name. Be off wi' yer! You're not welcome. Your type ain't wanted 'ere. Be off, or I'll 'ave yer fer trespass!'

We got back in t' car and drove back to t' lane end. As soon as we reached a passing place on t' single-track road Gordon pulled over and killed the engine. I stared numbly out at the swaying roadside grass. Gordon wor drumming his fingers on t' steering wheel. From somewhere overhead came t' plaintive cry of a lone peewit carried aloft on t' breeze.

The Sunday next wor Mother's birthday. It almost slid me by. I snaffled a box o' Quality Street and a card from a petrol garage while I wor out on t' round. I'd been in a bad mood all day. I found the page for Blandford Gardens in t' round-book and scored the address through wi' a pen 'til I'd made a hole. When I wor done, Eric said, 'What's all that about?'

'Nowt. It's nowt, all right? He's gone, ain't he? So I'm taking him out of t' round-book.'

For t' rest of t' round I wor fumed up. Eric didn't ask owt more, and we just got on wi' it.

When I got home late that afternoon I found Mitch in t' kitchen, taping up a brown-paper parcel.

'Where's Mand?' he said, breaking the sellotape on his teeth.

'How should I know? Unlike some, I've been out working all day.'

'What's eating you?'

'Nowt. Pig of a day, that's all. Maybe she's in town wi' her mates.'

'Well, she should be home by now. Your mother's over at Mavis's.' He held the tape up in front of his eyes. 'Now then, tape, what did I say about hiding your end?'

I said, 'I'll be upstairs.'

Mother showed up in t' early evening and flumped her shit-brown leather handbag down on t' kitchen table.

'There's nowt to eat,' she said.

'Thought we'd order in,' said Mitch.

'Order in, Mitch? Anyone'd think you'd had a win on t' horses.'

'I don't do t' horses, remember? Not like yer dad. He practically lived in t' bookies'.'

'Don't speak ill of t' dead. Sometimes, Mitchell, I don't know what day it is, never mind what you get up to. Where've you been all day?'

'Looking at televisions. We need a new'un.'

'We can't afford it.'

She laid t' birthday card Mavis had given her on t' draining board and said in a slightly excited tone, 'What's that, then?'

Mitch held the brown-paper package out to her like a small boy wi' a prize from t' fair.

'It's. Erm. I mean. Well. It's.'

When she didn't take it from him he put it on t' table and slid it toward her. 'It *is* your birthday.'

She frowned, tearing at the wrapping joylessly.

'Hair rollers,' she said wi' an edge of suspicion. 'But I've got hair rollers, Mitch. You remember, the third prize in that shampoo competition a while back?'

'Then it's time you had new ones,' he protested lamely. 'And these are heated.'

She rubbed the box lid wi' her sleeve and looked down on t' model's face gleaming back at her, all glistening lips and sculpted hair.

I wor trying not to split my friggin' sides. The other thirty or so boxes wor stashed in t' garage under a horse blanket. He'd had more, 'til I helped offload about half of them to some bloke in Shipley, along wi' a few hundred packs of ciggies all labelled in Dutch. Turned out that Mitch had bought the dog from this bloke's wife. He'd introduced me to t' bloke by saying, 'This is my lad.' Which made me feel strange. I shook the bloke's hand. He eyed me untrustingly, and grunted.

'From me,' I said to Mother, holding out the unwrapped choccies and the unsigned card. 'Happy birthday.'

'Oh, thank you, Ricky,' she gushed. She pecked me on t' forehead, opened the card and glanced at it briefly before putting it down next to t' chocs. Her mind wor still on t' hair rollers.

'Not knocked off, are they Mitch? You said you wor done wi' all that. Because if you so much as ...'

Mitch picked up the box and held it close to his mouth. 'Are we knocked off? Tell me, are we dodgy goods then? No? Certain? Oh, that's good, cos Mitch here wouldn't want his wife to have summat that wor nicked for her birthday.' He doffed an invisible hat at her. 'Not absolutely new, I know, I know, but this bloke I know had one box left, so I said, "I'll take those for my missus if you knock down t' price," and so ...'

Mother rented out a smile. 'You could have wiped the box.'

Mitch looked crestfallen. 'Well, if you don't want 'em ...'

He tried to take the box from her, but she batted him away. 'No,' she said, placing her hand firmly on t' lid, 'they're just fine.'

Over dinner (an Indian takeaway treat, so Mother didn't have to wash up on her birthday), Mother blathered on about Mavis's new decor. Don had spent t' past three weekends redecorating, and Mavis had invited Mother over that afternoon 'for an exclusive'.

'She calls it the lounge now,' said Mother sniffily.

Mandy grabbed the foil container wi' t' remaining chicken biriyani and upended it onto her plate. She'd rolled up just before dinner wi' a silver bracelet for hersen and a bangle for Mother. I guessed that she'd lifted it, but I didn't say owt. The bangle wor a thick, green wooden thing, and not Mother's style at all. But she acted dead pleased anyways.

Mother prattled on about Mavis's lounge having new curtains wi' matching wallpaper the colour of milky tea, wi' an orange floral pattern and whatnot. The doors and skirting boards had been painted mushroom gloss. New carpet too, wi' a swirly olive and ochre pattern that Mother said kiddies might like to imagine as roads for their toy cars. Shame, Mother said, that Mavis and Don had never had kids. Friggin' lucky kids, more like, I wor thinking, never to have been born. Mavis always wheedled summat out of Don after he'd battered her about and wor all remorseful after. Made me happy our place wor so scuzzy. Meant that Mitch worn't battering Mother all t' time. Except when she got it into her head that Mitch wor t' Ripper, and even then he'd took it out on t' crockery.

'Maybe she'll get the suite next time round,' said Mandy between mouthfuls. I tore into a naan bread and mopped up some lamb bhuna gravy.

Then Mother started reminiscing about back before I wor born, when she took a part-time job as a barmaid in a bowling alley. Mavis wor her co-barmaid back then. She got the times all wrong, like adults do, saying that she'd met Mitch while she wor working there. Mother wor always muddling her stories, mixing one bit wi' t'other.

I said, 'That can't be right. You must have met before that. Otherwise ...'

Mitch stood up at the table. 'What does it matter who met who, when and where?'

He scowled at Mother, who wor biting on her lower lip. I screwed up my face and reached across t' table for t' last scrap of naan bread. Parent lovey-dovey stuff always made me squirm.

Eric had said that people start dying when they live in t' past all t' time.

Gran had been refusing food, so they'd been force-feeding her. Mother wor going over more often, cos she wor afraid that every visit might be t' last. Gran sure had the family stubborn streak in her. That last cup in her cupboard wor t' one marked 'Let me die.'

One day I went wi' Mother on t' bus, cos she hated going on her tod and Mitch wor never at home and sis wor pretending she wor too squeamish so she could sneak off to see whoever wor her latest boyfriend. I had my own reasons. I picked my moment. 'What wor Gerald like?'

Mother pulled in her chin. 'Gerald? Different. Why?'

'In what way, different? I mean, apart from t' carpets and the posh house and all that.'

'Well, your gran didn't take to him. She didn't like folk who'd got on in t' world. "Puffed up", she called him.'

'Is that why she's always blathering on about "that man"? She must mean Gerald.'

'You think so?'

After checking that none of our fellow busfolk wor earwigging, I asked in a low voice, 'Did you leave him?'

Mother sighed. 'I stuck it for six month. But I wor like a bird in a gilded cage. I'd lie on his bed in t' afternoons while he wor out at work and listen to t' radio or just to t' house humming ... you know, that hum a fridge or air conditioning makes? Don't get me wrong, the house wor lovely, and Gerald wor always very sweet to me, but I wor lonely, Rick. I didn't have no friends nearby, and Gerald didn't like me hanging about wi' my old crowd, Mavis and Nora and all of 'em. He'd charmed me into marrying him, what wi' his dosh from t' carpet business and all t' restaurant dinners and work dos, but he wor nearly twice my age, and I wor just a slip of a girl. I soon realised I'd been a fool, and that I didn't love him really. I cared for him, but that's not the same, is it? That's not love. So one day I packed a bag, left him a note in an envelope wi' t' house key, and went home to Mum and Dad.'

'How did that go down?'

'Dad wor all right about it – well he would be, he just took life as it comes. But Mother wor livid. She told me I should lie in t' bed I'd made for mesen. She wor all for sending me back. At the time I thought all she cared about wor what the neighbours might think.'

I paused, pulling the question from t' depths within.

'Is he my dad? Gerald?'

Mother inhaled sharply.

I said, 'I worked it out yonks ago.'

'I knew you'd ask these questions one day.'

'Where is he now?'

Mother's voice thickened. 'I wor three month pregnant when I went back to Mum and Dad. Only I never told him. I half-expected him to show up at the house, but he never did. He didn't try to get me back. Dad went to see him one time, to clear the air, but Gerald worn't the type of man to try and win me back.'

'He wor too cowardly?'

'Too proud, more like. I'd made Dad promise he'd say nowt about me being pregnant, and he didn't. I broke Gerald's heart, mind. It's a hard thing to live wi', that.'

She looked down at the bus floor.

'So what happened to him?'

'Heart attack, so I heard. Well, he always did work all hours. Your gran spotted the death notice in t' paper. You know how she wor always reading the births, marriages and deaths columns. Kept her entertained. I'm ashamed to say that when I heard, I thought it wor for t' best.'

She glanced out the bus window at some passing shop fronts, then said, 'Do you know how you got your name? It wor Lionhearted Richard.'

'Eh?'

'When you wor born your granddad danced a little jig and said this wor his lucky day and he should make good use of his luck. So t' next day he went to t' races and put five pound to win on a horse called Lionhearted Richard in t' 2.30 at Doncaster. It came in at fifty to one. A grandson and a winning horse on t' same weekend. He said it wor fated. So you wor christened Richard.'

'I wor named after a horse?'

'A winning horse.'

Her lids fluttered as if she had an affliction. 'All I ever wanted in this life wor a proper family.'

I took her hand and she squeezed my fingers briefly as if to say 'That's that, then,' and then let my hand go. She fumbled in her bag for a paper hankie, but unable to find one, closed it again. We rode the rest of t' way to t' nursing home in a soft, shared silence. As we walked through t' gates and up the driveway, the gothic turrets seemingly bearing down on us like the building itsen wor leaning forward to earwig, I ventured one more question.

'So is Mandy my half-sister?'

Mother smiled weakly.

'Look at the gardens, Rick. Aren't them fuchsias beautiful?'

Back from his honeymoon in Jersey, Eric wor still in t' full flush of being newly wed. Anyone would have thought he'd been to Barbados or he'd had a win on t' pools the way he kept blathering on. The sunshine! The castle! The hotel wi' t' balcony overlooking the bay! The seafood!

I said he hadn't caught the sun much.

When I mentioned Eric's honeymoon to Mitch in an attempt to make conversation – it wor late one Saturday afternoon and we wor watching wrestling on t' box cos it wor siling it down outside – Mitch said poncily that marriage is like a mountain stream: fresh at the source where it comes out of t' ground, but as it scurries down t' hill it picks up all manner of nasty stuff along t' way. 'Which is why you shouldn't sup from lower down,' I said. 'In case there's a dead sheep further up that you don't know about.'

The first test of t' water quality in Eric's marriage would be t' sprog that wor due in a couple of months. The way I saw it, Eric wor so taken up wi' the idea of becoming a dad that he hadn't given much thought to *being* a dad. Lourdes wor doling out some unwanted advice on motherhood along wi' her horse-piss tea. Anyone could see this riled him.

'As if she knows owt about being a parent,' he fumed as we rearranged the van load. He paused, wi' a bottle of lemon barley water in his hand, seeking out the right crate for it, and said, 'You've got all this coming one day.'

'Not me, mate. I'm not getting spliced. No friggin' way.'

Eric chortled and shook his head.

It wor on t' edge of my tongue to tell him, but the words wouldn't come. As we worked, shifting empties to t' bottom and centre of t' van and moving full crates to t' open sides where they'd be easily reachable for t' coming hour or so, I blathered on to Eric about Mother and Gerald, and Mitch being my stepdad. I said it felt as if summat wor broke and summat else repaired.

He said it wor a good thing that the truth had come out, and from what he'd heard, Mitch worn't such a bad bloke neither. That's as may be, I said, but I'd always felt there wor a distance between mesen and Mitch. We wor chalk and cheese, as the saying went.

'Makes sense,' I said, 'learning we worn't common blood.'

'No,' said Eric. 'But he brought you up, all t' same.'

He made it sound like I'd been t' lucky one.

'I wish it had been Gerald. If it had been Gerald I would have had a better life, that's for sure. He wor rich. Or he wor before he died. You know, Eric, he didn't even know about me. If he had, he might have left me some dosh.'

'If he'd made a will. If he didn't, the tax man will have gobbled it up.'

For t' rest of that day I walked around feeling lighter than t' air, and seeing t' world in a wholly different light.

Vera Millward

16/05/1978

Ah. Diary sneak-read opportunity. I had to be quick though. Just summat about getting her ears pierced and complaining that neither Mother nor Mitch had noticed. So that's why you keep pulling your hair down one minute and then flicking it back the next. They're not going to notice, sis, cos that's what you want. Nowt comes of throwing petrol on a dead fire, does it? What's done is done. Or maybe they don't care. You tell me, sis.

Vera Millward had been done over in Manchester. She wor found in a sitting position, propped against t' fence in a car park by t' hospital.

While Eric and I sipped horse piss, Lourdes wor blathering on about t' undercover officers all over Chapeltown at night, and even a few during the day, pretending to be courting in strategically parked cars.

They wor doing t' same at other red-light districts in t' North too – I heard it on a Radio Pennine late-night phone-in show. One woman said, 'They've got it coming to them, haven't they, luv?' The next caller said it wor God's work – cleansing the streets of sin. There wor a discussion about God and the Devil. The man wor saying that God wor taking his revenge for all t' sin in t' world. The presenter suggested that the Ripper might be of t' same opinion. God man worn't sold on t' idea. There followed a radio barney about whether the Yorkshire Ripper was some Godfearing nutter or not, and then t' caller wor cut off and the next one wor on t' line. Some addled old biddy. 'I don't know ... it's terrible ... all these killings ... I don't know what to think.'

So t' presenter told her what to think, and moved on.

Camp David had invited me to a Saturday-afternoon barbecue in t' back yard of Radclyffe Hall. I cadged the day off work by swapping shifts wi' one of t'other van lads.

The barbecue itsen wor one of them cheap camping jobs that hold two chops and a porker if you're lucky. On t' kitchen table wor two big bowls of salad: yellow rice and nuts in one, and in t'other grated raw carrot, sultanas and grapes. A bit of lettuce, a tom and a blob of salad cream would have done me.

All t'other Radclyffe Hall inmates wor there: Fizzy, Fazel, plus a tall, shy Irishman called Gary who I'd seen at Gay Lib. The old dear I'd seen rattling the dustbin lid that one time wor there too – her name wor Hilda – as wor Spider, Fazel's new boyfriend, who he'd met in t' waiting room of a clap clinic. As always when there wor a crowd, Terry wor holed up in his room.

There wor also two Asian lads. One wor about eighteen, and his name wor Ali. T'other couldn't have been more than thirteen. Camp David said he wor Ali's cousin, fresh out of Pakistan, and that he didn't speak much English. The cousin wor dressed in brushed-cotton brown flares and a thick cable sweater, even though t' sun wor beating down. The clothes looked borrowed, cos they didn't fit proper.

Fazel whispered in my ear that Camp David had a thing about Asian youths. He wor always chatting to t' ones who hung about outside the Hyde Park cinema, or them that kicked a footie about in t' park, or sat on walls talking among themsens. They cadged his ciggies and knew what he wanted in return.

We all stood about or sat on t' yard wall. I wor supping from a can of Red Stripe and watching Camp David prod the porkers that wor already charred along one side and still raw on t'other. Some of them wor made of some veggie gunge. Fizzy had moved his stereo speakers by t' open window so that the sounds of Jimmy Cliff's *The Harder They Come* LP wor carried out into t' yard and up the back street.

In between t' banter about sex and sausages, the talk wor of Gay Lib and Rock Against Racism and whether RAR supported us queers or not, and about t' NF and all that. Camp David wor nattering wi' Hilda and batting his eyelids at Ali. Hilda wor saying that she'd never married. Camp David asked her straight out if she wor a lesbian, and she roared wi' laughter. She said during t' First World War she'd had a young fancy man she wor set to marry, but he'd never come back from t' front. Then her father died in t' flu epidemic and she had to look after her mother.

Ali wor looking a bit awkward and aloof, so I asked him if he wanted any sausage, but he declined my offer wi' an embarrassed smile that showed off his nice teeth. He wor a slim lad, wi' high cheekbones and dangerous, playful eyes. His jeans wor tight about t' crotch and showed his dick line perfectly. I let him see me eyeing him over while I wor piling my paper plate wi' rice salad. As he moved away from t' table, Fazel sidled over.

'If you want that one, you have to wear the kit.'

'The kit?'

'He drops in on David that often you'd think he's practically moved in. Only active, mind you, strictly no kissing, and David has to wear a dress, stockings and heels. Otherwise it's no go.'

I ploughed my fork through t' yellow rice and kidney beans.

'You're having me on.'

'And David's taken to shaving his whole body. The bath plughole's always clogged up with his body hair. I mean, all that stuff about gay liberation and radical drag, and then as soon as some randy Asian lad tells him he has to be as smooth as a baby's backside to get a shag he's at the razor and Immac before you can say "Heels over head in lust."'

'So, you're not joining the club?'

'Me? Look at me, dear. You'd need a machete. Either they take me as they find me, or they can fuck off.' Fazel placed his left hand on my lower ribcage. 'So what's the story I hear about some man you're shagging?'

'What man?'

The hand lingered there, the fingers dancing against me like he wor playing a piano.

'The skinhead you had in my room on the night of the party. You see, there are rumours flying about. Rumours about you. Some people don't trust you. Because of the types it's said you hang out with.'

I pulled away from him and put my plate down on t' table. I wor fumed up at Fazel for even mentioning Tad. It had been months now, I'd buried him in a dusty corner of my mind, but wi' one flicker I wor lit, and I could see him, smell him, almost taste him.

'Is that right?'

'Some are saying it wor you who put the NF on to attacking the Fenton.'

I took a large sup from my beer can. 'Honest to God, Fazel, I haven't seen that bloke since t' party. It wor a one-night stand, and that's that. He wor gone before I woke up in t' morning. I don't know owt about him.'

'So I guess you won't know that after the Fenton attack that fascist bitch Gina was arrested for GBH?'

'You're having me on. Gina? She wor in on it? Really? That surprises me, truly it does. She's no bigger than a pint of milk.'

'You really didn't know?'

'Like I said, I haven't seen any of them since that night. She don't even come to t' FK Club no more.'

Fazel grunted. 'She glassed this old woman in the face. And she threw a chair across the bar. There were two GLF people in there that night, having a quiet drink. One of them got a broken nose. They both recognised her.'

'Fazel, I promise you, I don't know owt about it. I've never even been in t' Fenton.'

I excused mesen, pushed past him and bounded upstairs to t' bathroom. My skin wor crawling, the demons bursting out of their burrows, spreading like a bracken fire up my arms and 'cross my stomach. I tore off my shirt, opened the tap and doused my chest wi' t' cold water. I stared at mesen in t' mirror. Breathe in, breathe out, steady, steady now. In–out, in–out. Dora, poor, poor Dora. What harm had she done anyone? Next time I saw that bitch Gina she'd get it from me, no messing. I dried my face and body wi' t' grubby hand towel, put on my shirt and stepped out.

Ali wor coming up the stairs. He grinned at me wolfishly, but I let him pass wi' just a nod.

Since t' ruckus in t' garage Mitch and I had been keeping each other at arm's length. He wor spending more and more time wi' t' dog. It gave him a reason not to be in t' house and to be somewhere other than in the Marquis or t' local working men's club.

Sometimes he wor out 'til late at night, walking Max out on t' tops above Bradford, he said. Other times he just let him loose in t' park and threw him a rubber ball again and again. Even Mother fussed over t' dog these days. Seemed that all

195

conversation between us had to pass via t' dog. Mandy wor less forthcoming, especially after Max chewed up her fave gonk.

But wi' me, Mitch just eyed me quietly, as if he wor waiting for me to say summat. So one day while he wor putting up a key rack in t' hallway, I said, 'I know. She told me.'

'Aye,' he said, keeping his eyes fixed on t' job before him. When I didn't say anything more, he apologised to t' key rack for keeping it waiting and then drove a rawl-plug into t' plasterboard.

Eric pulled onto t' grass verge and killed the engine. My ears popped, and in poured the squeals of kids playing on distant swings and the buzz of a light aircraft hanging in t' sky. For t' past two hours we'd been working this estate, circling, criss-crossing, backing up cul-de-sacs and inching along t' avenues and crescents of pebble-dashed semis and terraces, following the numbers (no number 13!) 'til we passed t' same abandoned pram I'd clocked earlier.

Eric said, 'Do you want to see where Jimmy Savile lives?'

I shrugged. 'He lives around here?'

'No, just over t' way. On t'other side of Roundhay Road. Come on, it's only a couple of minutes from here.'

He restarted the van and we drove out of t' housing estate and across t' Roundhay Road. Eric followed the edge of Roundhay Park, then pulled over and nodded at a block of posh flats opposite.

'He lives right there, in t' one at the very top. His old mum lived wi' him too, 'til she died a few year back. He called her "the Duchess".'

I screwed my face up at the block. 'Does anyone deliver to him?'

'Nah. Not that I've heard. Keeps to himsen.'

Mother had spotted Savile one time at Leeds General Infirmary, where he sometimes worked as a volunteer porter. He wor wheeling this teenage girl along t' corridor on a hospital trolley and chortling away to her in that way he had.

We climbed onto t' back of t' van to rebuild the load. I kicked a crate into place and said, 'My mother lived in a posh house once. When she wor married to that rich bloke before I wor born.'

This sounded, even as I wor saying it, like make-believe. Eric looked at me out of t' corner of his eye.

I said, 'Wouldn't you put your mum in a posh house? If you wor Jimmy Savile?'

Eric shrugged his shoulders. 'Aye, if I knew where to find her I would. But I wor brought up by t' grandfolks. Mum left us when I wor a nipper. She just walked.'

'Sorry. I didn't know.'

'Not that I remember owt.'

'I can remember stuff from when I wor two year old. I can remember the colour of my pram. Mother wor gobsmacked, cos all t' photos she has of me when I wor a baby are black and white.'

Eric mulled on this. 'Maybe somebody once mentioned it, and you just think you remember. I mean, I saw a photo of my mother once, and now I don't know if it's her that I remember, or if having seen t' photo makes me think I remember.' He banged a crate of cherryade into place wi' his foot. The bottles jiggled and protested. 'But I've never stopped looking for her.'

'And?'

'It's like she's fallen off t' face of t' earth.'

I dropped an empty bottle of Tango lemon and lime into a crate slot. We could still hear t' aircraft buzzing overhead. Eric looked out across t' open ground, deep in private thought. I didn't like that. When people wor thinking in my presence, visibly thinking summat, I felt shut out. Useless.

A breeze had picked up, ruffling the hairs on t' back of my neck.

'Sometimes,' Eric said eventually, 'I think I'm goin' to see her. When we're out on t' rounds. I knock on a door and then I'm waiting and I get this queer sensation, like I'm going to pass out. But then t' door opens and it's not her. It's never her.'

'What would you do if it wor her?'

'Dunno. I dunno what I'd do. I guess I'd grab her and never let her go.'

'Maybe she moved away? Remarried?'

Eric shook his head. 'We're Catholics. Mum would never get a divorce. Call it a hunch, call it what you like, but I think she's somewhere close by. She's my mum, after all. She'd want to stay close to her kid, don't you think?'

He wiped his nose on t' sleeve of his blue nylon Corona coat.

'Can I tell you summat?' I said.

Eric rubbed the sleeve against t' hip of his keks.

'All that stuff wi' Lourdes and the dancing and that, well, it's not who I am. Thing is, Eric, I prefer fellas. I'm gay.'

Eric jerked his head, as if avoiding a wasp. There wor a long pause. Then he said, 'I didn't need to know that. None of my business what you do. That's a game changer. That changes everything.'

'Why?' I said. 'I thought you, of all people ...'

'Well you thought wrong. I'm a Catholic, remember? And what you're telling me is wrong. It's against nature and against t' teachings in t' Bible.'

'The what?'

I'd been sure that Eric wor on my side. I knew now, wi' a cold and clammy certainty, that it would be gossiped around t' depot. But that Bible spouting got me fair riled.

'That's good, coming from you,' I snapped. 'What wi' Karen pregnant before t' wedding, and you knobbing other men's wives on t' round. I know ...'

I glimpsed the left hook an instant before I felt it. I dodged, and he caught me on t' side of my cheek, sending me staggering backward, catching a crate as I tried to stay upright, before falling off t' side of t' van and slamming onto t' tarmac and rolling over. I cried out, more in surprise than pain. His wedding ring had caught my cheekbone, and I could feel a warm trickle of blood running down my face.

When I looked up, Eric wor stood on t' edge of t' open van back, looking down at me, wide-eyed wi' hate. Using the wheel arch, I pulled mesen to my feet. My forearm wor grazed, my elbow wor bleeding and my nylon Corona coat wor ripped. Beneath my jeans my right leg wor stinging.

'All them times!' Eric shouted. 'All them times when I dropped you in town and I thought you wor giving some bird a seeing to, it worn't?'

'No,' I spat, tasting the blood that wor trickling into t' side of my mouth. 'It wor a bloke. A dead sexy bloke. The Matterhorn Man.'

'The who?'

'Blandford Gardens. The Matterhorn Man. One bottle of Coke and a tonic water.'

I wiped my face and spat onto t' ground. Eric's face had more creases than an unironed shirt.

'You mean it wor someone you met on t' round? On our round?'

'Aye.'

'Well, I'll be damned. But you've stopped seeing him?'

'He skedaddled back to Scotland. But not cos of owt to do wi' me. At least, I don't think so.'

'So that's why you scratched his name out of t' round-book t' way you did that time?'

'Aye. I wor riled up.'

'I wish you hadn't told me. It's disgusting, that. I wish I didn't know. Cos once I know summat, I can't unknow it, can I? And I don't like what I know now. I tell you, it ain't natural. I can't believe it. I thought I knew you. I thought I knew who Rick Thorpe is.'

'This is who I am.'

We pushed on wi' t' deliveries. Cos of t' bruised hip and grazed leg I wor walking wi' a limp. A few of t' customers remarked on my cut face, which I fibbed about, saying I hadn't been looking where I wor going, and one kindly young woman gave me an elastoplast. She insisted on dabbing on some Dettol and putting the plaster on my cheek hersen, letting her finger rest there a moment. I thanked her and made my excuses.

I wor feeling like my innards wor hanging out and I couldn't push 'em back in. I wor so cut up inside that I dropped a full bottle of Coca-Cola onto a garden path. What I'd wanted above all, I thought miserably, using a piece of wood to shovel the jagged pieces of glass onto some newspaper, wor approval. Eric's approval. After all, hadn't Eric shared shedloads of stuff about himsen which I then had to carry wi' me, stuff I could have spilled to Craner, Karen, Lourdes, anyone I wor minded to? What wor Eric always blathering on about friendship? Real friendship is cemented in secrets. Some secrets bind you together, and some tear you apart. Tell me yours, I'll tell you mine. Prick our thumbs and press them together. What shite.

To my mind, Eric should have been chuffed at being the first, the very first, person I'd ever told. Even just ... just what? What had I expected? 'Truth is, Rick, I'm gay as well'? Never once had I fibbed to Eric. Never once had I pretended to fancy birds, Eric had just assumed it. When he wor knobbing some housewife on t' round and I wor left waiting in t' cab wi' all my imaginings, Eric would say nowt afterward, save perhaps to utter a 'Best get on.' But it had been there, hadn't it, in t' complicit grins, the affectionate punches and teasing that sent lust and despair coursing through me?

Surely he'd now spill it all to Craner. And once Craner knew, the news would spread like wildfire. Most likely Mitch's ears would be burning even now. I might as well hang out a banner. Switch on a neon sign. I might as well hang mesen from t' next lamp-post.

I rolled the broken glass into t' newspaper and tipped the pieces into a dustbin. Eric wor watching me. As I got back in t' van, he said, 'Once the cat's out of t' bag, even t' devil himsen can't coax it back in.'

'Aye,' I muttered, only half-getting what the friggin' hell that meant.

We got on wi' t' round in silence-sodden truce. Every now and then Eric would catch my eye. I tried to thaw him out a little, asking him to pass me over a bottle of summat, or sorting out change. But as we pootled between one housing estate and the next, not a word beyond t' necessary wor uttered.

After a couple of hour of this Eric cocked his face skyward and said, 'The Matterhorn Man?'

I wor happy we wor speaking again.

'Aye. That's what I called him. Cos of t' mural of t' Matterhorn on his front-room wall.'

'So did he turn you?'

'What? Nah, course not. That's rubbish, that is. You can't turn people. You are what you are.'

'Then how do you know? I mean, if you've never had a woman, how do you know it's not better?'

'Cos I just don't fancy women. I look at men in t' same way you look at women. You could turn that on its head. How do you know, if you've never had another bloke? Never tried it?'

'Don't get funny wi' me.'

'I'm not. I'm just saying.'

'And how do you look at me?'

'Eh?'

'You heard me. I said, how do you look at me?'

I could see he wor demanding an answer.

'You're my Corona van driver. How am I supposed to look at you?'

'Well, I know which side my bread's buttered on, and it's not the backside.'

Craner scrunched up a piece of paper and fired it toward the waste bin. It missed.

'Mr Thorpe, you're staring at me like I'm Jane Fonda.'

'Could never mistake you for Jane Fonda, Mr Craner. I wor miles away, sorry.'

'Miles away, Mr Thorpe, is what you should be by now. Is your van ready?'

'Just about.'

'"Just about"? There are no "just abouts" in my depot. Only certainties, lad, certainties. Is it ready, or is it not?'

'It's ready. As good as.'

Craner threw his arms wide and rolled his eyes to t' heavens.

'We're a driver short today, that is a certainty, so I've divided his round up among everyone else. You and Eric are to add Quarry Hill Flats onto t' end of your round. You'll be paid £1.50 extra.'

'You can put me on someone else's round if it suits you, Mr Craner.'

Craner fired another piece of paper at the waste bin. He missed again. 'It does not suit me, Mr Thorpe. It does not suit me one bit.'

* * *

We got a new telly. Mother wor right, we couldn't afford it. Mitch said he got it on HP, and it would be paid off within two year. Then he tried to tap me for a tenner.

The telly wor an immense bugger, bunkered in its own cabinet in one corner of t' living room. The parchment sail lamp and Mother's two china poodles looked lost on it. It wor louder than t' old one, and lying on my bed I could hear it through t' floor, although I couldn't quite make the words out. The only place in t' room where I could sit or lie down wor on t' bed. The space between t' bed and the wall wor long and narrow, and lying on t' rug wor like a dry run for your coffin. I'd been miffed when we moved to this house six year ago, and half-sis got the bigger room and I got the box room. Mitch had said girls need bigger rooms.

I turned up John Peel on t' radio. Peely wor playing a lot of Sly and Robbie dub and some friggin' folky shite, but I wor waiting for t' live session by Siouxsie and the Banshees. I'd bought a portable casssette recorder and I had the C-90 tape sitting on pause, ready to record, wi' an external mic balanced on a book in front of t' radio speaker.

As luck would have it, Mand wor kipping already, so her usual clod-hoofing to t' Bee Gees or some such shite wouldn't interfere wi' t' recording. The heating pipes wor knocking, but I figured the mic wouldn't pick that up.

Half-sis wor twenty-two month younger than me, so Mother must have met Mitch pretty sharpish after I wor born. Three month after I wor born, or so she said, she took the evening job in t' bowling alley, while Gran and Granddad looked after me. She wor happy to be out of t' house and earning some keep, to be able to pay them a few pounds. What's more, Mother said, she met new friends, such as Mavis, who worked wi' her behind t' bar.

I thought about Eric, who'd been brought up by his grandfolk cos his mother had walked out and his dad had hit the bottle. And Gerald, my real dad, who wor long since pushing up daisies. I suddenly realised that Peely wor introducing Siouxsie, and I freed the pause button just in time for t' raw opening chords of 'Love in a Void'.

Next morn, while Mother wor ironing, I pushed her a little further about Gerald. She sprinkled water onto a shirt and pressed the iron down hard; it hissed and steamed as she held it down firmly, her knuckles almost white about t' handle.

'The past stays in t' past,' she said, 'dead and buried.' She flapped the shirt and hung it across t' back of a kitchen chair and said that I knew all there wor to know. But then she went on to tell me that Mavis had played matchmaker for her and Mitch. She'd resisted Mitch's attentions at first, having decided that no man would have her while she wor still married to Gerald, and her wi' a toddler dribbling down Granddad's lapels. Then Mavis took it on hersen to put Mitch in t' picture, so to speak, and to her surprise Mitch said he had no right to judge anyone, his folks and older sister having been killed in a bombing raid on Sheffield during t' war. He wor t' only survivor, dug out after someone heard him bawling. He wor just a three-year-old nipper. He wor sent to live wi' a great-aunt over Keighley way.

'Is that why he talks to things and sometimes acts so strange? I mean, cos he had a lonely upbringing?'

'I'm sure of it,' Mother said, stretching a Buzzcocks T-shirt of mine across t' ironing board.

I said I wanted to know about Mavis and the bowling alley. Mother said that Mavis wor all syrupy charm out front, and a bitch in t' back kitchen. I said she hadn't changed much in my opinion, and Mother snapped that Mavis had always been a loyal friend, and that it worn't my place to cast judgements on her.

So I didn't delve no further. I wor biding my time about summat else. The future. My future. I needed to move out, to have my own space. Find a bedsit or a shared house. It had been coming like a faint train whistle farways down t' track. Mentally, I wor packed and ready.

Girls might need bigger rooms.

But boys needed a world to play in.

It had been over six month since t' last Ripper attack. There wor speculation that he'd topped himsen, or wor inside for some other crime, or that he'd found a woman who worshipped him and so he didn't need to go murdering.

Now that the business wi' Gina and the attack on t' Fenton had blown over my life fell back into its steady furrow of t' FK Club, Gay Lib, Corona and the occasional foray to a gay bar or club. I wouldn't wear t' gay badges though, in case anyone back home found them or someone spotted me out and about. Even punk badges wor out of fashion now.

Not that the Gay Lib bloke wi' t' railway pins in his lapels gave fashion a second thought. Every time I clapped eyes on him he had a new one. In t' bar afterward Fazel and badge-vomit man wor confabbing about all t' demos in Iran to over-throw the Shah. I listened on, supping the head off my pint. Iran wor a country on another planet where things worn't done right.

As for Blighty, Mitch wor saying as we all sat down to watch *The Dick Emery Show* on t' telly that more strikes wor looming. 'Mind you,' he went on, 'now that the Tories have a bloody woman at the helm, they haven't a cat's chance of winning any election. I mean, who's going to vote for that stupid cow?'

'I might,' said Mother, without looking up from t' compe-tition on her lap for a two-minute supermarket dash. She sucked noisily on a boiled sweet. She wor trying to give up smoking again. The previous attempt lasted all of three week.

'Callaghan and his cronies wor ruddy-well daft not to 've called an election in September. I tell you, they had it in t' bag.'

'Did they, luv?' Mother said, biro poised aloft like a small dagger.

Mitch went on to warn me that when I wor old enough to vote I worn't to do owt daft like voting for anyone other than Labour. 'This is a Labour household through and through. It's in our blood. Your mother ain't really going to vote for that Mrs Thatcher. She's just saying that to rile me.'

Mother clicked on t' head of her ballpoint pen and then wrote summat down for her competition.

Wi' my Christmas bonus I bought:

The Only Ones – *The Only Ones*
Talking Heads – *More Songs About Buildings and Food*
Wire – *Chairs Missing*
Gang of Four – 'Damaged Goods' (single)

The Pistols wor washed up now that Sid had been accused of killing his Nancy, and all t'other half-decent punk bands wor signing up to t' corporates and selling their souls for a deal.

Punk wor dead. Silencer off. Bang. Bang.

Three days into t' New Year, the last year of t' decade, and Mitch and all t'other union lorry drivers came out on strike. But not us Corona men. We wor out all hours in it during one of t' rawest winters for many a year.

Mitch on strike wor a blessing and a bind. For t' first few days he wor a Santa sack full of plans: getting the airing-cupboard pipes boxed in, uprighting the leaning washing-line post in t' back garden, clearing the drive of snow, mending the latch on t' kitchen window. But after a few days he wor sloughing about barefoot in his pale-grey tracksuit bottoms and Leeds Utd shirt, pale-ale bottle dangling between his fingers, Johnny Cash or Glen Campbell twanging away on t' lounge record player. Mother badgered him into doing a few chores, but mostly he wor bored and moody. He footled about in t' garage, but it wor too cold to hang about in there for long.

So instead he took Max for walks – the dog must have thought it wor being trained for summat, it wor so knackered from trudging through t' snow – and smoked way more than usual. Most lunchtimes he spent in t' Marquis wi' Don and a couple of his lorry driver mates. Wednesday and Friday lunchtimes they had the added distraction of a rough-looking stripper and a bottle of baby oil to accompany their ploughman's and pint.

'There's this lorry driver,' Mitch wor saying one evening as *Opp Knocks'* presenter Hughie Green wor smiling smarmily at the camera, 'works for Clark's over Shipley way, who's known for keeping his lorry immaculate. Peter Sutcliffe's his name. A bit of a strange one, a bit standoffish, but the gaffer likes him cos he's such a good worker, and the other drivers like him cos he's dead helpful to t' new recruits.'

The clapometer at the foot of t' TV screen nudged toward seventy.

Mother said, 'I can't hear t' telly when you blather on so.'

'Women blather. I'm telling you summat. I heard about him from another driver who used to work for Clark's, and works for us at Maid Marion now. What I'm saying is, when it comes down to it, I wouldn't trust a driver like that in a strike. Likely as not he's nowt but a bossman arse-licker. A blackleg.'

Mother shrugged. 'He sounds lovely. Just what you want. The state of some of those cabs ...' Distracted by t' telly, she clearly thought the subject unworthy of any further consideration.

By t' end of January the public workers were out on strike an all. It didn't seem right that I had to crawl out of bed every dark, filthy winter morning at 5 a.m. and take two buses across town to t' Corona depot in Seacroft while Mitch snored on. Nor that us Corona men had to work through t' foul weather while others swanned about wi' nowt to do. It irked me that half-sis and I wor t' only breadwinners – her at Schofield's and me out on t' Corona round.

In such brass-monkey weather sales of pop plummeted, but it took just as long to finish t' round. I couldn't feel my feet in my boots, couldn't hold the coins between my raw fingers or grip the bottles easily. In t' worst of it the pop would freeze to slush in t' bottles. Out on t' round, the roads wor dangerous, especially where t' side streets hadn't been gritted, or paths salted, and carrying five or six bottles in t' crook of one arm, as we wor wont to do, wor a skittish business. Somewhere undercover, like Leek Street Flats – or any block of flats for that matter – wor a blessing, even wi' t' wind howling up the stairwells. It wor also a little easier cos no one wor buying. Pop worn't a winter drink. What's more, folk wor stashing their dosh. What little dosh they had. Eric said that in Liverpool, even t' gravediggers wor out on strike – no one wor being put in t' ground. Bodies wor stacking up.

I found Mrs Husk huddled in her chair beneath her grubby bedding, her swollen feet peeking toward t' mournful hiss of t' gas fire. Lord Snooty lay in t' blanket folds on her lap. Even though it wor late morn, Jack Frost still clung to her windowpanes. Mrs Husk didn't want no pop in this weather – just her bottle of Bell's to keep her own pipes lubricated.

Mid-morning tea wi' Lourdes wor a grateful pit stop. Lourdes didn't have much going on neither, and she wor happy to let us linger and thaw out our feet. She wor saying that over in Bradford the 'poleece' had given t' prozzies who worked at top end of Lumb Lane an 'amneeesty' so long as they wor only out working at times 'dem poleece' agreed. 'What punter go walking into dat bear trap?' She looked at me wi' a devilish glint. 'You's a growing boy – you's proper girlfriend material now, ain't he Eric?'

'Or boyfriend,' Eric said.

Lourdes' face popped. 'Bwoy? You mean you's a battybwoy?'

'A what?'

I glowered at Eric, miffed that he'd mouthed off. Lourdes slapped and wiggled her massive backside. 'Battybwoy?'

'I dunno, I mean ...'

'Cos if yous is, I knows dis man, Errol, married wi' two daughters, only his dumb wife she don't know, or if she does den she even dumber, but Errol sure has a taste for dem skinny white boys.' Lourdes cackled. 'If you's wanting Errol he always at the Gaiety ...'

'Thanks for the offer, Lourdes, but ...'

'You knows what Errol say? He say, once you ga wi' black you never go back. Dat's what he always say.' Lourdes laughed like it wor t' funniest thing in t' world ever. 'Ain't dat duh truth!' She laughed 'til she doubled over, as if it wor too painfully funny to endure, but she couldn't make it stop.

When I came in from work, Mitch collared me. He wor scraping burnt toast into t' sink.

'You're t' main breadwinner in this house right now.'

'I'm giving Mother half my money already as keep,' I replied, pulling off my boots and setting them down on t' sheet of newspaper Mother had laid out for t' purpose.

'While I'm on strike, you need to give her most of it.'

I tried to push past him. He stretched out an arm, barring my way.

I said, 'You went on strike, not me.'

'Solidarity, lad. It's called workers' solidarity. We're a family.'

'What about Mand? Is she giving most of her wages an' all?'

'She's got that coming.' He looked down at the toast. 'Happy now?'

One clear, cold night when Mitch and Mother wor out at a concert at the Batley Variety Club (on my workers' solidarity dosh, I shouldn't wonder), I snuck over to Radclyffe Hall. On t' way I ducked into a public lav that wor always unlocked, even at night, and picked up some young'un about my age. He wor very thin and pasty-faced and all bony elbows and knees.

We found an empty house in a short terrace that wor earmarked for demolition, boarded up at the front, but left open at the back. We clambered in through an unlocked window and headed to a rear upstairs room. The yellow glow from t' sodium backstreet light shone through t' bare window. He said he didn't like to kiss. He went down on his knees and unzipped my dick and starting blowjobbing me.

While he wor going at my dick like it wor a stick of Blackpool rock I took in our surroundings. I could see t' room wor nicely decorated, and the house looked in good order. Couldn't think for t' life of me why anyone would want to demolish it.

At my feet, the lad wor wanking himsen hard and making slurping noises. I stroked his hair to chivvy him along. News had drifted my way that Gina wor out and about again. I didn't want to get caught up wi' her again, but I got to thinking that maybe if I did see her she'd lead me to Tad. I closed my eyes and imagined that this lad, who wor going at it hammer and tongs now, wor really Tad. Wi' a sharp intake of breath I exploded all over t' skinny lad's face. Then he shot his load onto t' floor by my feet, convulsing like someone having an eppy fit. I wor glad my dick worn't in his gob no more, cos he might have bitten it off.

At Radclyffe Hall I found a proper commotion in full flow. Fazel, Camp David and Terry wor gathered in t' kitchen. Fazel wor seated at the table, face like a sick griffin. As I came into t' room he looked up at me wi' bloodshot eyes. Terry wor leant against t' stove, looking on, his thumb and forefinger under his chin like he wor solving a maths puzzle. Camp David wor sat beside Fazel, playing wi' t' fraying ends of his jacket sleeve.

Terry put me in t' picture in his usual deadpan delivery, wi' Camp David interrupting floridly. Turned out that Fazel's mother and two sisters wor about to flee Iran for Egypt. His brother wor already in New York. So Fazel had picked this moment to come out to his family over t' phone. The news went down like a body being dropped down a well. The next day his family publicly disowned him by placing an advert in t' paper, and his father withdrew his support money.

'They can do that?' I said.

'They've done it,' Terry replied.

'What are you going to do?' I asked Fazel, arranging my face into what I hoped wor a suitably concerned look.

'Don't know,' Fazel muttered. 'Maybe I'll join my brother in New York. In New York I will be free and no one and nothing can hurt me.'

'New York?' I said, wide-eyed.

'New York! New York!' trilled Camp David tunelessly. 'I'm going to wake up with somebody who never sleeps!'

'For God's sake, this is real life, not a fucking musical,' said Terry caustically.

Fate, I wor thinking, could not have dealt me a better hand. There would be a free room at Rad Hall. And the last person on earth who I thought might make that possible wor t' friggin' Shah of Iran. I could feel opportunities opening up. But course this worn't a good moment to say owt.

Terry looked down at the floor and said, 'Is that a semen stain on your boot?'

By early February Fazel's home country wor filling up the news. The Shah had fled, and some religious bearded bloke wor being mobbed in Tehran like he wor a pop star. Some of t' men in t' crowds wor braying themsens on t' bonce 'til they bled. I couldn't help wondering what this wor doing to their brains.

Before leaving Radclyffe Hall later that evening I asked Camp David if he wanted to go out for a drink the following night. His eyes widened.

'Just social, like.'

'My dear, I wasn't imagining for one moment you were asking me on a date.'

The next night I arrived outside Leeds Town Hall just as the clock wor striking nine, and waited, pacing along t' wide steps to stave off t' bitter cold. I hated anyone being late. Hearing the single strike of t' quarter hour, I wor just about to give it up as a bad job when I spotted Camp David emerging from behind a departing bus over t' road. He waved at me and trilled my name in a high-pitched squeal. As he neared he said, 'My, look at you. You look a pretty scary sight in that black leather jacket and those boots.'

'I could say t' same of you,' I sniffed, 'for different reasons.'

He laughed heartily, like for all t' world he wor pleased wi' this. He looked like a transvestite hobo. He wor wearing a mangy old brown ladies' fur coat that he said he'd picked up at Oxfam, a green bobble hat, black ladies' gloves and, wrapped around his neck, a paisley-patterned scarf. This jumble-sale outfit wor completed by a large brown sweater hanging loosely over crimson loons and dark-blue Doc Marts.

It wor too early for Charley's, so we decided to pop into t' New Penny first. Barely had we taken ten steps when from across t' street this goon started shouting and gesturing at us. He wor wi' a group of four others who'd just tumbled out of a nearby pub. They looked like bulldog office-workers who'd been out on t' razz.

'Hey! Queer boy!'

Queer boy. Singular. They wor striding across t' street toward us. There wor nowhere to run to, being so in t' open, so we just stood there.

'Well, lads, what have we got here? Quentin Crisp of Yorkshire?'

Camp David and I glanced at each other as if to say, 'You will stick up for me, right?'

'Are you a pouf?'

This wor directed at Camp David. It worn't looking good. I cast about for exit options. I sized them up, the whole group, trying to decide how fit or fearsome they wor. I wor sure I could take on any one of them on their own, but as a gang ...

'I am proudly of that persuasion,' Camp David declared.

Oh, friggin' 'ell, I wor thinking, just throw yersen into t' cauldron, won't you?

Like any gang of jackals, one led t'others. The head jackal wor a small, thick-set man in every thick-set man's clothes: brown leather jacket, dark office-suit keks, pale-pink open-neck shirt wi' a wide collar. He'd probably taken off his kipper tie as soon as he'd escaped the office.

Only a breeder, I wor thinking, would wear pale pink wi' shit brown.

'You people disgust me! Fucking shit-stabbing, fudge-packing queers!'

The bloke's lips twisted open, baring his yellowed lower teeth. The others, all of whom wor taller and less thick-set than this gnashing mutt of a bloke, looked hesitant and confused.

'Leave it,' one of 'em wor saying. 'Come on, leave it.'

Mutt man eyeballed me. 'And what have we here, then? His jobby basher?'

I kept my eyes on t' man's chest and said nowt.

'You know what your problem is, don't you?'

Camp David bit both the bait *and* the hook. 'Whatever my problem is, darling, it ain't half as big as yours!'

'What?'

Camp David's tongue broke loose. 'Nowt of yours can be half as big as mine, sweetie. Except maybe your gob. Only I use mine to better effect. In *and* out of the bedroom. You know what your problem really is? No? I'll tell you, sweetie. I turn you on.'

The bloke did a little jig on t' spot, and then his expression shifted.

'Euufff. Do you hear that, lads? He thinks I'm turned on. Turned on? By you? Fucking filthy nancy boy. You should be thrown into t' furnace wi' t' rest of your kind.'

I readied mesen for t' braying that wor surely about to happen. His mates closed in, and seeing the one closest to me drop his guard, I slugged him on t' chin. He tottered sideways, trying to steady himsen, then tripped over his own feet and keeled over. A gap opened.

'Run!' I yelled.

We pelted across t' road in front of two cars, then zig-zagged through t' shopping precinct streets and up an alley-

way that dog-legged past a pub, finally coming out on Lower
Briggate. Camp David stopped, one hand propping up a
lamp-post, bent double, breathing heavily.

'Wait! I think we've lost them.'

A young couple passed us by. She nudged her boyfriend
on t' elbow, turning her head to get a full gander, but he just
kept steaming ahead like he hadn't seen us. We walked the
rest of t' way down Lower Briggate toward t' New Penny. Just
before t' railway bridge, Camp David stopped and turned to
face me.

'How do I look?'

His face wor gleaming and his eyeliner had smudged.

'Just fine.'

He peered into t' barred-up window of a jeweller's shop,
tidied his hair and righted his hat.

'Thank you for defending my honour.'

'Your honour? Ha! You're t' one that dropped us in t' shit.
I'm just happy they didn't come after us.'

Camp David tucked his hand into t' crook of my arm.
'After that little escapade I need a stiff one. A drink, I mean.
Preferably a gin and tonic. You buying?'

I grinned. 'No, you are.'

We pushed through t' saloon-style pub doors to find oursens facing a DJ wi' a mic nearly kissing his tonsils who at
that moment wor introducing Manhattan Transfer's
'Chanson d'Amour'. I would never have ventured into t' New
Penny alone, it being a brash, two-fingers-in-a straight-man's-
eye sort of place, but wi' Camp David in tow, and wi' t' exhila-
ration of having dodged a braying, I wor feeling I could do
whatever I wanted.

Seated beneath t' DJ's pulpit wor a line of busty
middle-aged women, arms linked and singing along
raucously. Otherwise it wor what I expected: a few
tables of old codgers, a few younger loners standing about,

waiting to be picked up or just staring at the ends of their shoes.

Seeing us, the DJ garbled summat about fuckin' Sid and Nancy having just walked in, and one of t' women doubled up wi' laughing.

Camp David murmured in my ear, 'Plain-clothes are in tonight.'

'Sorry?' I wor thinking he meant everyone else.

'Those two, by t' pillar, propping up the bar.' He took off his hat and fur coat, which he tossed showily over a bar stool, then parked himsen on top of it. 'Plain-clothes cops.'

'How do you know that?'

'Darling, I just know.'

He looked at himsen in t' etched mirrors behind t' bar and patted his hair. The notion of plain-clothes cops in here wor a mite discomforting.

'So what do coppers want wi' this place?'

'Us. All of us. They want to know who we are. So they can pick us out when the time comes.' He leant into my ear and whispered, 'You are eighteen?'

'Aye,' I said. 'Just about.'

'You can let them see you drinking, but just don't snog anyone.'

'I worn't planning on it. You'd think they'd have summat better to do. What wi' t' Ripper still on t' loose.'

'Darling, the filth always have something else they should be doing, but aren't. I'll just say one word. Kickbacks.'

'This place?'

He nodded.

The opening bars of 'Hey, Big Spender' struck up behind us. Camp David let out a groan. A drag act mounted the tiny podium stage, someone called Ben Her. Lip-syncing that wor all pouted lips out of sync, deathly eyelash fluttering and Bassey-style flailing arms. The tape wor loud and distorted as Ben Her moved on to 'Diamonds are Forever', lips puckered up like a sex-shop doll.

'Do you like this stuff?' I shouted at Camp David.

'It's fucking shite! It's an insult to us all – women and gay men.'

'How come?'

'How come? Just wait for all the red-dress-looking-like-a-used-tampon, fish or chopped-liver jokes we've got coming.'

Camp David ordered a gin and tonic and a pint of lager and lime. The barman eyed me over, assessing my age perhaps, but said nowt. As my pint wor being pulled I said loudly, 'I'm thinking of moving out.'

'What?'

'Moving out. I'm thinking of moving out of home.'

'And go where?'

Ben Her wor wowing us wi' her 'Goldfinger'. It wor an effort to keep my eyes from flitting stageward. The in-between patter in a Doncaster accent included one 'In-that-red-dress-you-look-like-a-used-tampon' line, and three jokes about vaginas resembling chopped liver. Ben Her directed his entire repertoire toward t' group of brassy women and their gay mates strung along t' foot of t' podium, who wor lapping it up. Likely as not the Doncaster Ben Her fan club on an annual outing.

Camp David wor faced doggedly away from t' act, his elbows on t' bar, pretending it worn't happening. Ben Her's lacquered lids slid over t' audience, looking for a victim to slag off. Our eyes met for a split second, then he moved on wi' t' barest flicker of a smile. He must have read my alarm signals.

'My Way' came to an end like a drunk falling downstairs, followed by badly pre-recorded applause from *Sunday Night at the Palladium* or some such friggin' show, thanking the wonderful Miss Shirley Bassey, then t' noise level wor cut abruptly as the tape ran out. By now Ben Her had dismounted the podium and wor pushing through t' crowd toward t' ladies' toilet, elbow gloves already removed, before yanking off his wig to reveal a thinning, mousy mop. As he passed by I noticed the hands the gloves had been hiding. Bony labourer's hands wi' thick, half-crooked fingers.

The DJ tried to crank up the clapometer by rousingly asking for 'Another round of applause for Doncaster's very own Miss Ben Her!'

'Doncaster can keep her,' said Camp David. He swivelled round on his bar stool. 'I'd forgotten how fucking awful this place can be.'

'So why are we here?'

'It's the card we've been dealt. A single, low diamond. Or maybe a heart.'

I looked down at the floor. The carpet wor sticking to t' sole of my boot. The DJ wor playing Donna Summer's 'Love's Unkind'.

'I wor wondering,' I said, leaning into Camp David's ear, 'if there's a room going begging? At Radclyffe Hall?'

Camp David's plucked eyebrows arched.

I lay in t' bath, my ankles resting on t' taps, listening to t' tranny radio parked on t' toilet lid. We'd stayed at the New Penny 'til Camp David said he wanted some air, which had proved to be an excuse for him to walk along t' darkened streets near t' railway station and make a play for me. He said that when Fazel's room came free he'd 'smooth it over if I saw him right'. Seemed to me that everything in this world had a price, and nowt wor got for free. He led me into a fire-exit doorway that stank of old piss.

'Here?'

'As good as anywhere.'

I looked about nervously while Camp David wor caressing my unwilling crotch and trying to kiss me. The biting cold worn't helping me none. When a dustcart came rolling by I used the disturbance to step out into t' open. I hurried on to t' end of t' road, while Camp David lagged along behind. I saw my bus pulling up ahead. Camp David wor looking all flustered.

'I'd really like you to move in,' he said quickly, 'but it isn't just down to me. It has to be put to the house committee.'

As the bus pulled away he waved at me like a film star on t' aircraft steps and puckered up an air kiss.

I stayed in t' bath 'til t' water turned lukewarm. Mother tapped on t' door wanting to know if I wor all right and if she should heat up some dinner for me. I told her not to bother. I heard her clumping back downstairs.

The news came on t' radio and I paid little heed 'til, hearing the words 'Sid Vicious' and 'found dead', I sat bolt upright, sending a wave of bathwater over t' rim. 'Sid Vicious,' the Southern twat of a newsman wor saying, 'is believed to have died in a New York hotel room after taking a heroin overdose.'

I collapsed back into t' bath, sinking my head beneath t' waterline. When I couldn't hold my breath any longer I surged up again, gulping in air. Mother wor drumming her fists on t' door.

'Rick! What the heck are you doing in there? There's water coming through t' ceiling.'

That night I made up a shrine to Sid Vicious. I placed a photo of him between my Pistols singles and sank on my knees before my shrine as I contemplated my fate.

There wor a small tarn above t' town which Mitch said wor frozen over. He said we should go see it. We took the dog along for exercise.

The coldest recorded temperatures since '63, Terry had said. Canals, ponds, even some reservoirs had frozen over. Pipes wor bursting, cisterns turning solid, paths wor icy, roads wor dicey.

On t' drive up neither of us had said a dickybird. Mitch had driven intently, his unshaven jawline set, straining through t' gears as we funnelled between t' dry-stone walls either side that blocked our view of t' valley below. The town lay behind us.

We came to a stop on t' rough ground that wor t' car park. I ruffled the dog's head. The dog sat up, ears pricked, a breath patch forming on t' side window.

'Shush, Max,' I said softly.

There wor another vehicle in t' car park, an old dark-blue van. Mitch sat there, caressing the car-key fob between his fingers.

'Looks like we haven't got it to oursens after all.'

I peered up at the sky through t' windshield. What kind of clouds wor they? Cumulus? Or cirrus? Terry would know, Terry wi' his isobars and rain jars and thermometers. The dog whimpered to be let out. Mitch opened his door, so then I opened mine, the dog yanking hard on its leash to be let free.

We stood in t' crisp winter air, our breath hanging about our mouths. The snow glistened in t' sickly yellow of t' afternoon sun, melting now, save in those shadowed crevices beneath t' rocks and between t' tree roots. Soon there would be another frost.

Mitch surveyed the terrain like a woodland tracker, stroking his chin. 'It could be years,' he said, 'before she freezes over again.'

We set out. We passed a wooden tourist-information hut that wor shuttered up 'til t' spring. The tarn wor up ahead of us, out of view, hidden by an escarpment.

There wor two possible routes: either we could follow the upward path 'til we came to t' crest of t' escarpment, from where we could look down on t' tarn, or we could follow the path around t' tarn shore. Up on t' escarpment ridge the snow wor drifting like talcum powder, and the stunted trees quivered in t' wind. The cold bit into my bones.

Mitch said, 'We'd be best to stick to t' lower path.'

I let Max off t' leash and he scampered on ahead, nosing his way across t' ground, lifting his leg on rocks and bushes.

'Well,' said Mitch, 'let's go and take a look at her.'

The path wove between limestone rocks and bracken, then descended sharply toward t' shore. The ground beneath our tread wor compacted and slippery, and we had to be careful of our footing.

I picked up a stick and tossed it ahead of me. Max belted after it then brought it back in his mouth, his tongue lolling out the side. I tossed it again. And again.

We saw it now – a dirty grey sheet through t' skeletal birch trees. We stopped, so Max stopped too and turned his head, waiting on us.

It wor a force of will for me to speak, my tongue ungluing itsen from t' floor of my mouth, the skin of my chafed lips catching and tearing.

'There's summat I want to say. I'm thinking ...'

'You know, Rick, I used to bring your mother up here. When we wor courting.'

'Courting?' The very word seemed old-fashioned. 'Back in '62?'

Mitch raised his face to t' escarpment ridge. 'Did you know I met your mother at a ten-pin bowling club?'

'You've said. Thing is, now I'm grown I wor thinking that ...'

'I hung out wi' a few rockabilly lads, and sometimes we'd go bowling. It wor a good place to meet girls. One day there

221

wor this new lass waitressing there. She wor somehow different to anyone I'd met before, you know, shy, friendly, just summat about her. She worn't uppity or brassy like some of them.'

'Aye. Winter of '63.'

Mitch's brow furrowed. 'Remember the time I took you to see Leeds Utd? The one and only bloody time you ever came to a footie match?'

'Aye, I know, but what I want to tell you is ...'

'And then afterward – we won 3–0, for pity's sake – I asked you if you'd had a great time?'

'You didn't ask – you *told* me I'd had a great time. Well I hadn't. It wor boring. I wor ruddy-well frozen. Colder than I am now.'

'So what do you remember?'

'It wor yonks ago. I wor eleven. What should I remember? That my feet felt like blocks of ice? That all I could see wor t' backs of people's heads?'

'You don't remember what you said on t' way home?'

'That I hated it and wouldn't go again?'

'Aye. Well, that's when t' penny dropped, so to speak. When it dawned on me about you.'

'Which is what?' I said hoarsely.

'Family tradition, lad. You broke wi' three generations of family tradition. Broke it like a spoke on t' wheel.'

I kicked a loose stone irritably. As usual, Mitch wor fleet-footing his way around t' subject. We'd started walking again, stepping cautiously over tree roots and trying not to slip. This meant that neither of us had to look at t'other.

'1963,' I said. 'The last winter when everything wor frozen like this. That wor 1963, not '62.'

'Why does it matter which ruddy winter it wor?'

'Cos it does! It matters to me! Wor it really mine to break, this spoke on t' wheel?'

'What do you mean?'

But Mitch knew what I meant all right. He rasped, 'Things wor different back then. I did the right thing by you, taking you on. Damn you, I did the right thing. Brought you up like you wor my own flesh and blood.'

He removed his gloves, took out his penknife and prised a stone from t' sole of his boot. His fingers wor trembling. Strands of hair blew across his bald patch. He tossed the stone aside and closed the knife. Hearing raised voices, the dog came bounding back. It snuffled around Mitch's legs protectively. Reassured, it scarpered off again. Snow wor stuck to its back where it had been rolling in t' drifts.

'We've come to see her,' Mitch said, his voice almost choking. 'See t' tarn all frozen over and walk the dog. So let's go see t' tarn.'

We approached the shore, each of us carrying the weight of our own silence. Anger crackled inside me, trapped by Mitch's refusal to hear me out. Mother had said it often enough for it to stick in my brain: 'We met during that hard, terrible winter of '62.'

Except that it worn't '62. It wor '63. Terry had said so, and like as not Terry could tell you what the weather wor like on t' same day back in 1900, never mind 1962 or '63. It wor all recorded in his little black weather books. They met *after* I wor born. So maybe I worn't a freak for hating footie. Maybe I wouldn't lose my hair. But I needed confirmation. I needed him to look me in t' face and say it out loud: 'I am not your real father.' We squelched through t' trickle of a small beck and trudged along t' far bank 'til we wor nearly halfway round. Max came belting back wi' t' stick again, so this time I threw it further, launching it in t' direction of t' tarn. The stick scythed through t' air, a dark thing against t' aching whiteness.

'No!' Mitch shouted. 'Max, no!'

Too late. The dog wor already out on t' ice, his head up, his eyes fixed on t' somersaulting stick.

'Max! Max, come back here!'

Suddenly realising where it wor, the dog's feet began to slither, its legs splaying.

'Max!'

The dog blinked at us both as if comprehending its own doom. Then t' ice beneath parted a little and black, cold water slurped across t' surface. The ice made a hideous retching sound and started to give. The dog wor scrabbling its paws for some grip as the freezing water began to envelop it. We crouched down at the shoreline, both of us calling the dog's name. Mitch broke off a long, thin birch branch. I stepped onto a rock that protruded into t' tarn.

'Max! Max, boy!'

Mitch prodded the ice wi' t' stick, then eased one foot onto t' surface, keeping t'other on t' bank. Then he let the ice take his full weight. He kept his legs spread as wide as he could, edging out a little further, using his hands for support. Here, the ice wor thick enough that it held easily, but out there, a few feet beyond, out where t' dog wor struggling, we both knew it wor dangerous. That dog wor going to drown.

'Max, Max,' Mitch called out softly, calming it, encouraging it, cajoling it toward him. He ventured out a tad further. The dog pawed at the ice, whimpering. Mitch flattened himsen and stretched out the stick, trying to hook it through t' dog's collar. I looked on from t' rock.

The tarn just swallowed him. It creaked and complained, then opened its black jaws and Mitch flopped into t' water. I saw him thrashing to gain control, trying to haul himsen onto t' ice. Then he slipped under. Moments later he resurfaced, flapping his arms uselessly. His pleading eyes met mine. Then he wor gone.

I jumped from t' rock to t' shore. A raven flew low over t' tarn surface, cawing bleakly. I kept my eyes fixed on t' spot where Mitch had been only seconds before, half-expecting the ice to seal over and Mitch to reappear. Like a rewinding film.

The ice remained silent.

Somehow Max had struggled to t' shore. He wor shaking himsen and looking about for Mitch wi' nowt more than a dog's expression of having momentarily misplaced its master. The dog, intent on saving itsen, had not seen Mitch go under.

I pelted back to t' car park, Max bounding along behind me. I drummed my fists on t' blue van's side window. Max wor barking at my feet. Only when I stopped drumming did I see that the van had been abandoned. I slumped against its side and inhaled the crystalline air. I wor hot and clammy. I yanked my scarf away from my neck and tore at the top buttons of my jacket, letting the winter wind blast against my exposed neck. I stared numbly out across t' white fields toward t' arc of t' horizon. I must have stayed like that for t' longest time, cos I remembered later being puzzled at how much darker it had become. My limbs felt heavy, and I could not will mesen to move. Better to stay here, stay here, I wor thinking, and wait for someone to find us. I tossed my hat into t' snow. I tore off my jacket and chucked it aside. Max wor whimpering to be home. He barked once and then started to pad away, every so often stopping and turning his head, 'til finally he gave up on me and bounded out of view.

I smiled to mesen. I would stay here. I liked it here. Dusky mauve clouds wor skidding across t' sky.

Cumulus, or cirrus? Terry would know.

* * *

I came to in my own bed, pinned beneath weighty bedclothes, blinking slowly, letting the light bleed in. The sky through t' crack between my curtains wor t' colour of unwashed sheep.

I listened to t' murmurings of t' house. I could hear my alarm clock ticking, and the heating pipes knocking as the immersion heater cooled down. Every sound wor magnified a millionfold.

I moved my fingers and wiggled my toes. It wor an effort to push back the blankets. I wor wearing pyjama bottoms, a T-shirt and thick socks. The T-shirt wor damp, and clung clammily against me. It took an effort to swing my legs round and set my feet on t' floor. I clocked wi' a woozy horror that the pyjama bottoms I wor wearing belonged to Mitch. A flash recollection came into my head of his drowned and decaying corpse dressed in t' same pyjama bottoms. I cried out. Pushing on my hands, I tried to stand. I collapsed onto t' floor. I could hear footsteps coming hurriedly up the stairs.

It wor a bitter, bone-freezing day when Mitch wor cremated at Rawdon crematorium. Before that could happen there wor an investigation into his death by t' police, and then an inquest. I wor interviewed in a kindly manner. I told the policewoman what I felt I should remember. I didn't feel like embroidering it wi' extra stuff, like making out that I'd tried to rescue him or owt.

Mitch's death got a mention in t' *Bradford Telegraph and Argus*. Mand showed me t' clipping. 'Man Falls Through Ice and Drowns', followed by eight lines about him trying to rescue his dog. For some reason I worn't in t' story at all. That left me feeling all hollowed out. Mand said that a farmer, bringing in his cows before dusk and alerted by Max's barking, had lucked upon me collapsed by t' van. I wor taken to t' hospital, she said, kept overnight and then brought home. None of this I remembered.

On t' morn of t' cremation the house wor stealthily quiet. I could hear Mandy and Mother creeping about and speaking in low voices. Summat about shoes. Usually at this hour Mand would have been bouncing about like a beachball to Radio 1 and making hersen ready for work, while Mum would be hollering up the stairs that brekkie wor on t' table. Even t' dog just lay quiet in his basket in t' kitchen, eyes fixed on t' back door. Since t' drowning that was how it had been, this day and every day. I sloughed about, sniffling cos I had a stinking cold. I made mesen some tea and toast, but couldn't finish the toast so I threw it out for t' birds. A magpie swooped out of t' morning mist and snaffled it.

We followed the hearse in a taxi, all three of us sitting stiffly in t' back. Mother had wanted to keep the cremation simple – no flowers on t' hearse spelling out MITCH or DAD or owt like that, and she dismissed out of hand Don's suggestion that a US Confederate flag should be draped over t' coffin.

Waiting in a huddle at the crematorium gates wor Nora, Janice wi' little Damien in a buggy, Mavis and Don, who wor blowing warm air into his gloveless hands, and Mrs Fibak, who moved gingerly wi' t' aid of a stick since her fall, but no Mr Fibak, who 'didn't feel up to a funeral this morning'.

Craner pitched up an all, wearing black jeans and a pale-grey suit jacket peeking beneath a muddy-brown parka, which he kept on throughout. Just before t' service kicked off, a couple of Mitch's lorry driver mates shuffled in at the back, together wi' a small bloke wi' big square specs and an egg-shaped head who Mother whispered wor t' depot manager of Maid Marion Foods.

It wor all over in under fifteen minutes. Lined along t' pews, we stuttered through a hymn and mumbled the Lord's Prayer, then t' vicar, a fat little man wi' bulging blue eyes, doled out a few words about Mitch, his heroic and tragic loss, his devotion to his family. Then we all had to listen to Elvis's 'My Way', and I drooped my head and noticed a piece of chuddy gum stuck to t' back of t' pew. I wor feeling ill. Had I eaten summat bad? Had I eaten at all? I couldn't tell if my stomach wor wheezing in protest or pain. Then I remembered the toast, and wished I'd finished it.

Light-headed, I let my mind go on a gadabout, lulled perhaps by t' Elvis song or t' vicar droning on, or perhaps by t' mind-numbing otherness of it, 'til I felt a jab in t' ribs and saw Mandy's reddened, kohl-streaked eyes staring into me as if I wor stood hard on her toe, and I realised the coffin had disappeared behind t' curtains and folk wor wanting to file out.

'It isn't the cough that carries you off, it's the coffin they carry you off in.'

I sniggered. Mavis gave me a surprised frown, but said nowt. Why did that come into my head right now? Summat Granddad used to say in his teasing voice. A spot in time – dark, like a rainspot?

Outside, on t' steps, I heard talk about car space and travel arrangements. Craner came up to me and patted me on t' shoulder.

'Take your time, son, before returning to work,' he said in a low voice. 'Take a whole week if you have to.'

I don't recall the car journey. I recall getting in t' car, and my nose against t' side window as we u-turned, and then being back home, but the ride itsen never happened. Although it must have – this worn't *Star Trek*.

Once we wor back home we stood about in t' lounge not talking, a gathering in grieving. The table wor laden wi' sarnies, sausage rolls and cake. The dog had its nose up against t' table edge, its tail drumming on t' floor.

'It isn't the cough that carries you off, it's the ...'

I guffawed, placing my hand over my gob to stop mesen. Everyone wor looking at me, sorrowful and aghast. I saw it. Felt it.

Nora and Mrs Fibak went into t' kitchen to brew tea. Mavis followed them, and lit up a ciggie – through t' kitchen hatch I could see it burning down between her fingers. She'd painted her nails a dark plum. The men stood about, supping beer and exchanging remarks on t' weather, food or Mitch in low, rumbling voices. Mother kept a fixed stare out through t' window nets, as if she wor expecting Mitch to be coming up the front path any moment. Mandy sat beside her on a dining chair, her face set stonily in distress.

Then Damien started caterwauling to escape his buggy, so Janice moved it into t' hallway so he wouldn't be quite so loud. Motherhood had aged Janice beyond her years; her hair wor lank and her clothes wor what Mother would call 'practical'. Drew, I heard Janice say, had moved to Blackpool to work the summer season as a fairground-ride operator on t' sea front. Then he'd stayed on for t' Illuminations, then Halloween and Guy Fawkes' Night, then Christmas.

Mrs Fibak came through wi' t' tea in a large pot I didn't recognise, then fetched a tray of cups and various assorted mugs. One of t' mugs had been a Christmas present from Mandy to Mitch, a *Carry On* mug that laughed like Sid James when you cocked it toward your gob. Mrs Fibak must have found it at the back of t' cupboard.

'The snowdrops looked nice,' she said, setting the tray down. 'Peeking through t' ground.'

I excused mesen, went upstairs and locked mesen in t' bathroom.

'... carries you off, it's the coffin they carry you off in.'

I grabbed a hand towel and laughed into it 'til I wor dry-heaving and my eyes wor watering. I stayed like that for some time, steadying my breathing. Wi' my forefinger I stroked t' bath rim, then around t' sink and over t' taps, then along t' top of t' loo-roll holder. Someone tried the door, the handle waggling freely on my side. I coughed loudly, counted to five and then flushed the loo.

Whoever it wor had gone. I ducked into Mandy's room, opened the top right drawer and pressed my hand on t' cover of her diary, trying to feel the words through my palm. I closed the drawer again and went back downstairs.

As I turned the corner of t' stairs I came upon Mavis, backed against t' wall, and Don, prodding her repeatedly in t' throat wi' his forefinger, his face red and sweating, hers stretched and fearful. Don had been drinking all morning. On seeing me he hugged Mavis tightly and said loudly, 'There, there, don't worry my petal, don't you worry,' his fat arms covering Mavis's face while he nailed me wi' a cold, dead eye as I edged past. Behind me I heard Mavis thudding up the stairs and then Don saying loudly for my benefit, 'She's upset, that's all. She'll be as right as rain.'

After this wor all over, a routine of sorts resumed. Only it worn't a routine I welcomed.

Every night I'd been having t' same bad dream. I'd see a hand reaching out from t' water. The hand wor large and grasping and kept coming toward me, the fingers stretched wide like an eagle's claw. At the very last moment I'd jump back, and then t' hand would wither away and Mitch's contorted lips would appear before me, forming some word-less plea as he wor being sucked below. All t' while I'd hear Max barking like an echo in my inner ear 'til I woke up, knackered and basted in cold sweat. I'd lie there, my head on my pillow, staring around my room and thinking how friggin' unreal everything looked.

I slid out of bed, sloughed over to t' window and pulled back the curtains. Two of Mitch's freshly washed shirts wor flapping on t' washing line. I fathomed that this wor in readiness for charity, or to be given away. I wor wrong. Mother ironed them and hung them in t' wardrobe, just as she'd always done.

Each evening Mother laid a place for Mitch at the table, and chatted away like he wor there, shrilling his name up the stairs or over t' banisters into t' hallway below. On Saturday afternoon she asked Mand to switch on t' telly cos the wrestling wor on. We supposed it soothed her to hear t' wrestling or horse racing on t' telly in t' next room.

After about a week of this Mand let rip at Mother, her voice bursting into a sob. 'Why are you doing this? He's dead, Dad's dead! Why lay his place at the table and talk as if he wor still here?' She shoved her dinner plate away from her and stood up, then picked up the cutlery, plate and beer glass that had been laid for Mitch and stomped off into t' kitchen. We heard them crashing into t' waste bin. Mother sat there and wept.

As for me, there wor so much to do, I didn't have no time to think about Mitch being gone. Jobs about t' house. A kitchen-cabinet door had loosened on its hinges and needed tightening. I went to fetch a screwdriver from t' garage. I shouldered open t' garage side door and wor met by t' smell of oily rags, rusting tools and old rubber, of sawdust shavings and marinading paintbrushes.

'Hello hammers,' I croaked. 'Hello mushroom-head and claw. Hello paintbrushes. Rusting paint tins. Hello clamp. Vice. Saws. Tobacco tins of carpet tacks and screws and nails. Hello oil drum and bottle of turps. Tyres, ironing board, dartboard. Blunt darts. Bag of Xmas tree mishaps. Number 7 iron and driver, garden hose and taps.'

I stroked the surfaces of all these things as I spoke.

'Hello tins of car paint, bikkie tins and Royal tin tray. Hello *Sun* calendars 1973 and '76. Busty Brenda – wi' t' massive tits. Hello mono record player, needleless. Hello horse blanket covering old pram. Wigwam for my seventh birthday, never played in. Hello garden fork and spade, watering can wi' a hole in t' bottom, and all them flowerpots, never used. Hello. Hello old toilet seat, hanging from t' ceiling. Hello faded photos of Mum and sis. And me. Propped against a rusting tea tin. Hello.'

By t' time I'd greeted every object in t' garage I wor bawling my eyes out.

Back in t' kitchen, screwdriver in hand, I found Mother wiping a clean glass on a tea towel. Even though t' glass wor dry she continued wiping it.

'I want rid of t' dog,' I said to Mother's back, caressing the screwdriver handle wi' my thumb and forefinger. Mother stopped wiping the glass. She set it down and picked up another glass and started wiping that.

I put an ad in t' local rag offering to give Max away 'to a good home'. On t' first evening there wor a couple of telephone calls that led to nowt, and then after that it went silent. I wor planning on leaving Max tied to a lamp-post somewhere when a man telephoned 'to see if the dog's still going'.

The man rolled up in a rusting old Ford Zodiac wi' a loose rear bumper. He had his wife and three small kids in tow, and another dog, a terrier, wor yapping and throwing itsen against t' rear side window. He wor a bony-shouldered bloke who moved like he couldn't quite manage his limbs, and his wife wor a mousy little thing in black slacks and a blue anorak who wor constantly pushing her hair back behind one ear. The kids and the terrier stayed in t' car. The man kept nuzzling Max's ears and saying to his wife, 'We can't turn this one down, luv, we just can't.'

I could see that she worn't keen.

Mandy came out to ogle t'scene, squished her lower lip and went back indoors.

The man shook my hand and the deal wor done. I gave his wife Max's lead and dog bowl and a half-full bag of dog bikkies. They didn't want the basket. Max went without any fuss, but his tail wor drooped, and he gave me one last mournful look, like he thought he wor being carted off to t' knackers' yard.

When Mother came home from Nora's a bit later I told her I'd given the dog away. She smoked a ciggie down to t' butt and said I should try to get shot of t' kennel an all. Then she said she wor intending to visit Gran the next day. I guessed Nora had been blathering on to her about it. Mother said she wanted me to go wi' her. I reluctantly agreed.

At the nursing home there wor this empty space where Bobby's chair had been, and there wor a new girl on reception wi' dark-brown bangs jiggling before her eyes. There worn't no Mr Kipling cakes neither. The new girl had the radio turned up loud and wor filling out a crossword book. I asked her about Bobby. She looked blank, so I told here he wor t' man in t' wheelchair who'd been abandoned there as a nipper and who turned the pages of his book wi' a stick he held 'tween his teeth. She said she'd only started last month and that no one like that wor there then, so she knew nowt about it.

We could hear raised voices echoing along t' corridor, but no one wor to be seen. Gran wor in her room. She'd been got out of bed and plonked in her bedside chair. The bed had been stripped, except for a rubber sheet covering t' mattress. My thoughts wor snagged on Bobby. Maybe they'd done away wi' him? Or shipped him off somewhere where he couldn't read his books on t' music stand or listen to t' radio?

Mother patted the edge of t' bed to check that it wor dry, then sat down on it and took Gran's speckly hand. It lay lifelessly in Mother's palm like a small dead fish. I perched my backside on t' arm of her commode. She'd closed her eyes tightly, as if waiting for or willing us to be gone.

Mother looked earnestly at Gran and said, 'Mitch has gone. I'm a widow now. Like you. Rick's the man about t' place now.'

I breathed steadily, said nowt.

Mother changed tack. 'When I wor small, about seven or eight, I took a pound note out your purse. I knew it wor wrong, but it wor that wrongness that thrilled me. I remember standing by t' back door wi' it in my hand. It wor a bright, breezy day. I wor holding the note by my fingertips. Then I let it go, watched it swirl across t' yard and pin itsen to t' back fence. I ran after it, but just as I reached the fence the breeze tossed it high up into t' air and away it went. The next day, you and Dad had a proper barney over t' housekeeping money. I'd never seen him so mad. You wor crying and your purse wor on t' table between you, so I knew I'd been the cause of it.'

'What,' I said, 'is to be gained by this? If you want to confess summat, go to t' proper place.'

'This feels like t' proper place.'

She took a tissue from her handbag and sniffled into it. Gran's closed lids flickered.

Mother went on. 'Did I want too much? A proper family, decent kids, food on t' table – just like most folk. Wor that too much to ask? Maybe that's the trouble wi' this life – we all want too much, don't we?'

She clipped the handbag shut, smoothed her skirt wi' her palms and rose to leave.

In t' bus shelter outside t' main gates wor a poster that read:

Ignore the Ripper,
and he'll go away
... to kill again.

When we got home, I helped Mother collect all Mitch's clothes together and burn 'em in an old water drum. My own confessions would have to wait.

'Corona, Mrs Husk!'

Mrs Husk wor leaning against t' dining table, mashing up a small dish of cat food wi' a fork. Lord Snooty wor sashaying about her swollen ankles, his tail erect, the tip swaying gently.

As Mrs Husk turned slowly toward me I swore I heard the creak and strain of her neck sinews, like an old ship's timbers. I thought I saw t' hint of a smile cross her lips, and a flickering in her rheumy old eyes. She laid the fork aside and set the dish at the far end of t' table. Lord Snooty leapt up elegantly and, purring loudly, began licking away at the dish edges.

'So you're back.'

'Looks like it.'

'That lad who wor on while you wor off – I didn't take to him none.'

'Steve?'

'Never did get his name. In and out of here like a rocket on wheels, he wor.'

'Sorry to hear that, Mrs Husk.'

I set her ginger beer bottle on t' table, took the dish of cat food and put it down on t' floor. Lord Snooty protested briefly at his dinner being moved, then attacked it again.

'You're late this morning.'

As if Mrs Husk wor keeping anyone waiting save her maker. God must be tapping his watch wi' a frown. Not only had we been late starting out, but then Eric made a detour to sell ten crates of Coke to some newsagent. Only when we got there his missus said he'd gone to Pakistan on urgent business and she knew nowt about buying ten crates of Coke from Corona and shooed us out of t' shop wi' flaps of her painted hands, her gold wrist bracelets jiggling like sleighbells.

'Sit,' said Mrs Husk, motioning toward one of t' dining chairs. Her wig sat askew on her head, as if it wor about to slip off.

'Your leg?'

'The leg can wait.'

I pulled out a dining chair and sat on its edge. Mrs Husk clasped the teapot wi' both hands, then poured a cup. Lord Snooty cocked his head and miaowed.

'It's still warm.'

'Mrs Husk, I haven't got time ...'

The tea worn't for me. She held the cup in her left hand and slurped from it noisily 'til nowt save t' dregs wor left. Then she upended the leaves onto a saucer. The saucer had a crack running through t' rose pattern. She bent over t' saucer, staring down into t' leaves as if searching for a foreign body, her lips moving soundlessly. A fly clung to her hairnet, twitching the air, 'til she moved her head a smidgen and the fly took off sharpish.

'What is it, Mrs Husk? What do you see?' I wor itching to be gone.

When she finally spoke, her voice wor thick, the words gurgling in t' back of her throat. 'I see a girl, or perhaps a young woman ... an iceberg ... a knife ... a copse, no, not a copse ... tall trees ... yes, tall trees along a path, perhaps in a park. It's hard to see ... it's night. Wait ... Ah, I can see her better now, yes. She's happy, she's gay. But danger lurks.'

'She's gay?'

'Yes, yes, hidden danger ... the iceberg ... She's been to see her grandfolk, and now she's making her way home. Beneath t' trees. Yes, home.'

Her tea-leaf nonsense wor rattling me. Maybe Mrs Husk wor leaving the building. Wi' her left hand she gripped the table edge.

'A wolf, or someone wolf-like, is stalking her,' she said, her wheezy voice rising and tightening. 'Oh, he's closer. The danger is walking toward her, not she toward it. She's heading home. She has summat that she wants to show off, summat shiny ... like gold.'

'Gold?'

'Gold. It's time itsen. She wor showing her grandfolk time itsen, time all gleaming and gold, and now ... and now he is upon her, and ... Time stops!'

Mrs Husk wor sucking in air. Then wi' a sweep of her hand she sent t' saucer skating off t' table. Lord Snooty miaowed in protest and leapt away.

'Mrs Husk?'

I bent down to pick up the saucer from t' floor. It had cracked clean along t' fissure, split in two.

'Soon!' Mrs Husk breathed. 'Soon!'

I shuddered. 'I should be going, Mrs Husk. Time don't wait for t' living.'

I wor gone like a greyhound out of a trap, not waiting for her ginger beer money.

Josephine Whitaker
04/04/1979

How many Halifaxes are there in t' world? Some places are like that – you see t' name on road signs, trucks and vans, but you never think you'll ever visit. Not unless you end up there by happenstance.

There wor a Halifax in Nova Scotia, I'd seen it on t' globe in school. That's two Halifaxes. I guessed there must be others spread about. I pondered on how confusing that must be for t' post.

HE had gone to Halifax. Driven there wi' intent. It had been nigh on a year since his last topping, and it seemed that he wor fading from our minds, but truth be known he wor just cowering amongst all t' junk that wor stashed in t' attic.

The police took a few days to confirm that it wor HIM. The 'characteristics', confirmed the pathologist, wor t' hallmarks of HIM. She wor another innocent, as they said, a young girl on her way home from her grandfolks', where she'd been to show them her new watch. Josephine even worked for the friggin' Halifax Building Society.

It wor only some time later that I made the connection wi' Mrs Husk and the tea leaves. I told her she should go to t' cops, tell 'em what she knew, but she wor having none of it.

'What use would there be?'

I pleaded wi' her, and said that if she didn't, I would. She listened on while stroking Lord Snooty beneath his chin.

While we wor reloading the van, I spilled all to Eric about Mrs Husk and the tea leaves.

'Karen's really into all that stuff,' he said. 'You know, horoscopes and palm readings and the like. I didn't realise how much 'til we went to Morecambe for a day out. We left the little one wi' Karen's folks, and took off. We'd just done t' dolphinarium and wor sitting on t' pier when Karen spotted one of them Gypsy Rose palm-reading tents. I never put much store in it – you pays good money to be told all sorts of stuff and nonsense, but she thought it would be a lark, so in she went while I waited outside. When she came out, she wor in a black mood. I wor half-minded to stomp in there and ask for our money back. She wouldn't let on what she'd been told.'

'That's cos if you reveal it, it won't happen.'

'Well then, if it wor bad news, she should have said, shouldn't she, to break the curse.'

'No, you can't do that neither – it doubles the trouble.'

'Is that right? Well, maybe it did double anyway. We'd just left the pier when it started to rain. We'd had lunch already, so we went into t' wax museum. Have you ever seen that place?'

'Never been to Morecambe.'

'Oh, you should go. First week of September's good, when t' lights are on. But if you do, avoid the wax museum. The models of t' famous people are all tatty, and don't look nothin' like them. I mean, there wor one that wor supposed to be Neil Armstrong, but it wor just a mannequin in a space helmet – it could have been anyone. Then there's this separate inner bit – "the Macabre Torso Room". Really gruesome stuff, like models of pregnant women cut open so you can see t' babby inside. Who wants to see that? And others wi' their faces half eaten away wi' syphilis. I tell you, a quick shufty in there wor more than enough for me. But Karen

239

wor fascinated. After we left, she took me by t' arm, and she wor trilling like a budgie for t' rest of t' day. Womenfolk, eh?'

'I bet it had summat to do wi' t' fortune-teller. Only she couldn't say.'

'You think? On t' way out I told the man who sold the tickets what I thought about his Torso Room. He said it wor what pulled in t' punters. Without the Torso Room, he said he might as well shut up shop.'

Sis had left her diary on t' sofa, so I opened it at random and took mesen a peek. Since Mitch's death she didn't keep a proper diary no more, just a big exercise book that she scrawled and scribbled in. She worn't much cop at keeping it up to date. Sometimes months went by without an entry.

The page wor full of friggin' ticks. It wor all about her new boyfriend. Some goon called Marcus. Every entry wor numbered and followed by a tick 'til last one.

1. I have new boyfriend √
2. His name is Marcus √
3. He's year older than me √
4. He eats licorice sweets that make his tongue turn
   black and then he tries to snog me.

Then she'd written: 'Note to self. Must change that.'

I bet I could make his tongue loll, sis.

'We've all got inner rooms.'

Damned if I knew what Gordon meant by that. We wor taking a drive out of town in t' Humber. On t' way I'd been blathering on about Mrs Husk, and Eric and Karen in Morecambe.

At Blubberhouses Gordon swung a left toward Fewston reservoir. We parked up on t' bridge that wor also t' dam wall and got out. It wor a fine spring day, bright and blustery, the sunlight punching holes in t' clouds, and I stood there beneath t' restless giant sky, the wind tugging at my hair and making my donkey-jacket collar flap like a flag's edges.

We leant over t' parapet and looked down on t' sky reflecting in t' water. Gordon's ciggie smoke wor snaking away.

Gordon said, 'I popped by Radclyffe Hall and saw Terry. I thought it wise to put them in the frame.'

'Ta.'

'Fazel's still there, you know. His visa doesn't expire until July – the end of the academic year, I suppose. Poor boy. Do you think he'll get to New York? Apparently he has a brother there. Terry's suggested he should seek political asylum.'

'But they won't give him asylum just for being gay.'

'No, indeed. Maybe the Dutch would give it, but he would need to prove persecution. It helps that his mother and sister have gone to Egypt. That's where the Shah went when he first went into exile, incidentally.'

'Fazel told me he hates him.'

'The Shah? Right now, my boy, it's a case of lesser evils and self-preservation.'

A pair of ducks skimmed over t' surface of t' water, quacking noisily.

'Well, when he does go, I won't be taking his room. I can't now, can I?'

'Your mother ...'

'She'll have to go out and work. Get a proper job. Wi' Mandy and me both earning, we'll be right.'

The copper on duty at Mill Street cop shop had his elbows on t' desk, and his head bent over a form. On t' wall to his left wor a photo-fit poster of HIM. It looked a lot like Jason King.

The cop knew I wor standing there, waiting for him to look up, but he worn't going to hurry himsen.

241

I scuffed my boot toecaps against t' bottom of his desk. He continued to ignore me, so I hacked up a cough, and his shoulders tightened. He pushed the form aside, but only so far that he could get back to it as soon as he'd dealt wi' me.

'Yes?'

The whites of his eyes wor mapped in fine red cracks. He had a prominent wart on his temple.

On t' bus I'd been going over and over what I'd say – 'I know this old biddy who can read the tea leaves. She can see into t' future, and she knows when and where t' next one will be' – but now I wor here, it wor clear as daylight how gormless that would sound. Likely as not I'd be dismissed as just another barmpot.

'Sorry. I've made a mistake. It wor nowt. Sorry.'

The officer pulled the form back beneath his nose and resumed scribbling. I walked out.

When I got home, Mandy waylaid me in t' kitchen.

'There's this girl who's showed up. Says she knows you. She wor in a bit of a state, so I let her in and gave her a mug of Nescaf.' She nodded toward t' lounge. 'In there. I wouldn't let Mother catch sight of her. She looks like she's been dragged through a hedge twice over, and whiffs like she ain't washed in a while.'

I opened the lounge door.

'Gina!'

She wor huddled in front of t' gas fire, turned away from me. Hearing her name, she jerked her head slightly, but kept her face hidden behind her hair, which wor longer now, and had grown back to its natural mousy brown. I went over to her, and touched her lightly on t' arm. In spite of t' fire her skin wor cold and clammy. She wor sodden wet, soaked wretched. She looked up at me wi' mournful puppy eyes and wiped one hand 'cross her nose.

'Can I stay?' she said, barely whispering.

'Here?'

'Is she your sister? She's pretty.'

I kept shtumm.

'Please. Let me stay. Just for tonight. I'll be gone in the morning.'

'Gone where?'

She turned away again, as if the answer lay in t' glimmering plastic coals.

'You'll catch your death in them wet clothes.'

I fetched a towel for her hair and face, and a large white T-shirt. She undressed down to her panties, draped her wet clothes over t' arm of t' settee. Squatting in front of t' gas fire wi' my T-shirt stretched over her knees, her hair lank and without make-up, she would have made a pitiful sight, had I felt any pity.

'How did you find me?'

'Not difficult, poppet. I rang your work and said I was your cousin, and that I wanted to send you a birthday card but didn't have the address. It's easy to find people when you use a bit of gumption.'

'So I see.'

'I've been inside.'

'I heard. When did they let you out?'

'A couple of weeks ago. I went to my mother's for as long as I could stand it. When she drinks, which is most of the time, she loves me, hates me, then loves me in the same minute, like she's ripping petals off a flower. She thinks that if she says she loves me often enough, one of us might start to believe it.'

'So you just thought you'd pitch up 'ere? What about Victor? Why can't you go to him – he is your husband.'

'Was. Fuck knows what I saw in him. Opportunity, I suppose. He's still got three months to go in Armley jail.'

'And Jeremy?'

'I think he's holed up in Rotherham. He knows some of our people there.'

'*Your* people, you mean. So you've got nowhere else to go. I've always wondered why you latched on to me in t' first place. You know, at the FK Club.'

'Don't you know, poppet? You mean you really don't know?'

'No, I don't. Not really.'

'It was Tad.'

'Tad worn't there that night.'

She arched her eyebrows at me. 'Remember that girl I went off to see?'

'The one you'd snogged?'

'That one. Well, she wasn't there, but I did have a cosy little chat with Tad. He was by the DJ box, watching us. Of course, you didn't know Tad at that point. We couldn't decide which way you swung. So we had a bet. A fiver on which of us got to fuck you first. We tossed a coin for who'd have first crack at you.'

'So you won the toss and lost the bet,' I said. 'Where's Tad now?'

'How should I know?'

'Cos you just do.'

'Did you know my dad was in the Merchant Navy? I never met him. He left before I was born. Then a few years later my mother took up with this odious pub landlord. He had eczema, and fat red fingers. He made it clear I was in the way, except when he wanted me ... He'd creep into my room at night. Anyway, one day that bastard took off as well. Stole the pub's takings. Other men came and went. My mother took to drinking: women's drinking – secretly, silently, until she was drinking enough that people started to notice. She's been more or less drunk ever since.'

'Where's Tad?'

'Did you ever try that telephone number, poppet? The one I wrote on your chest? Oh, you did? Then you'll know it was a fake. We didn't have a telephone at Paradise Buildings. We hadn't expected you to latch on to us like that. You know, that time when you came running over to me and Jeremy like a lost dog.'

'Where's Tad?'

'Where *is* Tad? Well, now ...'

'You can stay, so long as ...'

'Oh, you're an angel, aren't you? An angel! An angel!'

'... So long as you tell me where he is.'

She sucked on a strand of her hair.

'Maybe he's in prison.'

'Or maybe not. If he wor, you would have have said so by now.'

'Would I, poppet?'

'Well?'

'The truth is, I neither know nor care where he is. As far as I'm concerned, Tad can rot in hell.'

'And as far as I'm concerned ...'

I stood up and moved toward t' door.

'He's in London,' she said quickly, pulling the T-shirt tighter about her.

'London? Have you got his address?'

She tugged at her tangled hair. 'Are you in love with him, poppet? Hmmm? Cos he never shuts up about you.'

'If you give me his address ...'

Her lips parted slightly. I fetched a pen, tore a sheet from t' pop-up telephone address book and stood over her while she scribbled an address. I snatched the sheet from her.

'Stockwell?'

'That was the last address he gave me.'

I folded it and tucked it into my back pocket.

Gina sighed. 'Now what, poppet?'

'Now you can get dressed and go.'

'What?'

'You heard. I don't want you here. Get dressed and get out. Now!'

She scowled at me, but seeing that I meant it, she struggled to her feet. As she pulled on her black jeans, which wor still damp, I touched her elbow to steady her.

'Don't touch me! Don't ever touch me!' she screamed.

I thought she wor going to go for me. I wor tensed up, ready for it. Instead, she put her face close to mine and whispered viciously, 'Maybe I lied about the address.'

'I'll risk it.'

She finished dressing without another word. I followed her into t' hallway. She stopped and turned. 'You're no better than the rest of them.'

'You're probably right on that score. I'll say one word. Dora.'

'Dora? I don't know any Dora, poppet.'

I watched her walking away down t' road 'til t' darkness had swallowed her. When I came back inside I found Mand waiting by t' door.

'Promise me you won't go to London.'

'Never ask anyone to make a promise,' I said. 'They'll only break it.'

For once I wor alone in t' house. It wor so quiet I could hear t' pipes knocking. When I wor small Mitch had told me it wor little men scurrying along wi' tiny hammers, carrying out emergency repairs in case t' pipes burst into our lives.

Sis wor getting careless wi' that diary. It wor on t' floor beside her bed, barely covered by a *Jackie* mag.

I crouched down and leafed through it, turning the pages gingerly 'til: *Friday*. I read quickly. Seemed that Marcus fancied himsen as a bit of a drummer. He wor even in some band, called Max Squid. 'Max friggin' Squid,' I chortled. What kind of a friggin' shite name wor that? They rehearsed in t' basement of a warehouse in Bramley. Sis described it. I knew it – I could picture the building.

I flipped back a week. Boring. Fast forward. *Thursday.*

Ah, more like it. Sis and Marcus had been having sex in t' rehearsal room. He'd had an extra key cut. He'd done her a tape of his favourite shite bands like Gryphon and Gentle Giant and Spooky Tooth and Budgie. I looked at the cassette lying on t' floor. 'Music from Marcus: For Mandy'.

I closed the diary and unfolded the scrap of paper wi' Tad's address on it, stroking my thumb across it thoughtfully. Then I flopped back on sis's bed and undid my fly.

Mother's new job wor at Clark's hauliers, over Shipley way. It wor just three days a week, doing paperwork and answering the phone. Mitch would have never allowed it. Mitch always believed that a married woman's place wor firmly wedded to t' kitchen sink. But then, this wor t' same Mitch who'd told me that no woman would become Prime Minister in his lifetime. What wor it I'd seen in a feminist pamphlet at a Gay Lib meeting? 'It starts when you sink in his arms and ends with your arms in his sink.'

By t' end of her first week you couldn't shut Mother up. She retold every last friggin' detail over and over: who said what, where, when and why. Who drank tea, who preferred coffee, how many friggin' sugars – the whole nine ruddy yards. I couldn't say how many sugars Craner had in his friggin' tea, only that he fair heaped it in. But it wor good to see her smiling again, although sometimes I'd catch a sadness in her eyes. Maybe Mand saw it too, cos one day she asked her, 'Do you think Mavis would miss Don if he died?'

'You get used to folk,' Mother said.

247

In July the DVLA finally transferred the car over to Mother's name, and she sold it to a car dealer who screwed her over on t' price – her being a middle-aged widow who didn't drive. I wor riled at her for not discussing it wi' me, but she said she'd just wanted shot of it.

After she'd paid off what we owed on t' telly, Mother said she wanted to eat out at a restaurant. A proper restaurant, where you sit at a table and get served. And so we did. The three of us. A small Italian place just up from Bradford railway station, wi' frescos of Sicily and wine bottles in wicker baskets hanging off the stucco walls.

We wor t' only people there. It felt like we'd invaded a stranger's front room. Mandy plumped for t' spaghetti Bolognese, and Mother and I both chose the lasagna. Two glasses of Lambrusco and a Coke. The waiter, a podgy Italian wi' big lugs and bristly eyebrows, put a small basket of white bread nestling in a napkin and a saucer of olive oil on t' red-and-white check tablecloth. The food arrived double quick, in stoneware pots that wor too hot to touch. The waiter then retreated behind a corner bar area that wor decorated wi' shells. He divided his attention between watching us eat and ogling a small black-and-white telly on t' wall behind his head.

I heard the TV news come on, the theme tune cutting through t' sixties Italian pop that wor spilling out of t' speakers above our heads. The headline bulletin wor all about HIM. HE'd sent a tape to t' police (if it wor him), that wor about to be played on t' news. When it started playing the waiter grimaced apologetically at us, 'til Mother asked him to turn up the volume. We stopped eating and turned in our chairs to watch. The waiter moved to one side so we could all see.

The camera zoomed in on Superintendent George Oldfield's face. Maybe it wor t' distorted small screen, but he looked friggin' haggard. A man hanging on t' edge of hope. He pressed the on switch of t' tape recorder. Camera bulbs flashed.

I'm Jack. I see you are having no luck catching me. I have the greatest respect for you, George, but Lord you are no nearer catching me now than four years ago when I started. I reckon your boys are letting you down, George. They can't be much good, can they? The only time they came near to catching me was a few months back in Chapeltown, when I was disturbed. Even then it was a uniformed copper, not a detective. I warned you in March that I'd strike again. Sorry it wasn't Bradford. I'm not quite ...

'Is that HIM?' Mandy hissed at me across t' table. 'Shush, will you!'

... September, October or even sooner ...

The waiter turned the TV down again. We heard the opening chords of Andrew Gold's 'Thank You for Being a Friend' being played at the end of HIS tape before it cut out. Mand continued to sing after it, 'til she clocked from our faces that somehow it worn't right. Mother straightened her shoulders and set her fork down on her plate.

'A Geordie then,' she said crisply. 'Does anyone want dessert?'

15 July 1979. The *Yorks Evening Post* published a special crime report. There wor a big black square containing a question mark, wi' t' words 'Face of the Ripper?', along wi' a whole set of friggin' questions for t' readers. Mother read 'em aloud to us.

'*Question 5: Do you have a husband, father, brother, son, fiancé, boyfriend or neighbour with access to a car whose whereabouts on the murder nights are not known or cannot be established?*'

She held the paper up, staring at the black square as if she wor waiting for HIS image to emerge out of t' blackness. Then she laid the paper aside and picked up her monthly competition magazine. 'Oooh,' she said. 'Win a holiday cottage in Wales.'

'If someone don't burn it down first,' I said.

Over t' summer the police interviewed 150,000 people. Sometimes they interviewed the same ones more than the once. They turned up at our house again one warm August evening. I wor out the front wi' a bucket and a soft cloth, cleaning the windows.

'Mitchell Thorpe?' one of t' constables asked.

'No,' I said. 'I'm Richard Thorpe.'

'Do you know where we can find Mitchell Thorpe?'

'Aye,' I said.

I set the bucket down, showed them into t' living room and pointed to t' urn that sat on t' nest of tables next to t' telly.

'He's right there.'

Simon Alexander: Expressed his intention to visit the scenes of the Ripper murders 'to pick up the vibrations'. These vibrations would lead him to the Ripper's door.

Alfred Cartwright: A clairvoyant and medical herbalist for forty-two years, offered the police a description of the killer.

Stanley King: A Yorkshire clairvoyant, saw the Ripper in a dream living in a small village in the Pennines. His vision was so strong he felt compelled to give the police a description of the place.

The *Sunday People* announced that the famous clairvoyant *Doris Stokes* had 'seen' the face of the Ripper. According to Mrs Stokes the Ripper 'is about five foot eight inches tall and in his mid twenties to thirties with dark hair and a scar below his left eye which twitches when he gets agitated'. She added that his name was Johnnie, or possibly Ronnie.

Mrs Tracey, another clairvoyant, derived her inspiration from studying the Ripper's handwriting on the letters received by the police. Her view was that the killer was a gentle person with a 'deep psychological mother rejection'.

On 26 July 1979, Manchester astrologer *Reginald de Marius* predicted that 'the Ripper will strike tomorrow'. He added, 'I've deduced that the Ripper was born on 15 September 1946.'

Mrs Nella Jones, clairvoyant consultant, was brought in by the police to apply her expertise to the Ripper case. She claimed that she had become 'locked into the mind of the Ripper' whilst sitting in her Kentish home with a South London policewoman.

Mrs Husk swirled the dregs in her teacup, emptied it and studied the contents. She gasped. 'My, my,' she said, looking down at Lord Snooty, who raised his heavy head momentarily from his resting place beside her chair. 'It's a rum world. It is that.'

The late-August sun beat down on us through t' Corona van windscreen. The concertina doors wor pinned open to t' elements, so a welcome breeze wafted through t' cab as we hurtled along.

We wor on a different round today, delivering to posher houses out in Roundhay. Each house wor detached or a big semi, often set back from t' road wi' a driveway and a double garage.

Sometimes I didn't know which door to deliver to, although t' rule of thumb wor t' back door, if there wor a back door. Posh folk bought less and took longer to do it. It seemed to me that it wor more important to them to be offered and say no than actually buy owt.

One hot afternoon when I wor delivering some orange squashes and tonic waters I surprised Billy Bremner on t' back lawn of his bungalow. He wor stretched out in his shorts on a sun lounger. There wor an ashtray beside him on t' grass. Billy Bremner wor a footie hero at Leeds Utd. I mumbled 'Hello,' and he looked at me nonplussed and then his wife came out from t' kitchen, deeply tanned and wearing a white bikini that barely covered her decency. I told Eric and he said that from now on only he wor allowed to deliver to t' Bremners, the sight of Mrs Bremner in a bikini being wasted on me. He never did see her in that bikini.

One day Eric asked me out of t' blue if I'd ever seen the Matterhorn Man again, and I said I hadn't. Him reminding me of t' Matterhorn Man made my cheeks turn tomato, cos he wor a straight man asking a gay man about personal stuff. I couldn't help but wonder sometimes where Jim had ended up, how he lived his life now. Being gay wor illegal in Scotland, so I supposed life up there couldn't be easy. I could still remember the scent of him, the skip of his Scots brogue, lying in his bed and listening to Pink Floyd's *Meddle*. I never bought that album, cos I never wanted to hear it anywhere else but in Jim's bedroom.

Prog rock had gone t' way of all dinosaurs. I found mesen sitting wi' Terry, Fizzy and Camp David in t' back yard at Radclyffe Hall, listening to Talking Heads' *Fear of Music* and necking Red Stripe. Unable to get a US visa, Fazel, I wor told, had gone to Amsterdam. Fizzy said he wor living in a big squat wi' loads of other folk. I wor to hear nowt more about

Fazel after that 'til, in t' savage winter of 1981, in t' same week that HE wor finally caught, I heard that his badly beaten body had been found face-down on a frozen Amsterdam canal.

Barbara Leach

02/09/1979

Our Corona van wor working its way through a housing estate in Hunslet when a police van sped by. On t' side of t' van wor a poster that read 'The Next One Might be Innocent'.

'A bit fuckin' late!' I yelled.

Wi' t' new footie season underway the Geordie tape wor being played at footie stadiums all over t' North and out of speakers lashed to t' backs of cars. There wor a humungous TV campaign, and people wor encouraged to ring the hotline and listen to t' tape. At Elland Road the footie crowds jeered and drowned out the tape, chanting 'Ripper 12, Police 0!'

When Garthy rolled up at work sporting a badge saying 'Leeds United – More Feared than the Yorkshire Ripper', Craner lost it. He yelled at Garthy that if he didn't take that badge off at once he'd be out on his ear. Craner wor snorting like a dragon on heat. He pulled everyone he cound find into his office.

'No badges of any kind! Any kind at all! Understood, Mr Thorpe?'

All eyes turned to me. Afterward, I went into t' bog and took off the small pink triangle badge I'd pinned to my Corona coat lapel. They should have employed Craner to catch the Ripper. He would have had it sorted by now. Nowt escaped Craner's beady eye.

The story went that Barbara Leach had been in t' Mannville Arms 'til nigh on 1 a.m., having an after-hours lock-in bevy wi' her friends cos she'd helped the pub manager clear up. She left her friends and chose to walk home. HE must have chanced upon her. Her body wor found in a back yard, half-hidden under a piece of carpet.

There wor a new guy in charge of t' Ripper investigation – Chief Constable Ronald Gregory. Poor old Assistant Super Oldfield, it wor announced, wor somewhat sickly and had been put out to grass. Gregory launched a media blitz, wi' billboards going up everywhere that said 'The Ripper Would Like You to Ignore This ...'. A four-page newspaper about HIM wor shoved through our letterboxes, the Geordie tape wor played in pubs, works canteens, schools, working men's clubs, on t' BBC and all local radio stations. We wor blitzed wi' t' Ripper 'til we wor buried by him.

I got stopped twice by coppers that month. The first time wor on my way home from an FK Club gig. A panda car pulled up alongside me and two coppers got out. They asked me where I'd been and where I wor heading. They wanted proof of my address, but I didn't have none on me. They asked me if I went wi' prozzies. I said not, and then pointed out that I wor only fourteen when Wilma McCann wor topped, and anyways I didn't drive and HE had a car. Coppers don't like you getting clever wi' them, as it shows them up for t' numbskulls they are, so they frisked me. Sus law. Search Under Suspicion. They said they'd seen me behaving suspiciously.

'In what way?'

The one copper glared at me like he wor set to punch my lights out. 'We ask the questions, sonny. You just answer them.'

They looked disappointed not to find any hash on me. I wor plain relieved they didn't plant none. If I'd been black they probably would have. Black guys wor always getting stopped even though t' Ripper wor plainly a white man. The panda car CB radio garbled summat and they said they had to go and that I wor a lucky young man to get away wi' it. It being?

The second time I'd just left the Gay Lib disco at the Guildford Hotel on t' Headrow together wi' this bloke who said between dancefloor snogs that he wor a rugby coach. This time it wor two coppers out on t' beat. The rugby coach wor frighted out his wits at being questioned. His chin wor wobbling and he could barely speak. I said we'd just left a straight club I knew of in t' shopping precinct. The cops seemed satisfied wi' that and let us go. As soon as we turned the corner t' rugby bloke pelted off like a witless hare.

Women wor warned to stay indoors after dusk.

Hospitals, unis and factories organised door-to-door transport for their women employees.

Bingo-session attendances plummeted.

In t' run-up to Christmas, the streets wor all but deserted.

It had been ten month since Mitch had drowned. Sometimes it would replay in my head like flashbulbs going off, stick-dog-reach-fall-look-ice-running, wi' me always on t' outside looking in, hovering above or alongside. These nightmares wor always soundless, Mitch's 'No–o–o–' as the stick somersaulted through t' air an agonised, mute howl. At least I didn't wake up on cold wet sheets no more.

If Mother had blamed Mitch's drowning on me I might have understood – after all, I reckon every other bugger did. Instead, she painted Mitch as a friggin' saint 'til I lost my rag and yelled at her to shut the fuck up about Mitch for once, and launched an ornament at the wall behind her head. How wor I supposed to know the friggin' thing had belonged to Mitch's mother? It wor only a honeypot shaped like a beehive.

Mandy wor another story. She never said owt outright, just scowled or snubbed her nose up at me. Dipping into her diary, I read that she blamed me. This riled me up. She had no right to go blaming me at all. I might have chucked the stick, but it wor t' dog that went scarpering after it, and it wor Mitch who went out on t' ice, worn't it? What could I have done?

When she worn't holed up in her room, playing her records, she spent all her time out of t' house. She'd discovered goth music, and wor hanging out nights wi' her new mates at the Phono in t' Merrion Centre, and in various pubs and cafs. She wor piling on t' pounds. Her small red lips looked like a bullseye in t' middle of her chubby cheeks. Her baggy black clothes hid her flabby body. She'd had her ears pierced three more times, and had dyed her hair an inky dead black wi' a single purple streak on one side. Mother didn't know these new mates, and wor fretting all t' time about Mand being out and about somewhere HE might be lurking. Like he'd be preying on goths mooching about late nights in a friggin' Leeds shopping centre. Anyway, sis didn't seem to care.

Mother's way of dealing wi' it wor to let sis have her way and then sit up late, fretting, 'til she rolled in, usually khalied and reeking of old smoke. Sometimes there'd be a row, wi' full-on screaming and shouting, then sis would clomp up the stairs and slam her bedroom door. Sometimes, on nights when she didn't come home at all, I'd come down for brekkie and find Mother asleep, her head resting on t' kitchen table.

The late nights and sis's new look had cost her the job at Schofield's, so now she wor working two days a week in a small goth fashion stall in Leeds market that never opened before 11 a.m.

'We are letting you go,' her manageress at Schofield's had said, 'because you are letting yourself go.'

So t' last Christmas of t' decade wor to be a muted affair. Mother made it known that she wor spending Christmas Day wi' Don and Mavis, and that Mand and I wor welcome to join, but she'd understand, she said, stressing '*understand*', if we'd made other plans. She wor feeling a bit sorry for Don, cos he'd been fired from Clark's last month. He'd been accused by Willie Clark of fiddling the books on his loads. He worn't t' only one – Clark's had got shot of all their drivers bar one. Don protested blue in t' face to anyone who'd listen that it wor just admin errors, but he had form in that department, so we all knew it wor a load of baloney. Mother had seen t' evidence lying about in Clark's offices.

'Only one driver,' Mother said, 'worn't given his marching orders. He's Clark's shining light. Never no trouble, keeps his cab and lorry spotless, and never complains,' she blathered on. 'He's even had his picture taken and put up in t' office foyer for all to see. Peter, his name is. Peter Sutcliffe. Lovely chap.'

So Christmas morn wor a day like any other – no Christmas-tree lights or tinsel. They stayed packed away in a Jubilee biscuit tin in t' garage. But we did have more cards than usual that year. I hung them on string lines draped over t' fireplace.

Mand opted to spend her Christmas wi' her goth friends. God knows how a bunch of wrist-slitting, pill-munching goths celebrated Christmas. Droning doom-laden carols and charring a turkey on an upended cross? So Christmas Day I found mesen alone in t' house. I took a walk, just to be out doing summat. Just to be walking. I headed the couple of mile toward Radclyffe Hall cos it wor somewhere to aim for. If no one wor home, as wor likely, then I'd walk back and spend the evening watching telly.

I found Christmas in full flow. All t' waifs and strays – all t' gay men who couldn't or wouldn't go home for whatever reason – had gathered there. There must have been about a dozen in all, some who I knew, others I'd never seen before. Camp David and Fizzy had been, as Camp David put it, 'stoving over a hot slave all day', and there wor two large roast chickens wi' all t' trimmings. It had been assumed, Camp David said, that I'd be spending Christmas wi' my family.

Terry gave me a paper hat and set an extra place at the corner of t' extended dining table. Even he wor a smidgen less glum than usual. I wor squeezed in next to Ali, who said he had nowt better to do, as his folk didn't celebrate Christmas. We wor all bunched up like at a school dinner, Ali's leg pressed hard against mine. I didn't complain. Turned out that Ali wor living half the time rent-free in Fazel's old room. Camp David's arms, I clocked, wor smoother than any plucked chicken.

By late afternoon, stuffed and wrecked by drink, I flopped on t' sofa between two men, drinking whisky. Only Ali wor sober, cos he didn't drink. For a moment I wondered how Mother wor coping wi' Mavis and Don, or what Mandy and her morose mates were getting up to. Whatever, it couldn't be as good as this. We wor all one big gay family, and this wor t' happiest Christmas of my friggin' short life so far.

Mother and I wor watching t' news when t' telephone rang. Mother stubbed her ciggie into t' ashtray on t' chair armrest and went to answer it. Through t' open lounge door I could see and hear all. Mavis wor having one of her legendary meltdowns. Only this one wor nuclear.

'Mavis, I'm sure ... Of course it's terrible, Mavis ... Don? Don? Mavis, no, come now, whatever he might have done ... I mean ... now Mavis, please.'

She wor holding the receiver a little away from her ear, as if Mavis's hysterical sobbing might leave a damp patch on her. Likely as not Mavis had stopped taking her Valium. That wor t' usual cause.

'Mavis, he can't be. Are you sure?' Pause. 'Well, that don't mean ...' Interrupted pause. 'And what did the police say?' Longer pause. The word 'police' lobbed into t' conversation made me feel like my ears had just popped.

Mavis wor obsessed wi' Don's whereabouts. She wanted him under her thumb, but out of sight. Don had built a life entirely outside t' home – the pub, the working men's club, the fishing trips (not that I ever heard of him catching owt), the rugby matches (supporting, not playing), the grafting. And now he wor out of a job, thanks to his dodgy dealings.

'Oh, Mavis ... surely, I'm sure that ... Don isn't ... he was?'

When he wor arrested for fencing stolen goods, Mavis hersen had fly-tipped the friggin' evidence onto waste ground in t' middle of t' night. The next night, after t' charges had been dropped, she went back for it, but it had all gone. The story goes that Don went ape and wor pulling her by t' hair and she kicked him on t' shins so hard he wor hobbling for days after and telling everyone he'd fallen off a ladder.

'Oh God, Mavis. No, I'm here, luv, I'm still here ... Yes, course I will, I'll be over in a jiffy.'

A jiffy! Still, it wor an age before Mother reset the receiver on its cradle. Her face wor as pale as milk.

'They've taken Don in for questioning. They think he might be t' Ripper.'

She gathered up her keys, ciggies and handbag, pulled on her anorak. 'You get yersen summat to eat, hear me? I'll be back later.' And wi' that, the front door slammed and she wor gone.

A few minutes later Mand came downstairs, sauntered into t' kitchen and opened the fridge door. She prodded the cheese, peered at the haslet under clingfilm. 'Where wor Mum off to?' she said, head still half in t' fridge. The fridge light gave her face a fierce and sickly glow.

'Mavis.'

'Does that mean we're having cheese on toast again?'

'Don's been arrested.'

'Oh,' said Mand, closing the fridge empty-handed. 'Maybe she'll get them new wardrobes after all.'

'Cos of Don being the Ripper?'

Mand's mouth changed shape. 'You don't think ...?'

'Nah, course not. I mean, look at him. He hasn't seen his own todger in decades.'

Mandy sniggered. She took an apple from t' fruit basket, examined the sticker on it, then put it back. 'I've told Mum not to buy Cape apples.' She pulled a pack of ciggies from her pocket and lit up. 'She shouldn't be out there on her own. It's not safe. You should have gone wi' her.'

'Mum don't like you smoking.'

'She knows. Just pretends she don't. This house is full of people pretending.' Sis exhaled like a seasoned smoker, the smoke drifting beneath t' kitchen striplight. 'Isn't it?'

'Is it? I don't know what you mean.'

'You don't know what I mean? I hate that you won't admit it to me, your own sister. I don't care who you go wi', Rick, but you must think I'm daft, and I'm not.'

'I've never thought you wor daft.'

Sis pursed her lips. Goth pout.

'Then don't treat me like I am.'

I had the shakes and my legs felt like they wouldn't hold me, so I plonked mesen down on a kitchen chair. I wor fumed up at sis, and worried that she'd open her gob to Mother.

'How did you know? I mean, it's not as if I go round wi' "I'm a pouf" tattooed on my forehead, is it?'

'Friend of mine saw you going into a gay pub. Then there's that little badge you wear, the pink triangle one. Mum might not know what it means, but I do.'

'You won't say owt, will you? Especially to Mum.'

'Maybe I will, maybe I won't.'

'You say one word and I'll half flay you, I will.'

Sis gave out a short, cold smile and said she wor going to take a bath.

'Do you hear me?' I shouted up the stairs after her. 'Not one friggin' word!'

After sis went to bed I stayed up, fretting about her knowing and whether I should say owt to Mother. I turned on t' telly and nodded off in front of some late-night rubbish film wi' Glenda Jackson in it. It wor nigh on midnight when t' phone jolted me awake. I almost fell against t' hallway table as I snatched up the receiver. It wor Mother, asking me to meet her off t' night bus and walk her back to t' house. It wor only half a block from t' bus stop to our door.

The bus wor late, and I had to wait an age at the stop. I *would* tell her, I said to mesen, but not yet. She'd enough on her plate, what wi' all this latest Mavis and Don business. As if anyone could think someone of Don's bulk wor t' Ripper. Having sex wi' Don must be like having a beer barrel roll onto you wi' t' tap jutting out.

As we walked up our road Mother wor saying that the cops had interviewed Mavis an' all, wanting to know if she wor covering up for Don. They'd nosed about t' house and inspected his clothes. They wanted to know about his habits, his sexual behaviour.

'They even asked her,' Mother said, 'if Don had any sexual deviances.' She uttered the words 'sexual deviances' like she'd bitten into summat spicy and foreign. 'Then,' she went on, 'they asked if Don had any hammers or screwdrivers, and of course he has, cos that's what men have. So they took some of his hammers away. Can you believe they even took some of his clothes for forensic examination?'

'Friggin' 'ell,' I said, trying to sound both shocked and mildly impressed. I'd never really understood what that meant, 'forensic examination'. Did they run a magnifying glass over his keks looking for stains? No man, it had been said over and over by t' cops, in t' papers, on t' telly, could top that many women unless someone wor shielding him. By 'someone' they meant a woman – a wife, girlfriend, daughter or mother.

I said, 'But any idiot could see that Don don't fit the description. And won't his job sheet show he wor at t'other end of t' country when some of t' women wor done over? By tomorrow they'll have just thrown him back in t' water.'

'There's more,' Mother said.

'More?'

'His car's been clocked kerb crawling around Lumb Lane.'

'Oh. No wonder they pulled him in.'

'The worst of it,' Mother said, 'is Mavis finding out he goes wi' prozzies. She could stand owt but that. She said it made her feel worthless and unclean. That wor t' word she used, "unclean".'

We passed a neighbour's house just as the bay-window curtains wor being drawn a tad too forcefully.

'So what you're saying is that it's OK for Don to knock Mavis about, it's OK for him to threaten to kill her, or to ogle strippers in t' pub, but it's not OK for him to go wi' a prozzie from time to time?'

I wor sounding like I wor defending prozzies, or even Don. Mother had no notion about Vanessa or Lourdes or t' rest of them. It didn't seem like owt that a woman should know.

'It wor t' final straw,' she said quietly, adding as we reached the front door, 'Mavis is wanting a divorce.'

By mid-April it felt like t' cold snap would never end. I wor flabbered to learn that Mavis had kicked Don out on his ear. Mother said that Mavis worn't for t' life of her going to give up a house that had cost her bruises and black eyes to get into such decorative order.

Sis wor another problem. From peeking in t' diary to see what she wor writing about me, I found out that she'd finished wi' Marcus, so when she blubbered it out over dinner I had to pretend that I wor dead shocked. He'd shoved her up against t' rehearsal-room wall and threatened to hit her, although she didn't let on about that bit. That bit I'd read in t' diary. All she said wor, 'Marcus is history.' A week or so later sis wor back together wi' him.

On my next day off work, Mother roped me in as muscle to help Mavis rearrange furniture and cart boxes of Don's stuff out into t' garage.

The house had been stripped bare of Don. There wor dust circles on t' shelves where his footie and fishing stuff had once been. There wor pinholes and picture-frame shapes on t' empty walls. The hallway wor lined wi' boxes of clothes and shoes and other stuff.

We padded gingerly along t' plastic runner in t' hallway and into t' lounge. I stood on t' darker bits of t' swirly carpet in case there wor mud on my boots. The plastic coverings were still on t' cream leather sofa and armchairs. The air whiffed of lemon-scent aerosol and the faintest trace of cold ash from t' fancy ciggie-butt stands next to t' armchairs.

The kitchen units looked like they'd been varnished yesterday. The cooker top gleamed, and the rotisserie above it wor spotless. Nowt looked as if it had just been put down casually, nowt had been allowed to pile up in t' corners, nowt pinned to a cork noticeboard or sellotaped to a cupboard door. Not a friggin' fridge magnet in sight. God knows how they'd celebrated Christmas. They must have sat there, all wrapped up in clingfilm and furs, picking at cocktail sausages.

I could tell that Mavis had been blubbing a bit, even though she wor brazening it out when we showed. She didn't want to talk much, 'cept to tell us what we should take. I wor to cart the packed boxes into t' garage. While I wor portering I tried to keep to t' plastic pathways that led through t' house. I didn't want my boots imprinting the shag pile.

I thought I should conversationalise wi' Mavis to cheer her up a bit, so I asked her what she wor going to do wi' Don's fishing tackle. I wor thinking it might be worth a few bob.

Then this couple pitched up, 'answering t' ad in t' paper', and nosed about, picking over things, holding them and setting them back down again, prodding and poking about and murmuring to themsens. He had a mottled, bulbous nose and she had a letterbox smile. Eventually they drove off wi' t' fishing tackle and some other boxes in t' back of their Volvo estate.

Mavis quietly tucked a tenner into her pocket. I asked her where Don wor kipping now.

'In hell.'

I picked up a cardboard box. It wor heavy and full of mags. Likely as not fishing mags or footie programmes. Eric had said the only reason men go fishing is to get away from their wives. I said that's the reason only straight men went fishing, and that gay men didn't need hobbies, to which Eric said, 'Antiques.' That made me laugh out loud. I promised him I'd never collect antiques. He promised never to go fishing.

I hadn't taken two steps when t' bottom of t' box gave way and all t' mags splurged out across t' lounge carpet. I stood there, mouth open, looking down on t' bouncy breasts of a brunette who wor smiling winningly up at me. October's edition of *Fiesta*.

Mavis let out a howl and fled the room. I dropped to my knees and scooped up all t' magazines I could wi' both arms, trying to stuff them back into t' busted box.

Mother appeared sharpish from t' kitchen, not wantng to miss the palaver. I wor still on my knees, surrounded by porn mags. Mother giggled.

'Sorry, I wor just ...' I wor blushing redder than a tom.

Mother said, 'Don't you go sneaking any of them into our house.'

'I worn't planning on it.'

'Not that I've ever found any. You must keep them well hidden. Better than Mitch did, at least.'

I ignored this. Mavis came scuttling back wi' a black bin liner. I collected up all of Don's mags and dumped them in t' dustbin.

The rubbish late-spring weather wor putting Craner in a crabby mood. Sales wor flatlining. That, and Craner learning that Garthy had secretly upped all t' prices on his round and wor pocketing the extra dosh. Then Garthy wor taken ill – appendicitis – so his appendix and the truth came out on t' same day.

Now that the FK Club had moved from Chapeltown into t' city centre I'd fallen out of going so often. Ultravox, Fad Gadget, B-52's, Human League, Psychedelic Furs, Cabaret Voltaire, The Normal, wor t' new bands of t' new decade, playing new electronic sounds. The Warehouse Club in Somers Street wor now t' place to see and be seen. It had plate windows, so from out in t' street you could watch those already inside dancing, see t' strobe lights swirling and hear t' cut-glass sound system.

One night the Radclyffe Hall brigade (except for Terry) made a trip out to t' Warehouse. We queued down Somers Street, underdressed, shivering, waiting to be chosen for entry. It worn't a case of first-come-first-served; the security goons patrolled the queue, picking folk out. 'You!' 'You two!'

We shuffled forward, waiting. Fizzy wor sporting a scraggy old fur coat over red PVC keks. The coat wor buttonless and looked like a million moths had gorged on it. Since he was both skinny and short, the coat hung down to his calves. I could never work Fizzy out. He never said much, never gave away owt about himsen except to say, 'Oh, you know ...' when plainly you didn't.

Camp David had on a friggin' 1920s flapper dress under a greatcoat, espadrilles, Joan Collins shades and a purple scarf around his head. I wore my usual black leather jeans and boots, but wi' a white muslin shirt wi' floppy sleeves that I'd filched from Camp David's wardrobe.

The security man, thick-set, Kojak slaphead, paused in front of us, then tapped each of us in turn on t' shoulder, as if we wor being picked out for execution. We strode in wi' our heads aloft, while t' rest of t' queue shuffled and gawped.

We knew that the club wanted us gays to spice things up a bit. The straight punters wor trying to act too cool to care, but you could see them gawping at us while they danced stiffly, hopping from one foot to t'other like they wor trying to avoid stepping on a hedgehog.

Just before midnight a band got up on t' stage to some futuristic fanfare playback, then spent the next ten minutes tapping the mic heads and adjusting the mix levels. The music wor all plinks and plonks on synthesisers. They had their hair quiffed up and wor all wearing heavy eyeliner. Somehow they still managed to look straight.

While t' band wor on, Fizzy skedaddled off somewhere. He reappeared much later, looking all smug wi' himsen. He had a man in tow. They wor coming toward Camp David and me. We wor in t' middle of t' dancefloor, shimmying to some Grace Jones number and checking out who wor eyeballing us. The man wor just a dark block outlined by a purple strobe, but when he stepped out of it I nearly fell to t' floor. It wor a good-looking bloke wi' loose, dark curly hair and neat-looking specs. He grinned at me knowingly. It wor my friggin' old schoolmate, Warren.

I pushed the pillow back and sat up in bed wi' my arms behind my head. My head thudded, I wor thirsty and my throat wor dry as sand. Warren wor leaning on his elbow. He leant across, picked up his specs from t' bedside table and hooked them back on.

I said, 'You know that time years back when you pitched up at Gay Lib? I thought I'd scared you off.'

'You sure gave me a fright. You said you were meeting a girl. I kept thinking, "Here, of all places."'

'I said that cos I thought you'd just dropped in by chance. I wor bricking it.'

Warren shook his head. 'I would have come back, only not long after I started at Manchester Uni and then I joined Gay Soc.'

'Gay Soc?'

'The University Gay Society.'

'Oh, right. I always hated you at school cos you wor a bright bugger. Way cleverer than me. Never had you down for being gay though.'

'I knew by the time I was twelve. Realising I was turned on by other boys terrified me. But you just know, don't you? So I kept my head down and studied. Going to university was my escape route.'

'For me it wor t' opposite. I thought, "Brilliant, I'm different. Special." I thought, "Yeah – this is all right, really." Cos it meant I wouldn't be tied down by all that girlfriend, relationship, family crap, and I wor free to do what I wanted. I knew enough to keep shtumm about it though. I couldn't see the point of school, cos all they did wor bang on about getting a job and marriage and supporting your offspring. The same old bicycle wheel going round and round. Remember that book we had to read in t' third year? *The Chrysalids*? Where these kids wor different, cos they had telepathic powers, and they knew they had to keep it to themsens? For me, that's what being gay is – summat special that you have to hide from most folk. I don't want the whole world knowing about me, if I'm honest.'

'Like the Masons?'

'If you say so. I can't say I've ever met the Masons.'

On t'other side of me, Fizzy slept on, flat on his back wi' his mouth wide open.

'So what you going to do? After uni?'

'I want to be an optometrist.'

'Sounds posh.'

'You?'

'Me? Dunno. I won't be working delivering pop, I can tell you that for nowt. I've got plans to be someone one day.'

Fizzy snorted in his kip like a choking piglet. We both started laughing. My laugh wor a dribble, and then Warren egged it on wi' his own little laugh, and then it wor like we wor trading laughs 'til we wor nearly crying.

'Oh God,' Warren said, wiping his eye behind his specs wi' his finger, 'I think the residue of last night's spliff is still in the system. Where did he get that from?'

'Fizzy? Dunno. I don't ask. I know he deals a bit. All he said to me was that it wor Moroccan black.'

'Whatever it was,' said Warren, throwing the covers back, 'it was strong stuff. I think I need a black coffee and a fag. I'm booked on the National Express back to Manchester this afternoon.'

I wor putting out the household rubbish when a shadow fell across me. I looked up. Even though he'd lost half a hog of weight, even though his clothes hung from him and his greying hair hung lankly about his lugs, there wor no mistaking him. I kept my hand on t' dustbin lid.

'Don?' I said guardedly.

'Hello Rick.' He spoke rapidly, in a hoarse whisper, like time wor pressing. 'How've you been?'

'Well enough. What brings you round here?'

He gestured like he wor mulling over t' answer. 'Have you heard from Mavis? I mean, how's she keeping?'

My left hand stayed firmly on t' dustbin lid.

'Bearing up, I hear.'

Don nodded. 'Not like Mavis to buckle under.'

I looked about t' street, trying to work out where he'd come from. 'So where are you kipping?'

'In t' back of that van.' He nodded toward a decrepit, dark-blue Leyland van parked on t' opposite side of t' street. 'I've got me a mattress, a camping stove, radio – could be worse. Got it parked up a lane toward t' tip. I wor on a mate's sofa 'til his missus got fed up wi' me.'

He closed in on me. He whiffed like a blocked drain. If he wor wanting to kip on our sofa, or even park up outside our house, it worn't going to happen.

'You know what I miss, Rick? Liver and onions. Can you believe that? I have cravings for braised liver and onions.'

'On t' menu in any caf ...'

'Not the same though, is it?'

270

'You didn't come here to blather on about liver and onions.'

Don fingered the ends of his hair.

'Did you know the bastards had me banged up for nearly eight hour before they told Mavis? She'd been going frantic, ringing around t' hospitals and everything, fearing the worst. I tell you, when this fucking jumped-up copper asked me if I wor t' Ripper I just lost it. Totally lost it. I wor panicking, thinking they wor going to fit me up for all t' murders. It took four of t' buggers to hold me down.'

'She rang Mum.'

'I know. Pam's a good'un, all right.' He ran his sleeve about his nostrils, then said, 'Will you get a message to Mavis? Tell her you've seen me? Let her know ... you know ...'

'That you miss your liver and onions ...?'

'Aye, well ...'

He nodded, as if this wor as much as he could hope for. He stuck his arm beneath his sweatshirt and scratched his belly.

'Living rough gives a man time to think.'

He produced a crumpled envelope that had been tucked in t' waistband of his keks and held it out to me like a kid wi' a sicknote.

I said, 'If that's for Mavis, I'll not be your errand boy.'

'It's not.'

I took the envelope, folded it, slid it into my pocket. 'I'll read it later.'

'You know, Rick, without me your mother wouldn't have got that job at Clark's. Christ knows, jobs are scarce enough.'

I lifted my hand from t' bin lid. 'At some point all t' back-scratching gets a bit raw.'

'We had a nice little business going, me and Mitch. Things ran very smooth for a while. Very smooth indeed.'

271

'Until you mucked it up and the law got wind of it.'

'There's still some stuff of mine in your garage, you know, that Mitch wor looking after for me. I'll give you half of what I get for it ...'

'I don't have it no more.'

'You didn't get shot of it? Cos, if you did, then I'm owed ... I ...'

'I burnt it. I didn't want Mother finding it. Or anyone else for that matter.'

Don's eyes roved about before settling back on me. Only he worn't looking at me directly, but behind my left ear.

'Burnt it?'

'Aye.'

'All of it?'

'All t' knocked-off stuff. The cops have showed up twice here already on Ripper business. That don't stop them sniffing about for other reasons. I'm not getting nabbed for it.'

Don gazed up at the neighbouring rooftops. A few pigeons wor nestling up on t' TV aerial, like we had a small audience.

'All of it?'

'As good as.'

Summat frighted the pigeons, cos they took off. I said, 'Can I ask you summat?'

Don turned back toward me and he blinked slowly. Like a reptile.

'About Gerald. I mean, that ...'

'You did know that Gerald's carpet business wor just a front? You don't seriously believe that selling a few fancy rugs would get him that nice house and car? He had a nice young dolly-bird wife, 'til she left him. A couple of years down t' line things had got a bit hairy for Gerald. He ended up owing some gang up in Tyneside. Some big fish he'd got mixed up wi'. They came for their money. When he couldn't pay up ... That letter ...'

'I'll read it later.'

'It's important that you do.'

He stretched out the fingers of one hand, examining his calluses. 'You think you know people, Rick? Truth be told, you never really do. Everyone's just putting out a version of themsens. The one they think the world should see. And that might be different to different folk – one face for t' missus, one for your mates, another for t' boss. Gerald ...'

'Heart attack. It wor in t' paper, Gran read out the death notice. She wor always reading the columns.'

'A heart attack? I never knew that. Is that what it said?'

Don's voice wor fraying in his throat.

A neighbour drove by. She tooted a greeting and I waved quickly. I said, 'Does it matter how he died?'

'The letter.'

'It's about Gerald, ain't it?'

'Every time I look at you I'm reminded of him. The older you get, the more I can see him in you. It half kills me. The past plays on your mind like some shitty song that won't leave your head. That letter ...'

'Am I supposed to read it right now?'

One by one, the pigeons wor returning to roost on t' aerial.

'You decide.'

Don turned and walked slowly toward t' van. I called out after him, 'Did he know about me? Did Gerald know he had a kid?'

Don's step broke for a moment, and he cocked his head a little. 'If it hadn't been for all this Ripper nonsense ...'

As his van pulled away I turned the envelope over and over, stroking it between my forefinger and thumb. I filleted it open and pulled the letter partway out. 'Dear Richard,' I read. I stuffed it back into t' envelope, went indoor and threw it in t' kitchen waste bin.

Gordon lived in a prefab. He'd been blathering on at me for yonks about wanting me to come over to his 'abode' so he could play me some of his favourite 78s. Finally I gave in, if only to get some sort of duty behind me. Truth be told, I wor curious to see how he lived.

There wor seven other prefabs on t' site, all wi' neatly turned-out gardens except for Gordon's, which wor hidden behind a humungous hedge. The prefabs had an air of permanence, like caravans on bricks. There worn't no bell, so I tapped a coin on t' porch glass. Gordon opened the inner door, then t' outer door, looking flustered. He said I wor a tad early, but that it didn't matter none. Clearly it did.

He tried a light switch, apologised, and footled wi' t' leccy meter. The room wor chilly and smelt of stale ciggie smoke and wet wood. I heard a coin clunk into t' meter box and the dull, cold light brightened slowly, revealing a room of solid dark furniture and threadbare rugs. In t' middle of t' room wor two faded leather armchairs, between which stood the 78 gramophone player like a prize exhibit at a show.

Gordon plugged in a lampstand wi' a fringed shade. All t' plugs wor dark brown and round-pin. He clicked on t' lamp, then turned off the overhead light, and the furniture retreated into deeper shadows.

'Tea?'

'Aye, if it's brewing.'

While Gordon wor in t' kitchen making tea, I nosied about, stroking my fingers along t' backs of t' chairs and upending ornaments. The place clearly hadn't seen a duster in a while. I picked up a paperweight, testing its heaviness in my palm.

Gordon called out from t' kitchen, 'Coconut slices?'

I set the paperweight back down.

'Not for me, ta. Don't like coconut none.'

I could hear t' kettle on t' gas stove starting to wheeze. I stroked the neck of a candlestick.

'So you didn't live here wi' Brendan?'

I crouched down before a wooden cabinet crammed wi' 78s in their paper sleeves. I lifted one out, tried to make out the faded silver-on-black lettering. Benny Carter and summat else. I slid it back. Just the thought of ploughing through this lot wor giving me a belly-ache. Why had Gordon insisted that I listen to a cartload of scratchy old 78s? He'd been so friggin' enthusiastic about it, gassing on and on, and then when I gave in and said I'd come, he'd taken off his specs and looked at me wi' eye-bulging astonishment and said, 'Wonderful!'

Maybe, I thought, it wor a test to see if I wor worthy of my friggin' inheritance. I flipped my fingers along t' lines of paper-bag-brown, dull red and green sleeves. There must have been hundreds of 'em. What would I do wi' this lot?

'I wor saying ... Brendan?'

'Brendan? Heavens, no, we'd gone our separate ways many moons before. Brendan and I lived together in Bristol.'

'Bristol?'

I stood up. Above a low bookcase of crusty old books hung two framed pictures of racehorses and riders jumping a thicket fence. I heard Gordon rooting around in a cutlery drawer. All I knew of Bristol wor that it had two rubbish footie teams and the Two Ronnies making a joke about Bristol being twinned wi' Brest. Which is in France. I could hear Gordon opening and closing cupboard doors.

'During the war I worked at Parnell's near Bristol on developing radio communications. Highly secret stuff!'

The kettle wor starting to whistle. Gordon wor still conversationalising loudly from t' kitchen.

'Brendan came from down that way – I met him while he was on leave. We kept in touch. After the war ended and he was demobbed, we rented a small terraced house in Bristol and moved in together.'

I heard water being poured into a teapot and then t' kettle being set back down on t' gas stove.

On t' dining table wor an empty vase, an ashtray, the *Evening Post* and a small wooden cigar box. I flipped the cigar box open, then closed it again. I picked up the vase, turned it over. It looked like it had been made by someone wi' unsteady hands.

Gordon reappeared, carrying a two-bar electric fire, which he plugged in. He clocked me holding the vase.

'That was a present from Brendan.'

'Really? I wor just thinking how nice it is. Yeah, I like it, Gordon. Is it worth much then?'

Gordon smiled frugally. 'It is to me. I might have some Rich Tea biscuits.'

He scuttled off again into t' kitchen, returning wi' a tin tray on which stood a Brown Betty teapot, a silver-plated sugar bowl, two bone-china teacups and an open packet of bikkies. His half-smoked ciggie wiggled on his lip, the ash about to drop into t' sugar bowl. He set the tray on t' floor between t' armchairs.

'There. That's better.'

I grabbed a bikkie. Gordon tapped off his ash and rattled the teaspoon in his cup. He seemed nervous. I wor expecting him to open the gramophone lid and start winding it up, but he didn't, and I didn't want to remind him none, so I said nowt about it.

'So, my boy. Here you are. You don't know how much it thrills me that you agreed to come.'

'Well, here I am.'

'Indeed. Here you are.'

276

'Inside my first prefab.'

'There's a thrill of sorts in that, I suppose.'

I bit into t' bikkie. 'So how did you come by this place?'

Gordon poured milk and then tea into two cups and handed me one of them. 'It was my mother's until she died in the summer of '68. Then it became mine.'

I heaped several spoons of sugar into my cup. 'Were you in love wi' Brendan?'

'Utterly besotted. I was twenty-one. Brendan was three years my senior. But living with Brendan was difficult. He found it hard to settle down after the war. The nightmares didn't help. He'd seen some bad things. Not that he would ever talk about them. Bottled it all up. He was a lovely man when he wasn't pressing the self-destruct button. Which he did more and more frequently. He was drinking heavily, and the pressure of concealment was eroding us.'

Gordon gulped, as if needing more air in his lungs.

'England was a hideous place in the 1950s. We were in the dark ages – we still are, in many ways. Brendan and I were going through a rough patch when he was caught with someone else. Caught in the act. He was arrested, charged with gross indecency and offered treatment to cure him of his homosexuality. He had no option, really – either go to prison or agree to the treatment. To this day I don't think he knew what he was letting himself in for. He thought it would be a few sessions on a shrink's couch, and then he'd be free. The treatment involved being locked up in a cell-like room. He was pumped full of nausea-making drugs, then shown erotic photos of men. There was nowhere to be sick. He asked for a bucket, but was told to vomit onto the bed. Then they gave him more injections, and each time he was violently sick. He had to defecate on the bed as well. For five days this went on; every hour they injected him with drugs that made him sick. He had to sit, to sleep, in his own shit and vomit.'

'Friggin' hell. But they didn't come for you?'

'He held out – didn't betray me. I guess his wartime training kicked in. He told them he was my lodger and that I was straight, and that I would be disgusted if I knew. We'd always had the spare room set up that way, just in case. After his release he went to live with his parents down in Somerset. The last I heard he'd emigrated to Canada.' Gordon smiled weakly. 'Finish your tea.'

I took a slurp. It had stewed. I wor still thinking on how friggin' big Canada always looked on school maps when I said, 'What was it you wanted to give me?'

'Oh, yes. I almost forgot.'

He rose from his chair, went over to t' sideboard and took out a brown-paper package, which he handed to me. It wor shaped like a book. I eyed it suspiciously.

'Well, aren't you going to open it then? It's nothing much, just a token of our friendship.'

I guessed it really wor a friggin' book. Likely as not a copy of *Urinals of Yorkshire*. Cautiously, I pulled apart the brown paper. It wor poetry: *The Poetical Works of Rupert Brooke*. I fed the pages through my fingers like a card dealer. On t' inside page Gordon had written in ink, 'For friendship'.

'Ta, Gordon. Yeah, I mean, very much.'

'I adore Rupert Brooke. Brendan used to read me his poems. Brooke was beautiful and brave and one of us.'

'Yeah?'

'Yes indeedy.'

Gordon took the book from me. 'And look, I've researched this for you.'

He slid out a folded sheaf of paper that wor tucked inside it. 'I contacted a professor at Leeds University, and he sent me a note on the Greek in "The Old Vicarage, Grantchester".'

'I looked on, befuddled. I'd hardly ever read a poem in my life, not a proper one. Not unless you counted the one about some Roman soldier fancying Jesus Christ that wor pasted to t' back of the bog door at Radclyffe Hall.

'Thanks, Gordon.' I put the book aside.

'One day you'll treasure that.'

I thought not.

I never read Don's letter. I couldn't think what wor to be gained from it.

There wor still t' thorny matter of what to do wi' all t' knocked-off stuff stashed in t' garage that I'd told Don I'd burnt. I decided to see if I could find that bloke Mitch knew over in Shipley. Maybe word hadn't got to him about Mitch's death, and he wor wondering why his little supply line had dried up. Maybe I could even take up where Mitch had left off. Come to some arrangement. Christ knows, we needed the friggin' dosh.

Time slipped a week or two before I headed over Shipley way. Cos I hadn't been paying much attention when Mitch had driven me over there, I couldn't remember rightly where it wor. I knew it wor a merchant's yard, wi' a line of offices on an upper storey wi' cast-iron steps leading up to an outside walkway. I knew it wor t' third door along.

I wor about to give it up as a bad job when I found it: a small industrial yard behind a row of shabby shops. There wor a couple of skips in t' yard, an old Ford van and a pile of scaffolders' poles and boards stacked along t' base of one wall.

I knocked and heard a gruff 'Yep,' so I went in. It wor t' same bloke all right, sat in t' same fake leather swivel chair behind t' same cluttered desk. An air-con fan rattled away in one corner, causing a pile of weighted-down papers to flap.

'What can I do for you?' he said in a bored drawl, leaning back so t' chair rolled a little way from t' desk. He had beads of sweat on his upper lip. His beer gut wor straining at his shirt buttons.

'It's about Mitchell Thorpe.'

He sat upright and frowned warily, as if trying to place me. 'And you are?'

'His son. Stepson. Or at least I wor.'

The bloke's eyelids flickered. 'Wor?'

'He drowned. Last winter.'

The bloke's eyes shifted from me to t' door and back again.

'So what do you want, a condolence letter?'

'He fell through t' ice trying to rescue his dog.'

The bloke picked up a stapler from t' desk, turned it over in his hand. 'And the dog? What happened to t' dog?'

'Dog wor fine.'

The bloke set the stapler back down, and seemed to deflate slightly. 'I like dogs,' he said.

'There's some stuff. I thought you might be interested.'

He cocked his arms half-wide, palms open, fingers spread. 'So where is it?'

'Back home. I need a van or someone to come and collect it.'

The bloke half-smiled, half-snorted. 'I don't do collect, sonny. You sort out a van and I'll take a look at what you've got.'

Eric wor updating the round-book and chewing on t' end of his biro.

'How's the nipper?' I said, making idle talk.

'Cries a lot. Karen's mother helps out, and looks after him when Karen's got hairdressing customers. That's the only good bit about her folks living around t' corner.' He bit his bottom lip and stared into t' middle distance. 'She's pregnant again.'

'But that's good, ain't it?'

'Dunno.'

'You dunno?'

'Dunno.'

'You'll need extra dosh then?'

Eric frowned. 'I could always do wi' a bit extra. Seems it's never enough. Prices go up every month.'

I told him about all t' knocked-off stuff that wor still in t' garage. He said he'd come and give it the once-over. He said there wor someone at Corona who could probably get shot of it. 'As long,' he said, 'as you put a bit my way.'

'Of course. Tell me it's not Craner?'

'You think I'm that daft? No, it's not bloody Craner.'

He closed the round-book and turned the ignition. 'Come on. Tea-break time.'

Lourdes wor sitting astride the low yard wall outside her house, enjoying the late-August sunshine. She had a wide-brimmed straw hat pulled low over her large sunglasses, a canary-yellow top and tight denims down to her calves. When she clocked our van pulling up she stood up and went indoors. Eric and I exchanged a glance.

Eric said, 'Take her a bottle of summat. She'll be right wi' you.'

She'd left the back door open, so I rapped on it and stepped directly into t' hallway. 'Lourdes! Corona!' I swung the Coke bottle between my fingers. 'Lourdes! Anyone?'

'Leave it on duh table, mi got business,' came a hoarse shout from t' back kitchen. I walked into t' kitchen. She wor leant wi' her back to t' sink, dragging on a ciggie.

'You no hear me, bwoy?'

'Don't see no business.'

She pulled her hat tighter across her brow and pressed her forefinger against t' bridge of her sunglasses. She wouldn't look at me. The corner of her bottom lip wor swollen. I set the bottle of pop down on t' small drop-leaf table near to me.

'Ta,' she said.

'You're welcome.'

She scratched the back of her calf wi' t' toe of t'other foot.

'What I owes you for pop?'

'You don't.'

'So what you's waiting for? Mi ain't doing business today, if that's what you's after.'

'You know friggin' well I'm not, Lourdes. Anyway, I thought you had business.'

'Well, I ain't. Ain't making no tea neither. Dis place no caf.' She pulled off the sunglasses. 'Dis what you's wanting to see?'

Her right eye wor puffed up and half-closed. Shades of dirty yellow and purple bruising bled into each other like a film of oil on a road puddle. Beneath her left eye wor a dark scored line.

'Jeez. Who did that?'

A brief, hollow laugh escaped her. 'Why, bwoy, what ya going to do about it?'

'I ... I ...'

'You's want some advice, bwoy? Stay out of what don't concern ya. You's remember that. Don't go telling people ya business, bwoy, and don't trust no one.'

She wor right. Punter, pimp, domestic. None of my concern. Mitch would have said the same.

'I have to go.'

Lourdes nodded. 'You go. Lourdes don't want you round here no more. I's giving up dis game. Maybe start a new life in a new town. You go, and leave Lourdes alone.'

On t' back of t' van someone had traced in t' grime: 'I wish my bird was as filthy as this'. Eric wor in t' cab, his gob full of sausage roll.

'Well?'

'Tea's gone cold.'

He wiped the back of his hand across his mouth. 'So we'll find another pit stop.'

'She says she's giving up t' game.'

Eric laughed sourly. 'They don't give up. None of them do. It gives them up when they lose their looks cos of all t' drink or t' drugs they're downing or injecting. Or they just plain get too old and get pushed out by t' young'uns. If they live that long.'

The 'someone' at Corona wor four-fingered Kev. He turned up wi' Eric in an old estate car. Mother came waltzing out of t' house to say hello, so I had to introduce her to them both, and then she blathered on for a friggin' age wi' Eric cos she'd heard all about him from me and it wor 'good to put a face to a name' and all that baloney, while Kev hung back wi' his hands in his pockets like he wor wanting to hide in t' nearest shrubbery. I told Mother that they wor helping me clear out the garage by flogging some stuff and taking the rest to t' tip. Mother nodded briefly, like she knew what wor going on really, but didn't want to know. She said she wor heading into town to do some shopping. That gave us a good two hour.

We loaded up the boot as fast as we could. The rear tyres wor half-flat by t' time the car wor fully loaded. It looked like it wor leaning back on its haunches. I told Kev that if he got pulled over wi' it I'd deny all knowledge. He gave me thirty quid, which wor way under t' value. Then I had to give a tenner of that to Eric. But at least I wor shot of it.

Late in t' evening the phone rang. I wor standing right by it, but as no one ever phoned me, I worn't going to answer it. Mother glared at me and snatched it up. She wor expecting it to be Mand. She'd gone to a Bauhaus gig at Leeds Uni wi' all her goth mates. Mother had been fretting about how she wor going to get home afterward, which had led to another barney. She didn't want sis even walking the short stretch from t' bus stop at the end of our road. This had riled sis, which meant another slanging match about keeping safe and avoiding HIM, and sis doing her usual shouting and door-banging stuff. I said that if HE came upon Mand in t' dark in all her goth clobber he'd probably turn tail in fright and run a friggin' mile. Mother told me to shut it. In t' end it wor agreed that Mand would stay wi' Marcus, and that she'd ring to say she wor safe. Sis wor happy about this, cos it meant she could spend the whole night wi' her boyfriend. Probably hanging upside down from a beam.

Only it worn't Mand on t' phone. It wor t' nursing home to say that Gran wor very frail and might not have much longer on this earth. Mother wor told that they'd 'keep her posted', and she thanked them. She sat on t' padded seat end of t' telephone table, cradling the receiver in her lap. She didn't notice that the caller had rung off and the phone wor buzzing 'til I said so. Then she set it gently back in its cradle.

Mid-autumn dusk wor a blueish tinge by t' time I reached the small prefab estate where Gordon lived. There wor three kids, nine- or ten-year-olds, sitting atop a flat shed roof, firing off small stones at the gnomes in t' neighbours' garden. One of them tossed one my direction.

'Hey, mister!'

'Ain't it past your bedtimes?' I kept walking.

'Fuck off! You don't belong round here. Hey mister! Mister! Are you going to visit the old bloke?'

One of them stood up and chucked a stone wi' more gusto. It whizzed past my ear and pinged up off t' pathway that led to Gordon's prefab. If I'd been wearing my blue nylon Corona coat and portering a few bottles of cherryade or dandelion & burdock, that would have been a legit intrusion. Cos I'd have summat they wanted. They watched me 'til I turned the corner and wor out of their sight, behind t' hedge. The Humber wor parked in front of t' lean-to garage overhang. I tapped my house keys on t' doorway glass.

The door opened a bit, and through t' crack I could see a slice of Gordon's face. On seeing me, his face lit up, but then promptly dropped, cos it worn't usual for me to just pitch up unannounced. He unhooked the door-chain.

'This is a mighty surprise,' he said in a voice that wor pleased and cautious at the same time. 'Not in trouble, I hope?'

'I need to talk to you.'

I followed him into t' lounge. Music wor playing. The gramophone lid wor raised, and a rotating shellac disc gleamed in a narrow shaft of sunlight and dust motes. Gordon lifted the needle arm and the music cut mid-note.

'A foxtrot,' he said apologetically. 'I used to dance the foxtrot rather well.'

He indicated that I should sit. I remained standing.

'I've been thinking, Gordon.'

'Have you now? Do you want some ...'

'No ta, not just now.'

Gordon lifted the record off t' gramophone, holding it by t' edges wi' his palms, then slid it carefully into its brown-paper sleeve.

'So what's all this about?'

285

'That time in that posh caf in Harrogate, you remember you said that after Brendan there wor another man in your life, a man who died.'

'Ah. Perhaps you should wait here.'

He went into t' bedroom and I heard a drawer opening. He reappeared holding a photograph.

'It was bound to come out someday.'

I took the photo from him. In washed-out colour wor two men standing on a hillock wi' their arms slung around each other, squinting at the camera. The one on t' left wor most certainly Gordon – a more sprightly Gordon, a lot thinner, wi' a side wave of dark hair and the inevitable ciggie between his fingers, while t'other – I tilted the photo toward t' lamplight – wor my granddad.

Gordon dragged deeply on his ciggie. 'You must appreciate that this whole business has been very difficult for me.' He exhaled mightily.

'So I'm right. About t'other man. The one after Brendan.'

'You know, my boy, when you walked into that Gay Lib meeting for the first time all those years ago it was a tremendous jolt, I can tell you.'

I looked up from boring my eyeballs into t' photo. 'You recognised me?'

'Not at once. I hadn't seen you since you were a toddler, apart from briefly glimpsing you from afar at Frank's funeral, of course. Then at the Gay Lib meeting I kept looking at you, thinking that you were familiar, but I couldn't think why for the life of me, so I asked someone your name, and then the penny dropped.'

'You wor at the funeral?'

He said he'd eavesdropped on t' service from t' church foyer, watched the burial from a distance, watched us all – Gran, Mitch, Mavis and Don, the smattering of friends – saw him lowered into t' ground and earth sprinkled on him, and then, when we'd all gone, he'd stood by t' side of t' grave for a long time and said his own prayer.

'I was with Frank when he became unwell. It was here, in this house. He started having chest pains, and his speech was slurring. I thought it would be quicker to drive him down to Leeds General Infirmary A & E than to wait for an ambulance.'

He paused, lit a fresh ciggie wi' wobbling fingers.

'He had a major heart attack right there in the hospital foyer. The hospital staff took over, and whisked him away. I knew I couldn't wait. I left details with the front desk on who to call. I didn't want to be there when you all showed up, but I couldn't desert Frank either. As far as the hospital was concerned, I wasn't a blood relative. I wasn't next of kin. So I sat in the car and waited. I prayed. I'm not a religious man, but I prayed all the same that he would pull through. Then I saw you all arrive in that old van your father drove. Some time later I saw you all leaving. I knew at once that Frank was gone.'

'Why didn't you tell me this before?'

'What was I supposed to say? "Hello, I'm your late granddad's lover"? I didn't know what was for the best. So I decided – wanted – to befriend you. I have to say that I expected you to tell me to get lost. But you didn't. Why was that, Rick?'

'Dunno. I admit I wor wary at first. To be honest, I think it wor Fazel who decided it for me. Just summat he said.'

'Ah yes. Fazel.'

I looked about as if t' ghostly traces of my granddad might be present in t' corners.

'Was my granddad often here?'

'Oh, he didn't mind the old prefab, if that's what you mean. Prefab house, prefab life. Of course, staying overnight was quite another matter. That's the trouble when you have

287

a wife who never goes anywhere. Never went away for a weekend on her own, or to see anyone, or anything like that. She had no relatives to speak of, apart from a half-sister in Hull, and they didn't get along. So she never went out unless Frank took her. Wedded to her house, she was. And she expected him home every night. Married duty.'

'So how did you first meet? Where?'

'Late fifties, and it was a public toilet. Where else could you meet anyone in those days? I couldn't bring him back here while my mother was alive, of course, so before she passed on it was all secret meetings in the back of the car, in woods, sometimes at friends' houses. I was terrified that we'd get caught. Before '67 it was illegal, for one thing, and if you were caught you risked imprisonment, ridicule, your name in the papers. I knew of men who'd killed themselves out of shame, others who'd had their marriages wrecked. But Frank was devil-may-care, and that terrified me sometimes. I'd lost Brendan; I didn't want to lose Frank too. People thought we were horseracing chums. Before I met Frank I'd only been to about one race meet in my life.'

'Don't you like horseracing?'

'Not especially. But it gave us an excuse to be together openly. Of course, Frank being married was perfect cover. Although your grandmother was always rather cold toward me. But that was her way, Frank said. I was merely Frank's racing buddy. You become the master of façade.'

I looked across at the horseracing prints on t' far wall.

'A present from Frank,' Gordon said.

'Do you remember when I was born, then?'

Gordon clapped his hands together, as if delighted. 'Of course I do! In fact, I was with Frank at the races the day after you were born. It was me who suggested that you be christened Richard.'

'You?'

'His first grandchild. I'd never seen him so happy. So we bet on an outsider ...'

'Lionhearted Richard.'

Gordon uncoiled a laugh. 'Lionhearted Richard, no less!'

'Richard Lionel Thorpe,' I said dully. 'I'd never made the connection wi' my middle name before.'

'Lionel was my suggestion.'

'Can't say I like it. Makes me think of that Lionel Blair.'

Gordon chortled. 'Then I apologise. Do you know, you have a few of Frank's mannerisms. I like that. It reminds me of him.'

'Such as?'

'Oh, that way you scratch the bridge of your nose when you're puzzled, the same gait.'

'My mum remembers going wi' Granddad and some other bloke to t' races when she wor little ...'

'Have you said anything to her?'

'Hell, no. I've not even told her I'm gay. Friggin' sis has worked it out though. Don't know if I could tell Mum – especially after all that's happened. I think she might know, but she don't ask none. Eric says women only ever ask you what they already know. Like they want to see if you'll lie about it or not.'

Gordon dragged on his ciggie and exhaled toward t' ceiling light. 'That Eric talks a load of baloney, if you ask me.'

'All t' stuff that happened before I wor born, or when I wor too small to know any better – all these secrets ...'

'Ibsen's *Ghosts*.'

'Eh? You've lost me.'

Gordon crouched beside me, grabbed my hand. 'No, my boy. I've gained you. Don't you see that?'

His fingers tightened about mine. I bit my lip, looked at the floor in a swirl of thought. A small spider scuttled out of t' shadows. Gordon stood up, went over to t' gramophone and started cranking the handle. 'Shall I play some music? What would you like to hear? Something uplifting?'

'You're daft, Gordon, you know that?'

'I'll take that as a compliment.'

I watched the spider scurrying for sanctuary under t' sideboard.

'Did you ever meet Gerald?'

'Only the once.'

'It's a shame that he died of a heart attack too.'

Gordon flinched. 'Gerald didn't die of a heart attack. Is that what you've been told? Gerald was found with a hosepipe connected to the car exhaust and the engine running.'

It wor late, so Gordon suggested I kip in his mother's old bed. The sheets wor crisp and cold, the pillows unforgiving. I lay on my back, pinned beneath t' scratchy blankets, my arms flat by my sides, my thoughts twirling like some nauseous fairground ride. Granddad Frank swore blind, Gordon said, that Gerald wor murdered and it wor made to look like suicide. But the death notice said otherwise. Maybe Gran had lied when she read it out. More likely, the notice had lied. I couldn't see Gran having the guile to hide summat like that. Although I reckoned she knew more than she let on. Perhaps she saw through t' horseracing façade. I'd been right not to read Don's letter. What use would it have served? Let the fat bastard stew in his own guilt.

Unable to sleep, I got up and dressed. Through t' thin partition wall I could hear Gordon's steady snoring. I crept out of t' house and set off down t' road 'til I came to a bus stop. A night bus took me as far as Lower Briggate. From there I walked toward t' canal, past the doorway to Charley's Club, past the Dragonara Hotel where Mother and Mavis had once waited an age in t' foyer for t' Three Degrees to come out of t' lift, on past the New Penny, which wor closed and silent.

Reaching the canal bridge, I paused. The wind wor getting up, scudding giant clouds over t' moonlit sky. If I had the dosh I'd take off for t' South, go in search of Tad. Somewhere without secrets and serial killers. But at the end of t' week my pockets wor empty these days. Below me, the water had a steely, metallic smell. Industrial foam shimmered in stagnant corners. The night water burbled like a beckoning tune. But it worn't a tune I recognised.

III

Jacqueline Hill

17/11/1980

As far as everyone wor concerned, HE had been dormant for nigh on fifteen month. Some said he wor inside, or that he'd topped himsen. Others that he wor in t' army, and had been posted overseas.

Gina had disappeared again. Mand had found a new job, working full-time at Scene and Heard record shop in Leeds. Mother wor still at Clark's. We got by, but it wor a struggle.

Then on Wednesday, 19 November, we heard that HE had struck again. In Headingley. We heard that two days before, a student had found a bag in t' street wi' a bank card in it. That the cops had made a search of t' surroundings but found nowt, and the bag had been recorded as lost property. That the bag belonged to Jacqueline Hill, a second-year student at the uni.

HE wor back in our lives.

'And how's Mrs Husk this morn?'

She huffed at me and pressed one hand to her wig, checking it wor on right. Lord Snooty, who in cat years wor just as ancient as her, wor by her swollen feet, his nose buried in t' foil container of t' meals-on-wheels dinner she'd been unable to finish.

It wor plain as day that Mrs Husk wor starting to go downhill. She no longer levered hersen out of her chair when I knocked on t' door and shouted my usual 'Corona!' She didn't seem as sharp as she once wor.

By her armchair stood a zimmer frame that social services had given her to help her get about. The pot of tea on t' table wor cold, and a cup upended onto a saucer. She'd been reading the friggin' leaves again.

'There's been another,' I said.

Mrs Husk flapped a hand, as if shooing me from t' room.

'You know, Mrs Husk, I nearly went to t' cops that one time. I actually walked up to t' desk and wor all set to say summat.'

Her thin lips quivered, as if she wor remembering how to speak. 'What do they know? Nowt, lad. It's a waste of time reading the leaves if no one's listening, ain't it?'

'I listened, Mrs Husk. I tried, didn't I?'

'Aye, lad. Seems that you did.'

'So you know that HE's back, Mrs Husk. Another innocent, they say.'

Mrs Husk's fingers nuzzled Lord Snooty's neck. 'I know, lad. I saw it.' She nodded toward t' teacup. 'In t' leaves. He wor never really gone. There've been others. Others that the police don't know about. Or that they don't think wor him.'

'Others? You mean he's done in other women?'

'Three in t' past few month. One wor a foreign lady. At least she lived.'

She turned her face toward mine, fixing me in her sights. I shuddered like I'd walked right through a cold spot. The bottle of ginger beer I'd been holding nearly slipped from my fingers. I set it on t' table.

'Do you think they'll ever get him, Mrs Husk?'

'We all get careless, lad.'

'The tape ...'

'Is the devil's own deception. That tape is not him. Get away wi' you.'

The mantel clock chimed the quarter to t' hour. Lord Snooty miaowed.

'Money's on t' table, lad.'

I didn't have the heart to tell her the price of pop had gone up again. I took what she'd left. She wor seven pence short.

The murder of Jacqueline Hill wor like one of them horror films where some hapless female thinks she's finally escaped the evil and is safe, only for IT to come rushing back in for one last friggin' hurrah. The cops had gone into overdrive and put together some Super Squad. Then came t' *Newsnight* prog on t' telly.

We all knew it wor going to be about HIM. The BBC had made sure we knew. Like t' first squall of winter ripping the last leaves from t' treetops. As it happened, though December hadn't arrived yet, winter wor already blown right in.

The programme kicked off wi' some poncy Southern reporter as always, standing outside t' bus station roundabout opposite Millgarth cop shop, talking about t' Northern folk like we wor an alien life form.

Mand said, 'Must we watch this?'

'You can go and play your records if you want,' said Mother, 'as long as it's not too loud or too late. You have to be up for work in t' morning.'

Mand folded her arms tightly, her endless silver bangles jiggling like a friggin' gypo's dancing bells. 'I'm off 'til Monday.'

The reporter wor now on a shopping street in Leeds, on a busy Saturday afternoon by t' look of it. I draped a leg over t' sofa arm and slumped back into t' cushions, feigning casual interest.

Mand said, 'What does tangible mean? He just said it.'

Mother shrugged briefly to mean she neither knew nor cared.

... DEEP REVULSION ...

Mand's bangles jiggled again as she reached for a toffee from t' bowl on t' table.

... WALL OF HATE ...

... PSYCHOPATH ...

... SEVENTEEN ATTACKS ...

'Seventeen?' I said. 'Nah – he's got that wrong. No way have there been seventeen ...'

'Have you been counting them?' said Mand, tossing the toffee wrapper toward t' waste bin. 'I think it's disgusting, counting them like that. Like knocking down skittles. Seventeen ruddy skittles, each wi' t' face of a woman on it.'

Mother shushed us both and shifted hersen to t' edge of her chair.

... HATRED ... SPAWNED ...

Now t' reporter wor standing in a terraced street. It looked like Harehills, but could have been anywhere.

... BOTTLED UP ...

The reporter wor saying that the relatives of t' victims wanted to talk to t' Ripper himsen. A woman's head appeared, sideways on. She turned to face us.

Talking Head 1: Mrs Irene MacDonald ... BEAST ... COWARD ...

Sis faked a yawn. Her tongue wor stained wi' t' toffee. 'Must we?'

I said, 'I wonder whose idea this wor? Getting them to talk to t' camera like this?'

Talking Head 2: A woman wi' short grey hair and glasses. She also starts sideways on, but facing t'other way. Then she's facing us. She hasn't turned her head, she's just suddenly staring out into our rooms ... NOT A MAN ... DESPICABLE ... DESPISE ...

Talking Head 3: The reporter introduces her as Mrs Olive Smelt, who wor attacked in 1975 in Halifax. This wor t' first I knew of her. I never knew there wor others before

Wilma. I gazed at Olive intently. One of her eyes wor very dark, much darker than t'other one, like she couldn't see out of it any more. But it could have just been t' camera light and shadow, I couldn't rightly tell. Her voice wor soft, kindly.

Then we got Talking Head 4: Her husband, Harry Smelt. Again he wor fully sideways on to t' camera, then face on, like he wor in a police photo-fit. His face wor like a boy melding into an old man ... PRETTY LOW SEXUALLY ...

Mother fidgeted, making her stockings rustle on her inner thighs.

Talking Head 5: The father of one of t' victims, murdered only last year ... LOWEST OF THE LOW ... TAPE TO POLICE ... GUINNESS BOOK OF RECORDS ...

'Mrs Husk says that tape ain't HIM. You know, that Geordie bloke on t' tape. Are you getting me, Mother? This woman on my pop round, Mrs Husk, she reads the tea leaves. She says the tape's a hoax.'

Mother got up and turned up the volume, then sat back down again. Without taking her eyes from t' screen, she said, 'I'd have thought you'd know better than to believe owt that some batty old woman on your pop round tells you.'

Talking Head 6: The mother. She has highly arched eyebrows and long sideways lashes. ... INADEQUATE PERSON ... PHYSICALLY ... MENTALLY ...

'Who wor it, eh?' I said. 'Who wor right there when that Wilma McCann wor found? Me, that's who. Who's sat and listened to all t' stories from prozzies on t' round ... and ... and ... we've all seen what happened to folks' marriages, haven't we, to Don and Mavis ... even to us ... what wi' all t' talk and deceit, all t' lies ...'

Sis grabbed another toffee and hissed, 'You of all people can talk about deceit and lies. Hiding yersen away, pretending!'

'You can go to hell. You're not even my proper sister. You're only ...'

'Enough!' Mother glared at us. 'Shut it! Both of you!'

Talking Head 5 wor Maureen Long, who wor attacked in 1977. She had such a deep, dark voice for a woman, it almost vibrated through t' telly speaker.

There wor a shift. The Talking Heads wor no longer addressing HIM directly, but the woman in his life, whoever that wor.

'How do they know,' I said, 'that there's a woman in his life? There might not be a woman in his life at all, which is why ...'

... HARBOURING ... LOATHSOME ...

Mother said, 'Someone has to be protecting him. Someone knows, and most likely it's his wife.'

That got me thinking about t' time when two coppers came calling and Mother covered for Mitch, but I said nowt.

Sis got up. 'I hate HIM. I hate the way he's part of our lives! I wish I lived somewhere else, somewhere right across t' country where he can't get at us!'

'And where are you off to?'

... GIVE HIM UP ... DESPISED ... EVERY WOMAN ...

'Why should you care?'

... US MOTHERS ...

'Mandy?'

... THE DEVIL ITSELF ...

Mother yelled, 'I can't hear t' telly! I want to watch this!'

A horn parped outside, quickly, like it wor a warning or someone signalling summat. I bounded upstairs and peeked through t' hole in my curtains. A white Ford van had pulled up outside t' house. Some young bloke, black hair, black leather jacket, washed-out grey jeans, jumped out, and Mand rushed out and threw her friggin' arms around him. Marcus. I watched them snogging forever, their tongues dental diving. Then sis came back indoor while Marcus leant against t' van and tossed a chew of some sort into his gob. A few moments later sis reappeared, dragging a bag. Marcus took it from her and heaved it into t' passenger side of t' van. Then sis got in. I suddenly remembered: Marcus's band wor playing some gig in Nottingham. I'd read it in her diary. Sis wor skedaddling off wi' Marcus to Nottingham. Stupid cow. By t' time I'd reached the bottom of t' stairs I could hear t' van pulling away. Mother came out of t' lounge.

'Who wor that?'

'I think Mand's just done a runner.'

Mother looked at me all nonplussed. 'In this weather? Oh, the stupid little fool. And HE's out there. Why am I always being kept in t' dark? Why don't no one ever tell me what's going on?'

'I'm sorry, Mum. I'm dead sorry. I'll get her back, I promise. I think I know where to find her.'

I bolted from t' house after sis.

I guessed that the band might have to load up their equipment at their rehearsal rooms, which were about a mile away. I set out, running at first, then slowing to a brisk walk so I didn't get a stitch. It wor icily cold. I crossed a main road and took a short cut through a park. The park wor frosted brittle and white. The branches of some of t' smaller trees wor heavily laden wi' snow, and looked as if they might snap. I crossed the gently rising open ground, my footprints crunching into t' snow. A small dog wor yapping somewhere, and on t' road beyond t' park gates the traffic swished by, white headlights tracing the yellow arc of t' streetlights.

The warehouse wor a rabbit warren of rooms that the management let out. No sign of t' white van, but then it might be parked up in t' yard or around t' corner.

I followed a narrow side ginnel. At the end, some steps led down to a steel door. I shouldered it open and found

301

mesen in a dank corridor, dimly lit by a dangling bulb. In front of me, three doors, all t' same.

'Mand!' I called out, my voice bouncing off t' pipes and unseen recesses. I could hear t' dripping of slow, fat water drops. I listened. This place wor giving me t' creeps. I blew into my palms and stamped the snow from my boots. I tried the nearest door. It wor padlocked.

'Hello? Anyone?'

Water plopped monotonously. Either I'd been wrong, or I wor too late. But I'd been dead sure that this wor where she'd be holed up. I opened the second door. It wor a store cupboard.

I thought I heard a sound. I listened breathlessly, my heart nudging against my ribcage. I hoped it worn't a friggin' rat. Some fat bugger bunkering down from t' cold. I'd encountered the odd rat or two out on t' round. Mrs Husk had had one once, lodging in t' pipes behind the sink, 'til t' council sent in some men to flush it out. 'Big bastard' wor how Mrs Husk described it. Gave her summat else to natter about.

I edged toward t' final door. I palmed it and it gave wi' a long, un-oiled screech. I groped forward in t' blackness.

'Mandy?' I whispered.

I could smell damp and stale ciggie butts and beer and an acrid trace of welding flux.

'Mand. You here?'

It wor like stepping into a soft velvet wall. As my eyes adjusted to t' gloom, I could make out egg boxes and bits of old carpet stuck to t' walls, just as she'd described it in her diary. Then t' big Marshall amp stacks stepped up, then t' bass and snare drums showed their curves and the cymbal rims winked at me. Then, lastly, an old sofa against t' far wall. Sitting in t' middle, in deep shadow, wor a figure.

There wor summat about t' figure that worn't quite right. It worn't Mand – too tall and thin. It wor probably a bloke, judging by t' slaphead or t' woolly hat he wor wearing.

'Hello?'

The figure sat, motionless, not saying owt. I could make out the outline of a head, a shoulder, a leg. I shuffled a few steps forward.

'You all right?'

I stubbed my boot against a metal box and stumbled into t' figure, which fell apart beneath me, limbs crashing down. Even t' head rolled off. Then the light came on.

I blinked in t' sudden harshness of t' bare bulb. In t' doorway, one hand still on t' light switch, which I saw now wor further away from t' door than usual, wor a scrawny bloke wi' lank hair. The same scrawny tyke I'd seen sis snogging earlier. Mand hersen appeared behind him, and looked at me all agog. At my feet lay the limbs, head and torso of a dismembered female dummy. The eyes stared up at me like glassy blue marbles. She had lashes like centipedes and painted-on eyebrows. She wor bald.

'Rick? What the heck are you doing here?'

'I've come to fetch you. You're not going off like this.'

'You can't stop me!'

Then t' thought struck her. 'How did you know where to find me?'

I grimaced. 'Read it in your diary.'

'You've been reading my diary? I knew it! I knew it! How could you do that, Rick? You disgust me! You utterly disgust me!'

'This your brother?'

'No, Marcus, it's the fucking Ripper. Of course it's my brother!'

'Half-brother,' I corrected.

Mandy eyeballed me hatefully. '*Gay* half-brother.'

'You're gay?' Marcus said.

'Christ, what planet have you just landed from? You heard what she said, didn't you?'

'Just that I've never met someone who's, you know, gay, before.'

'You have, you just didn't know it.'

'I don't know why you hide it, Rick. Mum knows. I started to tell her, but she told me to shut up and walked out the room. Course she knows.'

'So what? I don't want you to go on this stupid friggin' so-called tour. It's not a tour anyway, it's one pissing little gig in Nottingham. Sister, half-sister, who gives a fuck? You're still flesh and blood and I don't want you to go ...'

'You can't tell me what to do. Nobody cares. You don't care, Mother don't. No one.'

'She does. Course she does. We all do, it's just that we have our own ways of showing it.'

Marcus started to open his gob and say that he cared too, but Mand shut him up sharpish.

'You just want sex all t' time. If you really cared, Marcus, you wouldn't eat all them disgusting licorice sweets before you snog me. It turns your tongue black and it tastes horrible.'

On t' way home from work I spotted a poster that read 'The Ripper is a Coward'. Some loaded Leeds businessman had shelled out for eight thousand of t' friggin' things to be plastered everywhere. As we drove past a whole row of them, Eric said, 'That's really going to do it, ain't it? What a waste of money. What an utter waste of good money.'

By 7 o'clock every night the pubs wor nigh on empty, the streets wor dead, as if it wor a wartime curfew. Eric thought the businessman who paid for them posters must be suffering cos he owned a chain of pubs or restaurants, or a couple of nightclubs. 'Otherwise,' he said, 'why would he care?'

'Remember that Clark's driver?' Mother said as we wor watching *The Two Ronnies Christmas Special* on t' telly. 'You know, Peter Sutcliffe – that nice chap I told you about that always keeps his lorry clean and helps others out and ...'

'Aye. What about him?' I wor annoyed wi' her cos she wor blathering over a really good jape and I missed half of it.

'Well, t'other drivers nicknamed him the Ripper cos he'd been picked up for questioning so many times.'

'And?'

'He handed in his notice this morning. From one day to t' next. Just before Christmas an' all.'

I turned over in bed. The digital glo-red figures of my new alarm clock (Christmas present from Mother) blurred into sight: 6.30 a.m. I clicked on t' bedside light and lay there, blinking away t' dying strands of fitful dreams. Early January mornings wor always the worst.

I heard Mother coming out of t' bathroom. The hot-water pipes knocked as they cooled down.

I groaned softly, pulling the pillow over my face, and snuggled deeper down against t' winter. Moments later I heard Mother's foosteps clumping down t' stairs, and then t' kitchen radio come on.

Her cry wor one of shock, pain and surprise. Summat dropped. Not crockery or glass, nowt shattered or splintered, but a single, weighty object, like a cooking pot. I slung back the bed covers and tugged on my jeans, zipping up the fly as I bounded down t' stairs.

She'd been holding a kettle of boiling water when t' news came, news that had caused her to pour scalding water onto her hand, drop the kettle, cry out and slam on t' cold tap. She wor still holding her hand in t' water stream.

'They've got him! They've ruddy well got him!'

She turned away from t' sink and clasped me, pulling us both about t' kitchen in an unbalanced jig that nearly ended up wi' both of us on t' deck. 'They've got him, they've got him!' Her tears of pain and joy wor t' same tears. Her voice rose to a mouse-squeak. 'They've got him, do you hear me?'

'I hear you! I hear you!'

Her hand wor blossoming in a red weal. I took a tea towel, soaked it in t' sink, then wrapped it about her hand, saying, 'Wrap it once for me, twice for thee and three times for HIM.'

'It's over, Rick! It's over.'

'I'll get you some Germolene.'

I fetched the ointment from t' bathroom cabinet, then flung open Mandy's bedroom door.

'Mandy! Mandy! Wake up! It's the bloody Ripper! They've got him, they've ruddy well got him!' She raised hersen on one elbow, shielding her eyes wi' her other arm as the landing light fell upon her.

'What?'

'They've caught HIM! They've got HIM! The Ripper! It wor on t' news just now!' I wor shouting at her. I yanked the edge of her bedclothes.

'Who?' She pulled at her hair, tidying hersen. She wor staring at me like I wor an intruder. Then she seemed to register what I wor saying.

'They've got HIM!'

Her expression flick-knifed. She grabbed the nearest thing off her bedside table and slung it at me. It bounced off my arm. It wor her diary.

'Get out of my room! Get out! Get out, get out, get out!'

I slammed her door behind me. I heard her burst into tears.

* * *

306

All day we wor glued to t' news on t' telly and the radio. He wor being held at Dewsbury cop shop.

Mr Clark wor interviewed. Clark's long building and sign behind him, Clark wor saying, 'They've been twice and interviewed us, and we thought that we wor clean.'

Mother said that wor an odd word for Mr Clark to use. 'Clean'. She worn't due in at Clark's that day.

In t' afternoon we took the bus from Bradford Interchange to Dewsbury. The journey seemed to take an age. Mandy chewed her chipped nails. Mother wor messing wi' her face in a compact mirror. She wore a disconnected expression. I sat directly across t' bus from them, taking in all our fellow passengers. A silent charge choked the air, as if the whole bus knew, and we wor setting out on a mission from which we might not return. Could we all be headed to Dewsbury cos of HIM? Not the elderly couple in light macs, surely? Not the woman wi' t' toddler on her knee? Not t' teenager in t' Judas Priest baseball cap, his knees up against t' seat in front of him, tapping out a rhythm on t' seat rail?

Near my head, a small insect crawled over t' windowpane. I watched it make its way up, down, then up again, then across, and then back up again. Every so often it would stop and appear to stroke its feelers against t' glass. Did it know it wor crawling over summat solid, or wor t' glass like an invisible wall? Did it hurt when it had collided wi' it?

I opened the small top window and held my forefinger beneath t' insect. It seemed to hesitate a moment, then it boarded. I raised my finger very slowly toward t' open window, then flicked the insect away, out into t' cold air, where it could take its chances. Maybe in doing that I wor killing it.

By t' time we arrived at Dewsbury bus station it wor late afternoon, and winter dark had set in. Rain started to fall. Mother pulled up her collar against t' cold, looking about.

307

'What now?'

Mand wor tugging at her hair.

'Dunno.' Mother nodded toward a small knot of women across t' street. 'We could follow them.'

We set off, following t'others, who wor following others also, an urgency in our stride as we trudged along t' rain-shiny streets. We soon came to t' grey TV vans, arc lights, thick cables lying across t' road, noisy journalists and lines of jumpy cops. The air crackled wi' a nervous frenzy. My stomach churned over. Mother had taken hold of Mandy's hand. Ahead of us the hum of t' still unseen crowd grew, like we wor approaching a trillion bees. As we came closer, this hum of voices wor punctured by yells and piercing screams, shrill screechings. Mandy shouted to us that it wor like t' time she'd hitched to Manchester Airport wi' two school mates to scream at David Cassidy. Mother gave her a frown that meant, 'When wor this then?'

We pushed on forward, the way seeming to part for us. We wor in t' presence of evil, and that evil still had the power to strike any one of us. We hardened and emptied our minds 'til only an icy collective hate remained. Close by me, a large woman in a purple anorak and black headscarf gave out a hoarse, throaty cry. Beside her, another woman wor in silent tears. Placards proclaiming 'The Ripper is a Coward' bobbed and danced above our heads. A chant started, low, uncertain at first, a few lone cries of 'Hang the bastard!' cutting the air, then 'Kill him! Kill him!', a low rumble dredged from t' pits of our stomachs, growing stronger, growing ever louder, faces contorted so that on any photograph (and from t' flash of t' cameras there would be many) our mouths would be deformed, our hands madly clenched, our eyeballs bulging.

Mother fell in wi' them, at first only her lips moving to 'Kill him! Kill him!' as if she wor feeling her way into a tune she barely knew, repeating 'Kill him! Kill him!' like a runner exhaling, punching the air wi' short jabs of her bandaged fist. She wor crying and laughing at the same time.

It wor then that I glimpsed summat in t' far corner of my eye. Glistening in t' TV arc lights, the shaven pates of a group of skinheads. I saw t' rope, oily black against t' searing lights as it squirmed loosely upward toward t' top of a lamp-post, danced in t' air and fell. Then up it went again, this time snagging on t' light.

'Tad!' I said, aloud and to mesen.

Or someone who looked like Tad. I peeled away from Mother and Mandy, and pushed through to where I'd seen him. It had been just a fleeting moment, and if it wor Tad, then he'd shaven his head again and wor back in his skinhead garb. Then t' crowd swallowed him, and cops wor pushing through and gesturing at the fascists to take down t' hangman's noose. His mates wor there all right; that friggin' cabal of pasty-faced youths in their drainpipe jeans, wi' their Nazi insignia and Union Jack badges sewn neatly onto their jackets. (By who? By their mothers?) Again the rope swivelled skyward, a fleeting, shifting shape.

Sirens upon sirens.

A roar went up. The mass surged again, almost unbalancing me, and the women, for it wor mostly women, wor shoving, shouting, yelling, 'Hang the bastard! Hang him! Killer! Killer!'

There wor a mighty ruckus as a white police van drove through. HIM. It must contain HIM. Police helmets bobbed, a border of dark, glinting helmets, a poison toadstool line, two, three deep, as they linked arms to hold the crowd at bay. A woman's shoe flew through t' air, launched toward t' van. Arms, necks, shoulders, breasts, thighs pressed in on me. The crowd swelled again as the van doors wor opened, and a woman wor bundled out the back and into t' police station, her head hidden beneath a blanket. HIS wife.

I elbowed my way toward a small space, but as soon as I got there it wor gone. The crowd wor being pushed back by t' flanks of coppers. I heard Mandy call out, 'Mum! Rick!' but I couldn't turn my head, couldn't see her.

I used my fists and elbows to shove through toward where I'd heard her, standing on some woman's foot so that she screamed and swore at me. I could see parts of sis – her cheek, her elbow, her hip. I lurched forward and tried to grab her, but then t' crowd cast her away from me.

'Rick, get me out of here please! Please! I hate this!'

'I'm trying! Just try to stay upright!'

'Please! I can't breathe!'

I could hear her panic. The crowd swirled and I saw her again, up ahead of me. A sliver of space opened up and she tore hersen through it. Then t' crowd closed about me and I lost her.

I found mesen stood before someone else. We wor almost face to face, about ten feet apart. For a moment each stared at t'other, as if not quite taking it in. By t' look of him, he wor back in wi' his old tribe. His expression travelled from recognition, through disbelief, to astonishment tainted by shame. Like someone caught wi' his hand in t' bikkie barrel by t' very person he'd least expected. He opened his mouth and began to say summat, but just then two coppers grabbed him by t' crooks of his arms and dragged him away. He managed to turn his head so that our eyes met one last time. That look seared into me.

I wor never to see Tad again.

The next morn the news confirmed that HE wor t' Clark's driver, Peter Sutcliffe.

My breath hung in front of my face in t' icy air as I followed the high kerb of t' dual carriageway, lurching along wi' my bag banging against my thigh. The distant tower blocks looked like they wor dissolving in milk. Every so often I set the bag down and squinted up at the pale sun, slowly emerging from behind a gauze of winter cloud.

By t' time I reached the roundabout that fed into t' southbound lane of t' motorway my shoulder wor sore where t' bag strap had been cutting into it. I set the bag down, stretched my arm, feeling the blood tingling back into my fingers, and pulled up my collar against t' cold. A car passed, windscreen wipers swishing furiously. More cars, vans, trucks slowing down, gears changing, picking up speed as they hit the slipstream of t' roundabout and then out again, down onto t' motorway below.

I placed the bag a little out of sight and stuck out a thumb. I put my other thumb through my belt loop and let my fingers dangle about my crotch area.

I didn't have to wait long. A dark-blue Ford pulled onto t' hard shoulder a few yards ahead.

The passenger door fell open. A slim bloke, early middle age, salt-and-pepper hair, clean white shirt, suit jacket hanging against t' rear side-window – probably a salesman of some sort, probably out on t' road all week, probably had a wife and two snivelling kids in surburbia somewhere, probably picked up lone young male hitchers whenever he got the chance. I struggled toward t' car, half-running, half-limping, the bag knocking against my leg.

Acknowledgements

I have to thank the following people, without whom this book would still be languishing on my hard drive.

My MA tutors/authors at Kingston University, especially Jonathan Barnes and James Miller, for their support and feedback, and above all my dissertation tutor, Alexander Masters, for introducing me to my agents, RCW.

Rachel Cusk and David Vann for taking the time to read the whole book, and for their comments.

Thanks must also go to my fellow MA students at Kingston University, and to my good friends Marko Jobst and Alan Caig Wilson for either reading or listening to the novel in development, and for their helpful feedback.

Fanie (S.J. Naudé) for the long road travelled.

Thanks to my editors at Fourth Estate, Nick Pearson and Robert Lacey, for their energy, insightful comments and sharp editing. Also to Andy Bridge for the cover artwork.

Finally, I am greatly indebted to my agent, Peter Straus, and to everyone at RCW.